SAVAGE JOURNEY

by Richard Prygodzicz

PublishAmerica
Baltimore

ISBN: 1-4241-2751-3
PUBLISHED BY PUBLISHAMERICA, LLLP
www.publishamerica.com
Baltimore

Printed in the United States of America

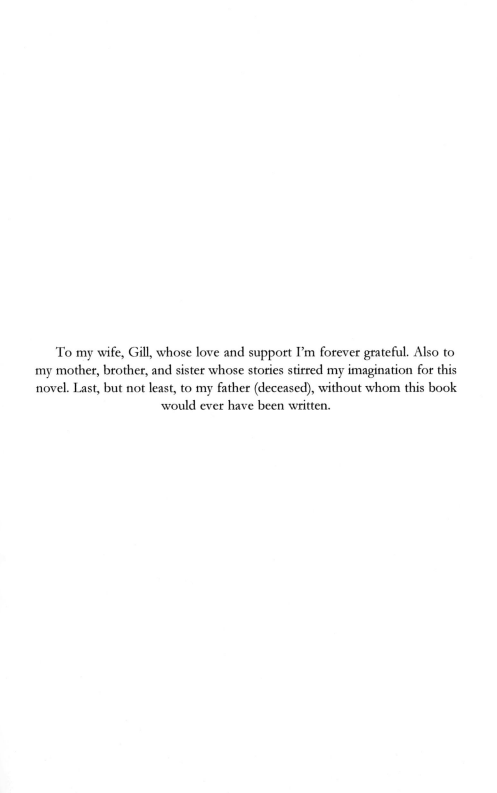

To my wife, Gill, whose love and support I'm forever grateful. Also to my mother, brother, and sister whose stories stirred my imagination for this novel. Last, but not least, to my father (deceased), without whom this book would ever have been written.

Acknowledgements

Thanks to the staff at Aberdare Library assisting with my research. Alan Bleasdale, the writer, whom I've never met but inspired me to write. My children who, occasionally as youngsters, sat on my knee and gave me a hug whilst I typed out the novel. PublishAmerica for providing the opportunity to get my novel published.

Author Note:

My name is pronounced "PRE-GOD-ITCH"

Table of Contents

CHAPTER 1

There was no choice but to swallow the first segments of the rich brown earth that had forced its way into his open mouth as he fell flat on his stomach. On reaching the freshly excavated area, he hit the ground hard, winding himself on the impact, his mental reflexes forcing his mouth to open wide to breathe the air he urgently required. He coughed violently spitting out the remainder of the liquefied mud from his mouth unafraid of being heard as the continuous sound of teeming rain and the heavier cacophony of weapon fire echoed all around.

'May God help us,' he whispered helplessly, his spluttering and regurgitation over.

Lying there he surveyed the bitter and bloody one sided battle scene that was continuing. Strangely the monotonous sounds, final to those who had been fatally hit, reminded him of how, in complete contrast, the day had begun.

With the long hard winter finally over the spring of 1940 was underway with thoughts of summer still a distant expectation. April had commenced. The trees, shrubs and the sprinkling of blooms they passed were prosperous in greenery and colour and the ambient scenery was altogether pleasant. The weather was unreliable and changed sporadically from downpours of rain to bursts of sunshine, but always the underlying temperature was chilly.

The march had been long, hard and strenuous. The three hundred personnel, the majority of them soldiers and Officers of the depleted Polish Army along with a minority of professional people, had been rounded up from the numerous prisons in which they had been kept, and marched by the Red Army further into the Soviet Union.

The columns of marchers were kept away from the large towns and cities, and many of the Polish Officers could not understand why this was so. The last town of any size they had been near, which was early morning, was Smolensk.

Pieter Sagajlo was a Lieutenant with his regiment and the questions he now asked himself made him stand out from the rest of the soldiers in catching the eye of his Commanding Officers. His potential to climb higher in the ranks was promising, though his prospects of doing so had been prematurely cut short with the invasion of not only the Germans but also the Russians into his country. 'Why do they not tell us where we are going? Why are we avoiding the major roads and towns?' he asked himself with his natural inquisitive demeanour resulting from such strange circumstances.

The cavalcades of army and civilian personnel continued their march into the afternoon. The April skies were again overcast. Rain was expected once more having accompanied them during the morning with a grateful interruption accepted by the captives whilst they ate the small amount of food supplied to them at midday. In many ways the changing weather represented the differing attitude of the Russian escorts, cruel one moment, understanding the next, but always volatile.

Suddenly the processions of marchers were carefully and controllably steered off the road they had been progressing along and re-directed onto a track which led through woods thick in foliage.

Walking was difficult in places as the rain, which had soaked the ground, made their gait slippery. More and more of the detainees now questioned one another as to why they were taking this route. Some more concerned than others.

'This is a strange route we are pursuing Sir.' Pieter now openly protested, unable to keep his curious mind quelled any longer as he spoke with his immediate Commanding Officer.

'Yes Lieutenant, it is unusual.' The Commanding Officer agreed. 'Tell your men to prepare themselves for anything unexpected.'

'Like what Sir?' Pieter asked, then replying to his own question though still directing it at his C.O. 'Like fighting?'

'I don't know Lieutenant. Perhaps we will have to do battle.' The major stroked his military moustache as he always did when making decisions or giving orders. On this occasion he was clueless as to what the Russians had planned. Like his lieutenant, he too, had thought the route they had taken on the journey so far was extraordinary. Since turning off the main track, his suspicions were enhanced.

'I say we fight now Sir.' Pieter continued with his enthusiastic patter, trying to persuade the indecisiveness of his C.O. to make a firm decision along his own line of thought. 'We are being taken further away from any population. We have seen or heard nobody since early morning except our guards. Something is awaiting us. If we fight we can take them by surprise. Yes, there is a risk that some of our men will die, but many will live and can escape.' He protested, explaining quickly the advantages and disadvantages for his course of action.

The major pondered on his subordinate's words then eventually replied.

'We'll wait a little longer and if we do not rejoin the main road soon, we'll decide on what course of action to take then. Do not forget Lieutenant there are hundreds of men here. To achieve maximum effect we would have to communicate with all of them. That means that I should first discuss with the other commanding officers. If we agree, they in turn will have to notify their men plus the civilians. That will take time. Carry out the original order I gave you Lieutenant.' Pieter walked on.

The major snapped the last sentence at Pieter giving himself strength in his wavering decision. At the same time he contemplated the deviousness and cunning of the Russians and, like his subordinate, felt sure they were up to no good. The lieutenant's course of action could be correct, he surmised to himself, and that eventually all the men would have to fight to escape whatever the Russians had planned for them. 'It was indeed a strange route for a body of soldiers to follow,' he murmured to himself, repeating his earlier thoughts.

Thirty minutes after departing from the road and twenty minutes after the two officers discussed their individual propositions, the captives together with their Russian escort descended upon a large clearing in the wood.

At the opposite end of the glade a dirt track road had recently been constructed leading away from the grassland area which lay in front of a large open ditch. The Polish contingent had no knowledge of its recent creation. On the dirt track beyond, two large transport lorries lay idle.

As they entered the glade, the rain which had threatened most of the afternoon finally emptied from the harbour of dark grey clouds where it had manufactured and stored itself throughout the day. Unknowingly to them, it was a portent indication to the unsuspecting men of the events which were about to befall them. Seconds after the heavens opened and when all the detainees had been ready assembled into the glade, the majority of the Russian guard furtively made their way out of the clearing leaving a splattering of soldiers behind.

Not for the first time the Polish Officers now gathered in small groups. After instructions to rest, they questioned one another as to why they had travelled on this path and been brought to this spot.

In one of the groups was Pieter Sagajlo, who noticed whilst the conversations were taking place, that the original escort of Russian soldiers had congregated on the side of the glade nearest to the newly constructed road away from the Polish personnel. Many had boarded the trucks which were moving slowly out from the area. The remainder walked. The noise of the teeming rain drowned the drone of the engines.

'Odd,' Pieter thought. 'They can't be leaving us alone.' As he made the statement he surveyed the surrounding area. It was too late to warn anyone.

Standing two sometimes three deep, a separate group of Russian soldiers advanced on them from the woods. Even through the blockade of rain Pieter instantly recognised their professionalism, totally different from the soldiers who had left. Their greatcoats appeared in pristine condition. Their stance was upright and their formation remained tight and cohesive like a dancing troupe. Many carried Mosin-Nagant bolt action rifles capable of firing five rounds of ammunition. To this they had fixed bayonets. The remainder carried PPD 34/38 sub-machine guns which were capable of firing seventy one rounds of ammunition. They walked forward like unstoppable robots firing relentlessly at anything that moved.

There was no time in which to react to defend themselves as a complete unit. Each man would have to fend for themselves. The more perceptive Poles like Pieter reacted before the shooting commenced. The majority noticed nothing. There appeared to be more Russian soldiers than Polish, in reality it was the opposite. Each captive ran hither and thither trying to escape the inevitable penetration, sooner or later, of the bullets which would unquestioningly bring death or mutilation on them.

Pandemonium immediately set in and the teeming rain which fell had been drowned by the sound of the fierce chattering noise of gunfire. Men ran directly at the persecutors, hoping somehow that they could beat the volley of bullets which were being fired and disarm the soldiers before the rounds of ammunition continued to echo their salvo. Others turned and ran in different directions only to be met by more Russian soldiers advancing side on.

Very few men reached their goal, falling short of their aim, crumbling in their pursuit or flight, dropping torn and twisted by first the impact and secondly the pain which the bullet had inflicted on them. Bright red blood flowed immediately from the wounds that were opened in the bodies. Those Poles, who did meet their adversary, did so for a minimum of time, as the nearest Russian soldier would turn and either fire at point blank range or mercilessly bayonet the attacker.

Pieter on seeing the advancement moved in the opposite direction making those he passed aware of what was entering the area. A plan was already beginning to form in his mind. The tight formation in which they advanced quickly decided that for him the best possible chance of escape was toward the area where the ditch was situated and the number of Russian soldiers present was minimal.

The carnage seemed to develop instantly around him, and feeling fortunate that as yet he had not been hit, he turned and ran toward the ditch, the reason for its construction he now understood. Passing the bodies of men who had already fallen, some of whom he knew and loved, he ran with great speed, sliding and losing his foothold on two occasions, only to arise and pursue his quest to reach the newly gouged out earth, awaiting all the time for the inevitable impact of the bullet.

Miraculously he reached his target without harm and before he was on top of the massive burial ground he fell down flat, spuriously dead. The first part of his plan completed. The rain continued to beat down and the sound of its relentless pounding on the floor continued to be shattered only by the merciless clatter of weapon fire.

The shooting and commotion continued for many more minutes. To Pieter it seemed like an eternity and he wondered whether it would ever stop.

The bursts of firing which became more and more intermittent, followed by lone single discharges from the rifles returned Pieter to the present. The next section of his individual escape plan must be concentrated upon, he told himself.

The firing eventually ceased altogether as if in command to his wishes for peace and quiet to enable him to concentrate on his plan of action. The rain continued however, unheeded in its unstoppable sound of vibrant downpour. The ground was drenched and sodden. The bodies lay there, dead and lifeless, finally at peace experiencing none of the emotions which Pieter was now going through.

He had fallen in such a way as to enable himself to see a large proportion of the activity going on around him. From his ground floor level he viewed the destruction of the one sided battle that had recently taken place.

The advancing Russian soldiers, themselves walked through the glade passing the dead carcasses. With each step they progressed, their boots sucked the mud as they came out of the sodden ground until they reached the other side of the ditch. The weapons cradled in the soldiers' arms, were now silent, quenched of the blood they had caused to spill. After watching the assassins exit Pieter turned his eyes once more to view the mass of dead bodies that had been mown down in cold blood.

Except for the falling rain, there was complete silence on the battlefield. The few Russians who remained, who were not part of the extermination squad, appeared to look on almost unbelievingly.

Mists of evaporation rose from the still warm corpses to the heavens only to be engulfed by the falling rain. The dishevelled uniform of the Polish army and the degrained garments of the civilians were further blemished by the blood which overflowed from the wounds diluting itself with the rainwater before falling to the ground. It would first stain and then eventually be absorbed into the earth to hide all evidence of the butchery which had occurred.

The glade which had originally been lush and green in texture and colour had now in large tracts been churned and swirled to a brown mud in the commotion to escape. The blood from the dead corpses contaminated the glade further. The area resembled that of an artist's pallet of reds, browns and greens. The whole scene was of complete destruction.

Pieter felt sick almost to the point of retching as he viewed the bodies of his colleagues, some of whom had been badly disfigured. 'Were there any alive, feigning death like me?' he asked himself.

Once again the glade was virtually clear of Russian soldiers. The scores of men which they had used to perform the slaughter had disappeared. Their duty for the day finished. A small contingent of soldiers remained to keep watch.

'Probably to finish the job if any men were fortunate to be alive after the first onslaught,' Pieter thought remorsefully.

The battlefield which resembled a mortuary was strangely quiet and Pieter pondered on the idea of making his escape now. His thoughts were broken by the sound of vehicles over and beyond the ditch. The trucks had returned. Men could be heard dismounting from the vehicles and those that had left the glade were climbing aboard to take their place. Once full the lorries moved off in the direction from where they had come.

Seconds later the smaller contingent of soldiers who had arrived were trampling over the battlefield toward the far end away from where Pieter was laying. The original small detachment of soldiers which were left behind to watch over the glade and its contents were ordered to leave and could be heard marching away in the distance.

Seconds after leaving the area, the new batch of soldiers proceeded to work through the field in line. Systematically bending over and firing their individually held Tokarev pistols into the back of the heads of all the corpses that were lying on the battlefield. If the back of the head could not be seen the cadavers were rolled over and then fired on.

Pieter now observed this hideous spectacle as he lay in the sodden earth, his clothes saturated as the rain continued its relentless helping.

The murderers advanced further toward him and he watched as their hands jerked backward with the recoil of the pistol after each bullet was fired. Then he noticed that the pistols were not of Russian origin. Those that were used were bigger in shape with an elongated thinner barrel and a larger handgrip.

'They're not Tokarev pistols,' he concluded to himself, clueless as to the reason why. 'The Russians always use their own pistols, why not on this occasion?' The reasoning was beyond him and his thoughts returned to what the executors were doing.

Again his emotions gnarled away inside him. He wanted to destroy those that were perpetrating this act on the dead, though he knew for him it was impossible. His concern now was to flee from the area as soon as possible. 'The rain would give me some protection,' he whispered to himself. 'They are still some distance away and with every moment they will be nearer. Act quickly Pieter,' he urged himself.

He turned his head to view the area behind where he lay. The last time he looked it had been virtually clear of soldiers. Turning once more he was not disappointed. Beyond the dead bodies, which, when alive, had managed to cover the same distance as him before meeting their final fate, only one Russian soldier, accompanied with a rifle, could be seen. 'With the element of surprise I may be able to overhaul him,' he reasoned with himself.

Returning his head to his original position he viewed the marksmen with their pistols still in the distance. Then as he was about to raise himself and flee the area as fast as possible, there was movement in the glade no more than ten yards in front of the approaching soldiers who were brandishing their weapons.

A Pole, who, like himself, had survived the attack, arose and fled to the west of the glade, in the opposite direction to where Pieter was lying. Running at speed, almost clearing the area and virtually at the entrance to the woods, a lone voice of Russian origin had shouted a warning before the man could make good his escape. Quickly following the vocal warning was the single crack of a rifle shot, which for a split second again cut the sound of the teeming rain before it continued pitilessly. The shot came from the same area where the shout emanated, somewhere behind Pieter. He watched as the Pole wriggled with the impact of the bullet. Blood spat forth from the wound, evidence that he had been hit. The victim stumbled two steps further and dropped slowly to his knees and then collapsed forward to the ground.

The soldier walked from behind Pieter and passed by no more than a foot from where he lay. Pieter's heart was pounding and he felt sure that the soldier would hear the noise it was making. He passed and continued walking to join the other soldiers who had now gathered around the latest dead body, and who, until the shot rang out, had not noticed the Polish soldier taking flight. They had viewed him first as he faltered through the impact of the bullet.

Without hesitation, lying in a puddle of rainwater, Pieter turned his head and looked behind him. The coast was clear. He returned his gaze once more to see the main group of soldiers congratulating the soldier who had fired the bullet. There was laughter in their voices as one soldier bent to certify death on the lone escapee.

Without further uncertainty and while they were still pre-occupied, Pieter arose and ran in the direction he had always planned to escape. As he ran he promised himself that if ever possible he would avenge the deaths of his comrades that afternoon and the name of Katyn would never be forgotten by himself or the Polish people. His determination had never been stronger and those thoughts decreed his body to distance himself from the enemy. He ran like never before and as he did so he awaited the discharge of weapon fire which never came.

CHAPTER 2

The shrapnel fiercely kicked up from the German shells impacting on its target cut the head clean away from Kovacs' body. Jacob Bryevski, who had the good fortune to have that extra speed needed to dive and crouch for cover, looked up to see if his comrade had made it to safety. His eyes could only focus on the open eyed severed head dropping through the air toward him. The uprooted disfigured cranium of his comrade in arms had been wrenched from his already dismembered body as simply as a child tearing off the head of a toy doll.

With instantaneous reactions and for no other apparent reason, Jacob dropped his rifle and reached out to catch the bloodied skull of the closest and dearest ally he had befriended since joining the military. A split second later the torso, as if trying to keep its attachment to the escaped part of the body, landed next to him supplying a quick nervous contortion perhaps in a final though useless attempt to live without that which commanded life before resting forever.

Jacob sat there unmoved, free of emotion, staring at the body which had been fully formed moments earlier with the part he was now cradling in his arms. The top of the sternum could clearly be seen even though the blood gushed from the veins and arteries which shadowed the white shaded backbone. His thoughts were simple. 'What fools we are but how we loved and still love our homeland which has been so cruelly invaded.'

Sitting there in seemingly macabre surroundings he remembered how the artillery from the German guns had found their range soon enough. The Polish defenders were under a deluge of fire early in the battle. Having regrouped several hours before only to turn and fight once again, those of full sight and sound along with the injured, some with limbs missing were full of passion to commence hostilities in a futile gesture of defiance.

There was nothing which could have possibly saved Kovacs from the cruel death that came to him. Facing his final death blow without discomfort was unlikely. Losing the use of his left arm during the early morning campaign, in addition to a badly deformed left leg, had resulted in a legacy of extreme pain. But as they turned, proudly, to face the enemy for the third time he ignored his own personal suffering and pledged the rest of his remaining short life to his beloved country.

Although it was early afternoon the smoke filled combat zone dimmed the surrounding area significantly bringing on the appearance of twilight. The light played eerily in the dugout where they had taken refuge. Jacob returned his gaze to the head he was still cradling. It appeared to be mouthing something at him, words which he could not determine. Another enemy shell landing close by averted his attention. When he looked back at the skull the mouth was closed and in an instant Jacob was propelled forward and out of his dream.

The vision which had left him all those months ago had now, for some unknown reason, returned to momentarily disturb him again. He sat upright in his bed. Unlike previous occasions, no perspiration, panting, or screaming accompanied him. He was calm and in control. He purveyed the room about him, his bedroom, like he did so on any other morning. Dawn had not fully broken. He contemplated arising and remembered that today was to be a holiday for him and that there were still several hours of sleep available to him.

Rekindling the dream he had moments earlier been a part of, Jacob knew that the sight, the sound, those memories, would live with him forever. For several months after that encounter, and after returning home from the war, Jacob had woken every night with the same nightmare. As Kovacs' head came toward his outstretched hands, the mouth would open and it would shout the words, 'Niemiecki! Niemiecki! Germans! Germans!' Before the skull would actually land in his hands he would awake, breathing heavily and perspiring profusely from his sleep. Sometimes he would cry out, when he did so he was always visited by either one or both of his parents. Even at his age they were a welcome comfort in times of need and they would sit with him until he either recovered his composure or drifted back into an uneasy and unsure remaining nights slumber.

As suddenly as the nightmares began they had ceased and the last six months had been clear, restful nights, except for now. 'Why had they returned now?' he asked himself. 'The dream...is different...longer. On this occurrence I hold the head, and the voice, although talking, is not shouting at me. And...the words, I cannot decipher the words. Was it Niemiecki he called this time? Or something else?' Whilst deliberating on what his imagination had conjured for him, Jacob returned to his slumber.

He awoke several hours later with renewed vigour despite the visitation during the night. If he had any concerns over the dream, the remaining hours of the night, whilst he slept, had hidden those concerns and allowed him to forget.

Jacob Bryevski leapt out of his oversized bed from the soft comforting warmth of the pastel coloured sheets which enveloped the mattress into the chilly spaciousness of the large bedroom. It was the sixth of ten such bedrooms in the large majestic house and Jacob's own personal domain. He washed quickly pretending to ignore the coldness of the water which had been standing in the English porcelain vase overnight ready for use in the morning.

Half dressed, he sauntered over to the window of the bedroom which was at the front of the house facing east and overlooked probably the most picturesque view available on his family's land. He began to reminisce about the period when he was of an age to appreciate beauty and how mesmerised he was with the scenery which greeted him each morning. Everyone who had the good fortune to enter any of the rooms on the east side of the house and feast their eyes on the panoramic splendour never faltered in voicing their opinions, occasionally enviously, to his parents. As a young boy on seeing this natural wonder he immediately asked his mother if he could move into the bedroom at the earliest opportunity. 'That would not be possible for many years, Jacob, as your great aunt is still energetic for her age,' she replied.

'I don't mind waiting.'

'You'll have a long wait Jacob.'

'It will be worth the wait Mama.'

And with the conversation ended his mother left the room smiling. Now Jacob Bryevski stood in the same position looking out the window of the bedroom he had first asked his mother about occupying eleven years earlier.

Five years after that conversation his great Aunt was dead. Old age had stealthily crept up on her and she died in her sleep proud and independent to the very last page in her life. She left behind a family who mourned her great loss. She was wise and affectionate and effortlessly endeavoured to pass on the special qualities in her life to those around her whom she loved dearly and not so dearly.

Jacob, now fully dressed, turned once more to view the scenery out through his bedroom window which he had opened. Each glimpse never failed to overwhelm him even though he had seen it a thousand and more times before.

The river which flowed through the land glistened like stars on a clear sky as the early summer sun shone its light onto the surface of the water. The last traces of the dew which had nurtured itself during the night were slowly disappearing revealing an abundance of emerald green grass rich in texture and thickness. Horses grazed nonchalantly in a cordoned off area to the left of his view. To the extreme right stood a gathering of trees, frequented by collections of crows, rooks and ravens and the infrequent jay, followed by grazing land leading into a meadow which reached out on all sides and wrapped itself around the borders of a densely wooded area. Beyond this could be found the cottages of the farm labourers who worked for Jacob's father, Pavel Bryevski.

The view he gazed upon belied the atmosphere that was present in his country. The Russians had arrived nine months earlier supposedly marching to save Poland from the German enemy. Within days of their arrival the original stories of why the Russians had come, and who, on every other occasion in the past had been the enemy of the Polish people, was found to be a complete fabrication of the truth. The people soon realised this. Almost immediately peasants were advised to take over the land and dwellings from their landlords. The Bryevski family had heard stories of many landowners being evicted by workers who until recently had worked for them and alongside them. The Russians had made sweeping changes in the short time they had taken root in Poland. They had not come to help the people protect their land but to help the Germans obliterate the state of Poland once and for all. To rape her people and the land of everything they possessed.

The deed was performed cleverly, very cleverly. The Russians cunningly used many of the Polish people to do its dirty work for them. Then, when the people who assisted the Russians were no longer of any use, they in their turn were set upon.

Fortunately events which were happening on many of the estates within the Soviet occupied regions of Poland were not repeated on the property of Jacob's father. The workers did not revolt and no person reneged to the Russians. The violators kept visiting and took stock of the belongings and valuables and were disappointed to see that the normal day's chores and duties were continuing on the estate with no disruption from the workforce. The workers had not risen and taken over and did not want to do so. Quite the opposite happened. Several weeks after the Russians invaded, and after the people had realised what they had come for, a delegation from Pavel's workforce arrived early one morning outside the house and asked to speak with him. Pavel duly obliged and immediately gathered his overcoat and guided the men into the large barn.

A deputation from the workforce had never occurred before on the Bryevski estate. If ever there were any meetings they were usually called by Pavel himself. Jacob did not want to miss this unusual event and quickly made an excuse to leave the breakfast table. In the hallway he pulled his own overcoat off the peg and made his way across to the barn situated approximately four hundred metres at the rear of the house.

Entering through the side entrance he quietly closed the barn door behind him and stealthily climbed the wooden steps to the upper floor. Any noise he did make was drowned by the gentle commotion of the men awaiting the commencement of the meeting. Seating himself on two bales of straw which were hidden by a wooden lattice, out of sight from anyone on the ground floor, but which had an acceptable view to the onlooker, Jacob could clearly see his father, the body of men and their elected speaker.

There the spokesman who represented the workforce stated the feelings of the men who worked for Pavel. He spoke clearly and concisely not wishing to embarrass anyone by over extolling the virtues of their landlord.

'We don't have much to say Sir but we want you to know where we stand. No man working here could receive a better wage or be treated fairer if they were to work elsewhere. Our homes are dry and warm, our wives and children are contented and happy and our stomachs never go hungry. For this we are grateful. We could no sooner rise up against you than rise up against our own families.' The speaker finished a short concise speech straight to the point.

There was several minutes' silence. Pavel was overwhelmed and taken aback by the support and warmth that his workforce and their families obviously had for him. Controlling his emotions, he cleared his throat and replied.

'I'm a very fortunate man because I not only have one family but several families.' A smile spread across his face. At the same time he opened his arms, reaffirming his affection toward them. There was a ripple of laughter in his audience. He continued. 'I will do my very best to continue the everyday pattern of our life for as long as possible. But I'm afraid to say that the changes which have affected so many others will probably happen here. When? I do not know, and when the changes come I do not know how big an effect it will have on us. But I repeat, I will do my very best to retain what we already have here on our land.'

He spoke to them willing them to believe that it was as much their land as his. Pavel knew that without them his estate would be nothing. The relationship between landlord and tenant on the Bryevski estate was unique.

There was a cheer around the barn. The men left and went to prepare themselves for the days work. Pavel sat for a moment and appeared to be praying. After several minutes he arose and made his way back to the house.

Jacob had witnessed everything. For him the unanimous decision of the workforce to support his father during a period when he needed it most confirmed to him that amongst men his father was truly an exceptional person.

Once again Jacob's mind and thoughts had drifted to the past of over eight months earlier. Perhaps it was something to do with the view outside his bedroom window. Perhaps it weaved a magic spell on those who were fortunate enough to ponder the beautiful panorama and take its viewer back in time to important events that had meant so much to them. The semi conscious state he had arrived at was broken by the melodic tones of his mother announcing from downstairs that breakfast was ready.

Descending the stairs his thoughts once again surmounted in his mind. He nourished the tide for they were thoughts of the woman he loved. His life had changed due to the effect of a young woman whom he had met approximately fourteen months earlier during a brief leave of absence from the military. His relationship with Sophie had commenced on a purely platonic association at first on his behalf. Over the coming months he had slowly and surprisingly fallen in love. Today they were to picnic at one of their favourite beauty spots. The thought of what the day might bring filled him with joy and happiness. Who was to know what a difference twelve hours would make to so many peoples lives, not least to his and that of his new found love.

Jacob laboured through breakfast. Even before commencing the meal his stomach felt bloated. He had never toiled over finishing breakfast or any other meal before and always prided himself on having a eupeptic metabolism.

'It's not like you to struggle with your food Jacob.' His mother remarked on the manner in which he ate.

Explaining to her how he felt, he slowly and deliberately surveyed his plate whilst slicing the contents into smaller pieces, hoping that somehow the food would disintegrate by itself. She smiled knowingly.

'What is it mother?' he asked noticing the amusement on her face.

'I think you know why you feel the way you do?'

'I'm not sure,' he said, feigning ignorance.

'Love Jacob, love,' she replied smiling.

Looking up at her, he smiled acknowledgement. When she smiled her face radiated warmth and happiness.

His sister wandered in. Noticing the smiling faces she enquired what all the gaiety was about.

'Nothing important,' he quickly retorted looking at his mother coyly out of the corner of his eye. Eva Bryevski pretended to be busy with the arrangements for that evening.

'I can have secrets too,' remarked his sister, pretending to be unperturbed by the behaviour of her mother and brother although actually annoyed at not being allowed to share their merriment. She wandered back out of the room in the direction from where she had come.

There was no reason for not admitting his love for Sophie to his sister. After all it was to be announced that night and Maria knew quite well how far the relationship had progressed, even to the point of catching them in the barn situated on the perimeter of the north field on the estate. Sophie and she were good friends from the moment they had first been introduced to one another along with Olga, Jacob's other sister.

'Must go mother,' Jacob whispered trying to hide the burning sensation in his mouth through swallowing the hot drink she had prepared for him and at the same time realising what little time was left for the rendezvous with Sophie, 'meeting Sophie in thirty minutes.'

'Picnic?' his mother asked.

'Yes,' he replied.

'You have arranged things with Papa?'

'Yes we agreed last week.'

Having fought against the German army on their invasion into Poland on the south western border, Jacob's regiment had been completely overrun with many fatalities and the cadre that remained were ordered to disband and either make their own way home or take refuge in that part of Poland under Russian control.

Arriving safely, after a treacherous journey, he had quickly settled into helping his father on the estate. Jacob had always enjoyed working on the farm from an early age, but, due to schooling, not on a full time basis. This had been his longest period working the estate, ploughing fields, tending to the animals and on the odd occasion organising the workforce. Despite the oppressed circumstances he had enjoyed the experience and considered it worthwhile even though the days were long and very tiring and many of the tasks were strenuous and the weather, especially in the winter, was hard and cruel.

During this period on his return from the Polish army he had been questioned occasionally by the Russians as to whether he still had any military connections. After the defeat against Germany many other soldiers on returning to their homes had been imprisoned. Some had been transported to Siberia. Jacob had been fortunate to escape the deportation because, as well as his services as a farm labourer to his father; their farm was one of the biggest producers of wheat in the region which also supplied the Russian army.

'When can we expect to see you? Don't forget the Ball tonight and the announcement.' Jacob's mother enquired and ordered all in one breathe as he left the dining room.

'I'll never forget that Mama. I'll be back at four 'o' clock leaving me enough time to get ready for the evening.' Jacob replied embracing her on the way out.

'Enjoy yourselves and take care.' She shouted after him.

Jacob's mother Eva always cautioned her children to be careful whenever they ventured out alone even though all but one of her children were adults and of an age to look after themselves, Kazik being the exception. Eva remembered her mother's warning long after the time that Eva had married. She thought it wise and dutiful to warn her children in turn. Her advice was more cautious now that the Russians were occupying their land.

Jacob's father Pavel had spoken often to his children about the countries bordering Poland, Germany one side and Russia on the other. Even Austria, a distant neighbour, who had also been a threat in the past but on this occasion, was taking a rear seat in the war. Austria had already been annexed by Germany meekly accepting their bordering hosts into their country. Pavel's prediction to his family about the Germans and the Russians both invading Poland had been correct. Hitler was a devious character, facinorous in his plans. He knew that Stalin also wanted to retake that part of Poland which he believed truly belonged to Russia. If Hitler could keep Stalin at bay until he could do what he wanted with the regions of Poland he desired then why not arrange an agreement with Russia in the interim period. Hence the signing of the Pact of Non-Aggression between the Soviet Union and Nazi Germany on August 23, 1939, closely followed by the German-Soviet Treaty of Friendship agreement on September 28, 1939, which provided for the joint action against the expected Polish resistance.

Despite Hitler's achievements, Pavel also warned that the greatest threat to the Polish people would come from the Russians. Stalin had already murdered hundreds and thousands of the intelligentsia within Russia including those aides and associates who were originally close to him. For one reason or another, very often petty, those people had now become his enemy. In addition to the murders similar amounts of people had been deported to Siberia to serve sentences in the labour camps. Stalin's enemies were never tolerated for long and were quickly disposed of by one foul means or another.

It was after the words his father had spoken, and how he had verified those words himself through seeing and listening to the events which were occurring all over his country, that Jacob had quickly grown to dislike the Russian invaders.

Today, however, Jacob had decided to erase from his thoughts all the worries that his family, relatives, friends and the majority of the Polish people were undergoing. He was on his way to meet Sophie, the woman who had become the most important person in his life, the woman who he wanted to spend the rest of his life with.

The route he chose was pleasing to the traveller, not only because of the view which was splendid in itself, but also because the Russians had not yet discovered all the paths and footways which one could take across his father's land. Therefore it was unlikely that Jacob would encounter the infiltrators on this day which he was looking forward to so much.

Collecting Sophie on time the young couple set off. She had already packed some food and her chestnut coloured horse was ready saddled and waiting when he arrived. Their affection for horses was mutual and the more they conversed on the subject the more he realised what an expert Sophie was on the equine animals. She was also a very capable rider. Whilst many of her gender chose not to ride horses, Sophie at every opportunity preferred to exercise her accomplished skills by riding horseback rather than travel by way of a carriage or in her father's automobile.

The time passed quickly on their passage to the area they had chosen to visit. The horses pace was one of a trot and for the whole journey Sophie and Jacob talked virtually non stop.

Arriving at their destination the view appeared more breathtaking than when they had last perceived it. The couple sat for several moments appreciating the beautiful scenery before them.

The valley they overlooked was virtually free of human habitation. In the distance toward the bottom end of the vale could be found a cluster of three small farmhouses. From one of these wisps of smoke could be seen drifting from the chimney to fleetingly discolour the deep green and blue beyond. The mountains either side of where they sat were small in nature and rose quietly but purposefully to meet the horizon of the blue sky. The different shades of green which grew lighter as the mountain became steeper finished suddenly as the deep blue shattered and changed, finally ending the assault of verdant growth that advanced to the heavens. The dark green trees hugging certain areas of the mountain tops continued to invade the secludedness of the untouchable expanse of shimmering blue. At the lower end of the valley, near the cottages, fields of differing shades of brown verified the planting and production of crops for the current year had already taken place.

The river wound its way down through the vale almost splitting the view of the land that lay ahead of them in two symmetrical halves. Sophie followed the sweep of water from the farthest distance which she could purvey, back toward its source to visualise how the flow appeared to disappear to the left of where they were sitting, no more than twenty yards away. Along the whole expanse, the land was broken and divided in almost perfect formation by groups of trees of various species occupied by their seasonal visitors who were now ready and waiting for their fledglings' next step in life, the flight.

Eventually both Sophie and Jacob broke away from the view which held them transfixed, disembarked and came around to stand in front of the horses. Their hands automatically and instinctively reached for one another. They held tight and he gently pulled her toward him smelling her sweet body fragrances as she willingly closed in, odours which he had become welcomingly accustomed to.

Standing there together, in a timeless warp, their eyes finally met, soon followed by their lips as they passionately embraced. After their caress they turned once again to face the stunning view they had come to visit, the view they had cherished from the first moment they laid eyes upon it and which stood on the borders of his father's land and that of his neighbour.

They both stood there together, side by side, seemingly without a care in the world only their love for one another to bother them. It was difficult to comprehend at that moment how their country was in such turmoil. Overlooking all that was before them now, the peace, the serenity, it was so far away from the hell they were soon to encounter.

Sophie turning to Jacob broke the silence. 'What would happen to us Jacob if the rumours became true?'

Jacob did not have to ask about the rumours. He too, knew what stories were being told by the locals. The Russians had already taken many of their countrymen. Surely no more would be forced to leave? 'We will survive,' he replied unknowingly. 'We will survive and our love will help us to survive.'

'Whatever happens I will remember moments such as these forever,' Sophie stated.

'The moments and this day,' Jacob replied, leading her by the hand he continued, 'shall we eat?'

They ate and drank a little wine which Sophie had managed to innocently purloin from her father's supposedly secret wine stock. After eating and drinking they walked down the slope to the river. Ambling along the riverbank on the soft green grass they talked continuously about their future together. How many children they would have? Where to set up home? Would Sophie continue to teach? She wanted to, at least until the moment arrived when they would have children of their own. They turned and retraced their steps back to where they had picnicked. On the way Jacob made a concerted effort to grope for fish and ended up falling in the water up to his waist. Sophie laughed uncontrollably at the escapade.

'I don't understand, I was an expert with these hands at catching fish when I was young,' Jacob said with a puzzled expression on his face which slowly turned to a grin.

'You have lost your touch Jacob,' replied Sophie still laughing at the thought of him falling in.

'Help me out,' Jacob said, toying with her.

Innocently she took his hand. He pulled her toward him asking, 'are you going to get wet with me?'

'No Jacob. No,' she pleaded, surprised that she had fallen for such a trick.

'Just a little and we can dry off together.'

He smiled at her wickedly and she returned the smile as he backtracked into the water. Before she could protest further their lips met and he lowered her gently in his arms into the water up to her thighs. The shock of the cold water as it came into contact with her lower body made Sophie break the kiss and gasp for air. Laughing he quickly lifted her and carried her to the riverbank, setting her down. She turned to help him. Taking her hand he allowed himself to be assisted by her and at the stage when his balance was in her control, she let go. He fell back making a large splash.

Twirling around on the bank she laughed at what she had witnessed as a result of her skylarking. He sat in the river up to his chest. After recovering from the initial momentary shock of what she had done, rather than the coldness of the water, he too burst out laughing. Then without warning he made a quick effort to pull himself out of the river and lunged at her. Still giggling, she turned and ran up the slope to where they had left their belongings. Jacob climbed out onto the bank and ran after her. Catching her, she screamed playfully as he held and teased her that it was her turn for a swim. Laughing and joking they reached the top of the incline, undressed each other, allowing their wet clothes to dry in the hot sun. Their jocularity was replaced with a more serious intent of love and passion. Their bodies touched and rarely parted. They made love whilst their garments dried in the warmth of the afternoon sun.

Sophie pondered on the days events as later she dressed into her dry clothing. Even though a cloud of uncertainty hung over the country she thought about how happy they had been that afternoon and how quickly the time had passed. No sooner had they arrived when it was time for them to return home. At that moment she yearned for time to stand still, though she knew that was impossible.

Jacob sat up and watched her dressing induced by her performance. She was pleased that she could captivate him so. Whilst Jacob dressed himself Sophie turned to him once again and sussurated softly, 'Will we ever visit this place, our place and our view again Jacob?'

'Of course,' he replied reassuringly and kissed her hand.

CHAPTER 3

Vladimir Stoich walked out of the vermin infested mud hut which had been his home for the past six months and looked across at the vast expanse of land facing him. Much of what he saw was unproductive and even the sections that did bear fruit of some kind only did so through careful preparation and hard work. Work that did not worry him or present any physical exertion for him, for his job alone was to oversee that work. The productive land was beyond the immediate horizon at least one hour's walking distance. For him longer, because of his size, though that again did not trouble him for transport was available to him.

Purveying the view before him, it held him transfixed. Although it was a hard land, a cruel land, the strange beauty which now emanated from the early morning sun over the northern steppes of Kazakstan mellowed his manner and he immediately thought of home.

He raised his hand and touched the left cheek of his face which had the remnants of a small cicatrice engraved on it. At the same time he cursed his insatiable desire for women, especially since the birth of his second born child and subsequent rejection by his wife. Before the repudiation Vladimir had been able to control his lust for other females. His wife loved him, he knew that. But for some unknown reason, she had rejected her own appetite for lovemaking after the second birth. As a result he had suffered also. For six months after he had controlled the urge. In the end it had overwhelmed him. His sexual desires filled every moment of his waking day culminating in him bedding many women of different classes. In the end, his lust and fornication had caught up with him and he had finally paid the price.

'Still,' he reflected with a wicked, lascivious grin, 'I've had a successful run which is still continuing to a lesser degree.' The grade of women was somewhat lower though he could not really complain.

He wanted to forget how he came to be in another world and pulled deeply on his large cigar. The intake of tobacco briefly blotted his memories and the number of sexual accomplishments from his mind. When his head cleared they returned stronger and more explicit than before, especially the last unfortunate incident. 'One slip,' he told himself, 'one slip and you find yourself here in another world.' A world which Vladimir loathed most of the time, but enjoyed occasionally.

Viewing the luminous yellow sun sparring with the white clouds for longer than an ephemeral existence, and perceiving the resultant strange though fascinating colours produced over the land as the different shades of light danced and weaved on the vista, he reflected back on the night in question when as a result of his actions he had been allowed no alternative.

The evening had been perfect until the very last moments. It had started with him meeting the Officer's wife on time at one of the more secluded restaurants in Moscow. The wine had flowed and the music was unending. The food eaten, had absorbed the wine, allowing room for more.

They left the restaurant late and the effects of the drink catalysed their happy conversation as they decided to walk the short distance home to her apartment. The weather was bitterly cold but their mood ignored the severe conditions. As they talked he could not help wonder what it was that she found attractive about him. He assumed that it was his jocular personality. The manner in which he could make the most beautiful or the ugliest of women relax and laugh in his company was an unexplainable rarity that his friends were envious of. Many women who were momentarily in his presence were taken by him. His physical attraction alone, he knew, would not give him any chance to compete with ordinary men. He was short with fine fair hair which had started to bald. His blue eyes sparkled continuously revealing the devil in him and his nose was sharp and pointed in the shape of a triangle. The plump cheeks disproportionately enhanced his roundness.

His physique had become larger since becoming a member of the NKVD. The delights afforded him and all members of the Russian secret police had astounded him, and he often thanked his brother, without his knowledge, for manoeuvring the position his way, making his selection a virtual certainty before he had taken the interview. All hospitalities offered to him had been accepted and his weight increased expanding the size of his waist.

On arriving at the entrance to her apartment block she invited him inside. This was no less than he had expected. They entered through the downstairs doorway still laughing and mouthing one another. He could not help but think that this was the night for the pounce, his expression for bedding a woman for the first time. He had looked forward to the prospect immensely from the first instant on meeting her. She, however, had proved to be his most elusive conquest yet. He, for his part did not mind. He was unstinting in his thoughts that this woman was definitely worth the long chase.

Entering her apartment he noticed the tasteful decorations, expensive furnishings from the border states of Latvia, Lithuania, and the Ukraine as well as more recently acquired chattels from Poland. It was as Vladimir had expected it to be and was a sign of the bounty that had been looted from those countries invaded by the Great Terror, Russia. Her husband was a major in the NKVD, who, sadly, was away for long periods.

She pointed out to him where the wine was kept and instructed him to open a bottle. Dutifully, he complied with her wishes re-entering the living area with two glasses and his choice of wine. She also entered the room several seconds later from an adjoining bedroom minus on this occasion her recently purchased French dress and petticoats. He was staggered at first but also extremely pleased. Never before had a woman appeared partly undressed in front of him without help from himself.

She moved toward him and he gazed at her well-proportioned body, especially her breasts. Taking the bottle and the glasses from him, she placed them on the small table in front of where he sat and bending forward with her back to him proceeded to pour the wine. As she bent her buttocks filled the slack in her underwear fully outlining her larger though attractive rear end. Her suspenders adjusted at the front and his erection hardened quickly as he perceived her stance. She turned to him and relieved him of his coat and jacket.

'I've got a surprise for you tonight.' She laughed and purred at the same time with a sparkle in her eyes. Vladimir could not make up his mind whether her attitude was due to the effect of the drink or that she adopted this playful mood whenever she entertained men.

He laughed at her and along with her contented that they were both happy. After she had put some music on she moved toward him, gyrating slowly, whilst at the same time finishing the contents of the glass. She placed the empty vessel on the table and her hands disappeared behind her back. Unclasping her brassiere she slowly lowered the garment down and away from her to reveal her large pink breasts which stood out firm as if still supported.

This is how Vladimir liked his women, larger in proportion but with curves to match. He didn't mind if they were plump and before he cast his eyes on the nakedness of his latest conquest he had himself visioned that she would look as inviting as she was now.

Still gyrating, her bosom moved in unison and resembled ripe fruit on a tree swaying in accord with the wind. She moved slowly toward him, temptingly fondling her breasts, hardening her nipples at the same time. He was both amazed and delighted at her performance. The pounce he thought was definitely worth waiting for and from what she was doing now a formality.

31

Whilst he sat on the couch she approached him, giggling all the time, and arrived in front of him with one stockingless leg. Raising her second leg and taking the stocking off she dropped it tantalisingly over his shoulder. Standing upright she caressed her breasts in front of him once more before easing her silk underwear down the tops of her thighs to reveal her light brown puberty.

The clouds continued to weave their path over the sun and the ever changing colours on the land before him reacted like a catapult heightening the vividness of that night in his mind. Thoughts of that far off encounter stirred his loins and his memory easily continued its recall.

He was spellbound his erection uncontrollable. Never before in all his womanising experiences had he come across a female like her.

She turned her back on him as the last piece of her clothing hit the floor and bent forward to pick up the silk material. The laughter had now ceased. Her manner, despite her inebriated state, had become more serious. Vladimir was pleased at this but for the first time since his encounters with the opposite sex he was unsure about what to do. He wasn't in control.

'Should he touch her and caress her now as she bent fully forward? He wanted to. Did she want him to?' His indecisiveness surprised him. To him it seemed to last a long time. Thankfully she made his mind up for him. Slowly standing upright she turned to face him once more dancing and revolving in front of him using her silk underwear as a sexual aid.

Concerned with his inability to decide what to do, the frustration of seeing this beautiful body perform in front of him, and the fact that she had not enticed him to come and touch her, he lunged forward at his target, grabbing her around the waist. The warmth and touch of her body only enforced his erection. Pulling her toward him he ignored the shriek that she let out considering it to be the result of taking her by surprise. Rejecting it he sank his mouth onto one of her large breasts concentrating on the rosy red nipple area.

She screamed again and on this occasion he was unsure as to the reason why. They struggled and rolled over onto the couch. Releasing her, he gathered himself and undid his trousers. As he did so she kicked out at him and connected with his groin. The blow was forceful enough to cause him pain and to unbalance him. He ignored the pain and considered the fact that she liked to be rough during lovemaking. She arose from where they were seated and he steadied himself to immediately pull her back toward him.

'No! No! Nyet! Nyet!' she shouted.

'What do you mean?' He raised his voice at her in exasperation.

'No contact,' came her reply.

Vladimir was still unsure and voiced his indecisiveness. 'What do you mean after that performance?' And then he thought to himself, 'She's an exhibitionist.'

With one hand he pulled the bottom half of his clothing away, revealing himself, at the same time holding her down on the couch with the other.

'That is my turn on,' she said.

'And what about mine, you bitch?' he questioned whilst his thoughts about her intentions became increasingly clear.

'Not with me Vladimir.' She kicked out at him again. This time he caught her right leg in flight and pulled it open. Catching hold of her other leg with his free hand before she could hurl that in his direction, he held them apart. The target opened up in front of him explicitly and without hindrance. In that fleeting moment he scrutinised her body instinctively. The softness he had briefly touched and the warmth which coasted through and emitted from her body elevated his excitement to the highest level. Thoughts of whether she wanted him or not evaded him. His eyes skipped back and forth at speed between her sizeable bosoms to her inviting genitals and lastly to her face. In the end the three visions became one. He knew then that he had reached the point of no return. With grace he lowered himself to pierce her womanhood and her fingers reached up to scratch at his face. He felt the pain as her nails cut deeply into his skin. The shock ruined his smooth manner and he fell on top of her with force, penetrating her lower body. She screamed then groaned. To Vladimir her latter noise testified to him that she wanted what she was now receiving. One of her fingernails broke and stuck in his cheek as her hand relaxed and fell to her body. The blood from his facial wound flowed and dripped onto her neck and ran down her chest.

He arose from her minutes later soft and empty of juices though richly rewarded. Immediately she began shouting and screaming at him. Her protests were getting louder and louder and he wondered how he could calm and quieten her. She was sobbing and he could not understand why.

The whole episode had been obfuscated to him. Still he was unsure whether she had wanted sexual intercourse. Then as if answering what he had asked of himself she shouted at him. 'You have raped me.'

He was shocked at the accusation. The realisation began to dawn on him. He had forcibly held her down surmising, incorrectly, that she had wanted intercourse with him. If that was not the case then she was correct and he was guilty of the crime.

She continued with her accusations. He tried again to calm and comfort her and as he reached out to touch and console her she screamed obscenely at him.

'Shut up,' he bellowed at her.

He arose, pulled up his trousers and gathered a coat for her to hide her nakedness. Ignoring it, she came at him fists clenched and punched him hard on the side of the face where she had earlier cut him with her fingernails. Her punch loosened the broken nail and it fell away. She burst into another tirade of verbal abuse and Vladimir knew then that he had lost control of the situation.

Pulling his right arm back and clenching his fist he threw his punch with medium force. It connected with her jaw and she dropped to the floor. He picked her up, carried her to the couch and covered her body with the coat she had rejected from him moments earlier. He sat down next to her. He could hear her breathing and pondered on what to do next. The whole affair had culminated in complete chaos and he could not think straight.

His thoughts turned to those people who could help him. His brother came to the fore. He picked up the receiver and dialled the number. 'He would know what to do, he always did,' Vladimir consoled himself.

'Come quickly,' he pleaded over the mouthpiece, 'I need your help. I'm in trouble. A woman is involved.' His conversation was hesitant. He blurted out the address and put the receiver down.

Within thirty minutes there was a knock on the door. Vladimir rushed to answer the call. His brother entered and guessed immediately as to what had happened after casting his eyes on the woman who was now slowly gaining consciousness.

'Pour a brandy,' Vladimir's brother ordered.

He did as requested.

'Did she dance in front of you until she was naked?'

Vladimir did not reply verbally. His stunned expression answered the question his brother had asked.

He handed the brandy over at the same time asking, 'How did you know?'

'This has happened on at least three other occasions to other members of the regime. Did you have intercourse with her?' Vladimir nodded his head.

'The others I know about did not touch her. You of course went all the way. You could never resist it could you?' He scornfully reprimanded him.

The woman came around as the brother slowly poured the brandy into her mouth. She sat up quickly coughing and spluttering as the drink took its effect. The coat dropped and even the brother noticed her large but firm shape. She covered her bare chest. The half emptied glass of brandy was offered to her again. Refusing it, she whimpered a little as she caught sight of Vladimir once more. He motioned toward her looking to comfort her, at the same time hoping that she would forgive him for what had happened, still unsure in his mind whether he had raped her.

'Keep him away from me,' she screamed, 'keep him away.'

Vladimir stopped in his tracks and stayed back from the woman with whom the night had begun in such a promising manner.

'Calm down, he will not hurt you anymore,' the brother assured her.

'I want him out of my sight for good.'

'He will go, though you too must promise to keep quiet regarding this incident Katrina. I know this is not the first and may not be the last. What would Rudi say if he knew what you were doing whilst he was away?' The brother played on the strength of her husband finding out knowing that she would react favourably.

'Do not tell Rudi. I will do anything, but do not tell Rudi,' she pleaded.

'You will not have to do anything. Just remain silent over this episode.'

She cried, nodding her head in agreement at the suggestion, relieved that the experience was over and that her husband would not find out.

'We will leave now. Will you be all right?'

Again she nodded. As the two men left the door was bolted securely from the inside.

They descended the steps in silence. Relief that the sordid event was finally over capitulated Vladimir who thanked his brother profusely. Normally he would not have been so fulsome but tonight he was more than grateful. He looked toward him but there was no expression on his face.

Then the brother turned to Vladimir and spoke. 'Tonight when you get home you pack a bag ready to leave for Siberia. I will find a position for you to take up there. The exact destination will be given to you when you arrive at the station tomorrow. I will be there to personally see that you get on the train. One of my aides will travel part of the way with you. After what has happened tonight it would be better for all concerned that you have a cooling off period. Do you agree?'

Vladimir nodded his head in agreement, taken by surprise he was unsure what to think. What his brother had suggested seemed sensible enough under the circumstances.

'Your assignment will be for at least twelve months, perhaps longer. You will be briefed on the train journey tomorrow.'

The two men had reached the entrance to the apartment block and now exited into the cold night air. The temperature was below zero similar to the warmth of their relationship.

'I bid you goodnight Vladimir,' and he saluted his brother as they parted company.

Vladimir thanked his brother again, but he need not have done so. The gratitude, although heard, fell on deaf ears.

He was awoken out of his distant thoughts by the slut who had slept with him the previous night. Coming out through the door of his new but temporary home she sidled up to him whispering in his ear and grinning at the same time. He looked at his watch but his urge had already decided for him. He responded by clutching her buttocks.

'Why not,' he cogitated to himself in silent response to her suggestion. 'There is sufficient time before the village awakens to prepare for the work which is to be completed today and thirty minutes will be ample time to perform the task in hand.'

He momentarily thought about his family and then instantly forgot them as the whore closed the door and immediately lifted her skirts. 'Would I ever change?' Vladimir asked himself, accompanied with a wry grin as his accomplice's garments fell to the floor revealing the prize which for now was his alone.

CHAPTER 4

The early morning mist lay in intermittent folds vying from a deep thickness to a thin veil but at all times hiding his view and enhancing the chilliness of the morning. The contact could see no further than three feet in front of him though he trod the path well. Having established himself in the area several weeks earlier he had come to know every step and stone on the route he walked.

The trees about him, although not visible, intermittently swirled and swayed in easiness, submitting itself to the occasional flow of the wind. The drawback of the momentary rustling of the leaves and branches hindered his potential to hear anybody who might be following. His normal course of ensuring this was not the case overlaid his minor concern of the noise from the foliage.

This weather was perfect for clandestine operations, allowing, if necessary, an easier escape for Pieter Sagajlo. The movement of all around was of a deathly silence broken only by the early morning calls of the birds which went about their business totally oblivious of the dangers to ordinary mortals.

At intervals Pieter would halt and listen intently, mainly for the sound of any footsteps but also for any other untoward movement. The conditions, as well as being perfect for his operations, were also advantageous to the enemy. Having carried messages and packages to the dropping point on many occasions before and knowing the area well, the mist, he felt, favoured him.

Since his escape from the Katyn forest Pieter Sagajlo had made his way back into eastern Poland finally joining the underground movement there. Its network was large and diverse and always on the look out for reliable men and women. His duties were varied as was the movement itself. One week he would find himself breaking into a Russian occupied establishment to copy secret documents. The next he would be leaving a note or a package at a designated safe spot for someone, who he would have no knowledge of, to collect at a later time. This morning his duty was simply to leave a white piece of paper at the pre-arranged place and to leave immediately. Even this task could end in failure. Several agents had been caught recently and all members of the movement had been warned to take extra care.

Darker shapes loomed in the distance on Pieter's right like some gargantuan excrescence. He knew them to be the giant oak trees which stood on the outskirts of the village he was heading for. On his left were open fields which he could not see. No shadows came forth on this side, only an occasional muffling sound from the cattle that grazed there seeking out the richer tufts of grasses for the first feed since dawn had broken thirty minutes before.

Continuing on his walk toward the village, Pieter crossed and hid amongst the oak trees which he had now arrived at. Waiting quietly several minutes to detect any foreign noises, he re-crossed to the side of the road on which his drop was to take place.

Taking only several more steps he heard in the distance a sound which drew ever closer. The rumble emanated from the opposite side of the village from where he was approaching. Without running, not wishing to bring any undue notice on himself in the unlikely scenario, in these conditions, that someone was following or watching him, he crossed back over to the side of the road which housed the trees.

Walking quietly along the grass verge which bordered the wooded area, he was no more than one hundred metres from the entrance to the village. The sound which had gathered in noise the closer he approached to the village now stopped. Pieter halted in strange unison.

He recognised the sound to be that of a lorry. Listening intently from his open yet unseen hideout he recognised the footsteps of two people disembarking from the vehicle and puzzled himself as to whom it could be.

'The Baker is usually busy at this time of the day,' he confided in himself, 'but today is his rest day, his wife looks after the shop.'

An earlier warning from his Direct Command came to him. 'No chances, anything out of the ordinary, retreat. Get away as quickly as possible.' Other words also echoed in his mind again from his Superior. 'The job although small is extremely important.'

The white piece of paper, one centimetre square, had been placed in the palm of his right hand only twenty four hours earlier. After it had been left in his safekeeping, Pieter had scrutinised it thoroughly for any signs or markings. To his naked eye there was nothing on the paper.

His thoughts returned to the present. 'The second set of footsteps?' he now asked himself. 'Who do they belong too? The baker or his wife usually works alone in the early part of the morning. The assistant comes in later in the morning.' Pieter was puzzled.

After waiting another twenty minutes and hearing no more unusual sounds but still unsure as to what had happened, he decided to enter the village.

The lorry had not left and the drop had to be completed within a certain time. That time was running out. Pieter had weighed up the odds. If it was the Russians he would simply state that he was up early to fetch the bread. His papers, although false, were in order and would pass the normal inspection, if they decided to take him in for questioning. What could they do to a man who had nothing incriminating on his person. At least to them a white piece of paper would not be any evidence. Unless….unless they looked at the paper more closely. Again, Pieter reminded himself that he did not know whether there was anything encoded onto the paper which could incriminate him. The Underground told its members and couriers as little as possible about the reasons why the task had to be performed and even less about the contents of a package. That way, if they were interrogated, very little information, if anything, would be forwarded. Pieter, like the others, never ever knew the identity of their superiors or contacts.

His approach was like that of a predator cat. Furtively and quietly he neared his goal. The mist which provided him with excellent cover was beginning to clear. The pulse and beat of his body now increased in tempo sounding to him like a grandfather clock, a normal occurrence and one which he controlled easily despite the intensified pressure.

Passing the few houses at the entrance to the village, he neared the end of the first row and peered around the corner with only a slight movement of the head. The lorry which he had heard was stationary and parked down the lane by the side entrance to the baker's premises, the first building in the next row of houses. Hardly stopping his movements, Pieter reconnoitred the lane and the lorry as he passed by. The mist had cleared sufficiently enough for him to see into the cabin of the vehicle. Not a soul was visible. He was ten yards away and the sudden increase in his visibility warned him that the ideal conditions for his line of work were disappearing quickly. 'Speed but extreme caution is now your objective,' he warned himself.

He crossed the lane and was now in front of the shop. He located the dropping point two houses along, a crack in the pipe which carried itself from ground level to halfway up the length of the building. It disappeared into the dwelling between the ceiling of the downstairs room and the floor of the upper room. The hole was approximately one foot from the ground. Perfect for the approach which he would adopt.

Pieter had worked out his plan hours after receiving his instructions. Dropping to his left knee and knotting the lace on his right boot, the square piece of paper was ready in the palm of his left hand. He looked up once before finishing the bootlace operation. The mist had now almost cleared. He had misjudged the rapidity of its disappearance and it had taken him by surprise.

Visibility was improving by the second. The sunshine which had been severed by the density of the fog burst through randomly in strong shafts lighting up areas of the village as if under searchlight. The warmth of the day followed it through. The village was still quiet. The surreal visions around projected an eerie atmosphere. Pieter had never experienced anything similar before. An ominous mood surfaced and for the first time ever, negative feelings within him started to flourish, feelings which he fought to expunge. 'There is sufficient cover to make the drop,' he told himself encouragingly. 'You've been successful on countless operations before and in more dangerous situations. Do it! Do it!' he exclaimed to himself.

He arose. On his way up his left hand opened. It was over the hole. From either side of him he heard footsteps. At first they were slow in tempo. Then they quickened turning rapidly into a run. He looked up and between the remaining sporadic patches of mist Pieter detected two men hastily approaching and heading straight for him. His hand was still over the hole. The whole operation took seconds; to him it seemed like minutes. He retracted his hand simply and naturally. Prior to placing his hand in his pocket he deliberately dropped the small white squared paper, watched it fall to earth and rubbed it with his foot into the ground below him. He performed the action as naturally as he possibly could. At the exact moment he motioned to walk away, the running footsteps he had heard behind, but which he purposefully had not looked for, clattered into him felling him to the ground. Winded and shocked the two whom he had seen running toward him arrived to assist in his bondage. They were shouting obscenities at him as well as questioning him. The stupid expression on his face volunteered nothing. After a short while, still pretending to be winded, he whispered at his interrogators who continued to ask the same question over and over, 'to the baker's shop.'

Two of the men left Pieter in the companionship of their comrades and searched the area around the pipe for any sign of its use. Probing frantically they widened their area of examination. One of the men picked up a small square dirty piece of paper turning it over to peruse the rear. The back was more dirt sodden than the front. Without any further investigation he ignored the scrap and allowed it to fall to the ground. He continued with his now pointless search looking back toward Pieter voicing scurrilous abuse in his direction.

Eventually Pieter was taken away for further questioning. The next twenty-four hours were crucial to him and he contemplated whether his last task with the Underground was worthwhile. The beating sustained on his body raised serious doubts.

SAVAGE JOURNEY

Jacob met her again that evening, eagerly awaiting her appearance as her transport arrived. Sophie's parents sat in the front of the vehicle whilst she sat in the rear. Jacob moved gracefully down the steps to greet his loved one and her parents. His future mother and father in law disembarked from the automobile. He received them warmly, for he had always had a good relationship with them both. The elderly couple moved off quickly in the direction of where the music was coming from and left the young couple to their own direction.

Next Sophie alighted from the vehicle and Jacob moved forward to guide her down from the step of the automobile. Turning to fully face him he stared in the partly moonlit sky at the goddess like appearance of the woman he was soon to marry.

For several moments Jacob stood mesmerised by her sheer beauty, then proceeded to cast his eyes along the length of her body inspecting her every curve, undulation and movement that she made as she adjusted the fall of her gown. Jacob resembled a scientist investigating a new found organism, unable to take his eyes of the find.

Sophie wore a full white gown made of pure silk bordered around the neckline with narrow edged lace. A shoulder wrap, also of white lace, kept the chill of the evening at bay. The gown hugged her figure in a delicate manner enhancing the upper and lower curves of her perfectly shaped body. Her long black hair, adorned with a tiara of semi-precious stones, was dressed and styled above her forehead and the colour of her mane complemented by the complexion of her skin, and by the choice of her gown gave an added effect of beauty, beauty that, Jacob felt, the goddesses of mythology would have looked on with envy.

Sophie smiled unashamedly at him. She knew with her slightest movement that she conveyed sensuality to him. She had seen the look on his face many times before, very often prior to them making love. It pleased her that she had this power over him and could satisfy him in this simple manner.

When he noticed that she was smiling at him, Jacob broke out of his trance and smiled in return.

'I'm sure that for as long as I live I will never see another vision like the one I'm seeing now,' Jacob whispered to her staring into her hazel coloured eyes.

She kissed him approvingly, and he wished that they could be alone together for a little while and proceeded to tell her so. He knew that Sophie was adventurous as to where and when they could, and would, and did make love.

'We've only just arrived Jacob, I cannot disappear immediately,' she susurrated to him with a glint in her eyes.

She was correct of course, and Jacob knew it, but how he wished that it was possible to do otherwise. He kissed her once again, curtly but affectionately. He winked at her as he took her hand in his and they both turned to follow Sophie's parents into the house where the gay and gaudy merriment reverberated throughout the abode and into the immediate surrounding gardens.

They whispered idle gossip to one another as they ascended the steps and Jacob asked, 'are you ready for the announcement?'

'I have been ready for the last fourteen months Jacob Bryevski,' Sophie replied in a stern tone.

'Fourteen months!' Jacob exclaimed, 'but we have only known each other that long,' he stated looking at her, then realising that she had loved him from the very beginning of their relationship. He smiled happily, and, still looking at her, purred, 'I love you Sophie Sagajlo. You look so beautiful. Does love do that to people?'

'Yes, you make me feel beautiful Jacob,' she replied. 'This is the happiest day of my life.'

They entered the house in time to hear her family's name being announced. Jacob's parents stood in the main entrance hall eagerly awaiting the arrival of Sophie's mother and father.

The aristocracy in Poland usually announced a forthcoming marriage in the family by arranging a Ball in the honour of the couple who were to be married. Pavel Bryevski was the father of six children, four sons including one stepson and two daughters which also included one stepdaughter. His wife, Eva Bryevski, had been married and widowed many years before.

Despite their land being occupied by the Russians, Pavel was determined that the usual custom of announcing a forthcoming marriage would continue. He had successfully managed to bribe the Official of the Russian Secret Police, the NKVD, who was assigned, as on every estate in Poland since the Russians had arrived, to periodically logging the assets of his property and making sure everything was running smoothly. This inducement had paved the way for the Ball that was in being that night.

Pavel did not say how grand an affair it was going to be, only that a few close friends were invited. The official was happy with Pavel's explanation and more than happier with his inducement and could see no harm in allowing Pavel to organise his little gathering for one night.

After the announcement of the Sagajlo family, both the hosts and the guests greeted one another with warmth, excitement and affection. Then both sets of parents retired with the future bride and groom to the library to discuss the announcement of their respective offsprings marriage which would take place the following year. As was the custom, the remaining guests would be told at the end of the dinner which was being held in honour of the young couple who were to be married.

Prior to leaving with her parents, Sophie had arranged to see Jacob in the garden before her departure. They embraced one another and made arrangements to meet the next day. The evening had been a great success and everyone present was delighted for the couple who had made their announcement to be wed public.

Holding her close, Jacob accompanied Sophie to the front of the house. They walked through the beautiful landscaped garden, across the lawn which appeared as though it had been specially laid, and was on many occasions used as a tennis court especially in the summer months, through the orchard comprising of pear, apple and plum trees of various types and out onto the steps which led up to the columned entrance to the front of the grand house.

Her transport awaited her, a four seated bottle green Ford, given to her father several years earlier by a very grateful and wealthy landowner for saving the life of his only son out of seven children.

'More reliable than a horse' the benefactor remarked after the animal of Sophie's father had become lame prior to attending to the sickness of the son. 'I'll give you some lessons too,' promised the landowner.

Sophie's parents were seated inside the vehicle patiently waiting their daughter's arrival. She turned to Jacob once more, and out of view of her doting parents pressed herself against his body. Again Jacob embraced her and touched the soft round lips that always took his breath away. They whispered their love for one another, like two doves whistling mating calls in the spring.

With encouraging calls from her mother that they really should leave immediately as her father was required urgently to attend an emergency outside Lyszcze (Wishche), Sophie finally pulled away from Jacob, and after reminding each other of tomorrow's meeting, parted company.

Jacob watched Sophie waving liberally out of the rear window of the vehicle as her transport disappeared down the drive and out of the tree lined entrance to his father's estate. Although she would only be leaving him temporarily, his heart and mind already ached her departing.

When Sophie was satisfied that she could not see her Jacob anymore she turned toward the front of the vehicle and joined in the conversation taking place between her father and mother as though she had been included in the dialogue since leaving the Bryevski estate. Whilst she conversed she unclasped the tiara from her hair and placed the object in the inner pocket of her coat which she had brought with her but left on the rear seat of the vehicle. She then loosened the grips on her hair and allowed her mane to hang freely around her shoulders.

'Yes it was a very successful evening under the circumstances,' Sophie's mother replied in agreement with her husband. 'It was disappointing that we had to leave so soon.'

'I could have stayed the evening mother,' Sophie stated, returning to the earlier discussion with her parents that she be allowed to remain at the ball, 'or borrowed a horse from Jacob and ridden home later,' she continued.

'Neither of those suggestions are sensible Sophie especially with the Russians swarming everywhere,' her father reprimanded.

'I would have been perfectly all right Papa; Jacob would have ridden home with me.'

Her words however were lost to her father whose face had turned a strange ashen white. 'What is happening?' he thought aloud.

Sophie noticed her father's expression change and faced the direction in which he was looking. The Doctor brought the vehicle to a standstill. From where all three were seated, the beams of light from the headlamps of the vehicle highlighted several columns of people marching toward them. The columns were in turn flanked intermittently by other men who were carrying rifles.

Two soldiers approached the vehicle walking at a faster rate than those they had left. Sophie's father could see that they were heading toward them. He switched off the engine, and, getting out of the car, issued orders to both women to remain inside the vehicle.

A Russian lieutenant, being the senior of the two men, approached the doctor, saluted and asked in Russian, 'Your name please?'

The doctor understood a little Russian and replied, 'Doctor Yuri Sagajlo.'

'Papers?'

He produced his documents and handed them over for the Lieutenant to inspect. The officer, after inspecting the papers, then turned to the subordinate and ordered him to produce the list of names to confirm if the name of Sagajlo was present. It was, and the subordinate replied so.

The Lieutenant inspected the vehicle and the two women inside. Turning to the doctor he asked, 'Your family?'

'Yes. Da.'

'Their papers.'

The columns of people had approached the vehicle and were now marching by.

After all documents had been checked to the list, the Lieutenant turned once more to the doctor.

'You will all come with us, Doctor. Take what belongings you have from your vehicle, you may need them,' he ordered.

As all three took what little possessions they had in the vehicle, including two blankets from the boot plus the medical bag, Sophie's father considered whether to argue over his appointment with the emergency outside Lyszcze and to demand that he be allowed to proceed on his journey. He knew very well that he would not be permitted to continue. To argue was futile. It struck him that his name had finally been included on a list, the famous lists drawn up periodically by the aggressors to rid his country of the cream of its countrymen. The men who would, one day after the invaders had been defeated, hopefully return and rise again to build and to guide its populace through a new growth, to a new Poland.

'You will join the remainder of your people, Doctor; we march into the night to meet the train which leaves tomorrow.'

'What train Lieutenant? Why?' asked the doctor innocently, belying the fact that he had heard of the trains which made neighbours, friends and families, all or part of, disappear to another place, another land.

'You will be told the reason why when we see fit to do so, Doctor, now join the column,' barked the lieutenant getting irritated by the questions which had been asked of him.

Sophie's father took his wife and daughter in his arms and gently but quickly led them into and amongst their fellow people who were a mixture, he now noticed, of military personnel and ordinary people. Of the latter, many were well dressed and he assumed that these were professional people. Those that were dressed in working clothes he assumed to be a mixture of craftsmen and peasants, though considered the fact that they could have been innocent prisoners before joining the march. He noticed that both his wife and daughter had begun to cry. Holding them closely and firmly to himself he hoped that somehow the small gesture would comfort them and make up for the catastrophic events of the last ten minutes.

The tears that Sophie cried became stronger. They ran down her face over the high arched cheekbones to meet each corner of her mouth. The abundance of tears overflowed her lips and dropped off the underneath of her jaw. She appeared as though her face was lashed with falling rain, only this rain was tainted with salt and the raindrops fell from her deep dark eyes not from the heavens.

They were urged on by the saddest feelings that no more would she cast her limpid eyes on the man that she loved and to whom she wanted to spend the rest of her life with. 'I promise,' she thought to herself, 'I promise that I will find him once more when this intrusion is all over.'

The soldier who had brought the list to the Lieutenant folded the three sheets of paper containing the names and addresses of scores of Polish people. He placed them in the left hand breast pocket of the blouson uniform he wore, only after the Lieutenant had crossed the three names off the list and handed them back.

Turning again to the Lieutenant, the soldier enquired, 'What shall we do with the vehicle Sir?'

'If we had time we would commandeer it for ourselves and our army. We do not have time and we do not want to leave it for the Poles. Burn it!' He ordered to his underling, pleased with himself that he had suddenly thought of the idea, and immediately ordered two other subordinates to help the first soldier to destroy the vehicle.

Without further orders the three soldiers set about their task instinctively and with relish, as if each had performed the job in hand on many occasions before. The first soldier tore handfuls of grass from the side of the road and compressed them down the funnel of the fuel tank. The second and third soldiers ripped an old cloth which they had found under the front seat of the vehicle into thin strips and tied one end of the first piece to the other end of the second piece and so on until all the strips were tied end to end. They then rammed the cloth into the fuel tank with the help of a wooden stick picked up from the side of the road. The strips of cloth were then pulled out again to ensure they were covered or partly covered in petrol. When this was confirmed the soldiers laughed excitedly and proceeded to ram the cloth back into the fuel tank, ensuring that there was enough material spilling out of the opening to act as a fuse and to allow the soldiers to retreat to safety without fear of the vehicle exploding within their distance. With the fuse lit the three soldiers retreated, waiting like excited children for the fireworks display to commence.

Their wait was not long, and the orange ball of fire which ensued, quenched the thirst of the soldiers excitement. With their good deed finished they turned and quickly marched toward the disappearing columns of people, whom they had been guarding over shortly before. At intervals they turned to see the simmering bonfire slowly evanesce out of view.

CHAPTER 5

Several minutes after verifying Sophie's vehicle disappearing off his father's property, Jacob looked up across the horizon and was surprised to see that a strange orange glow was breaking into the darkness of the night, as if trying to fight back the black shadows which the darkness was surely bringing forth. Jacob watched as the glow turned bright like a beacon then dimmed slowly until only a flickering was left, infrequently altering to a brilliant flash of light from longer periods of darkness, like a lighthouse warning passing ships in the night.

As he stood watching, he wondered whether Sophie would have seen the strange sight, as that was the direction in which she was travelling. He quickly calculated the time it would have taken for her to pass the area and decided that she would have been too late to notice the incident.

After watching the phenomenon for several minutes and being utterly confused as to what was the explanation for such a sight, Jacob turned and retraced the steps that he had walked arm in arm with Sophie not more than thirty minutes before. His thoughts were for her and her alone as he entered the house to rejoin the other guests that were present at the Ball.

Standing in the doorway, his memories turned to the events of the day and the evening and how it had been a great success. He looked around at the guests who were enjoying themselves and felt grateful to his parents for risking such an occasion under such oppressed circumstances.

He noticed the two of them on the far side of the room, dancing. Entwined and engrossed in each other, he remembered the many occasions he had seen them as they were now, like two lovebirds setting out on a long journey, though they were many years into their passage through life together.

Yes, Jacob thought, it had been an excellent day throughout, and he could not criticise anything about the day's events. If anybody could find fault, then perhaps the abundance of food was not present at tonight's affair as it had been in the past. But how many people also had to support the Russian army, for they had commandeered much of the crops and livestock from his father's farm, leaving him with the bare essentials in which to provide for his family.

Pavel learned quickly though, about how to retain the best crops and livestock for his own use, and to conceal the true weight of food stocks which had to be handed over to the Russians. Over a period of time an accumulation of essential ingredients were stockpiled for emergencies and to help other families who had fallen on hard times. It was out of this stockpile that Pavel was able to provide for the table that was presented to the guests on this night.

Jacob wandered through the ballroom still being congratulated by the odd guest who had not been able to bestow their salutary remarks earlier on the future groom. He nodded approvingly and smiled at the profferers, exchanged small talk with those who wished to do so, and then continued his walk through the ballroom into the hallway.

He stood in the corner nearest to the main door surveying the mahogany staircase as it rose at forty degrees toward the rear of the building and branched out either side of the hallway to meet the four walls that it glued itself to, like an old oak tree reaching for the heavens. He thought of the house and the happy memories it held for him. How splendid the building was, providing warmth and comfort, despite being spacious and open. Decorations within the dwelling were striking yet simple, no ostentatiousness was prevalent.

Many people of all walks of life would remark on the warmth they would receive on entering the house, whether it was a visitor for Pavel through the main entrance or one of the tenants entering through the servant's door. Jacob's mother, Eva, always believed that people whatever their walk of life, should be made welcome. And so it was, with the servants playing their part in carrying out her wishes.

Jacob was stirred from his thoughts by the twelve piece orchestra in the ballroom now playing one of his favourite Strauss tunes. The majority of the orchestra comprised of members of Pavel's tenants who had learned to play their instruments in their spare time, and who had been taught by their elder relations with the occasional lesson taken under professional tuition. They were capable musicians and along with the more serious members of the orchestra who Pavel knew on a professional basis, and who he had managed to persuade to attend that evening knowing they would not refuse a chance to perform, combined to play music which was pleasing to the ear.

With anything that would make sufficient noise, but mainly with rifle butts and fists, the front doors were hammered upon. The handle mechanism was turned impatiently and the door violently flung open. There was no warning, no knocking, no politeness, no gentleness, no courtesy, no respect, nothing. Yes, one thing. Orders. Orders which were shouted and bellowed at individuals and groups of individuals. The intruders came from all entrances and exits.

Chaos erupted within. Seconds had elapsed and pandemonium quickly replaced the atmosphere of merriment. People ran anywhere to escape the intrusion. Several guests who were congregating in the hallway made a sprint up the staircase only to be met by the oncoming invaders descending toward them. Jacob surmised as to how the offenders had entered from upstairs, and then remembered the outer balustrade, which was never used, leading to the guest's bedroom.

Watching the total commotion break out in front of him in the hallway and on the stairs, a fight suddenly ensued between two of the male guests and two Russian soldiers. Without warning, a third soldier in a bedraggled uniform produced a machete like sword and swung freely toward the two Poles. The first defender met the full force of the swinging blade and it scythed through the neck with little resistance.

Jacob lurched forward, more in shock than a planned attack, and immediately came to a standstill. He heard cries of grief from a female in the background. To him they were very distant. The severed head rolled down the stairs toward him, the mouth wide open.

The vision of the previous night quickly returned to him. It was then that he understood why Kovacs had visited him once again in his dream and the words he had mouthed were 'Rosyjski! Rosyjski!' Russians! Russians!' and not 'Niemiecki! Germans!' It had been a warning to Jacob, a warning which he had not understood. Now it was too late, and as if to enhance his formidable predicament, the second young Pole who had fought to get away followed the fate of his friend in being dealt harshly by the Russians. The bayonets of the two leading rifles pronounced death quickly.

The remaining guests in the hallway were aggressively ushered, some brutally, into the main room where the music was playing, orders being continually vociferated at them. A charivari of sounds emanated from the orchestra and then the music stopped, conclusively announcing the intrusion to everyone. The different instruments sounded their final notes out of tune and completely uncoordinated with the other musicians before finally becoming silent.

The guests who had been rounded up from the other rooms in the house now entered the ballroom where all were forcibly congregating. The result of the damage in the room caused by the sudden and unannounced intrusion by the Russian soldiers was witnessed by all. Several instruments lay strewn on the floor, one violin severely damaged, and another unrepairable. One of the two large glass doors which opened out onto the rear garden had been completely smashed where a number of soldiers had declared their unexpected arrival and several tables near to the glass doors had been overturned.

When all the people had been gathered in the one room, Pavel immediately looked to see that all his family were present. All were, except for one male member, Mikolai.

The third eldest of his four sons, Mikolai was known to have a quick temper and did not take kindly to intrusions which did not meet with his approval. On many occasions, especially up to and including his teenage years, Pavel had to reprimand him severely for his lack of discipline regarding his temper. As he grew older he seemed more able to control this emotion, but still occasionally he had to be reminded by Pavel and his elder brothers to curb himself.

Pavel thought the worse had happened to Mikolai now, and that he may be lying injured somewhere in the house as a result of one of his outbursts. However, he decided against enquiring as to his son's whereabouts and prayed that the former was not the case and that he had somehow managed to escape.

Soon after it appeared that all people on the property were assembled in the main room, the military officer in charge of the squad who had commanded the intrusion, a Captain, entered the room. His appearance was one of neatness and orderliness, unlike several members of his squad. He was tall and yet slightly overweight with a portly outline which suggested he had recently been alleviated of an easier job such as that of desk duties. His hair like his eyes were dark with wisps of grey beginning to creep through his mane, and his complexion was bone white, almost ghostlike with two rounded pouches for cheeks. He resembled that of a walking cadaver. The voice was loud and strong unlike his appearance, and could be heard clearly in all four corners of the room as he spoke.

He addressed his audience in Polish, with an occasional interruption in his speech to define in his mind the equivalent translation before continuing.

'We have come to free you and your people from your oppressors. We look upon this act that we have performed for you as one of decency and humanity.'

An elderly friend of Pavel's spoke up and denied the captain's words.

'What oppressors?' he asked. 'You are our oppressors.'

In anger the captain's face turned a crimson red. He issued a command in Russian to the two soldiers standing nearest to the elderly man, a command that many of the Poles in the room could understand, for they spoke Russian fluently.

The elderly gentleman was clubbed with the end of two rifle butts. The first blow hit him across the upper left cheekbone and the bridge of the nose, producing immediate damage resulting in a bloodied nose. The second blow fell, fortunately, and less severely on the right shoulder. The man fell crumpled to the floor. Several people, including Pavel and Jacob, motioned to the aid of the victim whose head was being cradled in the lap of his wife who responded speedily in her succour to the beating. With her small, inadequate, lace handkerchief she stemmed the flow of blood and wiped the mess from around his face.

The captain ordered the remaining helpers to stay where they were, otherwise more would receive the same punishment or even worse. Those warned moved no further.

The captain issued further instructions. 'You two,' pointing to two male guests close by the attended man, 'tend to his needs as best you can and do not disturb me while I speak.' He continued his rhetoric as if nothing had happened not even stopping to think where he had been interrupted.

The Officer went on to describe what the Russian people had achieved since the revolution and what it could give to Poland and its people. He talked for what seemed like an age but only lasted twenty minutes. During those twenty minutes the speech he uttered came across to his forced audience as though it had been learnt parrot fashion.

Gesturing once more to the captives he concluded. 'All you people present will be required to give your names, ages and addresses to the lieutenant sitting here.'

He walked in the direction of where his subordinate was seated. A small, ornate semi circled table made of oak was produced from the hallway for the lieutenant to carry out his instructions which had been given to him earlier that evening. Together with a comfortable Louis XIV chair, which another soldier had brought in from the hallway, the lieutenant, who was of a young appearance for one in such a high position, made himself comfortable and proceeded to note the necessary information which his captain had ordered each of the individuals to divulge.

Now standing next to his lieutenant, more orders came from the Leader who increasingly sounded like a loudspeaker the more he opened his mouth.

'Unless each of you cooperates, no man or woman will be allowed to leave until all present have complied with my wishes. Line up in an orderly fashion,' he instructed.

Several of the soldiers which were present in the room quickly and vigorously made those occupants, who were slow to react, carry out the captain's instructions, pushing them into line with their rifles which they used like truncheons.

There were approximately one hundred guests attending the ball that night. After taking into consideration the two men who had been murdered on the stairs, Jacob noticed two or three others were also missing. Like his father had detected earlier, his brother Mikolai was not present. Whilst all families congregated together in the queue Jacob turned to his father and enquired in a low whisper, 'where is Mikolai Papa?'

'I don't know,' Pavel replied.' Hopefully Mikolai and some of the other guests have fled the house by now and are in hiding somewhere.'

'Let us hope so,' Eva, who had heard the conversation between her husband and her son, concernedly whispered, 'and that no harm has come to them.'

'Quiet! Quiet! Teeshyeh! Teeshyeh!' one of the soldiers barked in Russian as the waiting people began to talk both individually and in groups amongst themselves and the cadence of the line of voices began to rise.

There was immediate silence, as if the whistling of the north westerly wind which often blew across the lands were suddenly cut off in its prime. Pavel's family spoke no more, but each member in unison seemed to bow their heads and offer a prayer for their loved ones and friends who were missing.

Eventually all names and details had been given, including those of the elderly gentleman who had been brutally felled to the floor by the wooden ended rifle butts. He was now shown some respect and allowed to sit on one of the chairs in the room to recover.

There was a long pause after all the names in the room had been taken. The unexpected respite from further proceedings increased the thoughts of uncertainty and fear began to descend on the minds of the innocent. The people once again began to gather in small groups discussing what was to become of them.

On this occasion the group gathering session was tolerated to a greater degree by the Russians. At this stage they were more interested in the information they had received as a result of their intrusion, and subsequent investigations. The captain, lieutenant, and several of their subordinates were relentlessly scrutinising the lists that had been freshly completed. These new lists were in turn compared and examined to a second list which the lieutenant had extracted from his person. Jacob noticed the expressions of the men in charge change to one of surprise and pleasure when they had located a name which was on the new list and then found on the list produced by the lieutenant.

After what seemed like hours had passed, where the Russians were poring over, comparing and matching the information on the two lists, the captain once more turned to address the captives present in the room. Clearing his throat loudly immediately brought the attention he desired and expected.

'We shall now call out the names of the people we want to interview elsewhere. When your name is called move quickly to the right side of the room.'

The process began and the names were called. As people moved forward to the required area of the room, they were forcibly ushered under a tirade of verbal abuse from two soldiers. This provided several other Russian soldiers with a good deal of mirth. Twelve people now stood in the group and all of them were over seventy years of age.

Again the captain spoke: 'You people are allowed to go.'

There was an instantaneous yet subdued joy emblazoned on their faces visibly witnessed by those unfortunates who remained. Their relief only quelled by the fact that their younger relatives and friends in the room were not amongst them.

Without further complications they were led out into the freedom of the night, overwhelmingly relieved of the fate they knew they had somehow, inexplicably escaped. A fate which was unimaginably perpetrated on fellow human beings which, they also remembered had unfortunately already befallen certain relatives and friends of theirs.

The second group of names were called. The gathering took up the positions that the first had only moments earlier vacated. This group comprised of farm workers and labourers whom Pavel and Eva had invited to the ball that evening. Some had played in the orchestra that Pavel had arranged. Not only were the men invited but also the women, some of whom found it impossible to attend as they had to look after their children. Those fortunate enough to find relatives or friends who would tend to the children while they were present at the ball were now unfortunate enough to be held captive by the Russians.

Once more the captain allowed the second group of people to leave. The expression on the people's faces was similar to that of the first group—one of great relief and easement, as if a death sentence had been revoked on condemned men. Happy utterances from relieved people tainted again by the thoughts for those they were leaving. The group started to whisper as they left the room. The susurrations were quickly dispelled by the Russian soldiers escorting them out of the house.

Approximately forty people were left between the ages of sixteen and seventy. Both male and female were represented. Jacob's mind worked overtime. He thought deeply about what would happen to them all. He had heard stories of people being woken at night and taken away. People arising the next day from slumber only to find their neighbours had disappeared during the early hours of the morning. Members of families going about their daily routines only to return home to find an individual or the whole of their family arrested and either imprisoned or deported.

The Captain looked up and with a serious expression walked slowly toward Pavel. Standing immediately in front of him no more than a foot from his face, the Captain directly addressed the host of the evening's event.

'Where are your other two sons?' he asked authoritatively at the same time raising his right hand in front of his face with two index fingers extended.

The seconds of silence between the two men seemed like an eternity. In the fleeting moment in which the encounter took place, Pavel realised and resented the fact that this man and the Regime he represented possibly knew the whereabouts of most of the Polish people. It was a direct attack on their freedom. The liberty of his country over the previous thirty years had been of immense importance to the Polish people. The Russians were now testing that liberty. Pavel was angry, an anger which he had controlled since the Russian invasion. It simmered, then warmed itself internally and now it boiled itself to a point almost out of control.

With all his composure, Pavel answered calmly, 'Henri my eldest has helped to manage a farm outside Bialystock which belongs to his uncle.'

Pavel's throat became dry and as he continued, dried even quicker. 'Keep up the pretence,' he encouraged himself knowing that what he was about to say was a complete lie. Any saliva in his mouth had turned barren and he forced his words out hiding the soreness in his larynx. 'Mikolai left this morning to help his brother on that farm.'

Pavel and the Russian Captain continued to stand face to face, eyeball to eyeball. Neither man looked away. The hushed silence in the room was electric. Pavel pondered on the officer's next move and desperately wanted to swallow, as the saliva which earlier had deserted him now returned. He knew to do so might show his guilt. After continuing the eye contact for several more audacious seconds the captain turned away to address the remainder of his dwindling audience. Pavel swallowed painfully but with great relief.

'This house is now the property of the Socialist Republic of the Soviet Union. The owners will be allowed sufficient time to pack some belongings before embarking on our journey. The remainder of you will not be able to take anything other than what you have brought with you. You will be allowed to collect your coats prior to leaving.' He looked at his watch then continued pointing directly at Pavel. 'We leave for the station in fifteen minutes, go now and collect your possessions.' Turning to two soldiers he barked orders for them to accompany Jacob's parents whilst they were carrying out their task.

The rest of the group remained in the room whilst Pavel and Eva left in great haste. The soldiers were clearing the carnage on the stairs and in the hallway as the host and hostess came out of the ballroom. The latter immediately sickened by the sight, knew nothing of what had happened. Only the clothes of the remaining headless corpse gave her any idea of who the victim had been. Passing the scene of bloodshed Pavel succoured her whilst she overcame the shock.

Whilst his parents were gone Jacob again pondered on the joyous times which had befallen himself and his family during the many happy years that they had lived in the grand old house. He thought about the future and what it held for them now. Would they see their home once again, or was this the last occasion that they would cast their eyes upon it? As quickly as he asked the question even quicker did the answer come back to him. No matter how great a defence he offered in his mind, the odds and the attitudes of the Russians weighed heavily against him arguing for his father's property to remain intact and to be properly supervised whilst the family were detained.

He remembered when the Russians had crossed the borders into Polish territory many months before. They were amazed to see the high standard of living in Poland and how the people lacked for nothing. At first the Russians had proceeded to buy virtually everything that they possibly could because they had not experienced such an abundance and variety of goods which was on display and for sale in the shops. Eventually the purchasing stopped; they became greedy and had little respect for people's possessions or property, taking what they wanted whenever they wanted without any form of payment. Jacob concluded that they would probably loot the house when the family had left.

The captain sat looking impatiently at his watch obviously wishing the minutes to pass. Well before the fifteen minutes expired, he arose, walked out to the hall and again barked instructions in Russian to his two subordinates upstairs. Within seconds the clatter of boots could be heard on the stairway mingling with the sounds of lighter pairs of shoes. Contented that his orders had immediately been obeyed and with a smug satisfaction on his face he returned to the chair which he had momentarily vacated.

Whilst the group were waiting for Jacob and Eva to arrive the coats were brought in and heaped on the floor awaiting dissection. The mayor of the village, Anatoly Popov who had been attending the ball that night noticed that there were more coats than people. While several people remained searching the pile for their garments and although he knew differently, Anatoly quickly beckoned others to pretend that they had not chosen the correct overcoats. Whilst this was happening the mayor whispered to several people to put on two garments instead of the one. The coats on the floor were all taken and the Russians noticed nothing unusual.

Jacob's parents entered the room carrying several bags in their hands. They lowered their load in front of the family so that the chattels could be shared amongst all members, and then prepared to leave the house.

The captain arose from his seat beside the lieutenant and spoke. 'We are leaving tonight on a journey which will remain in your minds forever, an important journey which will change the course of your life, the manner of your thoughts and the path of your country.' For the first time since addressing his captive audience his voice rose in excitement, the reason for which was lost on his listeners. 'A journey which will make you better people, more able to serve your country when the time comes. All this will be provided to you when you reach your destination. A new learning will be undertaken by you all, a learning which will be provided by the Socialist Republic of the Soviet Union.'

He ceased talking as abruptly as he had begun.

There was no expression on the faces of the people present in the room, except one of emptiness. Families and friends looked at each other seeking words which would describe their horror, but no words were forthcoming. Nothing could describe what thoughts were racing through peoples' minds, though each of their individual thoughts was identical. They had heard the stories, now they were about to succumb to the reality of those stories, stories which were nothing short of nightmares.

Whilst the words that the captain had spoken dwelled on the minds of the victims, the superior left the room and its occupiers in the charge of his subordinate.

The lieutenant, who had been seated throughout the whole of the proceedings, now rose to his feet. Speaking in a sibilant sounding voice and in a badly broken Polish pronunciation he commanded that the remainder were now ready to begin their journey and without any warning and for no apparent reason bellowed at the top of his snake like voice, 'Out! Out! Von otsyooda! Von otsyooda!' returning to his native Russian tongue.

People filed out of the room through the hallway which had been cleared of its two cadavers. Although evidence of what had earlier happened, remained, pools of drying blood staining the wooden floor. Out into the night in disorderly fashion the persecuted trooped. Soldiers ordered people to march in columns of three abreast. If they did not understand they soon received the message through physical pain thanks to the Russian soldiers in attendance.

Jacob was deep in thought about what he was leaving behind as they came out of the house. His family would be leaving beloved relatives and friends, even though many were now present with them having attended the ball.

No more would they set foot on their proud land. For how long would it last? Perhaps forever. Then he suddenly remembered the captain's words and tried to understand what he had meant by them, if indeed it was the truth that he spoke. He had talked of 'a learning,' a learning that would be of importance to your country. Poland! Perhaps some of us would return one day, to serve the country that had suffered for so long. The country we love so much. But if it was to serve alongside the wishes of Russia which had always been an enemy, then how many people would take up the quest? 'Not many,' Jacob thought to himself, 'not many under those circumstances.'

After they had descended the steps outside the house, his thoughts disappeared as he glimpsed people who were not in uniform. As his eyes became more accustomed to the dark he could distinguish who they were.

There were six men, who until several hours ago had worked for his father on the estate. They had been told of what had happened that night by the workers who attended the ball and had since been set free. The six men were members of Pavel's workforce who had not been present at the evening's event but had decided to come to the house to see if they could help.

The group of people approached the captives extending their hands in farewell gestures. At first Jacob thought this was odd because the first person that Wladek, who was one of the better known workers and who had been with his father since before Jacob was born, shook hands with and then embraced, had never set eyes upon him until that moment. Each of the six men did this to individual people in the group, picking people at random. Some they knew, others they had never seen before. They whispered encouraging words as they bade farewell.

'May God go with you.'

'Have great courage.'

'Be strong for your country.'

The Russian soldiers, surprisingly, made no attempt to stop these men.

A young man not much older than Jacob, who he remembered had recently started working for his father, then approached him offering his hand. Jacob accepted his farewell gesture similar to those before him. With his other hand free he placed a package quickly and carefully inside Jacob's coat pocket. In one singular swinging action the young man continued moving his arm up onto

Jacob's shoulder embracing him for several seconds before releasing his grip and moving to another person in the column.

After he had passed and after the six brave men finally bade farewell to the group of marchers, Jacob lowered his hand into his pocket to investigate the contents of the package.

When he opened the parcel ever so furtively, he was surprised and pleased to see that the virtual stranger had given him bread to help him on his journey. It was then Jacob realised why Wladek and the five other men, most of whom he also knew, had embraced total strangers. Soon it became apparent with the messages communicated between the people that other food, in addition to the bread Jacob received, had been passed to other members of the group. Cheese, salad, and salami, as well as tobacco, had also been supplied.

He felt strangely comforted hoping that if there were more people similar to those six men who had been brave enough to smuggle food under the noses of the Russian soldiers, then surely the country would still be left with citizens who would never betray her.

Approximately one hundred metres from the main entrance to the Bryevski estate Jacob turned and looked back once more at what had been his home for the last twenty two years.

A strong possibility that he would never see this home again dawned on him. What he looked upon made his anger swell inside. To vent that anger would have been suicidal. The annoyance subsided turning itself to sadness which shaped tears in his eyes. He cried quietly to himself not wishing his family to see that the animals, pigs, bastards, scum, for they were all those rolled into one and he could not find a substantial word to describe them, had carried the furniture and contents out to the front of the house and had set the building on fire. The possibility, within seconds had become a harsh reality.

Quickly Jacob averted his gaze away from the scene of wasteful destruction. He had seen enough and in the moonlit night which purveyed sufficient light, surveyed the rest of the land he knew so well. The river in which he swam and fished with his sisters and brothers, the trees where his father built hideaways for his children, the fields where they all played and when old enough to do so, reap in the harvest. Other memories came flooding back of his family and friends and the many happy occasions they had been fortunate to share together. These happy thoughts in his mind quelled the anger inside and kept his sadness at bay.

Turning back from viewing the estate which had been his family's concern for many years, and which now was no longer his father's land, something; some movement caught his attention out of the corner of his eye.

Near the entrance to the main driveway to the estate was a barn two levels high used for storing farm equipment and hay. The top level housed the hay. On this level was a window. Over the years the glass had become covered with dust from the movement of hay within the barn. A thin film coating obscured the transparency of the substance. At first Jacob could not make out what it was that he had seen. He blinked his eyes to peer through the window once more. Then it registered with him that there was a face staring out toward the column of marchers passing by. He assumed at first that it was one of the farm workers, and then as they marched closer to the barn and drew level Jacob noticed with great elation that it was his brother Mikolai. Jacob knew that Mikolai had seen and recognised him and he smiled in return, a smile tinged with sadness. Jacob acknowledged him by pulling the collar on his coat up around his neck and saluted in his direction. He then turned to face the front and for the first time since the intruders had invaded his home, over four hours earlier, and despite what was happening to their house and home, he smiled contentedly knowing that at least his brother was safe. The rest of the family marched out of the entrance to the Bryevski estate.

The long journey had commenced. The soldiers were strict and sometimes cruel which was in complete contrast to the weather. The early hours of the morning had slipped into being. The night was clear and the star clustered sky emitted sparkling shimmering light of differing degrees of brightness which spread over the whole horizon representing some massive glowing chandelier. The quarter moon boldly jettisoned itself in front of the celestial bodies pretending to be the guardian to the heavens ready to protect against anything that tried to invade its kingdom. Tonight the moon and the stars lit the path of Jacob's journey which himself, his family, his relatives and his friends were taking. To where? That they did not know. What was awaiting them at the end? Again they did not know, though stories were in abundance of the suffering that other people had endured whilst detained in the presence of the Russian regime.

Not too long a time had elapsed on the march when several people had started to complain that they could not proceed much further without a rest. Many of the elderly began to fall behind and before too long, two separate bodies of marchers were visible. As the rumblings of discontent began to slowly increase, the Russian soldiers became restless to punish those who were grumbling.

Pavel, who had said very little since the march had started, noticed the irritability of the soldiers, and after passing word amongst the front group to carefully and deviously slow the walking pace down, struck the tune of the Polish National Anthem.

The effect it had on all the marchers was quick and positive, one which Pavel had hoped for. Completely different to the perplexed Russian escorts. This solo singing was immediately followed by a chorus of other voices, who on hearing the anthem being sung, gained an energetic step in their walking. The elderly group which had fallen behind also struck up in tune with the front body of marchers, and whilst not being able to link back up with the main group, did not fall any further distance behind.

The Lieutenant in charge ordered that the captives stop singing. Every marcher continued with the rendition of the anthem as if no one had heard his orders.

Szabla adbierze my Marsz, Marsz Dabrowski
Zie miwloskiej do Polski
Za twoim przewodem
Ztacym sie znarodem

On! On! Dabrowski!
From Poland's fair plain!
Lead us on to greet our homeland!
Lead us back again!

Again the lieutenant bellowed at the people to refrain from singing. Again they ignored his ranting. Under orders, several soldiers thrust themselves in amongst the marchers pushing and shoving individuals, women as well as men, assaulting their victims with the aid of their rifles and inflicting pain on the bodies of the defenceless captives. Still the marchers were defiant, and persistently continued with their chorus.

After several minutes of further harassment it was the soldiers who were becoming increasingly disheartened as they began to realise that the brutality they were inflicting on the group was not producing the required effect. Eventually, the Lieutenant ordered his men to cease further hostility toward the people.

The columns of men and women along with the Russian soldiers continued their march into the night. The Polish contingent were happier in the knowledge that they were still strong and united in their stand against their enemy and pleased that they had won a small battle against their captors. They carried on the singing until they arrived at a village where they were to rest for the remainder of what was left of the night. Their sleeping quarters, a barn on the edge of a farm.

'Well the hay is clean and fresh,' remarked Pavel turning and addressing the rest of the party who were entering the barn, hoping to somehow encourage the group out of their obvious dejected manner.

'What are we going to eat?' Another member of the party grumbled in a whisper as he passed Pavel on entering the shelter. 'I know we have a little food but it will not sustain us all Pavel,' he complained further.

Pavel, who since his rendering of the anthem during the march when the elderly had been in danger of falling well behind the main group, now seemed to have taken on the mantle of protector for the people. He approached the Russian Lieutenant who had followed the last of the marchers into the barn along with several of his soldiers.

'We are all hungry and would like some nourishment before we rest for the night.'

'You will be fed in the morning,' the lieutenant replied harshly.

'But Lieutenant,' protested Pavel, 'your men are eating now.' He pointed to a building opposite the barn where the door was ajar revealing the soldiers sitting at a table already feasting themselves.

'We have covered the same journey as you. Look around; there are people who need food now.' Pavel gestured with his hands for the lieutenant to take notice.

The officer was totally disinterested. He turned once more to face Pavel. A cold, venomous look in his eyes was plain to see and he shouted disparagingly, 'If you want to eat, eat the hay that is around you, the animals do.' He turned away, laughing to the two soldiers who were left to guard the party and they too, joined in his morbid jeering. After giving further instructions to his men he left.

Pavel, sadly, faced his people. 'Come,' he said in Polish which the soldiers did not understand, 'eat what little you have and eat without our captors knowing you have done so. But be warned also that from now on the food we eat may be the last that we have for several days. Once you have eaten get as much rest as possible.'

The people tried to make themselves comfortable in the hay. Many of them had already taken out the parcels of food which had been secretly given to them at the beginning of the march. The small amounts of provisions were shared between those who had nothing. Different meats comprising of sausage and salami which had been packed in a greaseproof paper were passed around together with a quantity of lettuces and cabbage with tomatoes and fruit wrapped in different bundles of cloth.

Nobody went without food the first night. The group of Polish people ate quietly without any disturbance from the soldiers. Indeed, after Pavel's encounter with the Russian Lieutenant, the orders given to the two soldiers were to watch over the Poles by patrolling the outside of the barn.

During the small but welcome feast the younger men raised the subject of escape. The older men joined in the conversation pointing out the pitfalls and dangers of many of the ideas discussed. It was suggested that energies be conserved for the journey that lay ahead. Tonight, which had already been eventful, was not the best time to discuss the possibility of escape. Tomorrow's journey would provide ample opportunity for everyone to ponder on the matter in question. With that thought in mind, those who had not already done so, drifted into sleep exhausted from the night's experiences.

CHAPTER 6

Sophie's start to the journey was an uncontrollably emotional one. For the first hour on the march she could nothing more than think of what she was leaving. The more she thought, the more the pain hurt and the more the tears flowed, until in the end there was nothing more to shed. The tiredness wore down her thoughts and gave rise to new concerns as to whether she, herself, would survive whatever the journey held for her. Not just her but her parents too.

Sophie's mother, Helena Sagajlo, quickly recovered from the initial shock of what had happened to them. Acknowledgement that her immediate family were present, except her son, provided some comfort against whatever lay ahead.

The Doctor, Yuri Sagajlo, Sophie's father, was strong and dependable as usual and the solace extended to his wife had eventually brought the results he had hoped for. His daughter, however, was a different story. It deeply concerned him to see her in the state to which she had quickly deteriorated. 'How strong her love must be for him,' he murmured to himself remembering the last moment he had seen his daughter with Jacob no more than several hours earlier.

All three preoccupied with their own thoughts, although very similar deliberations for one another and their distant loved ones, were surprised to find themselves suddenly halted and commanded to sleep inside the building, outside which they had now arrived.

'You will sleep here tonight and leave early in the morning,' ordered the Lieutenant.

The Doctor helped his wife to console and comfort their daughter who had once again started crying. The parents took turns to comfort Sophie. For the mother it brought back vivid memories of the moments she sat up with her daughter through the illnesses that most children experience. When the father took his turn, within five minutes, her crying gave way to sobbing which became infrequent, eventually petering out. Sophie had fallen asleep.

'You always could get her off to sleep quicker than me,' whispered Helena with an accompanying melancholy smile toward her husband as she continued to remember the past.

He arose from his daughter's side and held a hand out to his wife which she accepted willingly. Together they lay down on the single canvas bed bordered all around by similar beds with very little space between each. He placed his arm around her and they drifted off to an uncomfortable yet welcoming slumber.

Sophie was the first to awake the next morning and she soon discovered that what had happened the night before was not a nightmare. As she sat up on her bed she gazed fixedly at her parents. Her stare eventually continued on from them around the remainder of the building.

Other people in various areas of what could only be described as a mass communal bedroom were awaking from their slumber into their own personal nightmare. All around makeshift beds had been supplied to cater for the hundreds of people who were crammed into a factory premises stripped of its machinery. When the number of makeshift beds ran out the remaining people were left to sleep on the floor.

The building was in a dilapidated condition. Every window contained either a partly cracked or wholly shattered pane. The roof had holes allowing the weather to invade. The roots of the machinery which had once occupied the building were in evidence everywhere. Nuts and bolts, screws and washers, wooden battens, pieces of concrete foundation had been uprooted and strewn across the floor.

After surveying all around her Sophie turned once more to look at her parents who were cradled together on the flimsy canvas bed which barely accommodated them. She thought that despite the circumstances they looked good as a pair. The brief vision of them interlocked together infused her with strength and well being. Although she could not remember too much about the previous night's events after they had been taken captive, except for her useless self, she knew that her father had once again been the strong pillar amongst them. He had pulled them through the first horrendous night. Her own behaviour during the previous night slowly returned to her as she looked upon her parents. She decided in those few lonesome, quiet but salutary moments to be strong, if not for herself then for her parents, her family and for Jacob.

The doctor began to stir. His eyelids wavered and blinked open, almost immediately closing again. He repeated the movement until his eyes adjusted to the bright light of the early morning sun which rose higher on its daily path into the sky, breaking and invading the large spacious, previously shaded areas of the inside of the building.

Sophie leaned over from her bed. Leaning toward her father she kissed him gently on the cheek and whispered in his ear gratitude for the prior night's benevolence toward her. He smiled warmly in response touching her lovingly as if she were still his very young daughter. She reciprocated and they exchanged a few words of idle talk.

After eating the little food which was offered to them as breakfast the people were herded out of the premises. Once again they were forced to march in columns which dissipated haphazardly no more than one hour after the morning's journey began.

During the morning march Sophie looked around to see if she knew anyone who was in their group. She quickened her step toward the front of the column but recognised nobody. Then she slowed her movement to await the end of the column advancing on her. Again it was to no avail. She could not recognise any of the people who passed. Eventually she rejoined her parents who were not in agreement with her temporary disappearance.

Her father, however, had allowed her to go explaining to Helena 'that it would be good if she became more independent of us as it will give her added confidence. No one knows what is awaiting us in the future and whether we will survive. If anything happens to us Helena she will have to manage alone.'

'Yes you are correct Yuri.' Helena reluctantly agreed with his reasons. She knew that his reasoning made sense.

As Sophie's party were advancing on the railway terminus at Pinsk a group of almost one hundred male prisoners joined their ranks of men, women and children of all ages. Word quickly spread that the men were not only prisoners but interned Polish soldiers who, like themselves, were to be deported to Siberia for indoctrination into the Russian ideology.

Not long after the group had joined the initial body of marchers a sharp shrill noise could be heard above the normal cacophony of sound which was emanating from the large band of people. Sophie thought she recognised the noise and strained her ears to listen. No sooner had she tuned into the sound than it had ceased. Then as she relaxed her senses, which accepted the normal noises that were constantly around her, the sharp shrill sound emanated once more. This time it was clearer than before and her adrenalin started to react to the clarity of the tone which she now recognised to be a whistle. Sophie turned her head in the direction from where she thought the sound was coming, getting more and more excited with each note projected across the warm air of the disappearing morning.

Not wishing to draw attention to herself from the scattered soldiers surrounding the marchers, she moved slowly at first, toward the area which she considered the noise was coming from. As she drew nearer to the source she knew the tune could only be whistled in that manner by one person. She had heard the tune so many times before and so many years ago had she heard it last. Able to curtail the excitement inside for fear of disappointment, her adrenalin raced through her body out of control almost lifting and carrying her to the source of the sound. Her heart beat faster than the gallop of her favoured stallion and she realised that she had quickened her step to keep pace. She fought to slow herself down remembering that she did not want to bring any attention upon herself. The idea was sensible, the body however, either did not want to or could not react as her pace quickened once more.

She collided with people, young and old as she brushed past them apologising profusely as she moved on being carried by this force within her to find the source of the noise which suddenly took precedence over everything else. Then as the whistling became clearer and she felt as though she could reach out and touch the notes with her bare hands, although she could still not see what she was searching for, confusion interrupted, other sounds, and other people starting to whistle the same tune, sporadic at first then gradually becoming regular. She continued to push past people in her desperate exploration, physically turning them around so that she might see their faces. Each body she turned and each face she gazed upon was a disappointment to her greater than the previous.

Frustration began to creep into her movements. She knew that somehow she must control herself. The soldiers would be watching if she caused too much of a disturbance. Her frustration led eventually to tears and she prayed that she might find the source of the first sound she had heard so clearly, the one which had now been drowned by all the others, but which, intermittently could still be heard above the other whistling. She pressed on. Now she noticed that she was turning and staring at new faces and assumed that they were the men who had joined them most recently that morning. Still she could not find the one she was looking for. There were hundreds of people around, how could she find him? The tears continued streaming down her face. As she wiped them away, she remembered too, how he had occasionally wiped them for her when she was a little girl.

In sheer frustration she cried aloud, sobbing his name, for she knew that she had to do something to find him amongst this multitude of people.

'Pieter! Pieter!' she cried uncontrollably. She could not be heard clearly as the calling of his name evaporated quickly into and amongst the normal sounds.

Again she cried out the name, louder on this occasion, using all her strength that her weakened body would relinquish to her.

'Pieter! Pieter!'

Please let him hear me Lord, she pleaded in her mind, and she continued to cry in exasperation at not being able to find him. Her pace had slowed in unison with the hope that was draining form her. Several people who passed her offered comfort. Politely she refused, beckoning them to continue with their journey.

Then, similar to the slow build up in which the whistling had started, it began to fade away. Sophie now purposefully walked slower in rhythm to the dwindling sound of the whistling and the ebbing away of earlier sanguine thoughts, until soon the noise had completely abated.

Seconds passed. The silence was ephemeral though to her it seemed longer. Then the original lone shrill sound which she first heard what had seemed like an age ago, sounded once more. The anxiety process for her started all over again. New hope as strong as before coursed through her veins. The adrenalin was up, quicker than before. She turned to see if she could recognise from what direction the signal was emanating. The sound was stationery like its orchestrator. She also halted. She revolved again, on the spot, to locate the noise and as she did so she caught sight of him as he came slowly but determinedly toward her, colliding with people as he approached, he continued as if nobody else were there. Sophie's tears, which had abated, slowly but surely came flowing back. This time they were gratefully accepted.

She called his name quietly as he came forward, disbelieving at first what her eyes was seeing. Blinking her eyelids open and closed to clear her sorrow and to ensure she was not imagining his image. He placed his arms around her and in complete silence, except for her sobbing, they held each other tightly. Now she knew it was for real. He could feel her tears slipping off her cheekbones and wetting his unshaven face and he remembered how she used to cry, due to a childish mishap, when they were young and he would provide solace to her then. Now the role was played out by him once again.

'We must keep moving or they will suspect something,' Pieter eventually whispered to her.

She had not heard his voice for well over a year. The last occasion when he had been allowed a weeks leave several months prior to the commencement of war with Germany. The cadence of its tone calmed her as it had done so many times before. Immediately it reminded her that there were other aspects of Pieter which verified that he was his father's son. Placing his right arm around her they continued walking.

'Are you well Sophie?' he asked. 'What have they put you through?'

'I'm well enough,' she replied now, able to control her flood of tears. 'I haven't suffered as you appear to have done so,' she announced as she examined his features more closely remembering his young face the day he left home. Now that face had gone. No traces of youth remained. Instead it had been replaced with marks of survival, of fortitude, of hardness and age. His eyes enhanced the process. They too had changed from happy, innocent, gleaming orbs to a melancholy haze and Sophie thought that amongst all the cruelty he had probably experienced, personally or second hand, he too, no doubt was capable of being cruel. This candid acceptance on her part, regarding her brother, surprised her. Despite this fact she still loved him dearly.

'You look much older than your twenty seven years.' She continued eyeing him at the same time, expecting a reply even though she had not asked a question.

'You always were straight with me,' he replied, smiling at her before continuing. 'There have been some difficult times.' He stated broadly knowing that statement covered many bad experiences and then shrugged his shoulders dismissing the worse moments of his life, for now anyway, hoping that she would not enquire anymore.

'Mama and Papa are with me.' She changed the subject realising he did not want to discuss the matter and managed a smile to ease his worries. She remembered how as children he relished going out on calls with their father and how he had always wanted to be a doctor like him.

A lump came to Pieter's throat as he confirmed what Sophie had told him. She nodded her head.

'Where are they? Take me to them,' he eagerly requested and they increased their walking pace toward their parents.

'There!' she exclaimed, pointing in the direction as they caught sight of them and moved nearer.

Sophie indicated once again toward her mother and father as they approached them from behind in the long procession of human beings. Pieter recognised them and smiled contentedly to see them alive and apparently well. He could feel his heart beating a little faster at the thought of meeting them again. Sophie told her brother that she would approach them first and break the news. Pieter hung back behind his parents no more than an arm's length away. He could if he wanted to reach out and touch both with an outstretched hand.

His heartbeat was now racing with excitement pumping at full strength as the pleasure of seeing them again mounted inwardly. He remembered the last occasion he had seen his parents, and the thoughts of his last encounter with them, waving farewell as he departed for the Academy, suddenly made him aware that he had missed them and Sophie enormously. In those split seconds a tremendous urge came over him to thrust himself upon them, to shower them with his love and affection. He decided against this in case the shock would be too much for either of them and preferred Sophie's idea that she should announce his arrival. He heard the distinguished voice of his mother addressing Sophie and the sudden emotion which almost overwhelmed him was verified by the inflated thyroid cartilage in his throat which felt as though it was rupturing his skin. He swallowed the last remnants of saliva in his drying mouth and fought back the tears which were eager to exhibit themselves.

'Where have you been Sophie?' her mother enquired, relieved that she had returned safely.

'Not far Mama. I've met someone we know and I've brought him to meet you.' She smiled as he announced her news.

'Who is this someone? Where is he?' her father asked, joining in the conversation.

'Not far Papa, in fact he's right behind you.'

The doctor turned expecting to see some long lost friend or at best some distant relative. As he turned his wife followed suit and all four halted in their tracks.

His expression turned to one of awe as he gazed on his son once again, the son who he had watched growing from a baby to a young boy to a young man and then finally into manhood, only to be snatched away by the military to prepare and fight for a war that was doomed from the start. It was an event that would deprive his son from the best years of his life. His only son who had kept him company on many visits to his patients. The son who left home to pursue his studies at medical school, had qualified, but had no chance to practice his prowess in the field. The son who was adamant that he too would be a doctor just like his father, and who, but for the outbreak of war, would surely have fulfilled his dreams to succeed in the medical profession. His expression turned to a happy smile and proof of his emotions, normally under control, welled up in his eyes and slowly fought their way out and down the side of his face.

Pieter's mother did not worry about her emotions and let nature take its course, as she usually did. She burst into tears immediately she caught a glimpse of her son and by the time she had turned fully to confront him her crying was in full flow. Her arms outstretched eager for his touch. Approaching him her motherly instincts came to the fore and remarked, 'How thin you are looking Pieter..'

Pieter smiled happily when his parents turned to face him and he cast his eyes on those who had loved and cherished him for as long as he could remember. His heart ached even more now realising that he had stayed away too long. How he wished that the clock could be turned back and he had been able to spend more time with them at the same instant recognising that that would have been impossible. His mother's reaction he knew only too well. That of his father's surprised him. He had never seen tears from the father he loved and respected so much and it gave him a warm feeling to know the strength of love that he had for him.

When his mother's outstretched arms offered the love and comfort which he had not received for a very long time, and which he now realised he had desperately missed, he motioned toward his parents, opening out his channel, taking them both in his grip and holding them tightly to him.

His mother's comment broke any apprehension and all four burst out laughing. Pieter, in particular, laughed loudly which almost conquered the battle he fought to shed any tears. Memories came flooding back to him when as a little boy she always made sure he had adequate meals. The satisfaction of seeing them alive again coupled with the memories now broke down the barriers he had created to fight off the emotions which he was experiencing. He wept with joy.

The three clung to each other refusing to let go, openly crying with their happiness and contentment at having found one another amongst all the catastrophic events which had happened to them and their country in such a short space of time.

Sophie, also crying as a result of the emotive scenes from her family, had been watching the soldiers whilst her brother and parents embraced. She noticed that several guards were aroused as to what was happening in the centre of the throngs of people. Closing up and putting her arms around the joyful trio, she explained to them that they must continue in the procession.

Pieter responded by thrusting one arm around each of his parents' midriff, catching Sophie's hand, and marched along with them. All four, despite their surroundings, were in a joyous mood as they continued their progress toward their journey's end. Each knew the joy would be ephemeral. They talked incessantly about the many happy memories they had shared together as a family. Sophie and her parents enquired what had become of Pieter since he had last visited them over twelve months before.

He briefly relayed his experiences of what had happened after joining the Academy. In more detail he talked about events since he had last visited them, including the fighting and capitulation in the battle of Warsaw. How they had ignored orders and remained for several months to help the Jews of the city and then belatedly obeying the command to make their way to Rumania where they would be given refuge. Whilst carrying out that order his small band of soldiers had been ambushed by Russian troops. Pieter and two other colleagues survived the ambush and were imprisoned, whilst another managed to successfully flee the trap. In the early spring, after the incident at Katyn near Smolensk, Pieter returned to that part of Poland occupied by the Russians. He had found refuge in the countryside where he met up with other soldiers including several from his old regiment plus the one who had escaped the ambush, all of whom no longer intended to make their way to Rumania and who were now connected with the underground movement.

Joining the activity himself he had recently been apprehended making a drop. 'That was yesterday morning,' he announced.

'What did they do to you Pieter?' his mother enquired anxiously.

'A few kicks, a few bruises mother, nothing to worry about,' he candidly replied, hiding the truth form her.

'It was worth it,' he continued, 'I was used as a decoy. With my capture the Movement were able to pinpoint the person who was passing on information to the Russians. I only learned of that this morning.'

'Why you Pieter?'

'It's a long story Mama which I will tell you about one day.' Deliberately he omitted to relate to his family about the massacre in the woods outside Smolensk and had made up another story for his forced visit there. As his mind began to relive the carnage once more, his mother disturbed his distasteful cogitations.

'Why did you not come to us Pieter?' She asked.

'I wanted to but if I had come they would have found me eventually. Have you not had Russian soldiers enquiring as to my whereabouts?'

'Yes,' replied his father, 'they came on several occasions to see if you had returned home.'

'We could have hidden you Pieter,' Sophie eagerly suggested.

Pieter smiled at her. 'There are too many communist collaborators to hide anyone successfully. If I had been found at my own home then you,' he said, looking at all of them and enhancing his feelings for them. 'My family, as well as myself would have been persecuted. No, it was too hazardous for me to return home. And it was more beneficial to remain where I was.'

There was a moment's pause then Pieter chirped in again. 'Now though, I'm home. Wherever you are that is my home and if I should ever lose you or be parted from you there will come a time when I will find you and we will be together again.' He reassured them, not completely certain whether it was his happiness at chancing upon them that made him confident in his announcement or whether he truly believed in his own ability to do so. 'Today I have found you and today we are a family once more.' He beamed a wide smile at them and they in turn smiled back.

It was the turn of Helena, his mother, along with his sister to inform Pieter of what had happened during his long absence. They told of the friends and relations who had disappeared and of those who still remained if still alive. The culmination of their update was the announcement of Sophie's intended marriage next year and what had happened the previous night.

'We tried to get word to you through all sorts of channels,' Sophie told him, 'but there was no reply.'

'Don't worry,' he replied, 'even if I had known it would have been dangerous for me and probably for all of you if I had made an appearance.'

They continued their journey, the four of them felt stronger in the knowledge that they were together again, and, for the moment at least, they felt they could cope with whatever the Russians had planned for them.

They talked virtually throughout the duration of the march until ordered to stop on the outskirts of Pinsk. There they were given instructions that soon they would be boarding trains to be taken to Russia. The group then marched into the station terminus at Pinsk and were immediately made to board the cattle trucks that were waiting to take them to their final destination.

CHAPTER 7

Two shots awakened the captives the next morning. Performed by a gorilla like creature that passed for a soldier he laughed at the shocked expressions which he had helped to create on the faces of the majority of his captors as they aroused from their sleep. He then proceeded to distribute freely, kicks from his ape like feet, on the bodies of those who were slow to rise from their slumbers as well as shouting obscenities in Russian to the same slow starters. The younger members of the group who were quicker on their feet proceeded to help those who were the centre of abuse. Even those who provided succour were abused in turn.

Wilos, a quiet young man of nineteen years and strong as an ox due to many years working on his father's farm, was one of those who aided and was then ill-treated by the soldier. He stood up quickly to confront the apish guard who suddenly stopped in his tracks surprised and a little afraid that anyone dared to object to what he was doing. Wilos's father had seen the whole incident and noticed that the rifle of the Russian soldier was being raised slowly but surely. Reacting quickly to the situation he thrust himself between the two instant enemies. At the same time turning to his son, winking at him, he hit him several strokes about the head followed by an obvious tirade of angry abuse. On seeing his father signal to him Wilos covered his hands over his head only freeing himself from the protection when the words from his father had subsided.

The intrusion by the father had the required effect on the soldier who slowly displaced the expression on his face from that of anger to one of mirth. Happy with what he had seen the guard turned and walked back to the door. As he motioned to the front of the barn the lieutenant entered.

Without any courtesy he proceeded to bellow instructions. 'Outside is a trough of water where you can all wash and clean up before eating if you wish. Two rows of women form here and two rows of men form her.' He gestured with his right and left arms pointing to where he wanted the rows to commence. 'Hurry! Hurry!' he barked. The two groups, each with two rows, formed quickly with little problem.

Once outside it was the first daylight view they had of the area having arrived during the night. The surrounding countryside appeared peaceful and serene. The fields in front of the barn stretched far into the horizon frequently broken by bottle green covered hedges where leaves had answered the call of nature during the spring and summer seasons. The majority of fields all around had been ploughed and sowed and evidence of the task was already growing. Those fields that remained uncultivated were left for animals to graze on.

The guards ordered the marchers to commence washing four at a time in the trough. Each of the four rows was given one towel, which appeared to be an old bed sheet, in which to wipe themselves. On completion of the communal bath they were led back into the barn. Several of the prisoners, as well as the wash, attempted to clean their clothes and smarten themselves only to experience great difficulty in doing so after having slept in their garments in unclean surroundings during the night.

The lieutenant returned and proudly announced,' now that you are under supervision of representatives of the Soviet Republic you will receive a proper breakfast, a Russian breakfast,' and he proceeded to open the barn door.

Five women walked into the barn with the most appreciative sight the captives had feasted their eyes upon since being forced to leave their homes the night before. The sight of the food brought a smile to most faces. It was more appreciative as the food was hot verified by the steam which rushed from the gaps in the lids of the two large earthenware pots carried by four women. It reminded the group of the gaseous water vapours of opened tureens revealing hot vegetables prior to the commencement of dinner. In addition to the sight of food, and especially to the gratitude of the younger men, was the appearance of the two women sharing the burden of carrying the first receptacle.

Jacob noticed his friend, Jan Pilochka. His young male instincts scrutinising the two girls either side of the container, paying particular attention to the one on the right. His eyes never left her as he first noticed her flowing brown hair around oval features which held two of the most beautiful brown objects he had ever seen. These were supported by an almost perfectly shaped nose, a little too sharp perhaps at the end, and lips which curved and rounded in all the right areas which invited moments of passion of which he had had little experience. Jan then reverted to her body. Gazing at her pear like breasts which hung firmly. Her posture more than complemented her overall appearance as she stood upright, shoulders held back naturally, like that of a mannequin, and she was the most feminine human being that Jan had ever seen. He was unsure as to what part of her body he preferred to look at and switched rapidly from her face to her trunk repeating the process for several long minutes.

The object of his desire and her partner lowered the large vessel to the floor unburdening them from the heavy weight. Standing upright her peasant dress fell in such a way that it clung even tighter to her body enhancing her perfect hourglass figure. She stood there completely unaware of the effect she had on Jan and several other young men in the group.

Jan continued in the queue which had formed in front of the two distribution points for food and then realised that when it would be his turn he would be served by the second of the two young women. This he did not want. Yes, he was hungry, but the first young woman was worth going hungry for he thought to himself as long as he could get close to her. Whilst he considered whether to allow someone ahead of him he did not realise that he was holding up the rest of the queue. People behind were beginning to complain. Jacob, who was standing in front of Jan, realised what he was agonising over and assured him that he would change positions if it was necessary.

Something about the young woman had been puzzling Jan since he had first cast his eyes on her. As he stood in the file getting closer to his goal it suddenly dawned on him who she had been staring at. He was disappointed at first that his obvious stare in her direction had not once been reciprocated and when he thought back to her arrival he could not remember her ever having glanced in his direction. All his vibrant, excited emotions had been in vain. He did not mind however, as his friend Jacob was the result of her gaze. Realising that he was wasting his time on the first of the attractive young women he turned his fancy to the second. To his pleasant surprise his first glance met with an even quicker response. She smiled at him immediately. Whilst she was helping to serve and not looking at him he scrutinised her as he had done the first woman. She was almost as beautiful with a small wiry frame though not as many curves in the correct places. She appeared younger than her friend, although not by too many years. Jan thought that her body was still developing and as she became older she would flower with age.

'Come on Jan take my turn.' Jacob guided him in front as he talked.

Jan, suddenly nudged out of his daydreaming by Jacob, replied hastily. 'No! No!' and proceeded to push a surprised Jacob back in front.

Both the young women began to laugh quietly at the two men in front of them. Jan and Jacob also saw the funny side and joined in the controlled merriment.

As the girls served the two young men Jacob enquired as to their whereabouts.

'You are on the outskirts of Pinsk,' the elder of the young women replied, 'on the south eastern side of the town.'

'How far from Pinsk itself?' Jacob continued.

'About five kilometres.'

The smile on Jacob's face had disappeared for he knew now what fate awaited them.

'Take one more,' ordered the younger of the two women and she proceeded to heap another spoonful of food on both their plates. They smiled and thanked the women as they moved away for the next in line to be served.

Jan glanced back over his shoulder and was pleased to see that his fancy was still looking toward him. He returned a smile in her direction whenever he knew she could receive it.

The atmosphere in the barn was more relaxed. The Lieutenant had left and there were still only two soldiers on duty. The captives talked freely amongst themselves in quiet voices. When the queues for the food had finished the women serving asked if anybody wanted second helpings. Most people replied and the servers carried the lighter weighing receptacles to those individuals in the group who had requested more. Jacob and Jan's hands were in the air and the two young women motioned toward them. Jan seeing their reaction excitedly pointed out the fact to Jacob.

'My mind is not for this woman Jan but only for the woman I have left behind,' Jacob responded.

Immediately Jan thought he was selfish and apologised to his friend.

'There's no need to apologise and there is no reason why you cannot enjoy a flirtation with her.' After a fleeting pause Jacob beckoned then enquired, 'Well?' The expression on his face encouraged Jan to continue with his courting games.

Without further prompting, and with a flurry of nerves as the two women reached the area and were serving them, Jan looked his female preference all of five minutes fully in the face. He pursed his lips and blew a kiss at the young woman who had followed him with her eyes the moment she had seen him.

'What are your names?' he asked hesitatingly.

'I'm Elzbieta and this is Malgotia,' she replied smiling with confidence.

'I think I love you,' he blurted out smiling from one side of his face to the other. The announcement even took Jacob by surprise and he almost choked on the mouthful of soup he had swallowed.

All four smiled and Elzbieta replied still smiling at Jan, 'You are teasing me.'

While Elzbieta finished serving Jan she in turn teased him with at first a smile and then a wink. Jan's expression was one of surprise which quickly turned to excitement and he nearly dropped his bowl. She started to giggle at him and again she blew a kiss at him. He returned her smile and again all four began to laugh quietly at what had just happened. The laughing was not quiet enough however. The second guard sitting at the rear of the barn was disturbed by their noise and arose to investigate the disturbance. In Russian he shouted, asking what was happening. The other captives hushed immediately and looked to where he was directing his words. Jacob pretended to cough violently and gestured to Jan to start slapping his back. Jan responded immediately. The two young women moved on with their stock of diminishing food. When the guard arrived at where the two men were sitting Jan explained in broken Russian to the soldier that Jacob had swallowed something which had nearly choked him. Eventually the soldier accepted the explanation and meandered in a wide direction before resting in the position where he had started from.

Once the soldier was safely in his sitting position Jan looked to see where Elzbieta was. He caught sight of her in the far corner of the barn serving the last contents from the large earthenware pot. As she picked the receptacle up with her accomplice and moved the lieutenant entered the barn once more and immediately ordered the serving women out.

Eagerly Jan fixed his gaze in her direction and hoped that she would glance toward him for the last time. In his mind he gave thanks to the Lord as the young woman whom he had never set eyes on until that morning did so. Out of view of the Officer and his guards she quickly and positively beamed an affectionate smile at him and left the barn for good. His memories of a moment of shared happiness with a young nubile woman would encourage him on his journey he thought. It would help him to think of the better rewards that there were to be had in life. Rewards hopefully which were not masterminded by the Russian oppressors but would one day be freely gained, perhaps in another country, perhaps even back in his own homeland.

The warm weather, which usually advanced early in the morning from the Black Sea, was kept at bay by a temporal spate of cooler air abnormally blown from the Arctic plains rendering the day chilly for the time of year as Pavel's group of internees continued on their journey. The previous night's sky had remained clear allowing a silver sheet of dew to nurture itself by daybreak and the leaves and grasses bathed themselves in the moisture which was provided for them by nature itself. The group of captives marched through fields which had begun to show the fruits of seed planted several weeks earlier, passed woods which had once been dense and were now sparser as a result of men chopping and sawing the contents to provide building material. They walked by meadows where cattle and livestock were allowed to eat their full of the nourishment the earth had provided, and they marched around hedges and hedgerows, the foliage of which was an abundance of colours of different shades of greens, yellows and purples. The calm, beautiful morning belied the melancholy dispositions of the marchers.

To many people in the group the overnight stay had quickly been forgotten, except to Jan, and still with a little excitement in his mind he speculated a question to Jacob.

'Do you think I will see her again?'

'I doubt it very much Jan.'

'I will never forget her face. The memory of it will remain with me for many years if not for the rest of my life.'

'I'm sure there will be others Jan then you will forget. But there is no harm keeping her in your memory while the memory is acceptable and comforting.'

'Yes, you're probably correct, but my thoughts of her have certainly made today's part of the journey seem like a walk on a summer's afternoon.'

A pause came over their conversation. Jan wanted to continue his chatter about the young woman he had earlier met. Then he remembered that Jacob also had thoughts for one special woman, one whom it was unlikely that he would ever see again. He apologised and asked, 'What of you Jacob, where are your thoughts?'

'My thoughts?' he repeated Jan's question pondering slowly, though he knew his answer. His deliberations were for one person. He had thought of her continuously since their separation and now he voiced his thinking unashamedly and with a desire so strong he could visualise her next to him as he spoke.

'My thoughts are for her and her alone. Like your thoughts they sustain me on my journey to wherever that may be. I ache every moment that I'm away from her and the ache is worse not knowing where she is. I long for the touch of her hand, her skin and of her body against mine. I long for the gaze of her eyes upon me. I yearn for the smell of her sweet distinguishable aroma around me and near me which fuels the emotions of love, fondness and affection in me toward her. I breathe life into myself hoping and praying that the day will come when I can meet with her once again and when that day arrives we will never separate. She is a part of me now and until that part is found I will never be complete.'

The tears which were normally so difficult for Jacob to render now flowed freely down his cheeks. Jan on seeing this asked no more questions clasped his arm around Jacob who in turn reciprocated. Both men marched arm in arm on their journey. They spoke no more that morning.

CHAPTER 8

The blackness of the deepest corners of the wagon reached out into the daylight and patiently welcomed the new intake of visitors to share in its delights of degradation and filth knowing that it would have their undivided attention for many more days, probably weeks.

Sophie's family boarded the cattle truck shocked and overwhelmed with what faced them once inside. The wagon was foul and putrid. The doctor surveyed what he could only describe as a hovel, noticing, almost immediately in one corner, the excrement around the hole in the floor near to the door. Realising what it was for he momentarily buried his head in his hands. Not wishing to show to his family his lugubrious expression and that even his tough, resilient spirit was slowly but surely being ground down, he summoned enough strength to collect his wife in his arms and usher her into an as yet unoccupied part of the wagon.

Pieter, who by now had been joined by some of his military colleagues in the feculent wooden dungeon, was instantly disgusted with the conditions in which they were to be travelling in and was already plotting with one of his associates to escape from the train.

'I'm with you Pieter but how are we going to get out of this pigsty when they close and bar the doors? And once outside where do we head for?' asked Witold, Pieter's friend.

Pieter had already monitored the details of the station yard in which they were herded, the layout of the buildings, the number of trains awaiting its cargo, which areas of the terminus occupied most guards and the approximate distance from the wagons to the best route of escape, plus the observation that not all wagons were chained or padlocked. He replied to his colleague's concerns answering the last question first.

'Once outside the wagon we aim for the sheds on the far side of the compound and wait until dark. I noticed them as we entered the terminus. The wagons on the left of us will provide cover on one side. This side, to the south, will be more open and therefore more difficult to escape undetected, but there are no guards present. They probably patrol the area at intervals but not permanently. As for getting out, the carriages we are travelling on are not locked until minutes before we leave the station, until then they are only barred. When they close the doors we need to create a space between them with this.' From the inner lining of the right side of his trousers Pieter pulled out an iron rod one foot in length and one inch in thickness.

Witold looked with surprise toward his liege.

Pieter continued. 'This metal rod should be enough to provide the gap between the doors and strong enough to raise the bar which keeps the doors closed from outside the wagon, but we must have a gap of one inch between the doors when they are closed,' he reiterated.

'Where did you get that from?' asked Witold, still surprised and taking the implement from Pieter's hand.

'The barn which we slept in last night, I noticed it as we entered. When the guards weren't looking I picked it up thinking it may be of use at some time. It looks as though that time has arrived.'

'What if the doors will not close with it in place Pieter?' Witold questioned having second thoughts.

'The section of the outside bar which locks into the metal bracket protruding from the body of the wagon has an overlap. I'm hoping that overlap is at least one inch. Hopefully there will be enough of an extension so that the outside bar still slots into its normal position.'

After a pause Pieter asked the question. 'Well do we go or do I go alone?'

Witold had nothing but admiration for Pieter. The speed and confidence in which he had worked out all the details of how they were to escape from the wagon and where they were to hide in the short term was typical of the man. He considered then how, in the past, he had at first doubted Pieter's ability to become a dependable soldier for one so young. When Pieter was quickly promoted, he was even more confused as to why the Generals had chosen this young man for the position. Now approximately twelve months later, with a short interlude where Pieter had been captured and imprisoned before making his escape and having fought alongside and watched the young junior officer at work, he had seen at first hand how quickly the youngster had turned into a confident leader. He always learned from his mistakes and never made the same error twice. The experiences, good or bad, he gained from each problem and concern were carefully recorded and used to his advantage at a later date. His detailed planning of a battle was meticulous and the cohesion he instilled in his men during combat had surprised even the generals who had chosen him. During the few months they had spent working for the underground Pieter had carried his perfectionist attitude with him from his military days into the movement. The high opinion that Witold now held for Pieter was in complete contrast to the feelings he held for him twelve months earlier. He felt sure that if Pieter would ask to follow him to Armageddon he would do so.

Witold looked around the filthy mess they had entered and then cast his eyes upon the people who occupied the miserable, offensive shelter which was to be their home for at least the next two weeks. As he viewed the disgraceful scene he began to realise that he would not last the journey under these conditions. Sooner or later he would have to get out, to escape. All his life, before joining the military forces, he had worked in the open fields, free as a bird, no restraints on where he went. Even a short train journey forced upon would gradually suffocate the life existence out of him. He rested his gaze on Pieter, defiance was in his eyes. 'We go,' he said. 'We go and to hell with this forsaken place.'

Pieter smiled with all the aplomb of an officer who knew his men well, confident that before he had asked the question he knew what the reply would be. Witold returned the smile and then Pieter's withered; his expression became more serious as he decided to tell his parents that he would be leaving them once again.

'Keep the rod hidden until we're ready to go,' he ordered Witold; 'I must spend the last moments with my family. You tell the other men what we are doing. Tell them only two go you and me. If all is clear when we have gone then the decision is theirs to do as they wish. They can follow us or remain here.' Pieter patted Witold on the shoulder signifying the conclusion of his orders and made his own way to the corner of the wagon where his family were now sitting.

'Are you all right?' He asked his parents and Sophie as he knelt beside them. They nodded their approval.

'What were you discussing with your colleague?' Sophie enquired knowing from past experience that he was already planning something.

Pieter looked her in the eyes not wanting to tell her or his parents what he had been discussing. He also knew that he could not keep anything from Sophie. Although he was the elder of the two, from an early age through to adolescence, whenever he had been frugal with the truth to her, she seemed to know instinctively. After trying unsuccessfully on many occasions to keep secrets from her and to cover up he had decided to always be honest with her. She had an uncanny sense of differentiating whether he was telling the truth or being dishonest. He decided not to revert back to his earlier pattern in life on this occasion. 'Escape,' he whispered, his voice registering a sense of sadness in his words.

He looked at his mother. Tears began to dominate her eyes and he took her hand in his. 'I must go Mama, Papa, whilst there is a chance. I must take it,' he said, almost pleading for their forgiveness for not staying with them. At the same time feeling guilty that now he had found his family after such a long period he would be leaving them so soon to fend for themselves in a world he already knew to represent some form of hell and which was disappearing further into a nonsensical creation of madness. The thought of his departure gripped his emotions and he swallowed hard.

His mother wiped away the single tear running down Pieter's cheek. In turn she looked at her husband, her daughter and son, and then she spoke. 'You've only just found us and now you are leaving again. But as you have said you must grasp the opportunity when it arises. Be careful my son so that one day you may find us again.'

She wiped away her tears with her free hand and Pieter put his arms around her one last time. As he held her tight, and without him knowing, she gently dropped her most treasured possession that she always carried into the breast pocket of Pieter's shirt. It had been given to her by her husband on their first wedding anniversary almost thirty years earlier. She hoped and prayed that it would provide as much good fortune for him as it had for her.

He released his grip on his mother and looked toward his father who was now standing. Pieter arose also. They looked at one another in complete silence. There were noises all around though they heard nothing except the increasing sound of one another's breathing. They threw their arms around each other with a firm embrace.

The father broke the silence. The tone of his voice clearly roused with passion. It was a time for simple words. 'Be careful my son and know that wherever you are you will be loved and constantly though about.' They loosened their hold and broke away from one another supplying the briefest of glances for fear that one would trigger the other's emotions.

Pieter turned to his beloved sister, also standing, and held her in his arms. 'Take care and be strong. I love you.' He whispered to her. Smothered in emotion she said nothing.

Then he knelt one last time by his mother, who remained sitting, and kissed the mane on her bowed head. He was interrupted by Witold calling him.

'Pieter they are closing the wagon doors at the front end of the train.'

Pieter straightened up and moved to the entrance of their wagon. Sophie followed. 'Do you have the rod ready? He asked.

Witold nodded. Both men smiled at one another, Pieter's more restrained, though ever confident in his plan. He noticed Sophie had followed him and turned to address her. 'Are you all right?' He asked.

'Yes, I'm fine.' She choked and hugged him once more. He placed his arms around her.

Sophie rested her head against his chest one last time before he left. She peered through the open doors of the cattle truck the hundreds of deportees in the compound and thought she recognised a face among the people entering through the large open metal gates of the terminus. She stood upright and gathered her poise, stretching her neck and standing on her toes to obtain a better view of what she thought she had seen. The person appeared again, was lost and then sighted as quickly as he darted in and out of the surrounding throngs. In a split second she lost her quarry again. The body had disappeared behind the gateposts. Her heart began to react and she tried to stem the impulse. 'Surely he would appear again,' she thought to herself. Seconds later the figure emerged and this time her view was clearer though still partially hampered by the rows of carriages which stood at a lower level next to the one she occupied. Sophie took a foothold on one of the wooden lattices of which the cattle truck was partially constructed giving herself a better vantage point to view outside. Her excitement rose in unison with her heartbeat.

Like a bird of prey she followed the body for several more seconds, positively identifying who she thought it was. She wanted to break her silence to shout aloud her astonishing find, but for several seconds she was speechless. Then she exclaimed, quietly at first, then louder. 'It cannot be! It cannot be! Papa, Mama, it is Jacob. Jacob has arrived.'

Her utterances were a mixture of excitement and incredulity. Her father motioned to confirm her sighting. Her mother remained seated, exhausted as a result of the marching. Her expression changed from one of melancholy to one of hope and she questioned to herself, 'Could it be that one son leaves whilst another returns?'

The Doctor, who stood over six feet tall, peered in the direction which his daughter pointed. Sophie was smiling and crying at the same time and had started to shout his name. 'Jacob! Jacob!'

As she called she could feel her emotions physically tearing her apart. Her husband to be was entering her life again she thought, whilst her brother who had entered for such a short time was now leaving.

The Doctor who had been scrutinising the people around the entrance to the compound asked Sophie whether she could still see him.

'Yes Papa,' was the reply, 'he is over by the first pylon.' Again she pointed in the direction she was looking and her father followed her guidance.

'Shout! Shout his name for me Pieter,' she pleaded of her brother, hoping somehow, that he could raise Jacob's attention and stem the agony in her heart.

Pieter responded immediately. 'What is his name? Jacob?' asked Pieter, for he had never met him and had only known of the romance that morning when Sophie had told him.

'Jacob,' she shouted again out of the wagon still hoping to gain his attention and clear enough for Pieter to understand her in reply to his question.

Pieter joined in the chorus.

'Yes, yes it is him,' Sophie's father chirped in with calm in his voice hiding his fervent desire for his family not to be alone on this trip, 'and his family are with him.'

Sophie had only noticed Jacob but now that her father had picked out his family she too became aware of them.

Amongst all the commotion in the terminus the shouting was useless. It would be impossible for Jacob to hear them from where they were situated and Sophie's father and brother realised this. Still they continued calling for a little while. Eventually it was one lone voice shouting the name which was as strong sounding as when it had first called.

Pieter closed up to his sister reached up and placed his hands around her waist. 'Come Sophie, he cannot hear you,' he consoled her.

Sophie wouldn't give in. She continued to cry his name aloud hoping it would carry on the warm air toward him. Nothing happened. The sound of her voice was drowned long before it came within earshot of Jacob. She knew deep down that it was useless and quickly sought other ways to signal her presence to him. She thought about jumping from the wagon and rushing to him. Then she remembered how other people had tried the same only to be badly beaten with the soldier's rifles or chewed up by one of the dogs and finally picked up and thrown back into the cattle truck. She decided against this and continued with her shouting. After a while she listened to Pieter and capitulated. The pain in her throat which she had ignored now throbbed in the depths of her larynx. After watching Jacob disappear out of sight, whilst still standing on the wooden lattice, she looked around for her brother, fell into his arms and sobbed as if all the will to live had been sucked away from her.

Pieter caught her and held her tight, physically holding her off the ground. She was emotionally drained which in turn had brought on fatigue. He held her until she had recovered sufficiently to stand and then passed her to his father for him to support. Worried, he asked his father, 'Will she be all right?'

'She will be well Pieter,' he replied. 'You must go,' continued his father urging him on, 'and take care my son, take care.'

The doctor helped his forlorn daughter back to where the mother was sitting and sat Sophie next to her. She collapsed into her mother's arms. Conditions were already cramped in the cattle truck but people on either side of Sophie's mother made space available so that they might sit together.

'Come Pieter, we must prepare,' Witold said.

Pieter turned his gaze from his sister to his accomplice who was peering out of the cattle truck. He was in two minds whether to continue with his escape then realised there may never be another opportunity.

'The guards will soon be closing the doors.'

Witold pulled the metal rod from his pocket and handed it to Pieter. The soldiers approached the occupied cattle truck. 'Stand back,' they commanded.

Pieter and Witold, who were closest to the exit, moved back as the doors were being slammed shut by the soldiers. Inside the escapees prepared themselves and Pieter pulled the rod up and positioned it between the gap just before the doors slammed shut. As the large shutters, which blocked their access to freedom, came together enclosing the inhabitants of the wagon and impeding the daylight, the shudder which resulted reverberated through the rod causing Pieter to lose his grip. The expression of both men sank to the lowest depths of disappointment. Before all hopes of freedom were thwarted and as he was about to utter his annoyance, Pieter regained his grip on the rod placing it between the doors as they came together a second time after the rebound. The gap was visible. The adrenalin was flowing, their hearts beat fast and as they heard the conversation of the guards shouting expletives about the outer bar not sitting correctly in its proper resting place, to them the pounding of their heartbeats sounded like that of a bass drum. Now was the time for concern. What would the soldiers do? There was silence on the other side of the doors. The two pretentious escapees looked at one another, their sight not fully adjusted to the interior darkness of the wagon, only just visualising each others worried expression. Their breathing seemed to stop and the pounding of their hearts abated as if the whole escape hinged on their very silence.

The quietness from outside seemed endless exaggerated by the people inside who also appeared to hold their breath. The two men inside the wagon could then hear mutterings of conversation from the Russian soldiers on the other side of the barrier. As they strained to listen for words which would identify to them what the captors were doing, the sudden thumping of wood made both men jump and Pieter along with the others in the wagon voiced a startled remark.

The escapees' visages turned to happiness as they realised the soldiers were hammering the outside bar into its location making it more rigid. Both men gasped air into their lungs, air which was already beginning to smell stale and stifling, evidence that the wagon was unfit for habitation. Still they breathed voraciously that which gave life. As quickly as the hammering started the noise abated. Their hearts began to beat a little faster when they realised they could no longer hear human voices outside. The soldiers had gone.

They waited five minutes which again seemed longer, enough time they planned for the guards to close the remaining doors of the two cattle trucks behind also occupied with human cargo. Pieter noticed prior to boarding that the last six wagons were empty awaiting tenancy, no doubt, in the near future. Until their occupation the train would not depart and the inhabitants in the remaining carriages, with the lack of circulating fresh air, would suffer the accumulating, strengthening stench in the truck. The seconds ticked away slowly, the atmosphere in the wagon was tense. Although only the two men planned to escape everyone present had become part of the break out, praying and hoping that it would be a success.

Pieter, who held the metal rod all along between the doors of the wagon, now levered the shaft upwards in search of the outer bar which had been hammered into its final position by the guards minutes earlier. As he levered the instrument upward he struggled momentarily where the gap between the doors had diminished. He lowered the rod slightly taking care not to lose the grip of it within his hands, allowing the rod to fall would close the gap between the doors, and forced the metal rod upward more sharply than he had previously done so. The instrument, with the help of Pieter's strength, pierced the narrower gap and finally the sound of metal on metal could be heard. Contact had been made with the outer bar. The nervous sweat which had accumulated on both men's foreheads abated immediately. The relief was instantaneous and rewarding. Both looked at one another. Smiling faces peering out of the grimy, dark surroundings, verified by the view of their white teeth, resembled strange white puppets playing against a dark background. Simultaneously they looked into the interior of the wagon and could make out other smiling faces. They were pleased for they knew they had the moral support of the majority of people in the cattle truck and this gave them greater motivation and added confidence in their quest for freedom.

They both waited and listened further for any voices outside. All was quiet inside. The smiling now replaced with a more serious intent. Nothing could be heard outside.

Pieter again drew the metal rod down underneath the outer bar and pushed up heavily against the obstacle. Nothing happened. The noise of metal coming into contact was heard but the outer bar did not move. Immediately he considered whether the guards had padlocked the outer bar in position. Without allowing any negative thoughts to gather and dampen his enthusiasm he lowered the rod and decided to use all his force to dislodge the obstacle on this attempt. He gripped the rod tightly and heaved it upward toward the outer bar holding them in captivity. He let out a muffled cry of strength as once again the metals came into contact. This time he felt a vibration through the rod which was not evident on the first attempt. He was sure he felt the outer bar move marginally. Next he moved the rod up slowly to where the metals touched. Once the connection had been made he raised his rod slowly upward. The outer bar lifted off its seating point and now rested on the instrument that Pieter was holding. He turned, with a wide grin on his face, toward Witold mouthing what had happened. Witold's serious expression changed immediately to copy that of his friend.

'Open the door,' Pieter beckoned to his colleague.

Witold gradually opened the left side door of the cattle truck and the daylight once more burst through into the dark and dreary interior.

Blinking to readjust to the light, Witold peered outside to ensure no soldiers were in the vicinity. The area alongside the length of their train was deserted but he could hear voices on the other side of the wagons next to theirs. 'More human cargo,' he thought to himself and his smiling face disappeared at the thought. Witold grasped the outer bar which had held the doors together and Pieter lowered his rod onto the floor of the cattle wagon where it was quickly retrieved by another of his men.

'We'll close the door behind us and seat the outer bar on its perch, then if soldiers do come around they will notice nothing unusual. Should any of you decide to follow, wait a few minutes for us to get away and then move. You,' pointing to his subordinate, who held the rod, 'hold the metal rod between the doors whilst we close them.'

Pieter jumped down from the cattle wagon and joined Witold who had already disembarked. He turned and looked into the wagon once more, peered at his family, verbally expressed his love for them and promised that they would meet again. Both men closed the doors and placed the outer bar in its correct location not fully rested in its metal extension. They performed this with rapid movement and the minimum of noise. Once completed they took cover under the cattle trucks gaining their bearings before proceeding with the next stage of their plan. The sheds could be seen no more than two hundred metres across an open expanse of land. Witold and Pieter surveyed the area and to their surprise could see nobody in the direction in which they were aiming for.

Preparing to make their move Witold heard voices somewhere behind. He pulled Pieter back in time to see two soldiers appearing from around the rear of the next row of wagons. They proceeded to patrol along the length of the train and approached the two absconders at a nonchalant pace.

'If we go now they will not see us between the wheels,' whispered Pieter.

'Wait,' urged Witold, 'we have time to let them pass.'

Pieter, noticing that the soldiers were not accompanied by dogs, relented and abided by Witold's decision.

The two men, not for the first occasion, held their breath as the guards passed by and then suddenly halted no more than five feet from where they crouched in hiding. They talked in Russian and one soldier could be heard asking the other whether he wanted to smoke.

Pieter and Witold's hearts were uncontrollable. One guard offered the other a cigarette. Both escapees heard the striking of the match followed seconds later with it being thrown to the floor. A medium sized military boot made sure the flame was extinguished. A chuckle between the guards followed as one made a joke about it being a shame should one of the wagons catch fire. As slowly as they had halted the two soldiers moved on, their conversation fading the further they continued their patrol down the length of the train. Eventually they disappeared in the opposite direction from where they had appeared.

Both men breathed long, deep relaxing respirations controlling their nerves and influencing their adrenalin to come under control.

'We go now Witold,' urged Pieter.

Witold nodded in agreement.

'We'll stay under the cattle trucks until the last possible moment.'

Both men crawled on hands and feet moving stealthily and silently under the length of the train which minutes earlier they had been seconded too. Whilst making their way Pieter could scarcely believe it was minutes rather than hours when they had been entombed in what could only be described as a living hellhole.

Pieter stopped abruptly at the point he thought would give them good cover from which to run to the sheds in the distance. As he did so, Witold crashed into the back of him causing Pieter to topple over. He sat himself up and dusted himself down anxiously enquiring if he was hurt. Negative was the reply and a comical smile quickly passed between them over the awkward incident. It helped break the tension and then a lengthy silence grew between the two.

Neither spoke. Witold had experienced this situation with his Superior on many occasions in the past. He knew what the silence meant and understood that Pieter was concentrating on the escape. He also accepted without question that the young officer had everything under control. He had complete faith in the younger master.

Pieter looked at Witold. Both felt the unseen tension that they had created. Their mouths had dried as if they had not tasted water for days. In the past they had called it the sandpaper effect. The internal turmoil of their stomachs had begun slowly but sped up the moment they had finished their crawl under the cattle trucks. The legs of the two men began to quiver intermittently. The internal and external signs of their apprehension had returned with ease. They had experienced all emotions before, prior to commencing battle, although the mind could never accept or overcome the signals that its own body participated in. The waiting, although not always extensive, exacerbated the feelings even more.

The confident Superior broke the silence first and turning to his colleague asked, 'are you ready?'

Witold replied with a nod of his head.

They both crawled to the large metal wheels which transported the wooden structure above them, the tomb which without question would have carried them to a strange land and almost certain oblivion. Pieter viewed the colossus he crouched under with the wheels balancing on thin metal lines which, in the distance, resembled discoloured parallel spaghetti.

They squatted behind the wheels hiding themselves from the open space and out of sight of any alien body which may be present in and around the area. The beginning of the boundary through which they had to run to achieve what they wanted was no less than ten yards away.

Both men surveyed the zone to the right and left thoroughly. Without any signal except for their own refined, intuitive understanding of one another, they bolted from the protective covering and headed for the open space between them and the temporary safety of the wooden sheds which would be their haven until the next part of the escape plan could be put into operation.

The perspiration from their nervousness was quickly replaced with tiny beads of sweat on their foreheads as they ran. Pieter, who was younger by many years, had forged ahead of Witold in the race for eventual freedom. He turned to look for his colleague, could see him ten feet behind, and immediately slowed for him to catch up.

Witold knew what Pieter was doing and, verbally as well as motioning with his hands, urged Pieter to keep running. As he did so Witold, who had gained another few feet, suddenly lost his balance. Stumbling to keep on his feet he eventually dived forward, out of control to the floor, resembling an athlete crossing the finishing line in a last desperate attempt to snatch victory in a closely run race.

Pieter stopped and turned back.

'Go on! Go on!' Witold cried out to his colleague.

Pieter was about to return to help his colleague then stopped dead in his tracks. Rounding the second line of cattle trucks were two soldiers accompanied by two guard dogs. Witold could see the expression on Pieter's face and knew before he turned to look behind that he would see something to his dissatisfaction. After gazing on the guards and their canine companions Witold turned back to face Pieter urging him to continue alone.

Then as quickly as he had responded to his superior, even quicker did confusion descend on Witold. He was unsure if the soldiers had seen him and pondered whether to get up and continue his run or lay where he had fallen in order not to attract attention. He froze with fright.

It would have been easier to listen to his comrade but in those fleeting moments Pieter remembered much of what the two of them had been through. Neither had deserted each other before. He was not going to be the first to do so now. He stood where he was. Seeing Witold's predicament he made the decision for him gently but hurriedly coaxing his friend to follow him.

'Hurry Witold, they have not seen us yet. We still have time to get away.' Pieter's voice did not sound as positive as usual. Even he knew this but again he repeated the command to give Witold the encouragement and confidence to move.

Seconds had elapsed though it seemed like forever. Time seemed to have stopped for both men. Their mouths were barren of saliva and their hearts once more beat to a crescendo. Consciously they were oblivious of their internal emotions.

Eventually Witold arose slowly. As he stood the dogs started barking. Both men looked in the directions of their captors. The escaped men had been seen. The dogs had alerted their masters and were now loose and running at speed toward them.

Pieter and Witold, who had now recovered his faculties, shouted at each other to run.

90

They turned and fled immediately heading across the remaining fifty yards of open compound which lay between them and the sheds. Again Pieter was quickly ahead of his colleague. In an endeavour to catch Pieter and reach the sheds Witold asserted all his strength into his shorter legs to carry him faster toward his goal. Although the mind was still young and active the body of the man was older. With twenty yards to go Witold again stumbled and fell to the ground and the dogs were on him before he hit the hard clay surface. Just before the dogs pounced and as he fell forward Witold looked up, noticed Pieter was slowing, and shouted as before for him to continue.

Pieter looking back for his comrade, and slowing down once more, heard his colleague's final words before the dogs altered the pitch of his voice. He could see the brutes already tearing at his friend.

'There's nothing I can do for him now surely?' he questioned himself and instantly decided to heed his forlorn companion's words and continue his pursuit for safety within the attainable buildings.

The victim raised his hands to his face as the dogs leapt at him. The first dog to connect and taste human flesh bit into the right hand of its prey. The pain produced a loud, howling scream from the man. This did nothing to deter the dogs from pursuing their kill but only seemed to stimulate the animals into continuing the frenzy. The second dog seized the right thigh of its prey knowing that it was trying to kick the first dog away from itself. The pain of the second bite was worse than the first and it surged through the body of the man who, moments earlier, had been in sight of freedom. Witold, angered as a result of the wound and incited by the instant pain inflicted on him by the second dog, managed to sit up and turn his attention to the animal which was larger in size than the first. He swung his left boot hard at the second animal which had briefly released its grip on the thigh only to attain a better hold of the same area. As the boot swung through almost ninety degrees, the second, larger animal avoided the blow and bit once again. More pain thrust through the victim's body. Anger more than cohesion made his left boot connect hard with the beast's groin on the second attempt causing the brute to react instantly. The dog released its grip on the thigh, howled with pain and at the same time jolted itself out of the reach of its prey. Witold sighed with relief.

The remission was brief and before he could gather his senses further the first animal now sought the left arm of the victim. 'Where are the guards?' Witold asked himself as he prepared to aim his boot now at the first animal. Swinging the right foot toward the canine brute the pain reared from the double bite inflicted on the upper leg by the second dog. Witold fought to keep the leg on course and not to succumb to the pain at the same time knowing that a further attack from the second dog was imminent. No sooner had the thought disappeared when reality struck home and the larger brute again pierced the skin, on this occasion, to the shinbone, catching the right leg in mid flight. Witold felt the teeth sink through the skin and tissue with relative ease and touch the bare bone beneath. The agony compounded out of all proportion. He felt nauseous and faint but his determination won through. 'Before I go one of you brutes must come with me,' he uttered out loud grimacing with pain. Gritting his teeth and ignoring the smaller animal he tried to pull the larger one off the lower right leg with only his right hand available. As he did so the animal ripped further through the skin, muscle and tendons of the area leaving a gaping hole down to the off white shaded bone.

Crying with pain, longing for the guards to arrive and summoning the little amount of strength which was left in his body, Witold ripped his left hand away from the other dog and thrust it into the mouth of the larger dog. At the same time he pulled the animal toward him with his partly mangled right arm. Forcing his left arm further into the back of the dog's mouth and into the throat the whining of the animal became at first louder then quieter. The brute fought to pull himself away from Witold's grip. The more he fought the more the opponent pushed his arm down the animal's throat. Witold could feel a tugging at his lower left leg from the smaller animal but ignored the milder pain that it produced. Concentrating his efforts on the larger brute which he still grappled with, he manoeuvred the dog's body to restrain it against his own and noticed that the jaws of the larger dog was now fully extended. Acting quickly, Witold loosened the grip of his right arm from around the front of the dog's body and brought it around to the upper jaw of the animal. Gripping it tightly and, still pressing the beast against himself, with his remaining strength he pulled the jaw up strongly and sharply, snapping the neck of the canine beast.

The animal which had been writhing violently in an attempt to free itself became limp and fell dead partly covering the offensive thigh wound it had inflicted on its victim. Witold was please and relieved. The relief was ephemeral and as he looked for the other beast the shuddering pain, the like of which he had never encountered before, revealed to him the whereabouts of the dog. There was no time to reach for the brute as the pain burst into his neck and forced its way up to his head. This was accompanied by a flashing light which seemed as brilliant as the sun itself. Before Witold passed into unconsciousness he could feel the smaller animal taking a second piercing bite into the already exposed neck which was sprouting veins and arteries into the open air. His body lay slumped on the ground blood spurting from the wound. Seconds after the fight was over, when the body was limp and offered no resistance, the second dog became disinterested.

The guards, who had been watching the event with elation, now approached. The smaller animal was sniffing at the pieces of human flesh around the open neck wound. They called the animal off its prey and firstly tended to the dog that lay dead. After a quick inspection of the dead animal the guards stood up and praised the remaining brute for performing its duty by stroking the animal. Then, without tending to the unconscious man, the first soldier pulled his rifle off his shoulder and cocked the gun ready to use. Witold felt no pain as the bullet pierced his heart and buried itself in the ground under the body. Death was instant.

Pieter who had succeeded in finding refuge in the sheds had tried to get out through the only other door at the far side of the building. It was then he understood why the soldiers had not run to catch up with him. The second door was locked. The only way out was through the door which he had entered. With his failure to escape he returned to peer out of the window and witnessed almost everything that Witold was going through. Crying with a mixture of indecision, fatigue, and desperation to escape he remembered his friend's encouragement for him to continue.

He sank to the floor with is head in his hands trying to comfort himself at the same time fighting to forget what had happened moments earlier to his friend. He tried to gather his thoughts, to work out a strategy, but visions of the dogs tearing at his colleague stayed in his mind. He considered that if he had returned to help would he have been able to do something…to stop the death of his friend. Deep down Pieter knew there was nothing he could have done. The odds heavily outweighed the two men.

'Come on Pieter, compose yourself,' he whispered and encouraged himself, 'or Witold's death will be in vain.' The haunting was interrupted by commands from the two soldiers outside who ordered him to come out or he too would die like his friend.

Pieter looked around, rose to his feet and ran to the door at the rear of the shed again. He turned the handle. The door remained locked. Frantic, he tried it again, to no avail. He pushed the weight of his body against it in an effort to force it open. When that failed he kicked the door several times in turn with both feet. He was tired. He could not invoke all his strength and the exit remained closed. Leaning with his back against the door for support Pieter surveyed the interior of the building for any further possible escape route. There was none. He had been through the whole process before. The only windows were facing in the direction where the soldiers were waiting outside. Again he heard the orders being shouted by the guards.

'Give yourself up or you will die like your comrade. It is the last time that we reason with you.'

Pieter walked slowly to the door through which he had earlier entered, composed himself and stepped out into the open courtyard. He was aware of shouting from the first row of cattle trucks, from where he had escaped, as he walked toward the soldiers and the one remaining dog. The occupants of the cattle trucks had witnessed all that had happened and were now voicing their anger by bellowing abuse at the soldiers.

When Pieter stood near to the guards he could not help but notice the piercing stare from both sets of eyes. The first soldier, of similar size to Pieter, had a squint in one eye and the strabismus unnerved him as he perceived the rapid movement of that eye. He was unsure as to where it was staring and it never stopped its movement for any length of time. The second soldier had carrot red hair with a similar growth around his chin. The two soldiers together looked an odd and dangerous pair.

Standing close to Witold's body Pieter was asked why he had tried to escape. As the first soldier talked Pieter gazed at the torn body and the gaping neck wound of his beloved friend. His eyes rested, lastly, on the clear bullet hole through the heart. He heard the questions put to him by the soldier and a distant screaming made him more attentive but before he could answer, the bullet from the second soldier's rifle hit his chest off centre. The force of the missile unbalanced him and he fell backward and rolled over onto his front as he landed on the lower part of his friend's body and up against the dead animal.

Without confirming whether or not the second escapee was dead the soldiers turned and headed back in the direction from where they had come.

CHAPTER 9

From the moment the two escapees had left the cattle truck the remaining occupants inside had only the interest of the two men continuously in their thoughts. The bars in the top corners of the wagon, which allowed a little fresh air, and a modicum of light into the filthy interior was now occupied with spectators from inside and mainly comprised of Witold and Pieter's comrades who had remained behind in the vehicles.

Everybody inside the prison on four wheels eagerly awaited the news of what was happening outside in the compound regarding the two former internees. Several minutes had elapsed since the men had left and the tension inside the truck was unbearable for those who remained. The sudden break in silence by the Polish soldier who was now doubling as a commentator took the majority of people by surprise, though they were grateful for the supply of information. The news, which was relayed to them, was positive as the two escapees made their way across the open compound toward the buildings in the far corner. The hopes of the people in the wooden enclave increased as the commentator stated that the two men had only a short distance to cover. Their ambitions were dashed and raised again in several seconds as Witold stumbled and fell and then raised himself once more to continue the escape.

After several more seconds the voice of the broadcaster changed to a low key modulation and before he had barely uttered any further statements his audience knew that what he was about to divulge was not good news.

Their thoughts were justified as the Polish soldier announced that the two dogs had restrained Witold. No further commentary was forthcoming as the reporter now witnessed scenes that he had never witnessed before. His stomach revolved with revulsion as the bestiality of the canine brutes was unleashed on his masticated colleague.

'Where are the guards? Where are they?' muttered the second polish soldier who was also witnessing the same carnage as the first.

A strange silence came over the wagon. Nobody spoke. Everybody knew, including those who could see nothing outside that the situation was not progressing well for the escapees. The long silence was interrupted by the commentator announcing that Pieter had made it to the buildings and Witold had killed the larger of the two dogs. The sadness of his tone, during his announcement, gave away the fact that still the battle was not in the latter escapee's favour. No mention was made of the final piercing blows inflicted by the remaining animal, rendering the man unconscious. Silence descended in the carriage once more. The discharge of the gun took everyone by surprise, except those watching, and people began to gesture the sign of the cross with their hands. Sophie, who had recovered some of her strength, arose from her seated position and went to stand behind the soldiers who had the best vantage point to see outside.

The second Polish soldier dropped down to the floor of the wagon. He turned to help Sophie up to the position against the bars which he had vacated and at the same time whispered to her that Pieter would be all right, hoping that the words would comfort her.

The second and final order by the Russian soldiers was given. Sophie gripped the bars tightly and prayed that Pieter had somehow managed to get away through the building. She surveyed the scene outside where the Russians were standing. Astonishment made her gasp and somehow she stopped herself from vomiting as she gazed on the wounds which the dogs had inflicted on Witold, rendering his body bloodied and ravaged. It reminded her of the time that her own dog, as a puppy, had played with one of her soft dolls. Sophie had to leave the room and on her return the doll had been ripped to pieces with the contents and clothing strewn around. Witold's incomplete and tarnished corpse had fragments of clothing strewn around. From the open neck wound which could be clearly seen from where she was, slivers of flesh, muscle and tissue hung in a disorderly mess from and around his body. She wondered how animals could be trained to do such things and then answered her own question knowing that animals in the shape of human beings had no doubt devised the idea.

The silence was agonising not just for Sophie and her family but for everyone in the cattle wagon. They all felt that somehow they were part of the escape. Their prayers were weighted heavily for two men one of whom was now deceased and the other still in danger somewhere outside.

Eventually, the door of the building opened. Sophie announced this, in a low, melancholy voice, to the occupants of the cattle truck but mainly for the benefit of her parents. Her father arose. Nervousness agitated him and he motioned toward where Sophie was balancing.

The silence which was evident both inside the wagon and outside in the compound was gradually shattered by people in the next cattle truck venting their anger at what had happened.

Sophie could see the first Russian soldier talking to Pieter but as a result of the noise from the next wagon she could not hear what was being said. Her expression changed dramatically as she noticed the second soldier prepare his rifle. She could do nothing. In fury she became paralysed to the bars which she was holding. She gripped her support with increasing venom cutting off the flow of blood to her fingers which turned from a soft pink to a dull cream colour. Her anger vented itself inwardly and she felt like a furnace about to blow. Her array of emotions had reached the depths of despair. There was no room for tears. In sheer frustration at not being able to help him and with desperation in her voice, she screamed aloud to her beloved brother, nothing coherent just a wild, lengthy shriek. She was in a rage. The sound of her lone voice would be drowned by the hundred voices baying their annoyance, and he will never hear me.

Ending her outcry she never heard the sound of the bullet being fired but knew it had been discharged as she saw the recoil of the rifle kick against the soldier's body. The sight of her brother toppling backward with the impact of the missile confirmed the worse to her. A part of herself died instantly then with him. An emptiness came over her leaving a void somewhere in her soul. She had never lost anyone so close to her before. An aunt or an uncle yes, but they had always been distant relations and though she had felt remorse and sadness it had never prepared her for what she felt now. She remembered being very upset at the death of her grandmother and had cried for many nights after, but that also did not compare with what she was feeling now. The death of her brother was instantly final. At once she knew what the effects of an immediate death such as this entailed, an emptiness which was unacceptable. The void rushed into and over her, as it did so, her grip on the bars became weaker. Sophie felt herself falling backwards uncontrollably and lapsing into a state of semi-consciousness.

The trickle of people gradually swelled during the morning until the numbers were too great for any single person to count. The tide of human habitation, forcefully clustered into a lengthy column, resembled the swell of a river after a deluge of rain. The flow of bodies meandered through the countryside in search of its unknown and secret destination. This adding to the masses continued with the original number of soldiers to guard the people also being increased disproportionately.

There was no special membership required to join the multitudes. Participation was varied and, too many, confusing. The majority were forced; some came of their own free will. Arriving home from work or after shopping, what little there was to shop for, they would find their houses empty of any family or relatives. With haste, and if remembering, they would pack what belongings they could and go in search of their loved ones. So it was, and throughout the march the throngs continued to acquire pockets of people along the way, usually forcibly, some voluntarily.

Pavel's original group were together but lost in the multitudes of internees. These people were mainly of Polish nationality from the north, south, central and eastern parts of the country now controlled by the Russians. The original number had swollen by the end of the morning to almost one thousand. Some had travelled not only on foot but also by train, crammed into cattle wagons fit only for pigs.

Rumours spread that they were all destined for Siberia to be re-educated into the Russian ways and beliefs. Most Poles knew that that would be impossible for the majority of them. Poland and Russia had never been the best of friends as historical records would testify. There was no conceivable way that Poles could be indoctrinated with Russian ideals. Many Poles thought the reverse would be easier.

The expanded assembly of mainly Polish captives, dishevelled and dirty to varying degrees through the harsh and often savage journey which they had so far undertaken, finally converged on the town of Pinsk, before the occupation, busy in people and industry. The captors routed the thousand strong internees via the outskirts of the town toward the rail terminus keeping attention from what they were doing to a minimum. Those Polish people who were free and had seen the marchers entering the periphery of the town, supplied food parcels for the captives to take with them on their journey. Those marchers who had journeyed the furthest, and who had suffered the most with lack of food, opened their packages almost immediately and ate something if not everything which had been generously given to them.

Prior to entering the town the columns had been halted on the outskirts and addressed by the lieutenant. 'Soon you will be entering the final stages of your journey. You will all be boarding trains to be taken to your destinations to undergo re-education into the Russian ways and beliefs which will make you a better person. Before boarding the trains you will need to relieve yourselves.' He omitted to mention that no proper facilities were available once aboard. 'You will be given your next meal tonight when the train stops for refuelling. You will then be allowed to disembark where you will be fed. After feeding you will board the train once again to continue your journey eastwards.'

There was a slight pause before the lieutenant dismissed the thousand strong group. Orderly columns were again formed and marched on toward the terminus.

The station was situated on the edge of the town and one of the entrances was accessed through large steel gates which led into a spacious compound. Toward the middle of the compound three separate rows of cattle trucks stood awaiting its human cargo. The rest of the compound was teeming with other internees and numbered approximately two thousand. Several carriages already contained human inhabitants. The guards ushered, often violently, the thousand strong marchers to one side and ordered them to wait.

Pavel pointed out to Jacob that the violence by the Russian soldiers had intensified. 'Now we have increased in number the soldiers will be worried that we will raise up against them. We must be careful Jacob and warn the others to be cautious. Even the slightest incident will trigger a violent reaction from them.'

As if to prove Pavel's point a disturbance broke out minutes after he spoke. Indicating in front, he bade his son to look.

Jacob turned to see two old men being beaten by a soldier of bovine appearance. The two elderly men were having difficulty in boarding the train due to the height of the wagon off the ground, and in trying to board were continually slipping from the wagon.

'Get aboard! Get aboard! Na Poyezdych! Na Poyezdych!' The Russian ox shouted in his native tongue. Frustrated by their initial efforts, to successfully embark, the soldier started to club the two individuals with the butt of his rifle.

Pavel, acting quickly, addressed a young looking Russian Lieutenant accompanied by two soldiers who were marching by their group. Speaking in fluent Russian he asked, 'Shall we help the two old men to board Sir?' pointing once again in their direction.

The lieutenant first looked at Pavel and then spun around to look in the direction at which he was gesturing. He immediately noted what was happening and after dismissing the two soldiers, who accompanied him, spontaneously replied. 'Yes, quickly.' The reply was voiced in Polish.

Jacob was surprised at the response and the excellent Polish accent. He looked at his father who winked at him knowingly then turned to hastily walk to the aid of the two old men. Running would have brought attention on him which could be mistaken for an escape, with severe consequences. As he did so he thought he heard the crack of a single rifle shot in the distance but ignored the noise. Pavel heard nothing in similar fashion to the thousands of captives herding behind in the compound.

Jacob reached the scene first in time to see the younger looking of the old men into the wagon. His father and the Lieutenant were close behind. The soldier was taken aback when Jacob arrived to help and as he raised his rifle to punish him for intruding the Lieutenant intervened, clasping the soldier's weapon firmly in his grasp preventing him from inflicting the intended blow on Jacob's skull. The soldier was even more surprised by the interaction of his officer. The lieutenant's expression was one of anger.

'What are you doing?' he shouted at the assailant.

'They will not board Sir.'

'No wonder you fool, look at them. They are probably older than your father and should not be on this journey.' The Superior turned to Pavel and Jacob and ordered them to help the second man onto the cattle truck. They did as told, willingly and to the relief of the two old men.

The Lieutenant could be heard reprimanding the soldier for his behaviour toward old people and then was issued with new orders to work outside the railway depot. After the Lieutenant had sorted the affray, and he could see the two helpers tending to the needs of the old men, he turned and left the area satisfied that the confusion which had existed minutes earlier had been sorted.

The two old men profusely thanked the strangers for their assistance at the same time looking around to ensure that the soldier was not returning to harass them once more. Whilst the four men talked the two old men checked one another's bruises. Except for gashes to their heads, one quite deep to the younger of the old men, they were satisfied that nothing was broken. Again they thanked father and son for their help.

'It is no more than you would have done for us in the same circumstances,' said Pavel.

'We must go Papa,' said Jacob, 'or we will be separated from the others.'

'Yes, let's go. Are you all right now?' Pavel enquired, turning to the two old men once again.

'We are fine,' replied the older grey haired man, 'you must go if you are to remain with your friends.'

Pavel and Jacob disembarked from the wagon. Neither was questioned by the replacement soldier having taken instructions off the Lieutenant not to do so. Immediately father and son went in search of where they had left their group.

'How did you know the lieutenant would help Papa?' Jacob asked as they made their way back to their party. Before Pavel replied a roar of disapproval came from voices somewhere behind the row of cattle trucks they were walking by, causing them to abandon their conversation. As they walked the louder the noise of disapproval grew.

Father and son looked at one another in surprise wondering what was causing the commotion. Then Jacob heard, above the shouting, a second discharge of rifle fire from the same direction where the bellowing emanated.

'Did you hear that?' he asked his father.

'Hear what?' As before, along with the throngs of internees, Pavel heard nothing out of the ordinary.

'I'm sure it was a gunshot and I thought I heard a similar noise earlier.'

Jacob dismissed the incident believing that few people took notice because they were experiencing their own difficulties and had enough to concern themselves without taking note of noises which didn't bother them directly. As both men resumed their search for their party Jacob returned to his earlier, interrupted conversation repeating his original question. The roar of people's voices continued but to a lesser degree.

'When we first arrived here there was a small commotion near the entrance to the station. One man was being beaten by two soldiers. It was that lieutenant who stepped in and saved the man from further punishment. Did you hear his accent also?'

'Yes, I did.'

'He spoke in fluent Polish. He's probably got Polish ancestry or perhaps studied in Poland, probably the latter. He's had experience of the Polish people for many years, living amongst them, and judging by his actions to the people he is defending and protecting he is one Russian who has no aversion and bears no hostility toward them.'

As they ended their conversation they heard an engine pull into the terminus. A short time later they heard the rumble of carriages pulling out and turned to see, in the distance, several of the last wagons empty of any cargo.

Eventually they found their family in amongst their group. Eva was relieved to see both return and complained about their temporary disappearance to them with concern. 'Where have you been Pavel? We thought you may have been in trouble and were worried about you.'

'No,' replied Pavel, 'no trouble.' He went on to relate their experience of the last ten minutes, lingering on the kindness of the Russian lieutenant.

Five minutes later Jan returned with news of what had happened earlier in the railway terminus. 'Two Poles had tried to escape after boarding one of the cattle trucks,' he related.

'How? What happened?' Jacob asked, taking interest.

Jan narrated the story he had heard omitting several minor details but making up for it by exaggerating others. Proceeding with his news, what became important to him was the attention he acquired from the group who were listening. All of them had now closed around Jan and were captivated by the story he was relating. Expressions of surprise and adulation and finally sadness had passed over their faces as he progressed through the different stages. Jan, who had never attracted an audience for this long before, revelled in the reception he was receiving at that moment.

'What happened?' An impatient voice shouted from the back of the group.

Jan cleared his throat before continuing, increasing the anticipation in the people's desire to hear the end of the story.

'Where was I?' he asked.

'You know where you finished Jan,' replied Jacob, losing patience with him, 'get on with it.'

'The second escapee was issued with a warning to give himself up or he would die like his companion.' Jan repeated again continuing with the story, at the same time prolonging the attention he received from his audience.

A silence fell over the group which had listened to Jan's story. A few women cried and many of the group gave the sign of the cross. Jacob now understood the reason for the rifle shots he had heard.

'Was that the reason we heard so much shouting earlier on Jan?' He asked his friend for confirmation.

'Yes. The people on the train who had seen what had happened protested at the Russian soldiers in the only way they could.'

'So that is why the train we saw pulling out of the station only had two thirds of its wagons full. The rear section of the train was empty, remember? The doors of the wagons were open but nothing was inside.' Jacob continued.

'Of course,' said Pavel now remembering what Jacob and Jan had seen, 'and the Russians ordered the train to leave as quickly as possible in case people who had seen the incident decided, somehow, to take matters further.'

'Probably Papa and some quick thinking officer quelled the situation. Rather than face some form of defiance he issued an order to get the train out of the station.'

'We must be careful,' warned Pavel, 'not all Russians are as slow thinking as we are led to believe. Someone had the foresight to see what a disaster the shooting of the two men could have caused. If the train was allowed to remain in the station until fully laden with its human cargo I wonder what would have happened.'

Their conversation was interrupted by guards ordering the people to board and suddenly the group was ushered toward the wagons nearest to them. As the people approached the cattle trucks several tried to flee from the area. They were either quickly refrained from doing so and held by a relative until on board, or failing that option, mercilessly clubbed to the floor by one or more Russian soldiers and dragged back to the train to be thrown aboard. If the soldiers didn't hold them the dogs were the last resort.

Pavel's group slowly embarked and each person's face despaired deeper than at any time before. Pavel's expression was indescribable and he was speechless as to what could be said about the sight which faced him. He had been aboard one of the trucks no more than thirty minutes earlier but could not remember noticing anything like the dirt and filth which faced him now. Was it the fact that he had helped someone else and his mind was completely preoccupied with the two old men, ensuring they were safe, that he had totally ignored the state of their wagon? Continuing to reflect he felt sure that he would have noticed the filth, the degradation of allowing human beings to travel in such circumstances. The wagons were not fit for cattle to ride in and here the enemy were allowing human life to do so.

Pavel stood there in the doorway of the cattle truck stunned and silent, disbelieving that any human being could allow this to happen to fellow humans. Other people boarding the truck nudged him as they passed and he awoke out of his living, nightmarish stupor. He looked to his family and to Eva who had tears cascading down her cheeks. He went to her and did the best to comfort her. She, in turn, buried her face in his degrained clothing and sobbed. Pavel held her tight to him, intermittently caressing her hair to console her and to try and stem the tide of tears. She gripped him around the waist, so tight that he could not remember her ever displaying such physical strength before. He could feel her grip fighting against the air which he was inhaling. 'Why? Oh why Pavel?' she wept.

Eventually she relaxed her hold and Pavel led her and his family into a corner of the cattle truck still vacant. After settling the family he once again turned to view the inside of the wagon.

If anything the second purveyance was worse than first. Most of the floor area was covered in straw which was not fresh but stale from many days, perhaps weeks of use. Underneath the straw damp patches were visible on the wooden floor. Here and there could be found lumps of mud or clay where people had walked in the cattle wagon with filthy footwear. It was obvious that it had been used before for transporting people but little cleaning had been undertaken.

Evidence of its earlier habitation by human life was supported by names written or carved on the wooden walls of the vehicle.

At either side of the wagon on its narrowest span were tiers of wooden planks on which people were already squatting. High up in the corners near to the roof were openings which allowed light into the cattle wagon. The openings were small in area and barred to prevent people from escaping. Near the doors at the front of the wagon was an opening in the floor to be used for relieving oneself. The thought of answering the call of nature in that undignified, free for all, open manner caused Pavel to wretch slightly. He contemplated whether the inhabitants, especially the old, would be able to accept the conditions in which they would have to relieve themselves whilst aboard the train.

He looked at the faces of the people still boarding. Each expression on the completely different visages, young and old, male and female, was exactly similar. Disbelief. Exactly what he had thought. Then, after a moments lapse of time and after the reality had sunk in, from the women and also from some of the men, tears. Tears of anguish, tears of sadness, tears for the unknown and tears for the thoughts of what might happen to them. They knew now as they boarded the cattle trucks that their journey into the unknown had begun. There was no turning back, probably no chance of escape. They were to be taken to a land, some of whose occupants had always been warmongerers whose leaders only wanted to see the overthrow of the Polish state. They knew that punishment awaited them for being Polish and not for any crimes they had committed, for they had committed none. But what form would this punishment take in this foreign land, the final journey for which they had commenced upon. Whatever sufferance they had experienced before now would be meek compared to what they would encounter from now on. The remainder of their passage, wherever it led them, would truly be a savage journey.

Only one thought made Pavel happy amongst the degradation and filth they had boarded that afternoon. The majority of people he was surrounded by were the ones he loved the most, his family and after them his group of friends. They all managed to remain together for the journey so far. 'Perhaps,' and he offered a prayer for his next thought, 'they would remain together for the whole passage until the day they could be re-united with their homeland.'

Even these aspirations soured quickly when he reflected on the ages of his friends that had accompanied him this far. They were not young any longer. Age was not on their side. Most were on the wrong side of life to sustain themselves through hardship. Pavel doubted whether any of the elder would survive and concerned himself whether anyone of any age would survive. Realising what hardships they had already experienced and what suffering they would surely endure in the not too distant future he was also grateful that those parents who had been separated from offspring as a result of attending the ball, had remained separate, and he hoped that as few children as possible would be spared the traumas and hardships which they would, he felt, undoubtedly encounter.

Another thought crossed his mind and brought a glimmer of hope to his life. The knowledge that two of his sons who had managed to escape this mess was able to continue their existence other ways. Henri was already out of the way and hopefully would never be interned. Jacob had told of his sighting of Mikolai in the barn as they left their land. This gave much pleasure to the rest of the family knowing he had escaped. Pavel felt sure that his son was not experiencing what the rest of the family were experiencing and once again offered a prayer for this piece of good fortune.

Disbelievingly, he turned to his family once more. They had quickly accepted the conditions which they were about to travel under. What else could they do. He was not as concerned for the younger as he was the older people. The young, he knew, would cope with the depravity and have a better chance of survival. Above all, he was concerned for Eva though for the moment she was quiet.

He was confused, bewildered and, he thought to himself, extremely fortunate. He remained perfectly still for several minutes. When, eventually, he decided to move, the fortuitous escapee slowly turned his head in the direction from where he had first seen the Russian soldiers approaching. He viewed in the distance several soldiers in conversation with an Officer of the Russian army. He could not make out whether the two perpetrators of the shootings were among the group but he would never forget their faces. Their unmistakable features would help.

Watching the group of soldiers from afar Pieter also surveyed the surrounding area and noted, as before, that nobody else was in the immediate vicinity of where he lay. Ever so slowly he moved his right hand up to the area where the bullet had hit him. Partly lying on the dead body of his friend, and against the animal, he could feel an object in the left breast pocket of his shirt pressing into his chest and in the area where he felt sure the bullet had connected. Still ever watchful, like a sentry surveying the territory ahead, Pieter kept his eyes peeled on the group of soldiers who were still in discussion in the distance. One soldier pointed in the direction where he lay which made his heart beat violently. He froze immediately, a score of questions raced through his mind.

'What had they seen? Had he moved too quickly? Had they been given orders to collect the bodies and dispose of them? Burn them or simply bury them?' Pieter watched and waited keeping perfectly still. 'Surely they could not see if he moved like a snail from that distance?' Pieter questioned himself hoping that the answer was negative. Finally he breathed with relief as the Officer among the group waved down the soldier who had been pointing. The Officer indicated toward the row of wagons in front of where they were standing and from which a crescendo of noise was emanating.

Satisfied that a detachment of soldiers being sent to deal with the bodies was over, Pieter continued moving his right hand ever so slowly toward the left breast pocket. At the same time he was mystified as to what the object could be. 'I cannot remember placing anything in the pocket. I never put anything in the pockets of my shirts,' he mumbled to himself.

Eventually his hand reached its destination. His two index fingers fought their way inside as his chest was pressed tightly against Witold's legs. Once again he looked up to check that the group of soldiers were still in discussion and to survey the remaining area to make sure nobody had intruded. On completing his surveillance he caught sight of Witold's gaping neck wound which, until now, he had managed to avoid looking at since first witnessing the scene after coming out of the buildings. He knew it was there he simply did not want to verify the butchery once again. Catching sight of the carnage that he now lay near to, and partly on top of, and even though he was used to such sights, it was all he could do to control his stomach from retching. Perhaps because it was his friend that he felt like this. He averted his stare to the soldiers one of whom had now gone off in the direction toward the east of the compound. No other soldiers followed. Pieter waited several more minutes before letting his fingers feel for the object in his breast pocket. Touching the article brought a grateful and gentle smile to his face. It slipped out of his grasp and he pursued the object again. He wanted to be sure that it was what he thought it to be.

Clasping it for the second occasion, he pushed his thumb into the pocket to join his other two fingers changing his grip so that he held the main body of the item between his thumb and forefinger. Gradually, feeling it all over, which did not take long, he perceived through touch that the bullet had flattened the middle part of the shaft and he smiled as he pulled the object slowly out of its refuge in the pocket.

He held it near to him. The chain, hanging over the back of his hand whilst the crucifix lay across the two index fingers, coruscated in the afternoon sun. He smiled happily and said a small prayer for his mother who had put the solid gold cross and chain into his pocket. He knew the ornament was of great sentimental value to her. Placing the object back into the breast pocket of his shirt, he scanned the area around him once more.

Several more minutes passed and as Pieter continued his periodic lookout, he checked himself to see if he had incurred any further injury. The cross and chain had saved his life but he felt pain in his left arm. He looked down to see the bottom half of his sleeve on his shirt and jacket had been scythed through by an object that had left a hole a quarter of an inch in diameter. It had also left an abrasion on his skin that had caused bleeding but had now clotted. Pieter concluded that the bullet must have deflected after hitting the cross and chain, pierced through the sleeves of his clothing cutting the skin which was traversing its passage.

'A very small price to pay for a life,' he muttered in comfort. The lesion stung Pieter when it was exposed to his clothing but he tolerated the minor nuisance. He was now looking for his chance to escape. Traffic in the area of the compound where he lay was quiet. This would not last much longer. He also knew that eventually the Russians would have to get rid of the bodies. When that happened, they would quickly discover that only one dead person was amongst the two potential cadavers.

He surveyed the area immediately behind himself including beyond the sheds which Witold and himself had been aiming for and noticed that there was foliage growing around the side and at the rear of the building. This view was not visible to the men before as the cattle truck, which the two had escaped from, had its view partially blocked by a barred and bolted second building situated nearer to the wagon than the building they had chosen.

'If only the group of soldiers would move out of my view,' he thought, 'I could make a run for the shrub land area behind the shed.'

He wanted to run immediately but was in full view of the soldiers. To do so would arouse their attention and increase the chances of him being killed. No sooner had he dispersed the decision to flee from his own mind when an engine approached at speed from the east side of the terminal. Hastily, the engine connected to the row of cattle trucks from where angry protestations were still being voiced and which housed Pieter's family and colleagues. Without marshalling of any sort, the engine pulled out of the station to commence its journey eastward.

Watching the proceedings Pieter did not need any encouragement. The area was clear of soldiers in the immediate vicinity except for the group who were now standing beyond the first row of cattle wagons that were to be pulled out of the terminus. Because of this Pieter was partially hidden from the soldiers. If the group could see him in between the wagons then there would be a chance he could be caught but this was a slimmer chance. He would have to take that chance. He decided it was now or never.

He rose quickly, the tension in his body tricked by the rapid decision of his mind, itself manifesting quicker than ever before, and turned and ran as fast as possible toward the haven behind the sheds. When he reached the shrub land area, he grinned widely in a mixture of nervousness and excitement as he dived over the barbed wire which had been laid only waist high. Picking himself up he ran into the increasingly thicker wooded area which lay approximately one hundred metres beyond and where he knew he would stand a better chance of surviving and getting clean away.

CHAPTER 10

The rumble of the wood and the screech of metal coming into contact with the bottom lining of the door runner that it moved upon enhanced the ultimate conclusion. The doors were slammed shut. To many it was imprisonment of another form even though the cells were transportable and outside in the open air. A hush descended in the carriage only to be broken several seconds later by the outside metal bar being lowered into place and locked only to be opened, according to the Lieutenant's orders, in the evening for the collection of food and water.

The jerking and jolting inside the trucks confirmed the arrival of the engine. An old man dressed in clothes which had seen better days urinated in his clothes, corroborating his worse fears of deportation. The woman next to him, of similar years, cried in support of those fears. They comforted one another with sympathy from those around. Then the old man cried aloud. Minutes later the train pulled out of the rear terminus to continue the journey. To where? Nobody knew. The earlier rumours of Siberia had now expanded to the East, but the East was a larger place than Siberia.

With the initial shock of their actual departure over the elders in the group, including Pavel started conversing about the conditions in which they were travelling. Their feelings, muted up until now, were openly expressed. Others started their own conversation, not only about the conditions but also about how if possible any could escape, until finally the majority of the occupants of the wagon were verbalising differing opinions in small groups. They now felt safe enough to converse without interruption from Russian soldiers. Quickly, what started as a private talk eventually grew into an informal meeting.

Pavel who was one of the senior members of the group sat on the right hand side of Anatoly Popov who was already sitting. Anatoly, a large man, not in height but in roundness, was the current Mayor of the town of Lyszcze, succeeding Pavel in the post. He was greying on the remainder of hair he had left and as usual his matching coloured moustache was in perfect condition. Even now in the last eighteen hours of arduous travel, he still paid particular attention to his precious moustache. Whilst he and his clothes, like those of the rest, became dishevelled, his moustache seemed to be weathering the conditions and appeared in pristine order. He was an authoritative man, one who kept meticulous notes of any meetings he attended as Mayor and any other function he served.

Stefan Waschenska followed Pavel by sitting on Anatoly's left. Stefan, a landowner of less acreage than Pavel, was a gentle, easy going man of average build. Many people said it was his wife who ran his life and particularly the farm they lived on, especially when it came to disciplinary matters. Often in the past, Stefan had dealt with farm labourers too leniently concerning offences they had committed. If ever the offenders repeated their performance it was not Stefan who reprimanded them, but his wife. She would allow them two weeks to leave their cottages and find work elsewhere. It was known that Stefan's ambition was to be the next Mayor of Lyszcze and would often perform menial tasks for Anatoly and other important people who lived in and around the town to gain favour with them. Again it was rumoured that his wife encouraged this side of his behaviour.

'We must bring this discussion under control,' said Anatoly addressing Pavel and Stefan. 'It concerns each and every one of us. It is important that those who want to speak are able to voice their opinions. They may have valuable ideas we can use.'

Pavel stood up and without shouting raised his baritone voice loud enough for every person to hear him in the wagon. Tall and upright in his stance, he had a pleasant not handsome face with a slightly oversized nose and wide nostrils. His ears were of proportionate size though protruded from the side of his face. It was this feature that gave him a comical appearance at first. People, who did not know him, quickly realised that he was no buffoon. The firm, stentorian tone of his voice, swiftly brought order in the compartment.

'People, it seems that we are all eager to discuss what has happened to us here today. Can everyone, if it is possible, sit and make themselves comfortable and then we shall continue in an orderly manner.'

The people who wanted to voice an opinion, and had already privately done so, did as requested and sat wherever possible. The remainder, mainly the young, stood around the sides of the cattle truck leaning against the wooden walls for support. There were still a number of people who did not take an active part in the conversation. In the main these were mothers who were accompanied by children of different ages and were alone without a husband or father. Their appearance suggested that they had been on the march longer than Pavel's group.

The individual conversations had dwelled primarily on the conditions of the cattle truck, especially the sanitation in the wagon with the hole in the floor concealed by a trap door which was situated in the corner near the main doors of the wagon. It was this which was to be used to excrete through. Everyone was disgusted with what was available in the cattle truck.

'We have to come to terms with the situation and what is available to us,' remarked Anatoly. 'There is no other means to relieve ourselves in this God forsaken vehicle other than that method.' He pointed toward the cut out section of the floor at the same time acknowledging with his inquisitive eyes.

'We must all get used to the fact that probably from now on, for many days and nights in this carriage,' he emphasised his disgust at the hovel they were travelling in with a forlorn gesture of his outstretched arms and a miserable flick of his eyes, 'we are going to eat, sleep, wash and whatever else we have to do to continue our existence for survival, and we are going to do these things together, every man, woman and child. The sooner we all understand and realise the situation the better for all concerned. Are we all in agreement?' Anatoly asked, scanning the interior of the cattle truck hoping for full approval.

The majority of people who were listening dejectedly nodded their heads in agreement.

'Good,' Anatoly continued. 'Then we can discuss the problems we are inevitably going to experience. Firstly, does anyone have ideas as to how we can solve the predicament of being able to relieve oneself with a little more privacy?' He gestured again toward the relevant area. On this occasion it was primarily for the benefit of those people who had not noticed before. 'I'm more concerned for the elderly in our group and for those who will find it difficult to do such a thing with so many in a confined space.' He looked up at those young ones standing around the side of the wagon.

One shy young woman in her early twenties, looking older than her years whispered nervously from the rear of the wagon. 'P...Perhaps for the different sexes we can form a line around the person who has to go.'

Murmurs of agreement to the idea were mumbled by other people in the wagon. Another person suggested that material could be draped around the area to act as a shelter. Again approval was sounded for this suggestion.

Jan chirped in with a further proposal for the second idea. 'Blankets could be used in the day improving the screening to the area concerned?'

'That was a good idea Jan for a change,' retorted Jacob.

There were pockets of laughter from the younger element of the audience. For those that knew Jan also knew that despite having a clever mind and many ideas, not many of them were fruitful, some being occasionally disastrous.

Anatoly brought the meeting under control again enquiring whether anybody had any spare clothing or blankets to use. Several occupants produced odd garments which had been used on the journey and had worn excessively. One elderly woman came forward and volunteered a large blanket on the proviso that she could claim it back when the journey by train was over.

Pavel, who had sat down, once again arose and smiled as he took the blanket from the old lady, promising that he would personally return the item to her. She reminded him of the two old men that he and Jacob had helped to board back at the terminus, old and frail, yet full of courage. As they talked, he could not help but wonder whether she would complete the train journey and he felt sure he would not meet anyone older on this passage which was progressing deeper into hell.

'Many thanks,' reiterated Anatoly. Pavel, who had already thanked the woman, seated himself once more after taking the item from bequestor. 'That is one problem solved. Now I will ask Stefan to discuss another concern that will affect us all.'

Stefan cleared his throat before nervously commencing his conversation. He was anxious partly because he did not know all the audience and partly because he had not prepared any notes prior to speaking.

'W...we all k...know t...t...that there is p...precious little to eat and t...the likelihood of any f...food being leftover is very remote. W...we all know there is no opportunity for acquiring food, other than what our captors will be providing for us, and that which some of us may have brought ourselves.' The nervousness had quickly and unusually disappeared from his speech which had now become more fluent. 'You and I are aware of these circumstances, and what I'm about to say may sound obvious to us all, but one relaxed thought could affect any single person here. I cannot stress, too strongly, that any food which you may have over after a meal, food which you do not want, but which someone else could use, should not be thrown away under any circumstances, whether it is a morsel or a crumb. Remember that someone else will need it. It could save a life. That life could be a loved one who is dear to you. Think carefully before what you do!'

Stefan continued on the same topic. 'As we already know food is in very short supply and what I'm about to suggest is against the very grain of our thoughts and manners as Polish people, but desperate times call for desperate measures. Each and every one of us must at any opportunity take whatever food we can lay our hands on, by any method. If that means stealing, then we must steal. Look around you,' he gesticulated with his hands. Several people in the wagon followed his movements surprised also at what he had condoned, but knew he was right. 'You can see people who are weak as a result of travelling under severe conditions, having been persecuted by savage people who are no better than beasts. They have continued their journey without the basic needs of life, food. Look at them. How long will they last? Look at us,' again he motioned with his hands toward himself, 'we have not travelled as far as them and we already feel weak after only one day of journeying on foot. We must find the means to carry on and live through this, so that when the nightmare is over, some of us will be alive to tell the outside world of what we went through. We must survive at all costs, by fair or by foul means. We are not dealing with a legitimate regime when we associate with the Russian soldiers. We must think as treacherously as them and act as underhandedly as they do. If any person has the chance to acquire more food then take the opportunity and if, and when, any of us obtain extra food we should try and share something with those who need it most. The children, the sick or whoever else it may be. I realise that what we are asking is a great deal of the individual, and nobody can force you to follow our ideas, but it may be you or a member of your family who will be in dire need on the next occasion.'

'What about the people who run the risk of getting caught?' A young deep voice enquired from behind a group of younger people standing toward the rear of the cattle truck. 'Don't they deserve some of the rewards?'

It was Wilos who had asked the question and who now came out from behind the group to await the reply. He had grown in maturity and confidence during the short journey undertaken so far.

Stefan, who had explained and voiced his ideas so well, first looked at Anatoly then toward Pavel as if for an answer to the question. Pavel was the first to speak.

'Stefan has already explained that we cannot force you to share whatever you acquire. We would hope that you and others like you would be willing to share of your own free will. We would hope,' Pavel stressed, ' that the person will share some of the bounty to those who are in need of it. In the end the decision is yours and yours alone. I pray that you make the right decision to help others who may not be as fortunate.' At this point he fixed his gaze on those younger people hoping they would heed his words. 'Remember some of us have greater advantages than others, especially those of us who are quick with their hands, then borrowing food, I prefer to say borrow rather than steal,' Pavel announced with a mischievous smile which generated a patter of laughter from his audience, 'will be easier for you. I will stress that you should not feel guilty if you decide to keep all the food. No person here can criticise anybody for making whatever decision they wish to make. Probably, eventually, we will all face a life or death situation.'

There was a short pause as he allowed time for his last words to penetrate their minds, before continuing. 'One final point on this matter, nobody should put themselves at great risk to steal. Weigh up the situation and act accordingly. Please, no heroics. If you are caught you can expect the maximum punishment from the animals that are looking after us.'

Silence fell across the people in the cattle truck. All were reflecting it seemed, on what Pavel and Stefan had said. The lone thoughts of those individual people were of very similar substance. As quickly as the silence fell, it was promptly broken by the sudden crying of a baby. Heads turned to see where the noise was coming from. It was a shock to the majority of the people in the wagon that one so young was on board and a poignant reminder of Pavel's last words.

'Does anyone have anymore suggestions or questions?' Pavel asked gaining the attention of the audience once again.

Wilos who had remained standing in front of the group whilst Pavel answered his question, now thrust himself forward and stood in front of Pavel.

'Take this,' he said, and pulled from inside his overcoat three large loaves of bread and handed them to Pavel who smiled happily.

'We are all hungry now,' continued Wilos. 'I would suggest that as this is mine we all have a share now.'

Most of the visages belonging to the bodies, which sat or stood in the wagon, took on expressions of incredulity confirmed by their open mouths. Even those who had not paid much attention were now suddenly alert.

Wilos smiled as he turned and now faced those behind him. He was amazed at the expressions on their faces. Everyone suddenly crowded around him awaiting their share of the prize. They wanted to ask how he had obtained his catch but their surprise rendered them speechless.

Eventually, Stefan enquired what everyone else wanted to know. 'Where did you get it?'

Wilos again turned back to answer the question. 'I will tell you how on this occasion, but nobody should ever ask me again for I will not say.' The latter part of his statement he addressed by staring at everyone in the cattle wagon.

Facing the main body of people he related his tale.

'Back at the station I pretended to have severe pains in my chest and held it like so.' Wilos acted out his experience whilst continuing with the story. 'I chose one guard who looked very young and inexperienced and asked him for water several times. I must have been persuasive because he seemed to panic and allowed me to use the toilet inside the station building. I pretended to heave violently and he helped me into the cubicle which was at the far end of the corridor. Once inside I locked the door and continued my pretence of heaving and vomiting. He shouted to me in Russian that he was going for help. I said that I would be all right after a few minutes of rest. I heard the guard walking down the corridor away from where I was. I waited until I could hear no more footsteps then slowly opened the door, still keeping up the pretence. I used the wall for support and passed several opened doors in the corridor on my way outside. The second door away from the main entrance opened out into a large kitchen. I stopped, pretending to rest, looked around the kitchen and again up and down the corridor. The only person to be seen was a woman in the kitchen bending over a stove in the far corner. The bread was stacked so high.' Again Wilos demonstrated with his hands how much bread was available. 'They wouldn't miss two or three I thought to myself, so I quickly lifted three from the pile and hid them inside my coat and continued walking down the corridor to the exit. The young soldier re-entered. He was alone to my great relief. At that time I could hear a lot of commotion outside, so perhaps he couldn't find anybody. Anyway, I walked in a healthier manner, not too healthy, in case he became suspicious. I was also afraid that he would help me in my walking. I informed him that I was feeling stronger and it brought a look of relief to his face which relieved me for I knew then that he would not help. He opened the door for me to leave and I stepped out into the compound and told him I was going to look for my people. I thanked him and we parted company.'

Pavel who was smiling broadly patted Wilos on the back and thanked him. Wilos managed a small grin in return.

Anatoly arose and shook his hand soon followed by Stefan.

Everyone wanted to shake Wilos's hand and queued for the privilege. All occupants who had listened to the story were overjoyed.

'We can only carry out your wishes Wilos,' Anatoly finally said and enlightened Pavel of one of the loaves and proceeded to divide the bread equally amongst all occupants. Pavel and Stefan followed suit.

'While we eat,' continued Anatoly, 'we shall carry on with our discussions.'

People settled again in their original seating or standing positions with their pieces of bread generously donated by Wilos, ready to continue their discussions which so far had been very eventful, informative and above all rewarding. Anatoly once again took responsibility for commencing the dialogue. He finished a mouthful of bread which he had broken off from his own share, cleared his throat and proceeded to speak.

'As we have all heard from Jan this morning, two of our countrymen were shot trying to escape,' immediately the joyous interlude was almost forgotten, 'killed in cold blood by our murderous captors. Our journey will not be an easy one, and events will get worse, much worse before they get better. We may all believe at some stage that any fate is better than what we are going through now and what we will be going through tomorrow, the day after tomorrow, next week or even next year. Sooner or later this nightmare will end. Some of us will live through it; others will fall along the way. But we must all strive to survive this journey and to live to tell the tale. It will be difficult, very difficult, but we should never give up hope that one day we will be free again to return to our homeland where we belong. Make no mistake, when that time comes, our country will need us just as much as we need our country. Believe in that and you will survive this journey. Survive as a stronger person for the experiences of which you are now suffering, albeit cruel, deceitful, horrendous, and inhumane as they are.'

His voice had gradually risen in sonorous, until at the end of his speech it filled every corner, every cavity and every space within the cattle truck.

There was a long pause, most of the people, even those disinterested at first, absorbed and digested what Anatoly had said. He looked around him into every corner of the cattle wagon, at every person who he could see. Many were quietly crying. Those that were not, were very close to doing so.

Jacob remembered what his father had told him about the effect Anatoly had on people in meetings during and after he had addressed them with one of his speeches. Audiences were spellbound by his oral effectiveness; they literally chewed over the words which sprung forth eloquently from him. The taste of those words which fell on open ears made the minds and hearts of the people work overtime in thought and beat profound feelings on what was spoken. It was like that now Jacob observed. He too looked around the squalid cattle truck that was temporary home to approximately seventy people including children. The people present were strangely tranquil. The speech had clearly moved and touched the thoughts and emotions of each and every occupant who had listened. The mood was one of great patriotism, of collectivism, of togetherness and of complete unity.

Anatoly continued, voicing another topic, all eyes transfixed on him. His words were softer now, supplementing more kindness and more caring. Those who knew him well also knew that he always cared no matter how he modulated his voice.

'If anyone wishes to escape, let us do it together. We can help each other. Between us it will be easier.' He used his hands and fingers emphasising his speech almost as if he were writing the text down for his listeners. 'We can all plan together, pool our thoughts to arrive at the best method of escape. Do not misunderstand me. There are people here, the children, the elderly for whom it is virtually impossible for them to get away, but the younger element has a better chance of freedom and of surviving afterward. You cannot however do it on your own. Not all of it on your own. That is why I say we should gather all our ideas, pool our resources and discuss the best method should any of us wish to do so. We have amongst ourselves, if not in this wagon, then maybe in the next, or the one next to that, the tools to provide a means of escape. Additional clothes, extra food, money, all these will be required to survive for an initial period after the actual escape. To reach safety, if there is such a place for us, a greater amount of the necessities will be required.' He paused, allowing the words to sink into the minds, especially those of the young. Allowing sufficient time to elapse as only he knew how to do so well, he recommenced. 'I know that some of you will have listened to what I have said, what we have said,' pointing to Jacob and Stefan sitting on either side of him, 'and will come and discuss it with us. There are those who will not think it necessary and will make their own plans. Again we cannot stop you and if you truly believe that is the best way, then we will respect your decision. However, if you have any doubts, need any advice; do not be afraid to seek our help. We may be old, but we do possess wisdom, cunning and guile when it is necessary. The last thing any of us want to see is one of our own people die whilst attempting to escape.'

Again there was a pause before Anatoly concluded, 'That is all I have to say. Does anyone else have anything to add? Does anyone have any questions?'

There was silence once again in the cattle truck. Many vacant faces looked on toward the three elders. Faces that were expressionless, not knowing what to do, still not fully accepting what was happening to them, the silence only broken by the clattering of carriage wheels over the railway tracks that carried the wagons to their unknown destination. Eventually the meeting broke up and people made themselves as comfortable as conditions allowed.

Jacob looked around the wagon endeavouring to come to terms with the squalor of the dwelling. He thought of the minds and deeds of the people who would do such a thing to other human beings. Did those who ordered the deportations know what the conditions of the wagons in which people were transported in were like? Not fit for animals let alone human beings he answered himself.

He observed the people who were shuffling around to their own areas within the truck as the meeting broke up. If the wagon should be divided into equal areas, each person would have less than three square feet available. Not enough to lie in. He wondered how people would sleep. We will manage; again he replied to himself, we have done so far. Some, those who had travelled the longest, and who had not bothered to listen to the whole meeting, had already stretched themselves out on the floor, on what hay was strewn around, and had fallen asleep. He looked at those men, women, and children and felt that they were slowly but surely breaking under the hardship of their passage.

Jacob also noticed now that several people were coughing intermittently followed by the odd splutter, mainly the old and the young, and wondered how much longer they could last. They had already been through so much. How much more could they endure?

His thoughts and worries for his family, his friends, and his people were infinite and there was no solution to any of them except one. Personally he was determined to see this through and to live to tell the tale. He tried to ponder on happy moments during his life and memories of the last day he had spent with Sophie gladly drowned his mind, their ride in the country, the picnic, groping for trout, their lovemaking and finally the evening. He wondered where she was now.

If only she were with him the journey would be so much easier. So many questions regarding her were floating around his mind. Where was she now? Had she escaped the deportations? If the net had been cast wide by the Russians then she too was probably on some train somewhere. Where was she being deported too? Suddenly another thought came into his mind. Maybe she had been taken captive that same night and may even have been in the railway terminus at the same time as the rest of them. This was definitely a possibility. He pursued his thoughts. Pinsk was the largest railway terminus in their area; surely everyone rounded up that night for deportation would be marched to that terminus. It must be he convinced himself and vowed that he would enquire of people on other trains that passed whether or not they knew the whereabouts of Sophie Sagajlo.

He retraced his thoughts in the opposite direction and contemplated in his mind whether her family had made it home safe that evening after the Doctor had made his emergency house call. If they had, then perhaps someone would have got word to them that Jacob's family had been taken captive and deported. If this had happened, Sophie's family would have had time to flee the area. This he eventually thought was pursuing hope too far and he settled for the first option in his mind hoping that somehow Sophie was on a wagon like him, not so far away. Deep down he prayed the latter thought was the actuality.

Again Jacob scrutinised the occupants of the cattle truck but decided, at this moment, against questioning those people, who he did not know, as to where they had come from and whether they had come into contact with a Sophie Sagajlo or any of her family. 'What were the chances of any of them knowing? Remote.' He thought and answered to himself. Anyway why should they worry and concern themselves about someone else. They had families of their own who they cared about and worried over. Despite these assumptions, he would follow his original ideas and question the passing trains for word of his one true love.

He was stirred from his thoughts by a cold draught which had begun to circulate around the cattle truck. He looked to find its source and noticed that it flowed from the four square holes in the upper corners of the wagon. The holes which were barred were no more than nine inches square in area, virtually impossible for anyone to squeeze through and escape, except for a small child perhaps.

More people began to feel the cold as the afternoon passed and the early evening was nearly over. The intermittent coughing he had noticed earlier was now replaced by stronger, prolonged bouts. The occupants buttoned coats and tightened scarves, padded holes in shoes with bits of hay from the floor of the cattle truck.

All people eagerly waited the moment when the train would stop hopefully signalling to them the arrival of their first meal. Uppermost in many peoples' minds was the fact that the journey had already proceeded too far and too long without any food to sustain them. The waiting was unbearable. The seconds turned into minutes and the minutes into an hour. Darkness fell and one hour elapsed to two hours. Children, whom Jacob had not noticed on the first part of the journey by train, began to cry, at first sporadically, then more concentrated. Some occasionally screamed.

Finally, the train started slowing, and eventually came to a halt. Noises could be heard outside the wooden tomb. Men inside scrambled to the four holes in the corner of the cattle trucks to see what was happening. Their facial expressions were indicative of their feelings. Relief and even a little sense of happiness. All those who had perceived the events outside, without uttering one word, told the good news through their visages. The train had stopped to collect food.

CHAPTER 11

Sophie awoke several hours later having exhausted herself in her fruitless efforts to warn her brother of the impending doom. She came around in the lap of her mother. At first unsure as to whether her reality was still a nightmare. As before, like thousands of other forced internees, she hoped with every ounce of her breath that it was a bad dream. She realised it was not as she felt the movement and heard the rumbling noise of the carriage clattering over the rail track. To confirm her worst thoughts as soon as her eyes opened she gazed on the sad identical reflections that the faces of her parents, who were watching their daughter to ensure that she had recovered, emitted. She knew that it was definitely not a dream. She smiled reservedly at them both. They in turn did their best to return her feeble but loving gesture.

All three were badly wounded in the bereavement of their son and brother. Not one felt a degree of consideration was easily forthcoming. Sophie noticed that her mother's face on either side was stained from her reddened brown eyes down to her jawbone. She knew what had caused the tarnishing and felt the grief inside her begin to stir once more. 'Do not cry now,' she ordered herself, 'for mother's benefit if not your own.' She looked too at her father, but could find no visible evidence about him of the grief that her mother showed. Sophie did not look closely enough. She sat herself up with the aid of her two loving, caring parents and remembered how she had promised herself that she would not be a burden to them anymore. Already, she knew, she had broken that promise.

'All right Mama, Papa?' she asked them quietly, fighting her internal emotions.

Both parents nodded. It was not a time for conversation.

Sitting there the events of several hours ago came flooding back to her. She tried to curb the thoughts that compounded in her mind. She reflected on the fact that she was completely alone with her two parents for company. Not even Pieter would be able to help them anymore she reluctantly accepted.

The grief that fused and united in her memory cells became physically evidenced on the outside with tears cascading down her face. She made not one sound while she cried and neither parent noticed her grief. That is how Sophie wanted it to be.

Eventually the outward signs of her distress subsided and she viewed the degradation of the internal contents of the cattle truck in which they were travelling. The filth that lay in front of her now was nothing like that which she had experienced ever before. Any comfort she had hoped for dwindled away into the obscure murkiness of the interior.

The drone of the train rumbling on over the continuous, demanding, unending and infinite layers of rail track, produced a drug like, soporific sleep on certain inhabitants of the cattle truck which Sophie occupied. This, plus the nauseating effect of the stench which quickly filled the inside of the wagon, due to the warm weather, and originated from the purported toilet area within the cattle truck had an effect on people which caused them to fall into and out of an hallucinatory light slumber. Very often the women would awake calling the names of loved ones, mainly the husbands, who were no longer with them. Realising on awaking, that they had been dreaming, they would slowly drift into sleep once more. Nobody bothered to disturb them or tend to them if they awoke in a dream. Some would shout obscenities in their sleep. These were undoubtedly directed at the Russian soldiers which they had encountered either on their journey so far, or whom they had experienced before, and who had treated them or members of their family so brutally. One woman, whilst sleeping, re-enacted the death of her husband at the hands of a group of Russian soldiers. The narration in her sleep was vivid and descriptive for all those who were awake in the cattle wagon to clearly understand. She awoke sobbing and alone in obvious distress. Nobody moved to console her. Sophie waited to see if anyone accompanied her on the train and when nobody moved she responded quickly and went to give succour to the young woman concerned. The stranger gratefully buried her head in Sophie's arms and cried uncontrollably for several minutes. All Sophie could do was to stroke the woman's mane, as if a mother would caress a forlorn child, hoping that this would have a soothing effect on her. Eventually the woman's sobbing subsided and she fell, still in Sophie's arms, into a second slumber which on this occasion was tranquil and comforting to her.

She awoke an hour later and spoke in a soft, gentle voice, so unlike Sophie thought, the verbal abuse she had earlier launched through her dream.

'Thank you, whoever you are.'

Sophie said nothing in reply but simply grasped the woman's hand and held it tightly.

The young woman turned and smiled at her female companion who had provided support and comfort when she needed it most.

There was a long silent pause between both women and then Sophie asked, 'Do you know that you were having a bad dream earlier on?'

'Yes,' was the reply. 'Was it about my husband?' she asked.

'You mentioned a man's name.' A pause, then Sophie continued, unsure whether to ask or not.

'Did they kill your husband?'

'Yes,' she replied, and then almost immediately she proceeded to relate her story a second time to Sophie in more detail than during her dream.

'He was working in the fields when they arrived. He could hear my screams and came running to my aid. Four of them held me down and were tearing my clothes off. My husband burst through the door and pierced the two nearest him with the pitchfork he had been using.' Her voice sounded free of emotion as she told her story. 'A fifth soldier stood behind the door. My husband did not see him. As he pulled the fork out of the second of the two soldiers and started to attack the third and fourth, the fifth soldier had prepared his weapon and shot my husband in the back. He tried to get up, the same soldier stabbed him with the bayonet attached to his rifle several times and he lay dead. The three remaining soldiers then took turns to rape me. When they had finished they brought me along to the nearest rail terminus to board the trains like the rest.'

Her voice still held no emotion as she finished relating her story. Her stare was of a cold yet calculating person. Her eyes were an icy glaze, yet determination burst from them at an alarming rate. Her features were taut against the bone structure of her face and her appearance took on a different outlook from that of moments earlier, an outlook of seething rage, even of violent retribution. Visualising the woman, Sophie felt an uneasiness exuding from her and yet fully understood her emotion.

Another brief silence fell between the two women and Sophie watched as the face of her peer changed back to its normal appearance. With sympathy Sophie broke the silence.

'Is that what you always dream?'

'Yes, every time.' There was another pause. This occasion the woman continued.

'You are the first person to whom I have spoken about the incident. I have never harmed anyone in my life and never wished to do so, but during the whole incident I prayed that I had some weapon to fight with. For during those minutes of torment I wished that I could have killed those five soldiers. I would have had no second thoughts.' There was another lull in their conversation before she continued. 'Strangely, I feel relieved now that I have shared my terror with someone. Perhaps the dream will not bother me anymore?'

'Let's hope not,' Sophie replied reassuringly.

Once again the Russians kept the occupants of the cattle trucks waiting. First fifteen, then twenty then thirty minutes elapsed. There was an abundance of Russian voices from outside. Hardly a word was murmured inside though the cries and wails of the young made up for the lack of vocabulary. The emptiness of their infantile stomachs eager for nourishment but too young to understand what was happening. Those old enough, keenly awaited the opening of the wooden doors. People began to concern themselves as to whether they would ever be opened. They knew now that the Russian authorities were capable of anything and persecution of the Polish people, no matter what form it possessed, was plentiful.

'They are opening the carriages one at a time,' said Pavel.

The distinct noise of wooden doors running along the metal guides underneath, first being opened then, after a short period being closed, was unmistakable now that Pavel had pointed it out to people.

When the doors of Pavel's wagon were eventually opened, the freshness of the incoming air, as well as sweeping the old, stale air outward, also acted as a catalyst and stimulated the occupants into action. Several women began to cry with relief as the opportunity had arrived for their children as well as themselves to be relieved of their tremendous hunger. Whilst crying they could also be seen and heard uttering prayers of thanks and gratitude. Others in the cattle truck stood up and ventured toward the opened doors, as if trying to get out all at once.

Two soldiers could be seen directly outside the carriage. The first of them jumped into the wagon pushed back the occupants and bellowed, to nobody in particular, his orders.

'Two men are to follow me immediately,' he barked in his native tongue, and then jumped down out of the wagon.

The two soldiers were not alone. The platform was spattered with groups of military men, two to three in each group. Some groups were accompanied by either one or two dogs. Those without canine animals gripped the strap of their rifles ready to pull down and quickly use if any problems arose.

Pavel reacted quickly to the orders of the Russian soldiers and pointed to two men to follow their instructors. One of the men was Wilos.

'Go on our behalf,' Pavel said in Polish, gesturing with his hands that they were representing the remainder of the people in the cattle truck, 'and be careful to obey their orders,' he finished.

The two representatives jumped out of the train and followed the Russian soldiers as ordered. They walked across the platform to the rear of the station into a large dimly lit room. On the far side, which was adequately lit, a counter ran along the width of the wall. Two men, not in uniform, stood behind the counter transporting two different sizes of containers which held unknown substances from a hatchway in the wall onto the well worn wooden counter. There were already two men walking toward them away from the area, outflanked by a Russian soldier either side. Each man carried one container. Wilos and his companion passed the men, who like themselves he instantly recognised as being captives, and approached the counter where one of their Russian escorts now stood.

Whilst waiting for the containers Wilos looked around and noticed in the dimness of the light that the room contained several soldiers who stood in similar groups as those on the platform. These groups, however, were more relaxed. Wilos also noticed that in the farthest, darkest corners of the room soldiers were sitting at tables eating food. As the two captives were given their rations for that evening both men noticed that they were being sneered and laughed at by several of the Russian soldiers.

Wilos bit his lip and thought that in different circumstances when the odds were equal, or even slightly better stacked than what they now were, he would give any one of their captors a fight for their money. He took what anger he felt out on the largest of the containers. Dismissing the obvious heaviness of the receptacle, he punched at it as he lifted it easily and swiftly off the counter as if picking up a small lightweight object. He turned with his colleague and retraced his steps back to the cattle truck from which they had disembarked.

On their return journey, Wilos noticed that the vessel his companion held was filled with water. He also could not help but think that what he was holding, if it was food, would not be enough in quantity to share amongst all the occupants of the cattle truck. He started to get angry again but quickly controlled himself. 'Let us get this safely to the others first before protesting' he thought.

Pavel and Anatoly were awaiting their return and both were standing near to the edge of the opened doors on the inside of the carriage.

When Wilos was within five yards of the wagon, he shouted toward the elders in Polish.

'Not enough! Nie dosyc! Not enough food! Nie dosyc zwynosc!'

124

Anatoly instructed him. 'Get aboard before we make any protest Wilos.'

'Yes, yes. Tak, tak,' replied Wilos still keeping his anger under control.

Wilos put his container into the wagon and Jacob quickly pulled it into the middle of the cattle truck. Wilos's colleague handed his container over to Anatoly. This time Jan pulled the second container into the wagon. The two men then boarded the cattle truck and immediately turned and joined in with Pavel and Anatoly who were already protesting about the quantity of food they had been given.

'There will not be enough to feed all these people,' declared Anatoly.

'We'll require more than this,' stated Pavel. Both men spoke in fluent Russian toward their captors.

The two Russian soldiers were surprised at the protest, and then retaliated, announcing, 'That is enough food to last until your next stop, Pig! Sveeniya!' and with those final words the doors of the cattle wagon were slammed shut once again.

The four men now joined by others in the group still voiced their protests until the doors could be heard being barred from the outside. Nothing further happened. The doors never opened again and those inside knew they would not open until the next stop.

The protestors now turned their attention to their own people inside the wooden jail. The food they had been given, they knew, was not sufficient to meet all their needs.

'What do we do now?' asked Anatoly.

'We will have to introduce a rote system of some kind,' Pavel replied. 'If there is not enough to go around what else can we do?' He shrugged his shoulders looking toward other people searching for answers. None were forthcoming.

'You are right,' Anatoly eventually said to Pavel, 'a rote is the only answer. Let us see what is in the container.'

Everyone could see the water in the smaller container. Jacob knelt to take the lid of the larger one. It was a container full of herrings. Despite the meagre offering the captives were grateful for whatever food was supplied.

Looking up from the contents in the larger container Anatoly once more turned to address the people. 'We all have to help and support one another,' he pleaded with the occupants. 'We must try and get through this together. If there is not enough food here,' he gestured toward the container, 'then those of us who can must take a turn to use their own provisions at some stage. We,' pointing to himself, Pavel and Stefan, 'will take our turn on this occasion to go without. Next it will be the turn of others.'

There was a pause. 'Do we all agree?' he then asked.

Most of those he knew plus a few strangers muttered their compliance. Those that did not answer either looked on vacantly or were too preoccupied with their children and young families. What he had said earlier during the train journey had made sense to them. He seemed a person who could be trusted. All three who spoke, what were their names? Anatoly, Pavel and Stefan, appeared as though they could be relied upon. Anyway, what did it matter to those minorities of mothers who were alone with their young children? Whatever people wanted, they would abide with the decision so long as their children were safe and would come to no harm.

The majority, those who were well known to Anatoly, listened and agreed with what he was saying, though all knew that it meant more hardship in addition to what they had already experienced.

A woman spoke up and asked, 'What happens when all the food provisions run out? Which shouldn't be too long?'

'We cross that bridge when we come to it,' Anatoly replied. 'We must ration ourselves and we must be truthful with one another,' he continued.

The rote was drawn up. No children went without. Those adults that were under-nourished, and who did not have any food, received something first. The first night on the train, the three elders including their wives plus a few other members of their families went without their quota. Many younger men in the party offered to go without but this was vehemently turned down by the original three. Each of them had to eat their existing supply of food which was barely edible after twenty four hours of storage, mostly in warm weather, and certainly not adequate in quantity for an adult.

After the meal the water was passed around. Some people had concerns as to whether it was drinkable or whether the Russians had tampered with it. Again those people who had journeyed the longest were not bothered with what others were saying and immediately drank their share. Most of the remainder soon followed. Those who were still unsure decided against drinking.

Another woman approached Pavel and requested if she could have the water rations that had been turned down. They were given obligingly.

Turning to go back to her young children she warned to nobody in particular. 'The time will come very soon when you will drink whatever becomes available. She held up the second quota of water she had been given. 'This will taste like sweet wine to what I'm sure you will have to drink sooner or later to survive.'

After the food and drink was finished the people prepared to settle themselves for what was, to many, the first night on the cattle truck.

With stealth as its character the darkness had encroached upon them and would now firmly establish itself with them for the next quota of hours remaining in the company of a people who had done nothing different for decades to warrant such acts of evil, and who, for their punishment for doing nothing, were now being deported to distant territories within one giant boundary known as the Soviet Union. The chillness of the night increased hour by hour, for although the days were warm, the full extent of summer had not fully arrived. The night temperature was certainly bearable however. The people were thankful they had not travelled earlier in February or March. Some of their relatives and friends had already done so, and they were now lost forever, perished in the extreme cold and freezing temperatures in which they had been made to travel.

Several people had already stretched out on the planks of wood at either end of the carriage. The elderly, of which there were many, had been given priority for these positions. Others lay down on the floor and slept on palliasses made of straw which had originally been strewn across the wagon. There was not enough room for everybody to stretch out over the floor of the carriage. Some had to rest in a sitting position leaning with their backs against the sides of the carriage or against other people. Many families slept huddled together for warmth with one or two children encased in the coat of a parent, usually the father if present, further protection against the chilly night ensuring that all had a better chance of sleeping. Those families who had only one parent, always the mother, would huddle their children, some of whom were little more than babies, in their capotes for the night. It was not unusual either to see strangers nestled together to keep the cold at bay.

With the first night on the train a strange tranquillity had overlaid the carriage which Pavel's family occupied almost as if the people had come to terms with what was happening to them. The cruel transference of multitudes of strong willed, intelligent and very resilient people, without the means to fight, had decided to make the most of whatever was going to happen and were determined to struggle on and survive at all costs.

The night was intermittently broken by the cries of the young wanting food. Miraculously, somehow, the mothers handled the problem with expertise and the babies fell into slumber once more.

The night came and went. Children, especially the young ones, awoke and immediately started crying with pangs of hunger and with the cold which had crept up on them during the dark hours and had greeted them at first morning light. Parents cajoled and comforted those children to the best of their ability faithfully struggling to retain what food provisions, if any, they had put aside before eventually succumbing and using those provisions on their children to quell the pangs of hunger.

There were inevitable queues for the toilet in the morning. The hole in the floor produced repulsive looks and turned the elder generation away simply by casting their eyes on the scene. The area was open for all to see rendering the act more degrading but as a natural function of the human body it had to be performed. The concern in performing this simple task affected different ages to various extents. The young did not encounter many problems, if any at all. Most of the middle aged experienced few concerns though more than the young. The elder generation of deportees faired worse of all. Unfortunately they could not bring themselves to defecate in front of strangers or even those that they knew. Despite concealing the area with a blanket and coat draped over a piece of string this simple duty remained one of great shame and extreme difficulty to them. As a result of this problem, and after several days of travelling, further problems arose with their bodily functions. They began to have pains in the abdomen followed by illnesses. Eventually, after much cajoling and enticing and a great deal of patience shown by members of their own families and friends, the majority of the elderly overcame this barrier and they were able to perform what was a normal function. The problem returned occasionally. Some, unfortunately, continually experienced great difficulty, until finally they had no choice but to succumb.

The hole in the floor of the carriage used as a convenience quickly became feculent and stank offensively. The blankets and coats hung around the area for some privacy kept the worse of the stench and certainly the sight at bay. There was nothing which could be done to counteract this problem. Very soon the disorder which was noticeable to those entering the screened area became acceptable to everyone. Occasionally several people tried to clean the area but with few materials available to perform a decent job, except a very old piece of cloth and less than a cupful of water, this task was eventually given up. The stench was more penetrable during the day when the heat was stronger. It stirred the excrement propelling the odour from the area through the whole wagon. Again people became immune to the smell and it was soon forgotten.

Most of the deportees in the cattle truck were slowly slipping into habits which were totally unacceptable to themselves less than a week earlier. Clothes which were slightly dishevelled on entering the cattle truck became even more soiled and dirty within forty eight hours of commencing the train journey. The straw on the floor which was not fresh at the start of the journey became filthy within seventy two hours. The packs of luggage, some of which were suitcases, and others simple blankets which were filled quickly in the time allowed with necessities that the owner thought would be useful during the journey, were becoming damaged and degrained by people accidentally knocking, bumping or kicking the packages whilst trying to reach the convenience area before soiling ones clothes. The latter occurred more often as the journey progressed. Due to the lack of food supplied in the most basic of diets, and as result of fish usually being served, many people soon contracted dysentery and diarrhoea doubling the use of the latrine throughout the night and day. In trying to get to the area several people would fail and defile their clothes on the way.

Sophie and her new companion stayed together for much of the journey from the late afternoon into the late evening. Eventually the train stopped at a small station to take on board rations of food and water. Whilst at a halt the people noticed, between the gaps in the wooden planking that the carriage was made of, that another train had pulled up alongside. Sophie watched as people arose from their seating positions and spoke, either through the gaps in the wood or through the barred holes at the top of the carriages, enquiring as to the whereabouts of certain people. Names were being called continuously between the occupants of both trains. People on either convoy were listening for a name before answering as to whether that person had been seen or heard of either on that train or others that they had passed and come into contact with along the way. Nobody had a success story to relate on either train.

One woman enquired about her husband whom she had been separated from at the station which they had arrived at together. They had deliberately been placed aboard different trains. A man on the second train, who had recognised the name, announced that he had spoken to her husband on the early part of the journey. Sadly, he relayed the news to her that her husband had been shot by a Russian soldier whilst trying to escape at an earlier stop. The woman, who was accompanied by her two children, broke down, crying hysterically at what she had been told. She was comforted by several other women who were all acquainted with one another.

Sophie learned quickly, and unhesitatingly joined in the questioning of people on the other train as to the whereabouts of her Jacob. There was no positive reply from anyone. Nobody had seen or heard of a Jacob Bryevski. At least there is no confirmation of his death Sophie heartily thought to herself. 'No news is good news,' she mumbled, 'but I will keep on trying at every possible opportunity.'

While the occupants of the train waited at the terminus for the two people from each wagon to board with the provisions for the next step of the journey, local people, from the nearby village, wandered between both convoys pushing food and supplies into the cattle trucks between the wooden gaps and also in through the barred openings at the top of the wagons. People uttered their gratitude and thanked the benefactors profusely. The trains were still on Polish territory and those Poles who did not have much themselves in the form of food, but were still free, gave generously to those inside the cattle trucks who were so unfortunate. In some instances those people who supplied the food were often chased away and threatened by the Russian soldiers but still they returned after a short while to try again to distribute their free donations, even though their lives were in danger.

These gifts were gratefully accepted and most occupants were fortunate to receive something from those who were contributing. Other occupants, by nature of where they were seated or standing, received several packages but quickly dispersed the residue to those who had nothing. The food supplied was used later on the journey when the train failed to stop and pick up the daily rations from the Russian authorities.

The whole time that these benefactions were being delivered the people in the two trains continued to swap names and pursue their enquiries about their loved ones. The second train which pulled in after Sophie's was the first to leave the station. The names which had been communicated to and fro from either train continued until it had disappeared out of sight. The distant shouts of names being called by the few could still be heard like an echo repeating its tune in a tunnel. Eventually the train and the names vanished forever.

The two men boarded the cattle truck once more and the convoy pulled off in search of its distant destination. 'Perhaps we will catch up with the train we minutes earlier came in to contact with,' Sophie murmured to herself. 'Maybe we'll meet another doom laden train full of infested passengers living in squalid conditions not fit for animals.'

Deep down Sophie felt there was one element of well being when contact was made with another train. The abundance of people of the same proud, nationalistic values, furnished Sophie with the feeling of comfort. Perhaps it was the strength in numbers which gave an added air of protection to her but undoubtedly she felt more secure when other trains came into contact with hers.

The rations which had been supplied by the Russians were not of sufficient quantity for everyone to receive a share. Those that went without were usually the elderly or the sick. Measures were taken to ensure they were given something to eat. After the food and water was issued and then eaten, the occupants began to settle themselves for the night.

Sophie herself had no time to worry or concern herself over her brother's death and any concerns she had for her parents she knew would be resolved by themselves. She had become responsible for the young woman who seemed to have befriended her and had certainly, for the interim period, become dependent on her.

'Will you stay with me with for the night?' she had enquired. 'Tonight only,' she emphasised. 'If I can get through one night I believe I will survive and get through my personal nightmare.'

'I will stay with you tonight,' Sophie reassured her, 'first I must talk with my parents.'

Sitting across the carriage from her, Sophie's parents now seemed to have settled themselves for the journey, supplementing one another in their support.

'I should know by now that nothing can defeat you two,' Sophie uttered to them smiling as she sat with them for several moments before returning to her charge for the night.

They smiled in return. 'You go to your friend we will be fine,' her father replied.

Contentedly she returned to her new found companion and wondered how long the young woman would need to recover from her appalling ordeal. Sophie also concerned herself as to whether she, herself, could endure the strain of having someone dependant on her. This was the first occasion in her life that this had ever happened. Yes, she was a schoolteacher but her children always returned at the end of the day to their parents. This woman, in all probability, would be her travelling companion for as long as this odyssey lasted, not only for the duration of the train journey but also for the period they were to spend at their final destination which looked like being a considerably long term. Perhaps several years Sophie sadly reflected. Only time would tell whether she could cope with what she had got herself into. Perhaps she was worrying needlessly and the young woman would be strong and resilient after a minimum amount of time.

The night descended quickly enough. It was chilly but strangely soothing. The stench from the toilet area lingered on the stale air which permeated inside the cattle truck, smelling stronger when a gust of fresh air blew in through the barred openings in the top corners of the wagon. Calmness hung over the wagon and its occupants were quiet and easy. People fell into a surprisingly easy slumber, occasionally interrupted by the wailing and crying of one of two babies which were part of the cattle truck's cargo. Their mothers would suckle them to their breasts and they would fall asleep, quickly followed by the parents themselves.

Laying awake waiting for darkness to overtake her, Sophie's mind became active again as her fellow companion had slipped into slumber. She was grateful to the one above that she was undertaking the journey during the summer though she knew the longer the journey progressed the harder it would be to endure as the heat of the sun strengthened with each passing day.

She remembered the stories of the poor innocent people who had suffered during the first deportations in February of that year. She had heard tales that occupiers of the cattle trucks had froze to death within the very first days of commencing their travels. Some had died before the trains left the stations. Many of those who had not perished suffered frostbite and limbs had been lain waist forever more, never to be used again. Stoves had been made available in the corners of the cattle wagons, but because of the unavailability of fuel in many instances the stoves themselves were either of no use or soon became unusable. The winter had been one of the worse ever encountered in Eastern Europe. People who lived in their own homes were hit hard by the weather conditions. How could it be possible for anyone, outside in the midst of the elements, without adequate protection or shelter, and in some cases with the very minimum of clothing, survive such hazardous and treacherous conditions. Sophie prayed to God for at least giving her a better chance to survive what she knew would be a difficult journey. With those thoughts in mind and a grateful heart, Sophie too, drifted into a welcome sleep.

The night moved on with little disruption to the occupants and the morning elbowed its way in to commence the start of a new day. The sun which brought with it the daylight burst through the openings near the roof of the carriage in great piercing shafts of brightness, diffusing itself inside the wagon like a searchlight breaking into the night seeking out its escaped prisoners. The shafts of light were followed elsewhere by smaller filters squeezing, creeping and pushing themselves into the carriage through the gaps in the wooden and metal cattle truck.

It was going to be another warm day and the wooden material which the cattle trucks were built of, would act as a conductor for the heat outside to be transferred inside the wagon. Before the day was out the inhabitants would suffer, some worse than others. The water supplied to the occupants from the previous evening, the majority of which had been used, would not be sufficient to sustain them through the day. People would be desperate for the precious liquid which gave sustenance and would eagerly await the hour to arrive when the train would once again stop to pick up its daily quota of water and food rations.

The brightness of the morning, verified by the piercing shafts of light in the carriage, stirred those occupants who were in the direct path of the rays out of their slumber. For them the day started early. Other inhabitants, half or fully waking, decided to try and continue with their sleep. After all what else was there to awaken for? Those who did not fall back into sleep sat there, quietly contemplating what the day would bring, reluctantly facing the truth, that there was nothing satisfying to look forward to. They were alive which made them more fortunate than those thousands who had perished on the journeys. That, they could be grateful for, or could they? Many people of all ages contemplated this question throughout their arduous, gruelling passage. Often they would ask themselves, their families, friends and colleagues was it worth continuing with the folly of such an everyday existence. Always the reply came back from those human supports that it was. The promises that one day they would be reunited with the people that were relentlessly missed and faithfully loved, and also that one day they would set foot on their homeland which was patriotically thought about, enticed the people to go on existing. The next day the roles were reversed. Those that had provided the support would in turn ask the same question to those who had asked it of them the previous day. Again the reply would be the same. In this way many people prolonged their enthusiasm for surviving the peregrination which they were enduring.

Sophie eventually woke from her night's sleep which had surprisingly been a restful one for her. She looked around the cattle wagon and purveyed all about her before resting her eyes on her parents who were awake but who had not noticed her on the first occasion she had looked across in their direction.

'Did you sleep well Mama, Papa?' she enquired.

They both nodded their head in agreement.

'Your friend is still asleep,' whispered her father loud enough for Sophie to hear.

She looked sideways toward the companion she had momentarily forgotten and verified her father's perception.

'That's good news,' replied Sophie whilst her father again nodded in agreement.

Moments later Sophie's charge awoke to greet her new day.

The Custodian again looked sideways toward her. 'How do you feel?' she asked.

'Under the circumstances,' she glanced around her, 'very well, and I didn't wake during the night with any bad dreams.'

Sophie smiled, and replied reassuringly, 'No you didn't. Is that the first time since the incident that you have slept undisturbed throughout the night?'

'Yes,' replied the young woman.

'That's excellent news.'

The woman smiled, pleased that she had overcome what to her was a major hurdle. Now she could perhaps build her confidence to confront whatever there was to face in her journey ahead. She felt that nothing could be worse than what she had already endured in her own home which before the tragic episode had been a safe and secure haven for her.

'We've known each other nearly a whole day and I don't know your name?' Sophie stated jocularly.

The young woman laughed and replied, 'It's usually the first announcement people make to one another. Juliana,' she concluded as she held out her hand to what she knew to be a true Christian, and a worthy friend.

'Sophie Sagajlo,' Sophie replied, taking her new found companion's hand in her own.

'I'm truly grateful to you Sophie for supporting and helping me through yesterday and last night. I'm confident I can survive anything which confronts me now.'

Their hands parted and Sophie smiled at Juliana convinced that her friend's words would not prove otherwise.

CHAPTER 12

The second day came and went followed by the night. The people once again eagerly awaited the hour when the train would stop and the doors would be opened. The hour never came. The train did not stop and the doors were never opened the second night.

The people who waited patiently, yearning for the train to halt, cried quietly in anguish and frustration.

'It could still stop,' sobbed one mother in everlasting hope that the train would eventually pull up at a station. She was comforted by another who had older children, and whom she had befriended on the journey before Pavel's group arrived. She, like others before her, dwindled into an uncomfortable sleep. Nobody ate that night except for the children.

Each time a sudden jerk of the carriage occurred it awoke someone with the hope that the train was stopping. Before sounding the alarm to others they waited several minutes to make sure. Their hopes were quickly extinguished. The train never stopped. This had the covert effect of getting people through the second night and slowly into the third day.

The existing provisions, for those who still had them, were again eaten into. Everybody cursed the Russians for what they were doing and the manner in which it was being done. Over and over again the same question was asked, 'how could humans do this to other humans?'

On the third night the same happened. Again people fell asleep praying for the train to stop. It never stopped.

The next morning people awoke and felt angry, bitter and cheated at what they had been deprived of for the second day running. Conversations broke out amongst small pockets of people wondering what could be done to alleviate the problem. The majority came to the same conclusion. Nothing could be done. They were in the care of the Russians, who, it was plain to recognise, did not minister for their captives' needs. When the conversations were over people settled once again to eat a little of their own provisions, if they had any, or simply went without.

One of the women who had a small child with her had no food left. She told of her predicament to Anatoly.

'When did you eat last?' Anatoly enquired.

'The first night we boarded the train,' she replied.

'Nothing since then?'

The woman nodded her head negatively.

'Your child, when did your child eat last?'

'The day before yesterday,' she replied.

Anatoly turned and spoke to Pavel and Stefan, who since the journey had begun were sitting in close proximity to one another.

'Do you hear?' he asked.

'We hear,' both men replied in unison.

Pavel immediately opened his package containing a small amount of food. He broke off some of the stale bread and gave it to the woman. Stefan followed suit, offering salami which was beginning to smell bad. Anatoly gave the woman an apple which had been given to him by an elderly woman who had watched the columns of people approaching Pinsk.

The woman smiled and thanked the three men profusely bowing as she left their company to return to her child.

Whilst the woman talked to Anatoly another could be heard crying in the corner of the carriage. Eva, Pavel's wife, arose and approached the woman who was now sobbing hysterically.

Eva managed to squeeze in next to where she was sitting. She was holding an elderly man, presumably her husband, close to her. Both arms held tightly around his body.

Talking gently to the woman, Eva comforted her as best she could. She detected no movement in the person that the woman was holding and assumed that he was dead. The woman's crying became more controlled as Eva talked to her.

Pavel had seen his wife tending to someone in the corner of the carriage and he asked Jacob to enquire of his mother what was happening.

Jacob made his way across to where his mother was situated and both held a brief conversation.

'Her husband has died during the night Jacob. Tell Papa that I must stay with her for the present,' she whispered.

Jacob arose and returned to his father who had finished his conversation with the woman who had no food. He told him of the bad news. The three elder men looked at each other.

'Our first death Anatoly,' Pavel said. 'The first of how many?'

There was silence between the three.

Eventually Pavel asked 'What are we going to do with him?'

The three men looked toward where the dead man lay. His wife, still sobbing rhythmically, continued to hold him tightly. At timely intervals she took turns in stroking his hair, caressing his forehead and tapping his back. Throughout this ritual she continued to gently rock back and forth, like a mother nursing a sick child during an illness.

Again Pavel spoke, answering his own question.

'We keep him until those doors open,' indicating with his head, 'and then we ask to bury him properly, decently, the Polish way.'

'They have not opened the doors for two days,' said Anatoly.

'We wait and see what happens tonight,' chirped in Stefan.

'And if they do not open tonight?' asked Anatoly concernedly, 'don't forget a corpse will start to smell after several days, perhaps sooner in this warm weather we are now experiencing.'

'We, probably all of us,' gesturing with his hands, 'smell badly now in these conditions, only we have become accustomed to the odour. Look what we have to put up with from that corner. Do you think that we will smell a corpse over and above what we already have to smell?' Pavel angrily stated, not necessarily directed at Anatoly, looking and pointing toward the corner of the wagon which housed the makeshift toilet.

Pavel continued after a brief pause, now looking at the woman who had lost her husband and who was now quiet in her grief.

'We have to ask her for his rations. There are children in need of food and this journey is far from over.'

After he had voiced his opinions, he felt sad. He felt a lack of compassion toward the man and his wife. Had the journey hardened him so soon, and was he preparing himself for worse to come? He pondered these questions in his own mind, and then, for what he had said, the feeling of remorse finally came to him.

Silence overcame the three men. Nobody spoke. Although there were continuous noises of different sounds around them inside the cattle wagon, they heard nothing. As they sat there, they knew not what each other was thinking, though all thought the same thoughts, wished the same wishes and prayed the same prayers.

It was Stefan's turn to break the silence.

'You're right Pavel, his rations are essential to the remaining survivors. We must ask her. I will ask if we are in agreement.'

'It would be better if Eva asked,' replied Pavel looking across at his wife. 'At this moment she is probably the closest human being that that woman has remaining.'

Anatoly nodded in agreement. 'That is the best course to take.'

'I will ask Eva to do so when she thinks the time is appropriate.'

Jan Pilochka, Jacob's friend had absorbed all the depravity, hardship and inhumanity of the events and happenings which had affected those herded together with him in the cattle truck. He had not been able to understand why the Russians behaved as they had. From the highest ranks of Officialdom within the Soviet Union to the lowest subordinates, although he never had contact with the former, to Jan they all appeared to be moulded from the same kiln. Their thoughts, mannerisms and behaviour were in favour of wickedness and depravity toward others. Only the exceptional few members of authority were different and showed any kindness.

What had happened on the march was nothing similar to what was occurring on the cattle truck on which he was now travelling. On the march they were in the open and even though the brutality was evident it was tolerated. On the train, brutality took on a different form. The filthy cramped conditions were unbearable, the sense of imprisonment had heightened though; fortunately contact with the soldiers was less frequent.

He himself had suffered very little, in fact not at all. He was hungry, he was dishevelled, but others in the wooden prison, those who had journeyed the furthest before being joined by his group, were close to madness he thought. Many others, who were sane, were mainly unconscious to what was happening around them. This worsened as the days passed. Though he felt for them and to a certain extent cared for them he was afraid that he would soon become like them. One day into the journey by train he was scared. Two days into the journey he wondered whether he could cope with the effect of what was happening to those around him. Three days into the journey he knew he had to get out, to escape. His priority was how to do so, and when to do it? He was adamant in his mind that if he stayed, he too would meet the same fate as some of the occupants already appeared to have met. Each day he had confided his worse fears to his friend Jacob. Each day Jacob had tried to quell those fears. They returned to Jan like clockwork every morning when he awoke.

This morning he discussed with Jacob his idea for escape. He had made his decision. He was leaving.

'We have already stopped at Bryansk, and from the direction in which the train is travelling we are heading toward Moscow. If we reach Moscow, I'm getting out there Jacob.'

'Why Moscow Jan? Why not out in the countryside? You will have a better chance of survival there with fewer people to ask questions. How are you going to get out of the train? The doors are barred. There are machine gun posts at either end. Usually the searchlights on the train come on during the night. You will be caught and shot if you are not shot on sight.'

A multitude of thoughts raced through Jacob's mind now that Jan had decided to go. He voiced them all. Thoughts that were all obstacles to him going. Not one encouraged him to escape if indeed he was going. Yes, Jan had talked to him about his fears on the train and whether he could survive and even the possibility of escaping, but he had not thought his friend was serious about fleeing. Jacob assumed that the sudden shock of being told that his friend was leaving was a barrier to supporting him in his escape. He decided to immediately change tactics.

'I will…'

'No, say no more Jacob and listen to what I have to say.' Jan cut his friend off in speech before Jacob could utter what he really wanted to convey.

'My mother has, or should say, had a sister who married a Russian. After they married she left our home town and settled in Moscow with her new husband. They eventually had a daughter, an only child. My mother and her sister wrote often to one another keeping in touch and updated on each others events. My Aunt always invited my mother to visit them in Moscow. So, eventually, my mother along with me, decided to go there for a holiday. My father would not go due to the problems between the two countries in the past and he never trusted Russian people, especially the men. I was about nine years old, nearly ten, and Wandeczka, my Aunt's daughter, my cousin, was just twenty years of age. We had a wonderful holiday and my cousin looked after me very well especially on two nights when my mother and her sister went out with my Russian Uncle to be entertained. Both families kept in contact until my Aunt died about six years ago, the uncle six months after her. My mother received several letters during the next two years from her niece. Since then nothing, even though she continued to write. But I remember the address where they lived or should say where she lived.' He quickly corrected himself before continuing. 'My plan is to get off the train as near to Moscow as possible, find where they are living and ask if she will help me.'

Jacob was still shocked. Jan had never done this amount of planning before he thought, and he had to admit, the idea was good and quite simple. He turned to look at Jan and stated with eager encouragement, 'I will help you all I can, but have you thought of everything?' Again Jacob repeated some questions he had already asked and others which had entered his mind since Jan had outlined his story.

'How will you get off the train? What if she is not at the same address? Where will you go then?'

'Although I have thought about escaping since virtually the first day, the plan came to me yesterday. Not a lot of time perhaps but there are several days left before we reach Moscow, and I think I have covered most eventualities. I cannot go through the door or through the ceiling,' he pointed with his finger at both options, 'but I can go through the floor.' Jan smiled and looked at Jacob.

'How?' Jacob asked.

'Think Jacob. Think.' retorted Jan.

It dawned on Jacob. 'The hole in the floor.' he replied smiling at his colleague.

'Is it large enough for you to get through?' Jacob asked becoming more serious.

'I have taken a measurement and it's a good thing that I'm slim and getting slimmer with the food which is being served here.' He smiled lightheartedly. Jacob grinned too.

'It will be tight but I think I can squeeze through. If I cannot, there is an alternative I have thought of, though I do not have the tools to carry it out.'

'What is that?'

'I extend the area of the hole and cut a part of the floor away.'

'For that we will need something sharp.'

'Yes, but I don't think it will come to that. I'm small enough, you will see. Your next question. If she cannot be found I will head for the countryside and slowly make my way back to Poland. Although I have no reason to believe that she has moved.'

'What about the Russian language? Are you fluent enough?' Jacob asked realising with every response that Jan's plan was commendable and that he did not want to part with his friend. Although Jan had not been one of Jacob's closest friends before this journey had begun, they had become closer than ever since. They were easily able to confide in one another, to listen and advise one another if necessary which in turn gave comfort to the other colleague. Although Jan had turned out to be the more doubtful of the two in terms of whether either could survive the trip, he had now devised a plan which was creditable and above all would allow him a chance to succeed and survive.

'My Russian has improved since this train journey has started. It's not as fluent as yours, but I will survive well enough.'

Jacob then remembered Jan asking him to only speak in Russian the day after they had boarded the train. He wondered was this the reason for that request and assumed that it was.

'The simple plans are the best Jan. This escape seems straightforward enough. Do you have sufficient food?'

'I will need very little. I do not expect to have to walk longer than one day to reach the address of my cousin. If I run out of provisions I will take chances and borrow food as your father says.' A smile crossed both their faces. Jacob scrutinised his colleague's visage carefully. Almost instantly he became aware of an easier and more relaxed attitude emanating from his friend's composure. He voiced his awareness.

'You look relieved Jan. Was this journey carrying such a weight on your shoulders?'

There was a short silence in the conversation between the two men before Jan replied simply.

'Yes. For some reason it was a great burden to me. You know I've never been one who can tolerate pain and suffering to anyone or anything. Thankfully I have found much solace in my plan. I know it will not be easy out there but I have a better chance out there than in here.'

Silence descended between the two again. Then he continued enthusiastically.

'I've had an even better idea than the first Jacob.' The two young men eyed each other excitedly. 'Why not escape with me?'

Jacob was speechless. It was a good idea he thought.

'I don't know,' he replied hesitatingly.

'Why?' asked Jan, still excited at the idea. 'Together we stand a better chance, whether we head for Moscow or out into the countryside.'

Jacob pondered on the thought. His first instincts were to go and take the chance with Jan. Their chances of succeeding were good. Both spoke Russian exceptionally well. They could get lost in a city as large as Moscow and if Jan's cousin was unavailable, or simply chose not to help, then Jacob had the background and training to survive in the countryside if they wished to move on from the city. Jacob looked up and across to his family. His mother and father, two sisters and his youngest of three brothers. He felt sure that they had as good a chance as any to survive whatever awaited them at the end of their journey. He however, wanted to be there with them to make the possibility of their survival even greater. He had done nothing exceptionally brave or commanding on the journey so far. 'No matter his father had said to him, your presence is as important. We know you are there if needed. We know we can depend on you.' Jacob turned back to his friend.

'I cannot go Jan. The plan is good and it has an excellent chance of success. If anything happened to them,' he pointed toward his family, 'I could not forgive myself. I have lost one that I love, whether I find her again is in the hands of the gods, but if it is in my willpower I will lose nobody else that I truly care for on this journey.'

Jan reached into his pocket.

'I understand Jacob. If when you arrive at your destination you need help remember this address and write to me there.' Jan passed Jacob a dirty scrap of paper upon which he had written the name and address of where his cousin was living.

'If there is anything that you want don't hesitate to send word. If I can help, assuming I arrive safely, I will do so.' He spoke with a gentle tone to his words which conveyed a certainty and an assurance toward Jacob which he thought Jan was incapable of several days earlier. Instinctively and with emotion they clasped their arms around each other unashamedly showing the affection for one another which had developed quickly in a short space of time. They had become like brothers since this odyssey had begun.

'One more point Jan. You cannot go through the hole with that coat on. The excrement you're certain to come in contact with will soil your clothes even more.' He looked at Jan and before waiting for a reply, 'don't tell me you have already solved the problem.'

'No,' said Jan quickly, 'What should I do?'

Jacob started to laugh and Jan followed suit.

'Wrap an old piece of material around you especially your shoulders as you go through the hole. Keep the material on, it will protect your clothes when you land on the ground outside after dropping from the carriage and if we can get a brown coloured cloth for you it will provide better camouflage for you.'

'Good,' said Jan pleased that Jacob had thought of the problem and solved it also.

'Before you go you had better tell my father of your plan. He may have suggestions which could be of use to you.'

Jan nodded his head in agreement.

Eva had spoken gently and with compassion to the woman for several minutes, endeavouring to persuade her, as yet unsuccessfully, to release her grip on the body of her husband.

'I cannot,' she whimpered full in bereavement, 'he will be alone in this terrible land afraid of this accursed journey. I must hold on to him. I will not be long for this world myself and then we shall be together again.'

'You must not talk of such things; he would not have wanted you to speak in such a way.' Eva encouraged.

'There is nothing for me now, nothing whatsoever. We heard only days before being forced to leave our home that our only son had died in a skirmish with some Russian soldiers. That almost finished my husband. Part of him died with our son. This journey has only accelerated the inevitable.' The woman started weeping again and in between her sobbing continued talking. 'My strength was his strength, his strength was mine. Now that he has gone my resolve is weakening too.'

Her grief was complete. She buried her face in her free hand and sobbed bitterly. But she was not finished. Her enmity flowed against all things Russian. Normally of quiet disposition, she cursed those unknown faces who had developed such a system and admonished those subservients who carried and supported the system without question.

Her words were heard by all in the carriage. Those who had paid little or no attention to what anyone else had said, now looked up, at first with surprise. Then their expressions changed to one of support. As the woman continued her acrimonious rhetoric it gave added strength to the onlookers. Someone was speaking out, voicing their abhorrence of the system and those who had anything to do with it. It afforded those spectators with hope. Although confined within the four wooden walls, it reminded people of times gone by when they were able to voice their opinions openly. This woman, deep in grief, opened the memories of the not too distant past. Her words motivated others in the wagon. Moved them, some like never before. Those who had been dormant looked and listened and eventually were the ones to speak next, and, similar to the woman, voiced their disapproval of what was happening. And still others joined in. At first quietly, then louder, until finally they were shouting their intense dislike toward the Russian soldiers. They did not know if their protestations could be heard. In those fleeting minutes they did not care. They were unified in their thoughts and as one in their aversion.

Their noise drowned out the rumble of the carriages over the rail track and the gasping for power from the engine fell silent as it carried forth its cargo of human misery. Misery which was rebelling and resurging on a different plane. It relayed above their heads and outside to the Russian soldiers sitting in the machine gun nests at strategic points on top of the carriages. It transmitted to forlorn neighbours inside those wagons either side. The occupants, again buoyed up by what they heard, accompanied their folk. In less than several minutes the whole train had come alive like an audience at the end of a poor concert. Baying their denunciation, the whole convoy was an uncoordinated yet responsive choir of human voices.

Although the occupants spoke in Polish a number of the Russian guards were able to translate some of the words. As the noise increased in crescendo, so to did the anger of the captors.

Those in command, who were located in a carriage behind the engine, had heard the uproar and come out of their quarters to investigate. In annoyance they barked orders toward the machine gun posts. It was to no avail. The instructions could not be heard. The outrage was too much for one officer who climbed onto the carriages and made his way across the roofs of the wagons to convey his orders to the first gun post.

All the time the protestations continued. Although only words, invisibly they acted as a barrier to his goal and the provocation prevented him easily reaching his initial target. It was as if the voices and the insults which came forth reached out at him to hinder his passage.

Finally after much inconvenience he arrived at the first position. Seething with anger at the continued abuse echoing all around he snatched the machine gun from the first of two soldiers, unclasped the safety catch and clumsily fired off a volley of bullets which ripped through the wooden plinth on the outside edge of the roof of the carriage directly in front which contained human cargo. The burst of fire was too close to the soldiers' quarters and those who followed him out, and now looked on, jumped back with alarm. Knowing the reason for his misjudged aim, the officer breathed deeply, directed the barrel of the gun out across the empty expanse of land they were travelling over and fired a second time.

The flowing voices stalled immediately but did not completely abate. The majority of inhabitants continued.

The officer gestured with hand signals to the other gun posts behind him to follow his example. They too turned their machine guns out toward a vacuum of space and pulled the triggers. The noise drowned the sound of protestations but only temporarily.

Again the officer repeated his earlier gesture leading by example. Again his men followed. After the second, longer volley was fired the disapproval had subsided considerably. Still a minority persisted. The third fusillade ceased any further outbursts.

The silence was deathly. Those inside waited patiently, eyes gazing upward, tense for the next round of fire which never came. The silence continued unabated for several minutes. No one made a noise, not even the young ones, as if they too knew that any sound would bring instant and final retribution. Breathing seemed to have stopped for everyone.

Finally the stillness was broken. Not hastily but slowly. First the normal sounds returned. They had always been there and had never left. The occupants had somehow blocked out their minds and ears to them and now they returned slowly. The rumble of wheels over the rail track and the spitting of steam from the powerful engine accompanied them once more. The coughing and spluttering of humans followed, with first one then two then the whole carriage at once seemed to whisper in careful voices. Minutes later the voices had reached their usual pitch and normality returned. It was as if nothing had happened. Though something had happened. Unexplainable, untouchable, and unreachable. It had happened to them and they were stronger for it.

Eva, who had joined the protestations, had experienced the same emotions as everyone else on the cattle wagon. Turning her attentions to the elderly woman whom she had been comforting she wiped away the tears which had continued their flow through the whole episode. Eva remembered what the woman had told her and was saddened on hearing the story. What could she say to comfort her now she thought? 'No words will make her pain any easier to bear. No words will unburden her suffering. There is nothing I can add to suppress her grief or her resentment.'

As if knowing what Eva was thinking the woman turned and faced her helper. Although she stopped crying an occasional sobbing interjected and, eased by her outburst, she managed a smile. Both women fell silent. Slowly the woman fell into a quiet slumber.

Pavel eventually came over, kneeled in front of both women and offered Eva a little food. She declined.

He continued to look at his wife admiringly, remembering how from the first time he had met her; he had immediately fallen in love with her. His was undoubtedly a case of love at first sight. His first recollections inundated his mind and he was grateful for the respite. He remembered how after several months courting he had to relinquish her. She was an aristocrat descended from the old Royalty of Poland centuries before. He was a learned gentleman without a drop of Royal blood in his body.

Despite being a perfect gentleman and a successful businessman, he was deemed, in her parents opinion, not good enough to partner Eva. When she had to choose one of the three eligible bachelors, she refused outright, until she heard that Pavel had gone. To make her decision and her life easier he had purposefully decided to leave Poland and travelled to America.

Years had elapsed. Then news was sent to Pavel by his family who kept studiously in touch with him that Eva's husband had died leaving her with two young children. Without further prompting he sold his business in America, which he had built into an established and reputable company, and caught the earliest available boat home to Poland.

Pavel met Eva approximately one year after the death of her husband. A mutual friend invited them to a Ball given by him and re-introduced them to one another. From that night she very rarely left him and six months later, with, on this occasion, no disapproving protests from her parents, he married his first and only true love.

They had come through a great deal together. Poland had always been a troubled land. Not from within its borders but from outside. Enemies continually fought over its territories and frontiers. Indeed the last nineteen years prior to the outbreak of the war were the most peaceful that Poland had experienced for a long time.

Here they were still together on a train to Siberia. Deported to a different land. Ignorant in the knowledge of what would happen there. What mattered was that they were together and that was the important ingredient.

He stared at her, still entranced by her beauty even though she had seen her best years. The deep colour of her auburn hair was slowly being replaced with silver strands and although Pavel thought the process had speeded up due to their laboured journey, her beauty remained as strong as her fluorescent brown eyes. He touched her cheek lovingly and whispered his love for her. A tear rolled down her face and he gently wiped it away. The last act he performed before temporarily leaving was to rid her of the vermin crawling in her hair. The act also quelled the romanticism he had moments earlier reminisced.

'Are you sure you will not eat?' he whispered.

'I'll wait till later, I don't want to disturb her.'

Pavel arose and returned to the remainder of their family.

After the unusual but exhilarating event early in the morning the remaining time before noon passed as usual on the train. Children seemed to take turns in crying. The parents and the rest of the people were used to the noise and nobody took notice. Mothers continued to console their offspring, but there was not a lot they could do to suppress their obvious misery.

In the afternoon Eva arose from where she had been comforting the woman all morning and walked over to her family.

Pavel stood up from where he was sitting as he noticed her approaching and enquired as he took her hand. 'Is she still sleeping?'

'She is dead Pavel,' Eva replied coolly and calmly. 'She is dead just like she predicted.'

Shocked, Pavel made the sign of the cross and whispered a short prayer. He put his arms around Eva. She comforted herself in them as she had done on so many previous occasions. Remembering those past events, she thought none were as abhorrent as the situation they were in now. There was a long pause. Pavel was horrified and surprised. Horrified at how the woman had died so quickly, and surprised that Eva was so very calm. 'Was she too becoming hardened to the journey' he asked himself.

Eventually, after a long silence, Pavel spoke, susurrating in her ear.

'We need their belongings Eva so that we can put them to good use.'

'Yes I know, and she knew. She knew she was going to die and she gave me her permission for all their possessions to be used in the best possible way and especially for the children. Wait till I call you before coming over Pavel.'

He understood and gestured with his head. Eva returned to the two corpses.

With difficulty she released the dead woman's arms from around the cadaver of her husband and proceeded to take the clothing from both bodies including the shoes which were well worn but still adequate for wearing. Whilst she worked she sensed others staring at her and what she was doing. Eva comforted herself in the knowledge that she was carrying out the instructions with the express permission of the dead woman. She continued with her work. When Eva finished what had to be done, the elderly couple were left with only their undergarments. 'How thin and weak they look without their clothes,' Eva observed to herself.

The bodies, especially that of the man, even with undergarments on, already appeared skeletal like. 'How long had they been journeying' she wondered. Eva looked at their documents and was shocked at first, then decided it was synonymous considering what they had been through. They looked much older than the dates of birth stated on their identity papers and must have aged ten years within the last few weeks.

She kept the identity papers and called Pavel. After a brief conversation he, in turn, called Jacob and Kazik, his sons, to move the bodies to an area near to where the doors opened. He hoped that that night they would be opened.

Eva turned to go back with Pavel to the area in the wagon occupied by their family. She glanced back once more to where the elderly couple had been sitting. Already another family had taken the opportunity to occupy the small area which had been vacated. Space was in very short supply between the four wooden walls.

The garments were immediately given to those women who were alone on the train with children to look after. The coats were given to those who were without any, again these went to women. Some of them cried with gratitude others looked up at the benefactor with empty, expressionless faces.

That night the train stopped to take on board additional rations. Whilst two men went to fetch the food the bodies were carefully taken off the train by another two young Poles in the carriage and laid by the wall of the station building. No Russian soldier was concerned about the bodies. Pavel requested that they be given proper burials by those in the cattle truck. The soldiers laughed and bellowed abuse at the requestor. Before the doors of the carriage were slammed shut, Pavel noticed as he looked down the length of the station that other bodies were lined against the building wall. He felt sick as he perceived the different size of the corpses, the majority of which were those of children, some only several months old.

On a similar train travelling in the same direction separated by only several hours, the same misery was experienced by Sophie and her family and those people around her.

The slow, snail like pace of the morning taking root and the gentle, sporadic awakening of the inhabitants of the cattle wagon was broken by a piercing, heart rendering scream from one of the mothers in the carriage who had aroused from her slumber to discover that her only child of six months old had perished sometime during the night. The other occupants who were still sleeping were immediately awoken by the earth shattering cry of shock and emotion. Her screams could be heard two carriages along either side. The first high pitched, penetrating lengthy utterance, was followed by a second lower pitched, quicker wail. As she gasped for breath in readiness to continue to voice her sad news, the cattle truck momentarily returned to a strange quietness. Friends who had woken as a result of her alarm instantly turned their attention toward her. A second woman, childless and husbandless, put her arms around the woman who was rocking back and forth still clutching the baby tightly to her bosom. A third woman crawled around to see if she could be of any help to the victim who had suffered a great loss. The carriage was quiet. Nobody spoke. Everybody felt the pain and recognised the agony that the woman was experiencing.

Sophie's father, Yuri Sagajlo arose and carefully made his way through the outstretched bodies, some still stirring from their slumber having been woken by the shattering sound. He knelt in front of the woman, who looked not much older than his own daughter, and gently spoke to her with his kind, melodic and soothing voice which had served him well whilst calming excited and irascible patients whom he had attended on many occasions in the past.

He told her of his profession, and she was still sobbing uncontrollably as he continued to speak to her. With every word he uttered, her crying relented slowly but surely. Within minutes she handed over the baby to him as he had wanted, but only after he promised to return the child to her after he had completed the examination of the infant. As the baby left her arms, her crying stopped. The doctor's eyes and those of the mother briefly met as he took hold of the tiny corpse. He detected in the mother's lugubrious eyes a glimmer of hope that, perhaps, somehow, he could perform miracles and breathe life back into her child.

Whilst he examined the baby, the expectancy in her eyes that he had perceived preyed on his mind. 'What can I do?' he asked himself. 'I have my professional tools but still there is nothing I can do for this woman. The baby has been dead for many hours, probably losing out on life during the early part of the night,' the doctor assessed. The small, frail body he gently held in his arms was cold to touch. 'It would take a miracle to bring this infant back to life,' he thought as the hope of the mother came back to revolve in his mind.

He looked up at the mother, nodding his head sadly.

'I'm sorry; there is nothing I can do.'

He wished more than ever before that if there was one occasion on which he could perform a single miracle this would be the time to do so.

The mother took the baby from the doctor and held it tightly to her once again. The tears which had now returned, multiplied in numbers. She cried aloud at first as she held the tiny corpse then somehow controlled her emotions.

The doctor arose, gently caressed the young mother's hair, hoping in some way that it would comfort her, and returned to his sitting area where his wife looked on. She was crying in sympathy as were nearly all the females in the wagon along with several men.

The doctor sat down next to Helena. She put her arms around him to console him, for she knew that throughout his medical career whenever he had lost a patient, he had also suffered, thinking that he had failed the family of the deceased that were left behind. Although this baby had not been his patient she knew that his feelings would be very strong and that something should be done to correct the situation and alleviate the nightmarish experiences that everyone was currently going through.

Eventually after a long silence between them she asked her husband what the baby had died of.

'It's impossible to tell,' he replied, 'a germ, starvation.' He raised his arms upward to the heavens looking for an answer.

'The conditions we are travelling in are deplorable. The baby could easily have contracted a germ in this hell hole which in turn, due to these conditions, will accelerate death.' There was a momentary pause before he continued. 'I wonder when the last time the baby received a proper meal was. When was the last time anybody received an adequate meal?' he questioned aloud to anybody, but in particular to his wife. 'For that reason the early stages of malnutrition could have assisted in the death of the baby. Either or both reasons could be the cause of death. If the infant had a fever, and there is no sufficient diet available to fight the fever, then it will die. I don't know what the true cause is. We will never know.' Disheartened, he turned again to his wife and they continued to console one another.

Resuming his conversation he wanted to warn Helena of what lay ahead. Now was the time to do so.

'There will be other deaths Helena,' he murmured to her. 'They will occur all about us. On the train journey, whilst marching, even when we arrive at our final destination where we will remain, perhaps for many years, there will be death all around us. We must be prepared. There will be little in the way of help from our Russian captors. The country is lacking in all necessities even the most basic of needs. What we want and need we will have to provide for ourselves by whatever means we can achieve it.'

He ended his conversation and looked at his wife intently. He smiled at her and it comforted her to know that they would be on the journey together; for she knew that with him by her side she would have a chance and could even survive the ordeal. If he died, she too would die.

CHAPTER 13

Jan was correct. Several days later the train had finally arrived on the outskirts of Moscow at a station called Lyubertsy situated south west of the capital. It had stopped to refuel, to unload another two corpses and to pick up rations for the next stage of the journey.

Each day that passed, since making his earlier deductions, he was sure that the train was travelling in the direction where he wanted to go, but he could not be positive. The waiting and hoping and praying for his single wish to be fulfilled had been impressed heavily on his mind. Finally his need had been realised and his gratitude was immense almost to the point of elation. An emotion, he thought, which would have been impossible to achieve when first setting out on this heinous journey. The unpretentious escapee was excited, apprehensive and relieved that the train had reached what was to be his final destination on this unholy pilgrimage.

No longer would he smell the dank, stale, fresh less air that permeated the wooden cabin. The air, which in daytime, suffused with perspiration off human bodies as a result of the heat from the sun beating down on the wooden tomb. The air that was mixed with the foul and filth which evaporated from the congealed mess of peoples faeces around the perimeter of the hole in the floor, and the air which escaped through the already dishevelled clothes of those people who had contracted dysentery and who had not been able to reach the hole in the time possible to pass their excrement. All this he would be free off. Above all this, which he felt he could withstand if necessary, the one thing he wanted to be liberated from more than anything, was the visual effect of all the suffering prevalent in the cattle wagon. The effect not only of when one was awake, but also when asleep. He wanted to be free of the wretchedness that people had, were, and would continue to be put through. He wanted to be free of the nefarious conditions which people ate and slept in. He, Jan knew, had been spared a great amount of suffering. Due to this he felt guilty and was concerned for those people who had others to care for, especially the solitary mothers who fought on against the odds which heavily outweighed them. Soon the experience he was going through within the wooden chamber would all be over for him.

But the question dwelled in his mind. Would he forget what he wanted to forget? The pain. The suffering. The anguish. Only time would tell.

'Come on Jan,' barked Jacob, who now stirred him out of his final thoughts of the train journey, 'it is time to prepare. The doors are closed and the train will be pulling out of the station soon. Are you ready?'

Jacob and his brother Kazik had already made sure that Jan was able to get through the hole after lowering him upside down into the opening the previous night when the majority of people in the truck were sleeping.

'I will never be better prepared,' replied Jan, looking forward to the experience more than he ever thought he would. He felt as though he were a little boy who was going on some adventure, excited and aroused, the adrenalin seething through his body. Despite frequent reminders to himself that there was extreme danger ahead he continued in a buoyant mood.

He remembered advice given to him by Jacob who had told him so many times since first revealing his plan of escape. 'If you are ever stopped by anyone and are not convincing with your explanation then get the hell out of there. If you have to, hit first ask questions later and make sure you hit hard. Run and don't stop running until you know you are safe. Stoop to the lowest means possible to save your neck.' What else had he said about the Russians? 'They put no value on human life, so treat them as they would treat you. If necessary, shoot first ask questions later.' Jan hoped that the last scenario would never occur, for if it did he was sure he would lose out. His mind changed from joyousness to seriousness and he warned himself to be prepared for all eventualities.

Jacob wrapped part of an old blanket, which had been provided by his father, around Jan's shoulders and pulled it down over the top half of his body. He secured the protective covering at the front of Jan's waist. Once again the activity jerked Jan out of his thoughts. The time had come for him to depart.

'You're not with us in these last few moments Jan, is everything all right?' asked Jacob.

'I'm fine Jacob, fine. Although I will miss the people, I will not miss this place.' he gestured with his hands, looked at Jacob, and put his arms around him. Kazik, Jacob's brother came to Jan, and he too, was embraced by him.

'Someday, when this is all over we will meet again. Now come, let us help you,' ordered Jacob with a trace of sadness in his voice.

The three men made their way to the escape hole. A few well wishers patted Jan on the back, bid him farewell and whispered words of encouragement. He returned his thanks and gratitude as best he could. When they reached the area the two helpers once again clasped their arms around the escapee. Jacob and

Kazik took hold of Jan under his armpits, one on either side and lowered him through the infested hole to the ground outside and underneath the train. He stood there looking up at his well wishers and two close friends once more. For the last time he purveyed the scene inside the wagon, with nearly all its occupants busy eating the rations which had been taken on board, and prepared for the train to pull out of the station. Whilst waiting he knelt to his knees to ensure that he could still lower his shoulders through the circumference of the hole. There was no need. As before when he bowed his shoulders inward he managed to squeeze through the opening, the edge of which had already soiled the old material which Pavel had supplied and his son had fastened.

'You need gloves,' Jacob suddenly realised, 'or your hands will become badly stained whilst you hold on around the opening and that may cause suspicion later on.'

Jacob turned to his father and asked whether any gloves were available. The answer was negative.

'What about some old cloth Papa?' asked Jacob.

Hurriedly Pavel tore two large strips of cloth from the remainder of the same old blanket Jacob had used to make the protective covering for Jan. He handed the strips to Jacob who in turn bound them around Jan's hands.

'Take them off when you are away from the train,' Jacob said.

Jan thanked them profusely.

Whilst Jacob was sorting the problem of hand protection for him, Jan looked underneath the wagon to see whether there were any supports he could use to rest his feet on.

'There are wooden slats underneath Jacob where I can press my feet against whilst holding on here,' Jan happily announced.

The soldiers outside broadcast the departure of the train and Jan looked once more toward his two closest companions for the last time. The train moved forward slowly and Jan trotted backward in unison.

Last minute instructions were given to Jan by Jacob.

'Do not forget to wait until you are clear of the station before dropping onto the line. We will give you the signal.'

'Stay down between the tracks until the sound of the train has disappeared.'

Jan nodded whilst listening, signalling that he understood the information given to him by his friend. The train had gained momentum now and Jan had taken grip around the filthy opening. His feet pressed against the two wooden supports he had located minutes earlier underneath the carriage. The back of his body rested against the perimeter of the opening.

As planned Wilos had taken up a position by the barred opening in the corner of the carriage near the roof and was waiting for the train to be clear of the station and out into the countryside. When that had occurred he would notify Jan who would lower himself down onto the ground feet first.

Several minutes elapsed then Wilos gave the signal for Jan to commence. Jacob and Kazik aided the absconder, a slight change in plan, and sat on the edge of the hole themselves on the last remains of the blanket which they had placed over the excrement. Gripping Jan under his shoulders they lowered him out through the opened floor using their feet on the opposite edge of the hole to act as a balance, at the same time stopping them from falling through. Jan still gripped with his hands on the edge of the hole. The perspiration poured from his face, not only because it was warm but also because of his body weight which had started to strain his arms. The threat of being caught was also prevalent in his mind. His excitement abated quickly only to be replaced, even quicker, by anguish. Jacob and his brother perspired too. They, however, had nothing to lose.

'Let go now,' ordered Jan.

The brothers let go slowly. Jan took the complete strain on his arms and immediately knew he could not hold his own body weight for long. He was not muscular and how he wished that for those few seconds he could be.

'Good luck. Powodzenie,' the brothers bade to their disappearing friend.

Both men arose then fell to their knees, peering through the hole to catch sight of the little view they had left of their colleague. His body was now angled to the floor notifying to them that he had dropped his feet which were now dragging along the ground and being jerked over the sleepers which kept the metallic railway lines apart.

'You must let go Jan,' urged Jacob, 'or you'll be damaged by the wooden sleepers when the train gathers more steam. Let go! Let go! Przeszkoda puscic.'

Tears came to the escapee's eyes as the pain in his legs increased and moved through his body. His threshold for pain was very low and this nurtured doubts in his mind as to whether he should have gone ahead with his plan. His lack of confidence lingered. As it did, his pain multiplied with each jolt his lower body experienced.

Then inspirationally he talked himself into action. 'One moment of bravery and you will be free,' he thought to himself. 'Let go before the train gathers speed. You cannot go back. You do not want to go back.'

He could also hear Jacob's words telling him, urging him and encouraging him to go on. 'Let go. Przeszkoda puscic.'

The pain worsened with each moment that passed. 'Let go,' his mind now told him taking the place of Jacob's instructions which he could hear no longer. His hands lost their grip. H could not remember telling them to let go. It was as if they had a will of their own and they acted of their own accord. He hit the ground and the pain was momentarily excruciating. He bounced once then twice. His back felt as though it had been cut in two. 'Turn over, turn over,' he ordered himself. Forcibly and with great pain he started to turn to his side and then he remembered to turn quickly in case of some obstruction hanging down from one of the carriages. Acting with speed and overcoming the agony, he turned onto his stomach and buried himself in the ground. The pain which he had ignored returned. He pulled the excess of the old blanket up over his head for camouflage and waited until the train would finally pass.

The thudding of the carriages echoed in his ears as they travelled over him on their continued odyssey. Mingled with the sound were the mournful voices of its occupants. Within seconds of turning he heard a distinctive noise and almost immediately felt something fall on his back. He dare not move, and tried to forget what it could be. He turned his attention to himself and stretched his legs to make sure he still had full use of them. 'At least I can move,' he said to himself as the pain, which he had temporarily forgotten, returned once more. His left ankle hurt badly and he decided against moving it anymore. 'Wait until the train has gone,' he decided to himself. He fought back the pain as best he could and tried to think of the good things in life. He remembered his acquaintance with the peasant girl in the barn several mornings ago. The simple fragrance of her body odour came back to him and thoughts of her smile brought a little relief. 'What would she be doing now?' he thought.

The wheels of the train skipping over the tiny gap in the rails as they butted together to produce an iron road broke the concentration of his happy thoughts. 'This train is a large one,' he murmured to himself. 'I have lain here for what seems like an eternity.' It had been no more than two minutes and the train was slower than usual because it was still picking up steam after leaving the station. Jan felt as though he was slowly choking with the cloth pulled up around and over his head for camouflage. 'I will have to pull it back soon for I cannot breathe,' his mind warned. No sooner had he concerned himself about those thoughts than the timely clatter of the wheels over the rails suddenly halted directly above him and the noise became more and more distant, until eventually nothing could be heard.

The escapee smiled with happiness but waited a good five minutes before he dared to move himself. Satisfied that he could no longer hear the train or any of the sounds it produced and carried, and whilst he waited for sufficient time to build up courage before finally pulling back the blanket to see, if anything, what was there to greet him, he listened for other noises which may give clues as to what was in and around the area.

The only other sounds he could hear were those which filled him with happiness, and which, until several days ago, he had taken as everyday occurrences. The different calling tones of various species of birds filled him with delight. 'Never again will I take them for granted,' he promised himself. 'I will cherish each sound individually.' The other noise Jan heard was the occasional whisper of the warm summer breeze which frequented the morning and which cooled the warmth of the sun now beating down through the clothes that he wore, onto the back of his body and legs. He perspired profusely, this time from the heat of the morning and not from the pain of his grip or for any other reason. 'Strange,' he thought to himself, 'but I don't feel fear toward anything which I may now come face to face with when I pull back my protective garment. Perhaps it's because I'm out in the open and at least have a chance of escape, whereas inside the cattle wagons there is no chance whatsoever.'

Two more people died during the night, an elderly woman and a pretty young girl of nine years. The bodies were discovered by the husband of the woman and the mother of the child. The spouse informed that his wife had not complained to him of any ailment, which made the bereavement more difficult for the family left behind to understand. People had their own views. Did the woman realise the depravity they were all going through and that the possibility of events getting worse was slowly turning to a probability? Had she therefore given up what little hope her life had and accordingly wanted to die? Those people who asked these questions also supplied their own answers.

As before, Eva was summoned to take care of the thankless, morbid task of undressing the corpses and taking whatever was useful from them to put to good use elsewhere. Permission for this was instantaneously and unequivocally granted by both parties of the dead people.

Enough had happened during that one hour in the morning to keep the occupants of the wagon occupied for the rest of the day. After Jan had left a strange silence had descended on the carriage. Those that were interested in his escape were at first tense, then relieved, that the train had not stopped. They knew then that Jan had not been discovered, at least not by any of the guards on the train. Nobody was more relieved that Jan's close friends, Jacob, Kazik, and Wilos. When a reasonable amount of time had passed on the morning's journey they became very excited and talked freely of the hopes they had for their escaped colleague after liberating himself from a terrible ordeal.

Throughout the morning pockets of people within the cattle truck continued discussing the events, and, as if someone alien had overheard the conversations and informed on them, the train prematurely stopped at a small station called Ramenskoye on the eastern side of Moscow. All conversation stopped. An immediate silence descended on the carriage as the dwellers inside listened intently to those on the outside to confirm whether their worse suspicions were true. There was an abundance of verbal noise with people shouting orders and others obeying them.

'Have they found Jan?' Kazik asked his older brother, afraid at the same time that Jan had been discovered.

'No,' Jacob replied. 'We are far past the region where he got away and I have not heard those outside mention an escape or that someone has been caught.'

The doors opened and people in the direct path of the sunlight shaded their eyes from the strength of the sun. Fresh air poured in through the opening. It was welcomed and appreciated by all occupants. The breeze that blew into the carriage smelt like a spring cleaned house, refreshing and unpolluted. Completely clearing the stale air inside, the residents half asleep were roused back to full consciousness.

Two soldiers jumped into the carriage. The first started calling names from a list he had extracted from the pocket of his uniformed trousers. After he had read half a dozen names and had been interrupted by the second soldier, who informed him that firstly he had to read out the instructions, he looked up from the list and roared, 'If any of you are on this list then you will stand and come with me. Should you decide not to come forward and you are found out at a later date your only retribution will be death before a firing squad. Do you understand?'

Nobody replied. Everyone understood. Those that did not understand were quickly made aware of the procedure and the consequences by their fellow prisoners.

After a brief pause, where the soldier allowed insufficient time for the captives to pass on the information, he again lifted the list and commenced from the beginning. Repeating the first six names once again he continued. Surname first followed by the initial.

'Fibak, P. Stolwitz, S. Zenyatin, W. Pulsitch, K. Wersierski, P. Latchka, W. Bryevski, J. Bryevski, P....'

Five minutes after laying perfectly still and quiet in the middle of the track, the sound of the train having long disappeared, Jan moved his hand up slowly toward the garment, pulled it back down over his body and revealed his face. His eyes blinked open and closed several times before finally adjusting themselves to the strong sunlight which he had not seen in such strength for several days. His opened pupils now flicked upward toward the blue sky and he smelt the fresh summer air coast through his lungs. The freshness was exhilarating and the vivid colours inspiring.

Suddenly, the sun was blotted out by a figure which cast a shadow over his face. The abrupt change of sunlight made Jan suspect the worse. His lack of fear minutes earlier now disappeared. His face was shaded and he froze and blinked his eyes tightly shut awaiting an impact from the expected body that blocked the light to him from the sun.

'Had the Russians known he had escaped so soon? Had they come back to reclaim him?' Questions raced through his mind. The blow he anticipated never came. His perspiration attacked his body once again, this time it was as a result of fear and not simply the warmth of the day. 'What are they doing?' he wondered. 'Are they waiting for me to open my eyes again? Where is the punch? The kick? Where is it?' He asked himself brusquely. His mouth dried in anticipation. It was abrasive like the desert sand. His stomach knotted. He listened intently and heard nothing except the original sounds. The whistling of the birds, the gentle bluster of the summer breeze and nothing else. He waited another minute and opened his eyes. The sun had emblazoned itself on his face once more, and then, suddenly, it was again cut off in its prime. Again Jan blinked his eyes closed, but before he closed them on this occasion, he caught sight of what he immediately knew to be the object, the figure which had blocked the sunlight from his path. He opened his eyes and out of the corner, to his right, he could see the branches of the tree which had caused him all the concern. Relieved at what he had discovered and not wishing to experience anything like it again, he decided to find out now, whether anything alien was in the vicinity. He turned his head for the first time since he had buried himself in between the rail tracks. First to the right of himself and then to the left and finally behind. He smiled a deep, broad smile, sat himself up, looked around once more and laughed aloud. It was a combined laughter, one where the mind was unsure whether to laugh or cry. All the tension which had coagulated inside him from the very first thoughts of escape to its final conception disappeared. He was unburdened. The strain had discharged itself from him like a volcanic eruption. His laughter turned to tears as the tension evaporated from his body to be replaced by indescribable relief.

He was completely alone in the middle of the track. Behind and in front of him the metal lines of the rails disappeared in either direction. On either side were green fields occasionally inhabited with trees of varying sizes. The tree Jan had been obsessed with was of small size with complete green foliage. The gentle summer breeze had swayed the branches causing its clustered bloom to block out the rays of the sun which had beat down on Jan's face as he lay on his stomach.

Happy, contented and relieved, Jan got up, took off the blanket which had protected him from the griminess of the hole in the wagon from where he had made his escape, pulled off his makeshift but useful gloves and threw them to the floor. As the blanket landed, he noticed the foul mess present on the back of the garment and remembered that it was this excrement which must have come through one of the other openings in the floor of another of the cattle wagons.

Amongst all the happiness that Jan felt he also realised that he should get away from the railway track as soon as possible in the event that another train came along. In some pain he hobbled to the right hand side of the line and climbed over a ramshackle wooden fence into a field. Hiding himself amongst a small clump of trees he firstly checked himself over to see that no other filth had found its way onto his clothes and secondly, confirmed that there was no further damage to his already bruised and battered body. There was none except for the swollen ankle.

Jacob froze, his bottom lip quivered and his mouth dropped, his stomach turned uncontrollably. He felt sick and nauseated. The shock of his and his father's name being called so far away from home was a dreadful surprise. Despite the remaining names being called he heard nothing after that of his father's name. He had listened for the next but was spared the further shock as Kazik's was not called. For that he was grateful. Disinterested in all other names, he was completely unaware that both Anatoly Popov and Stefan Waschenska had also been called further down the list.

Sensibility returned. Thoughts raced through his mind. Questions burst into his now active brain. 'Why had they called them now? What did they want from him and his father? Why the separation from the family?' He considered how organised the Russians must have been to pull people out of trains heading for Siberia at this late a stage. 'There are clever people in the Soviet Union after all,' he concluded.

When he recovered from the shock, he looked across at his father who was already holding Jacob's mother in his arms. The sisters began to weep as did Kazik. Jacob arose fighting back the tears. 'I must be strong for the rest of the family,' he said to himself determinedly. Emotion was colossal inside him. There was so much to say and no time to say it. Pavel arose after he had kissed each member of the family and returning to Eva he whispered, 'Take care of them. We will meet again soon, that I promise. We'll be together again,' he reiterated positively after a short pause.

Immediately Eva reminisced. Pavel had never broken a promise to her. She had complete faith in him and was confident in her anticipation that he would not break this one.

Jacob followed his father in embracing each member of the family. Kazik arose and stood by both men he admired.

Jacob turned to Kazik and gave him the slip of paper he had been given by Jan before his escape.

'You know what Jan said. If there is anything you need write to him at this address. It is worth trying.' Jacob pushed the dirty scrap of paper, the address of which was barely legible, into Kazik's pocket.

Kazik nodded and with tears in his eyes he gripped his elder brother tightly. Jacob reciprocated, though as much as he wanted too, without the tears.

Father and son made their way to the exit of the cattle truck followed by Anatoly and Stefan.

Eva, thinking and acting quickly handed her husband and her son a share of what useful provisions were left, small items such as tobacco and matches which she had packed before being ejected from her home. She had learned quickly in her short excursion so far into the Soviet Union that its population had a great affinity toward tobacco, especially the men. Whenever the train stopped and if there was a need, she had bartered for extra food with the chattels her family had brought with them. Very often it was tobacco that was sought after by the Russian people. This was probably the only similarity that the population of the two countries had in common, their partiality to tobacco. Pavel and Jacob refused all except the latter knowing that if any commodity would be useful, tobacco would be the one.

Jumping from the train they cast a final glance at the occupants of the cattle wagon whom they had accompanied for the last five days. They were leaving an enlarged family, for most of the occupants were affectionate friends who were captured along with them. Although they had never set eyes on the rest of the inhabitants before the train journey, in the time they had travelled together, different members of the same family had made acquaintance with most of the strangers in the wagon, so that if one member did not know all, then the likelihood was that a brother or sister had befriended the remainder.

Their final glance was a forced and almost tearful smile toward their true family and loved ones. Without further words or gestures the heavy doors of the wagon were closed and they had disappeared from each others view. For how long? No one knew. Eva and her children, momentarily fighting back the tears, now capitulated. As the doors closed, synonymously the blockade which held the tears at bay burst open.

CHAPTER 14

The journey on foot had been a difficult one for Jan. The left ankle he had damaged whilst dropping from the train severely hindered his progress. He had rested for a short while after escaping, taking refuge in the small clump of trees. He questioned whether he should eat before commencing on his expedition to the capital and quickly decided against doing so, concluding that the euphoria surrounding his escape left no room for hunger. He was also looking forward, with mild trepidation, to the next part of his plan.

Jan walked in the green bordered fields separated and protected from the railtrack by hedges of differing heights. The corn was fruiting in readiness for the harvest payable in less than two months. He followed the same route of the railway line that the train from which he had escaped travelled on, making sure he was able to get out of sight should another pass at any moment. As he walked he absorbed the cleanliness of the country air into his lungs and thanked his God for allowing him to breathe such purity once again. Not for the first occasion did he remind himself that so many people take this simple natural existence for granted. 'Never again will it happen to me.' Breathing the air, he also breathed another fouler smell with him. The odour of the cattle wagon which had permeated through the vehicle was still encapsulated on his clothes and he decided to wash them down as best he could, whenever fresh water was available to him.

Twenty minutes into his walk he heard a rumbling in the distance somewhere behind him. Turning and crouching at the same time, behind the hedge he was walking next to, he looked back along the railway track in the direction from which he had been advancing. The noise was getting louder and louder. He was sure he knew what caused the sound, though he still wanted to positively identify the dreadful vision.

Minutes later the large, black, iron monster drew down toward where Jan was hiding, heading straight for him almost as if the metal demon knew where to look to seek its prey, and he was the victim. The off white coloured steam emitted into the air from the black funnel formed its own range of stained white clouds blotting out the warm blue sky directly above itself. Jan's stomach turned over as the iron horse pulled in its wake a multitude of carriages constructed of wood and iron similar to the one he had escaped from. He watched intently as the wagons passed. As he assumed on immediately seeing the type, they too were full of human beings. Arms were hanging out of the barred openings at the top of the structures. Behind the arms were the white, ghostlike features of people's faces. Eyes ready to pop out with the slightest touch. Bones protruding, severely in some cases, through the stretched skin of the victims. Jan was so close, he felt he could reach out and touch the pale extensions of the occupants. His emotion swelled inside him and he wept freely and outwardly as the train to hell passed in front of his eyes. He cried continuously as the carriages filed by. As each wagon passed he could hear the cries and occasionally screams from those inside. To him it seemed that each one was directed at him. He lost count of the number of carriages after ten as the train sped past in search of its destination.

Jan watched as the train pulled out of his view, the tears still flowed from his now bloodshot eyes. He lay back on the grass border, looked toward the heavens and mumbled a prayer for the innocent occupants of such hovels. Evidence of the train, although out of sight, still hung in the sky as the unnatural white clouds, which had produced portent excrescences, slowly disintegrated allowing the blue heavens its rightful existence.

To be in such a dungeon was soul destroying Jan knew. Witnessing such a vehicle whilst free was almost as awesome he concluded. After recovering from the experience of what he had just seen, and wiping his face down, Jan continued, nervous and hesitant at first then gradually becoming more positive. His confidence, temporarily crushed, slowly returned as he trekked onward toward the city which, for him, held endless hope.

No matter how hard he tried he could not forget the passing of the train. His memory returned to his experience on board and the death of the old man and lady. 'How many more had died in the short time he had escaped,' he wondered. 'How many more would die before they reached their journeys end.' His terrifying thoughts were disturbed by another problem, the pain throbbing in his ankle. He pondered as to how long he could progress and decided to rest his ankle every hour although he wanted to press on and arrive at his destination as soon as possible. Ignoring the pain, he took of his coat and jacket, wrapped them around his waist and to the best of his capabilities continued walking. He turned his attention to the warm and beautiful morning for which he was truly grateful to be free to enjoy.

Jan always scrutinised well ahead as he walked and kept watch of all that was going on around and about him. When he noticed people in the fields ahead of him, he would change his course and revert to walking on the other side of the hedge on or near the railway track. Several labourers working in the fields would wave toward him as they caught sight of him walking by. Not immediately sure as to what he should do, he eventually responded by returning the acknowledgement as calmly and naturally as he could. The labourers would return to their work happy with Jan's response. When he had passed the fields which were occupied with men and in some instances women, he would revert back to the fields where he was more confident of being able to quickly hide himself should anymore trains come along.

In his second hour of travelling on foot, two more trains with human cargo passed by. He cried on both occasions unable to stop the flow of tears. To shake himself out of the horror of what had passed, he would quickly continue on his passage.

The morning moved on quickly as did the afternoon. Whilst passing a field during the afternoon, Jan came across a spade lying against the hedge. Looking around to see if anybody was about and satisfied that nobody was, he took the tool in his left hand and walked on as quickly as he possibly could. He felt guilty about what he had done and continually peered behind for several, nervous kilometres afterwards, in case anybody was following him. The spade would come in useful he thought as he proceeded to use it as a crutch to support his ankle.

The evening developed and the warmth of the day abated. Jan's progress on foot slowed to a snail's pace. His ten minute rest every hour had become ten minutes every half hour by the mid afternoon. He ate nothing while he rested as the excitement inside him was still strong. He found his stream of running water and washed his clothes to the best of his ability. 'The sun will dry them as I walk,' he told himself, satisfied that he had washed the odour away. Several more trains passed by which he could not bring himself to look toward. Hearing them approach he hoped that they were not the death trains he knew of, but as the transport neared and passed, the unmistakable cries of human voices which emanated from the wooden enclosures, and which echoed in Jan's direction, continued to refurbish bitter memories he had of travelling on such a convoy. Endeavouring to blot out the nightmarish cries which were projected from the carriages, he held his hands tightly against his ears and cast his memory back to the happiest thoughts he could find of his short but eventful life.

The evening was slowly disappearing and the twilight zone had begun. Jan had been walking a long time and although his injury had severely limited his progress, he felt that by now he should not be very far from the outskirts of the city. He decided to enquire from the next person he made contact with, how much further he had to travel. Jan had not walked too far before viewing, two fields ahead of him, four men tending to the crops. Approaching the field from the side of the railway line he had quickly switched to walking by, his stomach once again began to circle in nervous expectation. The nearer he approached the men the more apprehensive he became. For the first time since escaping from the train he realised that he was truly frightened. Questions nurtured in his mind, a sign of his anxiety and self-doubt. Would his Russian be sufficient to understand these people? Would they understand him? Would they suspect where he had come from? What if they found out who he was? 'Calm yourself Jan, your caught before you have given yourself a chance,' he reassured himself. Jan breathed deeply several times. He was now at the gate entrance to the field and one of the men was slowly approaching toward him. Jan's heart beat to a crescendo. 'Calm yourself Jan. Calm yourself.' He begged and beseeched his mind and body into some form of self control.

As the man came toward him Jan spoke, staying as composed as his nerves would allow him. 'Good evening, Dobroyeh vetcher,' he said in perfect Russian.

The stranger said nothing but simply looked directly at Jan.

Having settled his nervous imbalance, the silence of the stranger acted like a catalyst and Jan's uneasy metabolism responded once more. 'He hasn't replied. Does he understand me?' he asked himself, at the same time noticing a second man approaching.

'Good evening, Dobroyeh vetcher,' Jan repeated the greeting at the first man. Still silence from him.

Jan stiffened. 'Perhaps he's deaf,' and immediately dropped the thought and seriously contemplated moving on. Then, as he was about go, in a language he could understand came a greeting from the approaching second person who was in earshot of both Jan and the first man.

'Good evening, Dobroyeh vetcher,' was the greeting from the second man.

Jan replied with great relief, blurting out in not his best Russian the same greeting that he had already offered to the first stranger.

The second man came nearer and he spoke in a foreign tongue to his colleague. Jan had heard the language before but could not remember where. The first man returned to the field to continue his work.

The second stranger, older and bigger than his fellow worker, now took up the uncommitted conversation that his colleague had with Jan. He noticed the spade in Jan's hand and the name which had been engraved untidily into the shaft of the tool.

'Ah, you must be one of the new workers on Shepko's holding?' he instantly announced drawing the wrong conclusions.

Jan had seen him looking at the spade and picked the implement up to look at it himself. He too had noticed the name on the shaft but had not given it a second thought. After a brief pause Jan pounced on the stranger's conclusions and answered simply, 'Yes, I am.'

'Is he good to work for? I've been told he is a slave master.' The man laughed as he answered his own question.

Jan laughed too, deciding not to answer but simply nodded his head haphazardly up and down and from side to side.

'You are not answering I do not blame you, trust nobody,' the man said in a deep rough voice, and laughed aloud once again. Jan followed suit, now feeling strangely at ease.

Whilst the two were united in laughter, Jan decided to quickly ask the question.

'This is the way to Moscow?' Jan emphasised pointing in the direction with his index finger.

'Yes, yes, Da, Da,' replied the man. 'Didn't Shepko give you instructions?'

'Yes,' replied Jan, 'though I seem to have been walking forever.'

'You will not have long to go, three maybe four kilometres.'

'Do I follow the track?' Jan asked.

No sooner had he asked the question than a familiar noise could be heard approaching in the distance.

Jan, who had surprisingly relaxed quickly whilst in the company of the stranger, mainly due to the fellow making him laugh, now became edgy as soon as he heard the advancing sound.

'Follow the track for two kilometres, and then take the path which leads off from the left side,' replied the man.

Getting closer and closer the sound it made became louder. Jan knew what to expect. The trains affected him badly. He tried to block his thoughts that were mustering in his mind. 'Concentrate on what he is saying or you will get lost. Concentrate.' He forced himself.

'Continue along the path until you come to the factories. That is the start of the city from our side of the country.'

The words were growing faint to Jan's ears. The train was upon them. He rested on the spade, his face turning a lighter colour as the train encroached on him. The usual sounds could be heard emerging from the carriages that passed behind.

The man was still speaking, his lips moving continuously. Jan thought he was speaking. Yes, he was, or was it the voices behind? He could not distinguish what was coming from where. He could hear Russian and he could hear Polish. What language were the cries of help spoken in? What language were the directions given in? Everything could be heard. Nothing was understood. He was confused and he felt light-headed.

In unison with the height of the noise, Jan fell backward to the ground. The Russian stranger bent over him. Jan heard the entombed Polish voices disappear out of earshot followed by the distant, decreasing drone of the train. As he stared into the sky, again the only evidence, as on previous occasions, of the train having passed was the disappearing cloud formation, this time allowing a very faint, pale moon to reappear.

'Are you all right?' asked the man.

Jan's senses returned quickly. He sat upright.

'Yes, yes, thank you. My ankle,' Jan continued, rubbing his painful limb at the same time, 'I damaged it in the fields today.'

'You should be resting it tonight,' stated the stranger. 'What are you doing out?'

Thinking quicker than ever before, Jan replied, 'I'm going into the city to find a woman for the night.'

The stranger's serious face turned to a mischievous grin. Jan was pleased to see the smile for it immediately relaxed his hardened inward emotion making him feel comfortable once again.

'All that pain and you are walking to find a woman.' He laughed loudly as before. 'You must be desperate,' replied the man.

Jan did not reply, but again simply laughed aloud like the stranger, at the same time raising himself with the help of the man.

'I must be going for Shepko has told me to be back early ready and fit for work in the morning.' Jan turned and retraced his steps to the railway track.

'What did you say again, follow the track for three kilometres...' Jan repeated what he had remembered of the instructions to ensure he had heard correctly.

The stranger, interrupted him, corrected what Jan had said and at the end laughingly shouted to him, 'Good hunting, good hunting. Dobroyeh Okhota, Dobroyeh Okhota.'

Jan turned back, waved once more to the man and hurried as ably as he could on his way.

The smoke filled room enhanced the haziness of the already dim lights in the club and together with the obscure shadows projected in the area, mirrored that of a dark cold night on a freezing Moscow street during mid winter. Inside though, despite the visual affect, the building was warm and cosy with an atmosphere of excitement which spread through the single, large rectangular room.

Bedecked with a stage against one wall covering over half the length, a drinking bar situated opposite with nests of tables and chairs interspersed between and stretching toward the two remaining supportive structures, the building, inwardly, appeared vice like. Around the corners and against those walls unoccupied by the stage and the bar, alcove seating in soft red colours were available where the salacious male clientele accompanied by even lower salacious women resided. Officially prostitutes were not allowed in the club. Though for a fat fee from the accompanying male members, and depending on the disposition of the owner on the night, one or two were allowed to cross the threshold. The stage area ate into the wall to a depth of almost five metres with access to the dressings rooms below gained from both wings. The curtain covering the area, and hanging flush with the wall, was a dark devilish red which only served to enhance the seediness of the club, though most of the clientele were respectable. The atmosphere increased to a hung silence as the customers heard, from behind the curtain, the deep, clear voice of the master speaker introduce the act they had all come to see.

Her outfit was not revolutionary. Though too many visitors of the club, whose travels had been limited and who returned time and again, it appeared so.

The manager of the establishment had copied the idea for this show, as he had often done so before, from the nightspots of the bars and clubs of other western European cities that he had travelled to and visited. Enlarging on those ideas he then used them, usually with some variation, to retain successfully the attraction of the large clientele in his own club which had steadily increased over the years. This was not the first occasion on which he had introduced the Cabaret idea within his own nightspot. After witnessing the magnificent Sally Bowles performing the act during the early years of the Nazi era, he immediately returned to Moscow and copied the performance with less than satisfactory results. His choice of girls then did not have the charisma required. Then several months ago, after pondering on how to replace the current show with something new, the theme of the Bowles' act returned to him. Sally Bowles was excellent he remembered, though to him, the woman performing the act now was equal to her, if not better. Since casting her in the role almost six months earlier, usually an act was changed every three months sometimes sooner, he knew she would be a greater success than in any other portrayals he had put her in.

He waited now as on many previous occasions for the favourable reaction from the audience.

The lights dimmed even further, impossible some members of the audience thought, and seconds after the music struck up, a long, sturdy limb appeared from behind the curtains enhanced by a single bright beam emanated from a lonely searchlight. A mixture of awe and delight was uttered by the onlookers as they perceived the movement of the leg. Covered as it was in a sheer black material almost to the top of the thigh and then to be suddenly severed in perfect roundness revealing her bare skin, only seemed to heighten their impression. A larger approving wail from the audience, followed by an immediate ovation, accompanied the singer come dancer onto the stage as she appeared flawless and intact from behind the curtain. Wriggling and writhing in measured movements and in perfect tempo with her cooing and laudacious singing voice, the audience, mostly men, were spellbound by her performance.

Wandeczka Ludmilla Tcharakova was not a strikingly beautiful woman although there were aspects about her which made men glance in her direction a second time. She was attractive with a pretty face and a body to match. The fact that she was half Polish explained her excessive height for a Russian woman. Her legs were of longer than normal length, neither slim nor big and it was this facet of her body that her husband of two years had found extremely attractive about her at first. After seeing her sing and dance at one of the most popular, yet perhaps, in many peoples' eyes, seedier nightspots of Moscow, he had been mystified by her.

Overcoming the obscurity he had wrapped her in, through his own doing, he decided to breakdown the barriers and started forming a relationship with her. Wining and dining her on the opulence which was afforded to members of the NKVD, the Russian secret police, of which he was a member, he had quickly fallen under her spell and six months later had asked her to marry him. She had grown fond of him, and although it was not true love, she felt it was the closest she would come to finding her perfect match. After all she was not getting any younger. She was then twenty seven years of age and did not want to grow old by herself.

Before agreeing to wed Andrei, she stipulated that she would not give up her career. Fortunately, and unlike most Officers of the NKVD, Andrei did not insist that his wife give up her job. He knew that if there was a choice between him and her job, there was a strong possibility that he would lose. He also knew she had grown to enjoy the affluence which had resulted from her involvement in the singing and dancing business and which was now a part of her life.

For her part she realised that an appealing factor of the job was the number of men whom she seemed to have power over simply by being what she was, performing a task which she enjoyed. The thrill of them looking at her supplied an added attraction to her feminine ways. Although she knew she had some sort of power over men she was not a whore. Yes she had taken two or three lovers outside her marriage, never the same person a second time and always men who were staying in Moscow overnight on business and not actually residing in the city. This sideline was purely to stem the loneliness whilst her husband was away completing his duties as an NKVD Officer which was often, especially since the pact with Germany where both countries had invaded Poland. Now, nearly two and a half years into her matrimony, and despite what to her were small infidelities, she enjoyed her marriage.

Wandeczka was surprised how much she had changed since her parents had died. Although religion was not allowed in Russia, her mother, who was of good Polish stock, continued to practise Catholicism in their apartment after herself and her new husband had moved back to Moscow from Poland. When Wandeczka was born she painstakingly taught her daughter about the Catholic religion and the Polish traditions and ways of life. Wandeczka had kept up her religion after her mother had died. Within nine months of her father passing away she had quickly turned to what her mother would have called 'the wickedness of the singing and dancing world which went on in such bars and clubs throughout Moscow.'

It had not taken her long to fall to such temptation, though to her it was not an attraction, not at first. Loneliness with her parents deceased, time on her hands and the extra money were the reasons she pursued a job and nothing else. Her mother had died nearly six years ago, her father six months later of a broken heart. When they were alive her life was filled with chores and duties to perform for her parents, as well as leisure time to continue with her dancing lessons. After the deaths of her parents, a void had opened up in her life giving her more than enough spare time to perform her normal daily duties. In the six months after the death of her father she was persuaded by a friend at the dance lessons she attended, to seriously consider the possibility of dancing for money. Before turning the offer down out of hand she had decided to investigate first. After all her friend had been performing for several months now and she enjoyed every minute of the job.

After much deliberation, and another three months had gone by, Wandeczka decided to pursue the matter and went along with a friend one night. The owner took one look at her and signed her up on the spot. Events snowballed and within six months she had become one of the top performers at the club which included a singing spot.

Each night, prior to her performance, her adrenalin slowly and steadily cultivated itself inside, until seconds before the curtain came up it coursed through her veins almost catapulting her onto the stage. It became like a drug to her and she looked forward immensely to her polished performances. Her reputation grew along with that of the club and both profited in unison. There were nights though when she felt that something was missing from her life, and tonight was one of those nights. She felt lonelier than she had been for many months. This had been the longest period that she had been separated from Andrei, her husband, who had been on duty and away for six weeks. Thankfully he would be home in four weeks time.

It had been over a year since she had been to bed with another man beside her husband. Tonight she would accept one of the many invitations proffered nightly by the male attendants at the club and had singled out a tall, distinguished looking gentleman of between the age of forty five and fifty years. She had noticed him at the bar several months ago and he had requested her attendance at his table then. She remembered her attraction toward him on that occasion even though they did not make contact as she had declined the offer. Tonight he had again propositioned her and this time she had accepted. She would make it plain to him that tonight's offer was simply a one off and he should not, under any circumstances, ever acknowledge her again, not even if the remotest possibility ever occurred that they might pass one another in the street.

She finished her second act to the same delirious approval from the crowd that had followed her first rendition and selfishly went in search of her chosen company and enjoyment.

CHAPTER 15

Walking along the platform away from their closed and barred carriage which they had earlier occupied, Pavel, Jacob, Anatoly and Stefan joined several other men who had also been taken from the other carriages which made up the long procession of wooden tombs from the train to Siberia. The wagons toward the end of the convoy which they were passing held the same ritual which they themselves had been through earlier. After a reading from a list of names any number of men then being taken from the carriage and separated from their families. The same bewildered look at being parted such a long way from their homeland had appeared on their faces also. Some carriages, miraculously, had no occupants taken.

No matter what age the men were in the trucks they still feared their names being called. Words could not describe the relief on their faces when the soldier finally completed his reading and an individual's name had not been called.

The four men joined the other detainees who had already been taken off the train and who were assembled at the exit to the station. One or two men were crying. To identify those that cried as men was incorrect. They were still boys easily young enough to continue their schooling. One was accompanied by a male family member who tried to console him. The other was completely alone and controlled himself when he saw that the soldiers were mocking him.

Jacob viewed the group of captives awaiting the commencement of another march. His gaze descended upon Stefan Waschenska whose face was fraught with concern and worry. Pavel could also see the emergence of distress clearly encroaching on Stefan's countenance. Along with words of comfort and determination he thrust an arm around his friend's shoulder and strove to temper the anxiety that surged inside the man.

The group waited another thirty minutes before marching. They watched the train they had disembarked from pull out of the station. Most men, with lumps in their throats, said a short prayer for the loved ones who they had been forcibly taken from.

Jacob pondered at length on whether he would ever see his family again and thought now that he would never find the whereabouts of Sophie and know for sure whether or not she had joined the great peregrination of Polish citizens to a land so vast, that many people had not even read about leave alone visited. He had tried to find out where she was as he had promised himself. Calling to the trains which had passed by in the same direction he had enquired of other occupants as to the whereabouts of Sophie Sagajlo. Though his enquiries had been in vain, he, as always, had consoled himself in the knowledge that no news was good news.

There were about fifty men in the group which Pavel and Jacob now occupied and not long after their march had commenced the party swelled to several hundred as they joined up with an army of men who were primarily of Polish and Lithuanian nationality. Approximately half were professional people accompanied by male relations, with the remainder having military connections, not of a high rank, but considered a danger to the Soviet Union nevertheless. They marched all that day stopping only twice. Many of the elderly men collapsed as a result of the exhaustive ordeal. Depending on which Russian soldier was nearby, some were shot where they fell, others were left, after inspection by the soldiers, to die in their own time. Some were picked up by complete strangers and carried along. Although a great burden to the helpers, they continued to persist with their encumbrance and many survived thanks to the complete unselfishness of those who risked their own lives. Those who were fortunate to be accompanied by members of the family were taken care of and again usually survived the march thanks to their relatives.

The first night they slept in an open field which had lain fallow all summer. Although no food was supplied they fell asleep quickly through sheer exhaustion and were awoken early the next morning by shouts of abuse from the soldiers. After feeding on the usual diet of herrings and bread, which had been delivered by lorry, they again continued on their march.

During the latter part of the morning people especially the elderly and weak fell by the wayside. Again the families intervened. On this ocassion they were not always successful. Younger relatives, who would not leave their elderly fathers or uncles and even friends lying close to death on the roads, were shot along with their relations. Those who felt they could not continue and would not survive the trek jumped of bridges to certain death as and when the columns of marchers crossed them.

Amongst those who jumped was Stefan. Before any of his three associates could restrain him and console him he made his move with surprising swiftness. The bridge was no more than ten feet away. Breaking ranks with ease, he tossed himself off the low wall which marked the edge of the overpass and the beginning of the drop and fell, he thought, to certain and instant death.

Unfortunately, it was not to be that quick and easy. The drop was only six or seven metres and on impacting with the ground both his legs immediately broke. Feeling the excruciating pain, he endeavoured to raise himself and somehow flee. As his legs took the full weight of his body, the pain easily conquered him and he fell over and backward taking in the full view of the two soldiers that peered over the bridge down toward him. He noticed the sun briefly reflecting off the bolt of the first soldier's rifle as he prepared the weapon. Every move they made appeared in slow motion. He watched, in agony and frustration, as the soldiers aimed their weapons and squeezed the triggers of their Mosin-Nagant bolt action rifles. Even the glint in their eyes was detectable to him before their final touch established his inevitable and now certain death. The last sounds he heard was two individual bursts of rifle fire from the guns which pointed at him. The last feelings he experienced was the impact of the bullets arriving, microseconds between one another, exploding and tearing with severe pain into two separate areas of his body. He passed into unconsciousness before death finally arrived. To those around the silence was instantaneous immediately the bullets were fired, signalling also the discharge of a life.

Others, who jumped, occasionally left younger members of the family alone. To those remaining, although it did not occur to them at the time, it provided a better chance of survival, for now they only had themselves to look after.

From afar the partly clothed bodies and the numbers which made up the columns resembled those of centurions in Roman days. There the similarity ended. Where the past legions had worn brightly coloured fine woven material, the current marchers, although perhaps commencing their journey with clothes made from the finest fabrics, had since turned to rags and had all but finally worn and withered from the very bodies they had earlier protected. Replacement material was always sought. It could only be found and was taken, whenever possible, from the dead bodies of their colleagues who had died on the journey so far.

The men marched in files of four abreast, shabbily dressed in dark grey uniforms. They appeared as uniforms not because the Russian regime had provided outfits but because each individual's attire had taken on the similar dank, grey colour as a result of the hardships encountered whilst travelling on their long journey. The darkness of the clothes together with the gaunt, ghostlike appearance of the men's' faces reminded the ordinary people they passed, of an army of undead cadavers returning after an arduous journey undertaken on behalf of and for the devil himself.

After travelling through the countryside on the first day, the route they had taken on the second was mainly through the back streets on the eastern side of Moscow. The strange yet sad eyes of the poor people of the city who looked on at these even poorer and sadder multitudes of men struck out a note of pity and compassion, confirmed by the small amounts, though of great significance to those who received them, of food which was thrown into the cavalcades of men marching to a certain but unknown terror. In addition to food, articles of clothing was occasionally given and quickly utilised by the receiver.

Finally, after nearly a day of further marching, the monstrous structure that was to be their shelter, for how long nobody knew, stared down at them from a great height. The darkened walls of the outer perimeter of the prison verified to the marchers that although they were not the devils' disciples, the building they had now been brought to was surely the devil's home. The huge brown wooden doors swung open before the columns of men were allowed to slow their rhythmical march even by a tempo. As the doors opened their jaws to greet and to hold the intake of men, they were accompanied by a high pitched screeching whine, corroborating the fact that very little maintenance had been performed on the hinges that the doors sat and swung open and closed upon.

The men progressed through into the inner courtyard and before Pavel and Jacob passed into their private hell, they both looked up one more time to the beautiful blue sky. As if a sign from their known god were throwing down a warning to them of what they were about to enter, the blue sky was suddenly blotted out by a cloud formation of extraordinary shape which appeared to manifest from the colossal building itself. Before entering they were greeted from the rapidly developing clouds to a downpour of such magnitude that it caused a mini flood as it fell, soaking the columns of marchers as it finally found its way to the ground.

Assembling in the vast courtyard, the rain continued to pour down and visibility diminished to a short distance. Men at the rear only stopped because those in front had halted assuming, rightly so, that they had been ordered to do so. The bellowing of orders which came forth from the Russian soldiers were drowned and inaudible to those prisoners in the rear half of the columns by the sound of the abnormal deluge of rain. Again the men did as those in front had done, copying every movement by turning right, arms down by their sides and feet apart. Minutes later they were led off in sections of four abreast and three deep.

All the time Jacob hoped that he and his father would not be parted. In this respect fortune had seen favour with them. As the groups were now called away, Jacob again was not to be disappointed. Right alongside him was his father Pavel.

The directions given to Jan by the stranger proved to be accurate on every account and he found the outskirts of the city with relative ease after he had taken the dirt track road which led away from the railway line. He passed the area housing the factories and as he did so he contemplated ridding himself of the spade he had used as a crutch fearful that it would arouse suspicion if he continued to use it. He decided against losing the implement and suggested to himself that it would be useful as a weapon in the event that he should run into trouble.

The night had long descended as he soon found himself in the sprinkling of back streets still on the outskirts of the city, unsure as to which direction he was heading, though hopeful that he was on the right course. The nebulous night was dark and breezy and the clouds covered the sky preventing the stars' nebula and a diminishing moon from casting their luminous light over the path that Jan walked. He was grateful however, for the arrival over the last two nights, of the warm weather. He knew now that the summer had arrived.

The buildings he passed were tenebrous in nature, resembling that of a ghost town without the smashed windows and broken doors. An occasional shout or verbal noise echoing from an opened window verified to him that the area he was walking through was definitely inhabited.

Hobbling along through the denser built up areas he reminded himself that he should now be more careful than at any other time since escaping. He also reminded himself that sooner or later he would have to ask someone the directions of where he wanted to go. Moscow and the place where Wandeczka lived were a distant memory to him and he would have to locate the district in which she lived.

The further he walked, in what he thought was the direction toward the centre of the city, and despite the late hour, the more populated it became. He tried to look inconspicuous, though felt quite the opposite, surmising that everybody who passed him was looking at him. Continuing with his trek he became both nervous and hungry and hoped that he could find his haven quickly and safely. 'What if she were no longer there?' his mind asked. Not wishing to think of the consequences and problems it could cause for him, he ignored what his brain was enquiring.

Thirty minutes later and after passing the same coloured building twice he decided to ask the next person directions to the address he was seeking. Walking with increasing pain he rounded a corner and not ten metres ahead came across a group of four men approaching toward him walking in an ungainly manner. They were talking loudly amongst themselves, at times almost shouting at one another. This was followed by an occasional louder burst of laughter followed by a song, only for them to relapse several seconds later back into conversation. Jan approached with caution and drew near to them noticing that they were elderly in age and extremely unkempt. The stench of liquor around and about them verified to Jan what his initial thoughts had been on first seeing them at a distance. They were drunken vagrants. As he passed the four men, one of the parties had dropped behind the other three. Jan hastily decided to ask the last of the vagabonds the directions he was now urgently seeking.

Worse from the effects of drink which was usual for the man at this time of the night, he turned; startled that he had not noticed the questioner approaching him. He looked up at where the voice had come from. In order to get a better look at the young face he could vaguely distinguish, he peered through screwed up small eyes to counteract the diminished visibility the effects of the drink had bestowed upon him.

Jan looked down on the man. He noticed that his face was heavily wrinkled and lined, evidence he thought of his many years dedicated to abusive drinking. The stranger now opened his mouth revealing large gaps where his teeth had once taken residence. He smiled upward toward Jan and speaking in barely audible words uttered meaningless vocabulary which lost their identity on the stench of alcohol which accompanied them through the vagrant's mouth. Jan turned his face sideward too late to escape the foul breath. He repeated the question talking louder to the man. The raising of his voice now focussed the attention of the other three vagabonds on himself. They stopped, turned and backtracked on themselves toward where Jan and their accomplice were standing. Jan watched them approach and noticed that one out of the three men walked with more control over his footsteps compared to his friends. Whilst they approached, the steadiest of the three enquired as to what Jan was asking.

Jan repeated his question now a little nervous that there were four men around him. Yes they were drunk but they could quite easily cause trouble. He remembered Jacob's words of warning given to him whilst on the cattle truck together. He tightened his grip around the spade he held and prepared himself for all eventualities.

'What have you got to give us in return for the information?' asked the steadier of the four vagrants now holding out a four fingered left hand expecting his reward before the information had been divulged.

Jan was taken aback. He had nothing only a little food and no money whatsoever. He remembered his writing implement and offered that. He did not want to offer his food which he intended to eat later.

They declined the barter.

'What can we do with that? We cannot write.' the soberest of the four stated, laughing at the same time. This triggered his trio of drinking partners who followed suit.

Jan remembered that he was holding the spade and offered that in acceptance for the information.

'Agree,' the same man replied and held out his hand to take the tool from Jan.

Jan, shocked at the suddenness in which the deal had been made, was about to hand it over, and then refrained from doing so.

'Information first,' Jan ordered.

'What if we give you wrong directions?'

Jan looked around, as he could not find a street sign he took note of the area and the distinctive red coloured building which they were standing opposite and replied.

'I will find this place again quite easily if I have to. Should you choose to give me the incorrect information I shall return tomorrow night in search of the four of you.'

Jan kept calm and spoke eloquently toward what to him appeared to be the ringleader, at the same time making sure none of the other three were out of his view. He continued.

'You will not find me so amicable when I eventually meet with you again, should you decide to supply me with the wrong directions. Members of the NKVD do not like having their time wasted by lazy vagabonds.'

After stating the last sentence Jan swallowed heavily and wondered what the reaction of the foreigner would now be.

It was instant.

The stranger who spoke for his party blurted out the directions willingly.

Jan was obliged and held back the tool he had originally offered.

'How far is the street from here?'

'No more than one kilometre,' was the frightened reply.

Jan realised that not only did the mention of the NKVD frighten the Polish people, it frightened the Russians too. He felt sure that if he had asked the man to show him exactly where he wanted to go he would have done so.

Jan bade farewell and the four men turned and left. He watched them go and then called back the one who he had conversed with.

The stranger approached more frightened than before. When he was no more than an arms length from Jan, the tool was offered to him. At first he would not take it.

'It is yours,' ordered Jan and he placed it in the man's hand.

'Now go.'

The man turned and hurriedly walked back to his colleagues turning occasionally to see that Jan was not following.

Jan waited until the party of reprobates had turned the corner and disappeared out of view and then proceeded to follow the instructions that had been given to him. He recalled his journey on foot during that day and how it had been a success so far with very little disruption, except the passing trains, and no trouble from anyone. He asked himself as to how long his luck would last? Reminding himself of the conversation he had moments earlier undertaken with the soberest of the four destitutes, he managed a mischievous smile for being so bold and pretending to be a member of the secret police, the only regime he, himself, was running and hiding from. If the four men had not been so badly dressed and so drunk he would not have pursued such an outrageous avenue of conversation. Still, the words had been spoken and they had the results he hoped for. Jan broke out into a cold shiver as he further realised what he had got away with. He wondered was it the meek, mild Jan that he knew himself to be or some inner being which was beginning to develop inside him? He left the question unanswered because he did not have an answer. He put his thoughts behind him and now looked for the sign of the first street he sought on his route to what he hoped would be his final destination.

Fewer people passed him and since his encounter with the four men he concerned himself no more whether anyone was looking toward him. He realised that he had grown in confidence.

Despite trying to keep the event in its proper perspective, the memory of what he had said to the vagrants continued to dwell in his mind and as a result of this he progressed down one street before realising he had taken the wrong turning. He retraced his steps concentrating his mind on his immediate objective. He passed premises from which music was emanating and which he could not remember passing before even though that was the route he had taken. The music confirmed to him that the building was a nightclub. A dim maroon light shone outside. As the light, for some strange reason, held him captive, he did not see the elderly gentleman and his younger female companion coming out of the entrance. Catching sight of them out of the corner of his eye at the very last moment, Jan collided heavily with the male member of the party of two.

Almost falling over, the man steadied himself and regained his poise quickly. The woman who was unhurt stood by and looked at the two men. Jan came off the better in the collision hardly losing his balance and immediately apologised, careful to speak in Russian.

'Sorry! Sapyotv!'

He motioned toward the man and offered, by gesticulating with his hands, to help. The man waved him away bursting into a quiet tirade of verbal objections against Jan. Jan was scared, unsure what to do. Should he run or should he remain hoping that the abuse would eventually subside. Again he apologised and turned to look at the woman.

She stood under the dim light outside the entrance to the club, and as Jan caught sight of her, she was looking at him fully for several seconds before she turned her attention to her gentleman friend. Jan eyed her nervously, and despite his edginess he could not help notice how attractive she was. She immediately reminded him of someone he knew, but in the confusion that was now going on he could not remember who and dropped the thought from his mind.

The woman now brushed past Jan and gripped the arm of the gentleman companion who was still uttering objections. Her actions seemed to comfort the man and as she whispered something to him which Jan could not hear, he ceased verbalising his protests at once. They moved off arm in arm together. Walking away the man continued to correct the crease in his jacket and trousers, as he did so the woman turned to look fully at Jan once more before finally turning back and pursuing idle chatter with her companion.

Jan could not help but notice the rear view of the woman's figure as they walked off and when she turned to look at him again he was shaken out of his gaze. Not waiting on this occasion for them to disappear he continued retracing his steps.

One hour later, exhausted and very hungry, he found the address he was seeking. He pressed the bell to her apartment. No answer. He repeated his action once more again without reply. 'She must be out' he thought and quickly prayed that she had not permanently moved away from the premises. He decided against pressing the bell again, it was late and he feared it would arouse someone unnecessarily. Now that he had reached this far he did not want to fail at the last hurdle.

Descending the steps he wondered where to spend the night and looked around for a suitable area near the apartment block. At the side of the steps to the entrance of the apartments ran another flight of steps down to a basement. Jan walked down these steps. The basement showed no signs of being occupied confirmed by the windows which were coated both on the inside and outside with a film of dust and grime. Relieved that this was the case he sat down and made himself as comfortable as possible. Taking the small package of food which had been given to him by his friends in the cattle wagon before leaving, he opened the package and first ate the salami which was at least five days old. The stench emanating from the piece of meat was strong but his continuous pangs of hunger overcame the odour and he ate ravenously. He then devoured the apple which again was as old as, if not older than the meat but which had kept itself reasonably fresh. With food inside him and successful yet dangerous thoughts strong in his mind of what he had survived during the day, Jan fell into a well earned sleep.

It was late morning when Wandeczka awoke and rolled over in the double sized bed of suite number twenty two in one of the more selective hotels in Moscow. Turning over, she extended her arm in search of the man she had spent the night with and was surprised to find the bed was empty beside her. She sat up and the soft, warm bedclothes slipped down uncovering the nudity of the top half of her body. She looked around the room for a second occupier in addition to herself. The room was silent. She was completely alone. Continuing her search without motioning out of the bed, she finally noticed on the bedside cabinet next to her a lightly coloured envelope. Picking it up, she reminisced about the night before and how, despite making love to another man and enjoying it, she had missed her husband immensely, not only his companionship but also his lovemaking.

Wandeczka opened the envelope and picked out the contents, a single sheet of white paper. The message simply read 'Thank you.' She smiled to herself, grateful of the gesture bestowed upon her by the complete stranger, and remembered again how they had satisfied one another during the night.

She arose from behind the sheets and walked into the bathroom to run the hot water. Whilst bathing she remembered her performance at the club and subsequent events leading up to her time of leaving. She pondered extensively on the encounter with the young stranger outside the entrance to the club and decided that it could not possibly be who she thought it was. After she bathed, she dressed, decided against calling for breakfast, preferring to eat at her own premises, and left the hotel.

Jan woke at five in the morning to a dawn which had already broken, bringing with it an abundance of light. He had slept solidly for three hours which surprised him under the circumstances. He looked up toward the pavement to see whether he had a good view of anyone who passed by and was happy with the results. He was hungry again but fought the battle his stomach waged inside. 'Keep what food provisions you have for later,' he told himself. He tried to relax and fall asleep but was unsuccessful. After much thought about his past life, the happy and unhappy times, he eventually fell into a light slumber. He was awoken by a middle aged couple who were arguing as they came out of the apartment block above him. He wondered what time it was and assumed that the working day had begun due to the increased content of traffic, both people and vehicles that were now busy in the street. Jan remained where he was until the middle aged couple, oblivious of him, moved out of his view.

Deciding to ring the bell of the apartment again to seek the occupant, he arose from where he had been resting and shook his legs into action flexing out the stiffness which had taking hold of his limbs through sitting in one position for such a long period. Walking up the steps he looked in the direction he could see the furthest, which was westward down the street, and concluded that the people were going about their business in a normal manner. He was sure why he performed this observation but unsure whether he would be able to distinguish anyone who may have been suspicious of him anyway. Finally, as a quick check, he peered in the opposite direction before speedily walking up the steps to the apartment block and pressing the required button. 'Please Lord let her be here,' he prayed. There was no reply. He rang again for a longer period the second time without success. He turned and walked down the steps mulling over in his mind what to do. Knowing that nobody had yet answered at the apartment, he concluded that she had not yet returned to her abode, if it was her abode. 'Perhaps she was away on holiday,' he guessed. 'Perhaps she was spending the night with friends. Perhaps it was not her apartment anymore.' Ideas came and went. He took up his earlier residence and elected to sit and wait until at least somebody in the apartment answered his call.

Jan, unsure of time, but assuming it was well past mid morning, once again ascended the stairs to the residence above. Several people had come and gone from the premises throughout his last period of waiting. None of the females he recognised as being that of his cousin. They did not even appear of similar age he thought. His spirits were low as he rang the bell, taking his disappointment out on the contraption which notified the presence of someone calling; he relentlessly pressed the doorbell over and over again each time without an answer. Eventually, the ringing did bring someone out of the building.

An elderly woman opened the door and started to question the young dishevelled person standing in front of her. This was the last thing Jan wanted at this moment in time. He was tired and hungry. He felt nauseous. Her verbal attack took him by surprise. All these provocations compounded even further as his nerves expounded, assaulting him inwardly. He kept quiet refusing to answer any of her questions and at the same time decided against even speaking. The muted attitude he adopted angered her even more. Her facial features screwed up resembling that of a witch and she continued her haranguing and threatened to call the authorities.

'What do you want? Was it you who rang late last night? This is the second time you have called this morning.'

Again amongst her rhetoric, she threatened to contact the authorities.

This frightened Jan even more. His infirm stomach, which he had managed to partly control, erupted once more and he decided to leave quickly.

Turning to go down the steps he stopped at the top of the flight almost in mid movement. The elderly woman from the apartment block continued her ranting for a short while. Then as she watched the two people in front of her staring at one another she halted her philippizing. Jan gazed in astonishment on the young woman who herself was about to ascend the steps of the apartment block, and who was also rooted to the spot after sighting him. He knew where before, in the past, he had seen the same female he had collided with the previous night and who he looked upon now. It was his cousin Wandeczka. His anxiety from the conflict with the elderly woman vanished. All he could think of was that she looked more lovely than the last time he had perceived her all those years ago.

She stood perfectly still not believing her eyes. Eventually she called his name in a surprised and questioning manner.

'Jan?'

He smiled. She smiled.

'So it was you last night?'

Her smile gave so much comfort to him it overwhelmed him and his smile turned to tears. Immediately he thought his journey for now was over and the relief to him was limitless and unbinding. In those few seconds on meeting his cousin, with, it seemed, her approval all the anguish, all the worry he had carried, lifted from his body.

He faltered at the top of the steps.

She ascended hastily and caught around him.

He reciprocated like he had never done so before with anyone, throwing his arms around her, almost violently and with little control. He had never been so grateful to see someone in all his life.

'I didn't know last night that it was you,' he said in a quaking emotional voice. 'You reminded me of someone though I could not place you until now.'

'Come,' she said, 'let us go in.'

Moving past the elderly woman, Wandeczka made an excuse that it was her long lost cousin who had been expected several days ago. On hearing this the woman aided the couple by opening the door for them, apologising at the same time to Jan for her rudeness.

Jan and Wandeczka continued their ascension up the inner stairs to her third floor apartment. She supported him as they climbed. 'What had he been through?' she wondered. 'He looked exhausted and smelt disgusting.'

All Jan could smell was the freshness of her scent which reminded him of odours from the past. Warm comforting odours which had made him feel good then, and made him feel good now, but where before had he smelt them he could not remember, and at the present moment it was unimportant to him. He allowed the reassuring aroma to engulf his thoughts and ease his mind as he basked in their consoling powers. He was oblivious to everything else around.

The door of the apartment swung open with the help of Wandeczka's leg after she had turned the key. Jan remembered crossing the threshold to the flat still pondering on his aromatic thoughts before collapsing in a heap on the floor. Wandeczka tried to break his fall but he was too heavy for her.

Unloading her shoulder bag she dragged him by his arms into the bathroom, undressed him and washed him down. Then she pulled him into the bedroom and struggled for several minutes, pulling and pushing him from different angles, until she finally succeeded in getting him into the bed. She pulled up a chair and made herself comfortable. 'This could take a long time,' she concerned herself.

CHAPTER 16

They had been on the cattle wagon for over two weeks maybe longer. It was difficult to keep track of time as the mornings, afternoons, evenings and nights rolled on, one after the other, barely distinguishable from each other except for the light of the day and the darkness of the night. It did not matter to the people whether it was dark or light, they slept a large amount of the time. Sleep brought a welcome escape from what they were experiencing.

Conditions became worse and carriages were infested with vermin. Bugs and lice were rampant. People, at first, tried to control the filth and clean themselves and the carriages that they travelled in, but this was impossible with none of the basic necessities available to help them. Not even water was in sufficient quantity to wash oneself. The smell in the cattle wagon was inhaled on each intake of air that every occupant breathed. The stench hung over the carriage and permeated into the clothes of the internees. The odour glued itself to the back of the throat, suffused itself in people's lungs and contaminated the skin and the hair with its invisible yet persistent presence. The clothes became more dishevelled and people now appeared completely destitute and impoverished. In the end it became part of their existence and it was simply accepted. What else could they do? As the days on the train progressed people hoped and prayed that the time was not too far in the future when the journey by train would be over.

Despite all the filth and depravity within the cattle trucks, the people firmly believed that one day they would return to their homeland. No matter what conditions no matter what cruelty they had been or were going to be subjected to by any regime, their hope, both individually and collectively, were strong, determined and resilient.

Their home towns and villages were a distant but still a strong reminder to them. The ports of call along the way had been visited and left behind. Moscow, Murom, Arzamus and Kazan had come and gone, and they were now heading into a region of land which few people new anything about. Uppermost in their minds, in addition to the question of when they would return to their homeland, was what would be waiting for them at the end of their passage. Strength was gained from the luxury that the majority of those members of the family who had started the journey together, continued on the journey together, except for those who had died along the way.

The schedule to take on board rations became more and more random as the voyage progressed. They would stop for two consecutive days and then not stop for the next one or two days. Sometimes, and since they had been travelling on Soviet soil, they stopped twice in one day. On those occasions when the train halted, people's expectant hopes of receiving additional food and water would be dashed when it turned out that the train had only halted to take on more fuel or to change the guard.

When travelling on Polish territory the inhabitants of the cattle trucks had been given food free of charge from their own people who were complete strangers to them. After crossing the Polish border into Russia, they now found that they had to make a payment of some form, usually barter, for food or for other goods which they required. Whilst trains waited to be refuelled at various points along the route other than those scheduled stops which were mainly at the large towns to take on rations, Russian peasants would approach the cattle trucks and barter their food with those held captive who wished to exchange for their belongings. There was not a great choice of eatables, but all was welcome. One of the most popular sources of food the Russian peasants exchanged was 'suhary' or toasted bread. This was bread which had been allowed to dry in the sun by the peasants to enable them to keep the food for longer periods so that it could be eaten at a later date. It helped to sustain the internees in the cattle wagon during their journey. What they now had left in the way of provisions was very little if anything at all. Their individual belongings consisted only of what they had been allowed to scramble together in the short time before leaving their homes.

Occasionally, very seldom, a Russian peasant would take pity on the interned people and give food free of exchange. Much gratitude was verbally communicated by those fortunate enough to receive these donations.

When these peasants came and went amongst the carriages they were often asked whether or not they had contact or word of Polish people who had journeyed this way before on other trains. No peasant was able to help with any information. The peasants themselves led simple lives and were in the main preoccupied with their own existence, not wishing to get involved in the whereabouts of strangers from another land. They too, like the Polish people were oppressed, although not to the same degree.

Nearly all members of the cattle wagons inscribed their names on the wooden walls of their portable dwelling. The more the wagon was used the higher to the ceiling the inhabitants had to reach in order to leave their entry. At times they would also insert the names of loved ones who had not been able, for one reason or another, to accompany them on the journey. Even the elderly inscribed their names. It was a task which although did not take long to perform, helped pass the time.

Deaths continued on all the trains which carried forth their cargo. Very few, if any of the carriages reported immortality on the long journeys under extremely foul and filthy conditions which became worse as the days progressed. At each stop dead bodies were unloaded to be dealt with by the Russians. Relatives of the dead occasionally refused to release the bodies at first, but eventually they were persuaded to do otherwise. Occupants at every opportunity requested decent burials for their Polish compatriots. Whether this request was granted was never known. Most people knew that it was extremely unlikely. Despite these horrific conditions the Polish people had great faith in themselves that sooner or later their country would come to its aid. They never believed that the State of Poland would ever be overthrown. It was this belief which sustained the Polish people during all the suffering they were experiencing.

Thoughts of escape were occasionally discussed but where in this land of immense size would they escape to. There were great expanses of land which they had journeyed through with no visible evidence of occupation until they actually arrived at the destinations of the interim railway stations. The only man made observation they cast their eyes on to verify that man had been there at all, was the very rail track which their train was travelling on. On occasions it was possible to view through the barred openings, the two definitive parallel lines of black spaghetti coming to meet them in front, and then disappear in the distance behind. A continuous expanse of beautiful but hard land broken by the only man made object visible for miles.

The Ural Mountains were passed through by hundreds of thousands of people and signalled the arrival of the multitude of deportees in another world, for the infamous mountain range was recognised as the physiographic boundary between Europe and Asia. It spread out of the earth like some gigantic abnormal growth and spread as far as the eye could see to the north and to the south. The beauty and colours which emanated from the colossal monument was pleasing to the eye and one wondered how a landscape of such magnificence could be found in a country which had very few pleasures.

The trains drew ever nearer to the mountain range with its occupants wondering how the colossus could be breached. From a distance the rail track seemed to disappear into the very earth, and the constant mirage tricked the inhabitants into thinking that they were approaching a dead end. As the trains neared, the great mountain opened up allowing its iron visitor with its non paying, compulsory human cargo, the privilege to pass through. Once through the Ural Mountains, the remaining journey to one of the main clearing centres, Sverdlovsk, was but a fraction of the time.

It was at the clearing station at Sverdlovsk that Eva's family, minus Pavel and Jacob had arrived in the middle of June. They were made to disembark immediately the train stopped. After refuelling, like a snake slithering away having fed, the train returned with the long, empty, silent row of carriages being pulled along in its wake, in the direction from where it had come, probably to bring another batch of deportees for indoctrination. The family, still with the majority of their friends, were told that they were to wait until another train would arrive to continue their journey to their ultimate destination.

Disembarking, the clean, fresh summer air which coasted through their infected, polluted lungs breathed new life into the bodies, endeavouring at the same time to cleanse the organ of the filth and grime it had breathed relentlessly for the last twelve days and more. The life it pumped into the body was overwhelming and stirred the captives out of their remorseless, unrelenting existence. The people were grateful that they were able to stretch their legs and touch solid ground once more. Still closely watched over by the soldiers they were not able to stray far from the terminus building.

Again they attempted to rid themselves of the bugs and lice which they had come into contact with whilst on the train. Some were more successful than others at doing this, usually as a result of cutting hair to the scalp. Even this did not always produce the required results as the vermin was also found in the clothing of the people. No antiseptic was available to help rid themselves completely of the nuisance.

Whilst awaiting the arrival of the train to take them onto their final destination, Maria, Kazik's sister, amongst the thousands of people in the station, spotted Sophie and her family sitting in a distant corner of the terminus. She was excited as she pointed out the discovery to her mother. Eva and her two daughters decided to contact them without raising the attention of the guards. Kazik also expressed a wish to talk with Sophie and her family, though it was he who elected to remain behind and watch their belongings whilst the three women ventured toward their goal. If there was time later, then Kazik would meet them afterward.

Although the distance was not far, no more than one hundred yards, there was still great danger. If a train should pull in to the terminus, very little warning was given, and groups of people would be expected to board immediately. In this way many people were parted from their families with no hope of reconciliation. This was not the only method of dividing groups of people. Very often the soldiers would deliberately separate families and force them to board trains which were destined for different areas within the Eastern Soviet Union. If people refused, then they were either taken out of the station and shot or dealt with on the spot.

Sophie, the Doctor and his wife were delighted to see the Bryevski family and all members of both households embraced one another affectionately. An instant tempered joy was radiated through the lives of both groups. Despite what they had been through it gave them new strength to carry on with their journey. Sophie, after introducing Juliana to the Bryevski family, immediately enquired of Maria as to the whereabouts of Jacob. Whilst the two younger women talked between themselves the remaining members of the two families discussed one another's experiences.

Maria explained the course of events which had occurred after Sophie had left the ball that night which now seemed so long ago. As she related the story, memories of the whole day came flooding back to Sophie. She specifically remembered how Jacob had looked at her as she alighted from her father's vehicle, and now looked down toward the remnants of the gown that she had worn that night and which she still wore. Tattered, and in places, shredded beyond description. The garment had undergone a complete transformation from the evening in question a little over two weeks earlier. When Maria came to the point where Jacob and her father had been taken off the train Sophie's concentration became intense. Her heart pounded hoping that what she was about to hear would not be bad news, her ears were impatient as to what Maria would say and her eyes were searching for the words long before they rolled of Maria's lips.

'He is still alive then?' Sophie asked of her friend after Maria finished her story, at the same time confirming to herself with enormous relief what she had already heard.

'Of course,' replied Maria trying to hide her own concern from Sophie of the possibility that even now her brother and her father could find themselves in worse circumstances than what the remainder of the family were experiencing.

'As long as he is alive, then we still have a chance of being together once more when this is all over,' Sophie said with immense hope.

The two young women embraced one another once again as Kazik called to them from a distance. With tears in her eyes Sophie had enough time to recount to her fleeting companion that her brother had been shot and killed. Maria tightened her grip on Sophie. That action was enough to relate to her that Maria was both saddened and deeply shocked by her bad news.

Kazik called once more. The two young women parted, tears in their eyes. Sophie waved to Kazik and smiled through her regenerated grief. He returned the compliment waving profusely, ever watchful that no soldier was paying attention.

The families parted company and the Bryevski's made their way back to where Kazik was waiting. Before Eva returned she placed several items of clothing, which she had unpacked before crossing to meet the Sagajlo family, into the hands of Helena. Gratefully Helena thanked her.

Forced to embark on the train which had now pulled into the terminus, Eva scrutinised the inside of the cattle truck and concluded that there was no difference from the earlier wagon they had travelled in. It was still frowzy and disgusting, 'but of course we have become used to these conditions' she muttered to herself. She settled her family near to one of the corners in the wagon. From experience she knew that this was the best place to sit during the warm weather. The breeze that blew into the cattle wagon through the barred openings provided fresh air which was a small luxury to those that were fortunate to be in its direct path.

The Bryevski family strained their eyes to glimpse their last view of the Sagajlos'. They sighted them in the same area where they had left them. Both parties waved at one another as the heavy wooden doors were again slammed shut. They were to be opened on five more occasions during the next seven days that it took to travel to the Barnaul region within Kazakhstan, passing on their way the towns of Tyumen and Omsk, before finally arriving at a small station not far from Barnaul called Suzun.

Vladimir Stoich arose from the woman he minutes earlier had been abusing. He cared nothing for the woman he had been fornicating with, for he knew that she used him just as he would use her. Indeed his attraction to her was purely physical for the body and facial features she was fortunate to possess, bared no resemblance to her personality, which was vicious and corrupt and she herself was a complete termagant with little or no morals depending on the occasion. For a small favour such as an extra meal or a portion of tobacco, her sexual donations were limitless and the choice for a man bearing gifts, in this case Vladimir himself, within the spectrum of sexual fantasies was inexhaustible. He used this woman whenever he wanted to experiment and explore, in reality, the sexual deviations that conjured in the darker side of his mind.

Having satisfied his large sexual appetite, at least for the next two or three hours, he now had to prepare for the fresh contingent of deportees which were due to arrive at his small kingdom. They were scheduled to arrive the previous evening, and unknowing to himself, although concluding correctly, he deduced that the new group of internees had been held up due to transport problems. It was essential to Vladimir that he viewed personally the arrival of the internees. He did not want to overlook any possibility that there may be one or two women who would eventually succumb to his wishes and there was always one, occasionally two, in each contingent who made his loins quiver with lustful passion.

Pulling his well worn brown corduroy trousers up around his overgrown stomach, and after tucking his matching coloured, perspiration stained shirt into his lower garment, he hitched the leather belt into its last sprocket, only after taking a deep breath to do so. Casting the flimsiest of glances down to his recent but all too ready conquest, he was in time to catch her covering her dark coloured puberty, and his animal instincts produced an immediate vibration deep within him despite the minimum amount of time which had elapsed since his last ejaculation.

'Your meal will be on the table within five minutes,' he barked at her, nodding at the same time in the direction of the stand. 'Make sure you are decent before it arrives,' he ordered as he pulled on his jacket, patched at the elbows, before disappearing through the door which he slammed shut behind him. Any affection he had for her had been evanescent and had vanished the moment he had dismounted her.

Once outside he remembered his wife, the other women, and not for the first time, the reason as to why he was condemned, although temporary, to the outside world he now found himself in. This was his punishment and if he were truthful with himself, and taking everything into consideration, it was not nearly as unpleasant as he had originally thought. Certain aspects of the position he had in the village were extremely favourable, especially now that a number of female detainees had arrived. There had been a steady stream of women of all shapes and sizes. Although it was extremely difficult to progress a relationship with the respectable women, many of those females who had committed crimes and had been sent to his area as punishment did not fall far short of being prostitutes, some worse than others. His policy was never to remain close to one woman for longer than necessary, especially those who, whilst not declaring to be whores, certainly performed as one. Vladimir knew that several of his acquaintances were also sleeping with other partners. His policy was to act quickly with the new, less respectable arrivals that took his fancy. Staying no longer than necessary, one month being the longest, and then moving to someone else. That way there was less chance of catching unwanted diseases. There was still a possibility that he may contract something, though he was prepared to take the risk, and he thought that the policy he adopted was suitable, safe and so far very rewarding.

He walked around the village policing the small area that it covered before relating his instructions to the people who were in his charge and who had been ready assembled during his walkabout. After discharging his underlings for them to commence with their days work he returned to his own dwelling in time to see the harlot he had spent the previous night with entering her own temporary abode whom she shared with another Kazak family. It was an unwritten law of Vladimir's that any woman he had bedded the previous night was allowed to eschew the following day's work duties.

Vladimir entered his own premises and opened the remaining bottle of Napoleon brandy he had brought with him from Moscow. Emptying the last contents of the vessel into an earthenware cup he drank a mouthful savouring its taste before finally slowly swallowing the cherished drink. 'Hopefully there will be more of that when the next batch of deportees arrive,' he wished to himself. He belched, placed the empty vessel on the table and walked out onto the front of his premises.

Opening the door his lingering concluded immediately as he noticed on the perimeter of the village a soldier dressed in a uniform he instantly recognised as being Russian. He smiled to himself knowingly. The next batch of deportees had arrived. As the soldier drew nearer Vladimir noticed a parcel under his arm. His smile turned to a grin. 'Another consolation for being in this backdrop' he whispered to himself. He beckoned the soldier to hurry along toward him and immediately invited him into his dwelling. The soldier placed the parcel on the table and Vladimir opened it with extreme impatience tearing at the wrapping with a serious expression. The grin which had momentarily disappeared now returned with interest as he held the two bottles of his favourite brandy in either hand.

'Drink?' he said to the soldier who instantly looked stunned at the request.

'Yes,' he quickly replied totally surprised at being offered such a luxury by an NKVD official.

'How is the world out there?' asked Vladimir contented that he had the opportunity to talk with somebody from the real world.

'Things are good. The pact between Russia and Germany is strong.'

Both men smiled and drank another measure whilst they exchanged further conversation before Vladimir realised that this may be the last two bottles of brandy he would see for a very long time and should therefore conserve it for himself.

Suddenly taking on the role of authority and completely changing his temperament, Vladimir barked into action.

'Where are the captives?' he enquired.

The soldier jumped to attention making sure he had drunk the last drop of brandy before placing the cup on the table and replying.

'They are being escorted into the village with the two remaining soldiers Sir.'

Vladimir walked out onto the veranda and watched as the new arrivals approached in his direction. From first casting his eyes on the group he had immediately spotted what to him, despite her poverty and obvious wretchedness, was the most attractive sight he had laid his eyes on since leaving Moscow. The nearer she approached the more beautiful she appeared to him. He grinned pruriently at her as he followed her every move. She was, he thought, a woman of class and purity. Attractive, beautiful and very appealing and even though she appeared too thin in size for his usual preference in women, and despite her obvious indifference to him, he continued his gaze toward her.

The second and final part of the Sagajlo family's journey, although they did not know it, had followed that of their friends, the Bryevski's. Not long after meeting them and once again being parted from them at the clearing station in Sverdlovsk they were again pursuing and following in their tracks across the steppes of Kazakhstan. The Sagajlo's did not travel as far east as their friends and after passing through Kurgan disembarked at Petropavlosk. There the hundreds of deportees were made to wait by the authorities to determine the final destinations of where the people would be settled.

After waiting approximately six hours for transport, the soldiers then decided to march the captives to the next town. It was five kilometres walking distance over hard terrain. The sun beat down on the columns of marchers making the journey more difficult, slowing the advancement to a snail's pace. No water was available and no food had been offered to the deportees for nearly twenty four hours. The elderly fell by the wayside and the soldiers did not even bother to inspect or help those that had collapsed. They knew that death was close and nothing could save them now. Occasionally, for no apparent reason, one or two of the guards would help those who had fallen, enticing them to their feet with the promise that water would be available at the next village. Some arose to continue. Others having arisen and having walked several hundred metres further again collapsed, this time never to get up again.

Having arrived at the next town the authorities allowed the internees water and a little food to sustain their strength. After eating they once again awaited transport before continuing. Different forms of transportation arrived depending on which village people were being sent to. Those who were to stay at the nearest village were given a cart drawn by an ox, or an old ramshackle lorry to travel on. Those who had further to travel had to wait for suitable transport to appear to carry them to their distant settlement. Eventually lorries came to take the Sagajlo's and their companion along with thirty other people to their final rehabilitation area.

The people unceremoniously bundled themselves into the back of the small convoy of lorries which had arrived, dragging their bundles of possessions in behind them. They sat in the rear of the trucks on badly assembled wooden frames which passed for very uncomfortable seats. People were grateful that they were not walking and at least they were out in the open air. Progress was slow as there were very few roads to follow. The terrain was uneven and undulating in places and the occupants wondered how anybody could find their way about in such a vast area of land. The scenery the captives gazed on was contrasting. For miles they would look upon a land of beauty and a richness they did not expect to see. Then it would suddenly become barren only to change several miles further on to one of beauty once more. The sights they perceived helped pass the long duration that the journey took.

The convoy of lorries suddenly came to a halt and one soldier from each of the vehicles who had been sitting in the front jumped out of the cabin, notified to its occupants in the rear that a sandstorm was brewing, and that everybody was to remain inside until told to do otherwise.

The sun which had beat down on the unprotected land for much of the day suddenly became blotted out by the whistling, whirling sand which blasted its way into every nook and niche where it could find a safe home. The scenery disappeared from view and the blue and greens of the near and distant horizons were quickly blocked out. The light brown sand, which the storm carried, descended on everything in its wake. The transformation camouflaged all natural colours to a duller tanned imitation of itself. Visibility outside was reduced to inches. Inside the lorry, even with the flaps down and tightly strapped by the soldier, the sand invaded and contaminated the viscera of the human body. The people learned quickly but not quick enough, and the hastily made protective coverings could not keep out all the intrusions of the ingredients that the sandstorm had manufactured in its manifestation. In as short a time as the storm had displayed itself, it disappeared, leaving in its wake a yellowy brown powder which appeared to have been dusted lightly across everything it had come into contact with.

The soldier again came out of his hideaway in the front cab of the lorry, dusting himself off as he made his way to the rear of the vehicle to undo the protective covering. The convoy once again continued on its way over the terrain in search of its final destination. The night came and the monotonous sound of the engine drove people into an uncomfortable slumber. Those who awoke passed lights in the distance which verified to them that there was habitation in this wilderness after all.

The small convoy of vehicles complete with their passengers motored on into the night. The morning dawned and the sun grew ever stronger and more remorseless in emitting its endless internal production of heat onto the open steppes. The people awoke to the drone of the lorry's engine just as it had lulled them into sleep the previous night. They stopped again for several hours due to a breakdown to one of the other lorries. Some people alighted. Others remained inside the rear of the truck taking refuge from the heat of the sun and eventually drifted into sleep once more. They were woken several hours later by the roar of the engine announcing the pursuance of their journey's end.

The Doctor, Sophie's father, wondered whether they were returning to where they had started the previous day as the scenery they now passed resembled that which they had seen twenty four hours earlier. After voicing his thoughts it was pointed out by one of the other passengers that surely not even the Russian soldiers would put themselves through such a pointless action.

Eventually, and to the immense satisfaction of the internees the convoy stopped at a remote village to unload some of its passengers. Only two of the lorries were unloaded and the rest of the convoy continued on its journey still further, so the detainees surmised, into the depths of the unknown country.

The captives unloaded themselves and their baggage which had diminished in size since the commencement of the journey from their homeland. They organised themselves into a small column before the soldiers had ordered them to do so, and awaited further instructions. The soldier in charge walked off in search of the official of the village to announce their arrival. The remaining two soldiers marched slowly into the village with the deportees.

Sophie surveyed all around her shocked to see that the houses were small and structured in mud, a dark richer brown in texture compared to the sandy coloured brown of the ground that they were built upon. Between each house the backdrop of the blue horizon interspersed like giant blue fingers reaching out to grab menacingly at something which didn't belong to it. There appeared to be nothing else of significance in the area. Mainly local women came out of their dwellings to view the new intake of Poles. The majority of these people were poorly dressed in dark clothing. Their facial features magnified contrastingly with small, slant eyes which peered inquisitively at the new arrivals. Amongst the many who gazed was a handful that appeared facially like them.

Progressing through the village Sophie noticed that halfway along one building stood larger than the rest of the dwellings and realised as they drew nearer that this was because the house had been constructed on a small hillock. On the outer wooden veranda, which had been added to the original mud structure, probably to allow an easier access to the premises, stood two men. One was the soldier who had accompanied her group on the last leg of the journey; the second was a large man, not in length but in roundness. His features were similar to hers and she knew him to be not of Kazak origin. His clothes were unkempt but she understood why and how it was possible. He held himself upright against the wishes of his large stomach which obviously weighed him down. Sophie surmised, correctly, that he was probably the authority of the village, the law that everyone had to obey. Purveying him from a distance, she also felt that she herself was being scrutinised in turn by him. He seemed to grin covetously at her. In between the yearning stares she also glimpsed a wicked boyish smile which mellowed her original thoughts.

As the group of people neared toward where he was standing Sophie averted her eyes away from him. She was unsure whether he repulsed her although his final stare had been unobjectionable to her. She knew his eyes were on her but for now she did not want to look upon him.

CHAPTER 17

After collapsing over the threshold on entering Wandeczka's apartment and after she had struggled to put him to bed, Jan had slept continuously for the next seventy two hours. A doctor, who was a close friend of Wandeczka's family and who could be trusted, had been called by her to examine Jan whilst he still lay unconscious. He had contracted a virus which in addition to the lack of sleep and the stressful circumstances he had been through; multiplied to compound the illness and intensify the effect it had on him.

Since awaking Jan had made a rapid recovery and within seven days of arriving at the apartment was out of bed and walking around. Any damage sustained to his ankle had healed as a result of his lengthy rest period in bed. Wandeczka refused to go to the club for the first three nights that he lay sleeping, but after Jan regained consciousness he made her go, guaranteeing that he could do no harm whilst he was lying in bed recuperating.

A further three weeks passed and the day soon arrived when Andrei would be returning home from his ten week assignment with the Peoples Commissariat for Internal Affairs, the NKVD. As an Officer he was expected to give priority to the department before his own family, and it was fortunate that he and Wandeczka had no children as she would have put pressure on him to be at home more often. Like her mother before, that is how Wandeczka would want it, believing that a father should spend sufficient time with the children.

She had missed her husband tremendously. Even though Jan had arrived to break her loneliness she still looked forward to the arrival of her spouse. She always excelled in presenting both herself and their apartment in perfect order on his arrival home after a period away on duty. On this occasion there was another reason to do so and she had made an extra effort to please him. Because her long lost cousin had turned up quite unexpectedly Wandeczka wanted to help him, especially after the story he had related to her. If anybody could help then who better than Andrei.

Jan was one of the lucky ones he had informed her. The weak and the old suffered the worse and several had died en route whilst he was on the train. She wondered as to what her mother would have thought about the events which were taking place in her homeland and what catastrophes its people were undergoing. Without doubt she knew that her mother would have cursed the Russians for what they were doing. If Wandeczka could help one of those poor, suffering people, that is what her mother would have wanted. Above all that, she had grown fond of her long lost cousin and he had certainly been excellent company whilst her husband had been away.

Wandeczka had everything planned and she knew how Jan, despite being Polish, could survive in Moscow as long as he was willing to pretend he was of Russian and not Polish origin. She had recognised immediately his grasp of the Russian language and how he spoke as good, if not better, than many people she had acquainted herself with. Language was certainly not a problem. She knew also, from earlier conversations with Andrei that accommodation was available in the city and that the secret police often found somewhere to live not only for themselves but also for visiting dignitaries and such like people who needed accommodation at short notice. This was another luxury that higher officials of the NKVD could call upon when needed. Jan would also require new papers and once again, where further to look than to her husband. Again, this was easily attainable within the structures of the NKVD although she realised that the danger lay in charging as few people as possible with the secrecy and keeping the information quiet.

All she would have to do was to persuade Andrei to help Jan. By helping him he would be doing her a great service. As a woman she knew how to manage that perfectly. In her husband's case her turn on for him was with very few clothes and a lot of sensuality. She looked forward to the challenge immensely, for despite satisfying him sexually she was also looking forward to being satisfied in that way. The only drawback as far as Wandeczka was concerned was her husband's blind refusal to help any of the Poles who the Russians were deporting, but she was also confident that eventually he would not refuse what she wanted. He had never done so since they had married and she felt no reason to assume that it would not continue in that manner.

The farm holding that Pieter Sagajlo had taken refuge in was occupied by a woman and her baby. Ownership was originally tenured by a Polish family who had been deported long ago when the Russians had first invaded. A peasant family who had worked for the original owners had then been put in charge to oversee the land for the Russian regime. Several months after having been instructed to take charge the man had himself come under suspicion for falsifying food stocks to the authorities and for his punishment had been deported to

Siberia. Travelling on the infamous trains to commence his ten year sentence in lagier, he had died halfway through his journey in the severe weather conditions of February that year. The winter of 1940 had been one of the coldest temperatures recorded. Snow fell up to the roof levels of the cattle wagons and even small houses and buildings had been covered.

The wife of the man had been left completely alone with her baby to fend for themselves with no help from the Russian authorities. Seeing that the farm was becoming rundown, the Oppressors ceased paying visits to her after a short while and left her to her own devices assuming that eventually she would return to her original family. After she recovered from the initial shock of her husband's death she decided to labour the farm on her own.

Her first decision was to work that part of the land which she knew to be of good soil and which would bring about the desired results quicker. Having taken this decision she had virtually cut the area of land on the farm down by half. For the next several months she toiled continuously, her baby always by her side. The days were long and hard with very few breaks except for the nights. She eventually attained the standards on the holding that her husband had previously set. At the end of her task she was pleased with her efforts and the final outcome.

She had found Pieter sleeping in the barn early one morning several weeks ago. Fetching an old shooting rifle which had belonged to her husband, she awoke the unknown intruder by prodding the barrel of the gun into his chest. He sat up quickly, rubbing his lunar shaped eye sockets as a result of suddenly being awoken from a slumber which had eluded him for seventy two hours previous. He cursed himself and his carelessness and was surprised to find himself being woken by a woman. After he had told her his story of how he had been avoiding the Russians since his miraculous escape from the train she had lowered the gun and invited him into the house to eat.

From the earliest moments of their meeting, there was some attraction between the two of them. Both related their experiences to one another and their respect and admiration grew in similar proportion. Pieter, in gratitude for the food she had provided for him, had offered to help with one or two jobs he had noticed needed doing on the farm whilst waiting the previous evening before furtively using the barn to sleep in.

She had gratefully accepted his offer and he duly obliged. It was the baby who had helped to break down the barriers of remoteness that exists between two strangers when first meeting. After returning to the small farmhouse in the early evening to inform her he had finished the relevant work and would now continue on his path, the naked infant was crawling out of the house through the opened door. Pieter picked up the baby and was gently playing with him. The infant was laughing at the faces this stranger made as Pieter first called and then searched downstairs in the house before the mother turned up as he became concerned for her whereabouts.

'We were wondering what had happened to you,' Pieter said looking from the mother to the baby.

'I was fetching his bath water,' she replied.

The baby laughed at Pieter again, and the mother, putting her jug of water down on the table and gently brushing her blond mane back over her shoulders with her hand, approached them both. As she was about to take the baby from Pieter the infant decided to relieve himself over the newcomer to the house.

Pieter's face took on a shocked expression. The baby continued to laugh and the mother, on seeing the completely different expressions on Pieter's face and that of her son, started laughing too. Pieter seeing the funny side joined in the merriment. The woman, now standing next to Pieter, looked into his eyes. In the short time she had known him he reminded her in many ways of her late husband, kind and unselfish, strong and hardworking.

Pieter held the baby safely to him still peering at the mother. Her face was rounded in shape and testified to having once held immense beauty which had slowly ebbed away from her through the hardened life she had been made to follow. Her large pale blue eyes glistened forlornly, reminding him of shimmering pools of water that the sea abandons on its way out with the tide. She raised one of her chafed and bruised hands, substantiating her earlier testimony to the burden she had pulled herself and her son through, and gently touched Pieter's face. Stretching up toward him she gently kissed his rough, broken lips once, then twice. The baby playfully tapped Pieter's cheek as if reminding him that he had been the only person to hold his mother's attention until now. Their lips parted and they both looked toward, and laughed at, the young infant.

Pieter had remained there ever since, which for him, was a long duration in one place. In that time she had made him feel like a man again and he chose to forget the amount of time he had spent living like a convict always on the lookout for the Russians and always trying to keep one step ahead. Despite what had happened between them Pieter knew that the time would eventually arrive when he would have to depart.

Wandeczka knew her husband well and he was always happiest when he was slightly inebriated. He was not a heavy drinker unlike many members of the NKVD and for that she was grateful. The stories that had been related to her by many of the Officers' wives after their husbands had been drinking horrified her. These stories were verified by the bruises and impressions on the bodies of the women even to the point of their limbs periodically being broken. If Andrei ever treated her in that manner she knew that the marriage would have to end. However that evening she had plied him with enough alcohol to keep him happy and she continued to fill his glass with the wine as and when she thought necessary without rendering him totally drunk.

The final part of her meticulous homecoming was about to be played out and as she undressed in the bathroom, and prepared to change into her outfit which she knew would please her husband enormously and round off a perfect day, she reflected back on the evening's events.

The shock of Andrei meeting her long lost cousin had been softened by the niceties which she had prepared prior to her friend bringing Jan around at the prearranged time to meet him. For tonight only she had arranged for Jan to stay at her friend's apartment. She had plotted the evening very carefully and had agreed that Jan should be introduced to Andrei after she had told her husband that her cousin had visited. She planned to break the news to him over the dinner table. Enough time she had calculated to feast him on his preferred meal and soak him in his favourite wine.

The plan had worked perfectly. She had dropped the information in after the main course had been eaten whilst they were conversing on the duration of his leave.

'My cousin turned up unexpectedly whilst you were away.' she mentioned filling his glass once more ensuring his insobriety was maintained.

'Oh! How unexpected?' he had asked.

'Well I haven't seen him for about ten years?' she said dryly.

'That is a long time.' he replied with a confused smile both through her changing the course of conversation and the amount of time she revealed since last seeing her cousin.

'Anyway, when will you be returning to duty Sir?' she joked with him arising out of her seat and sitting down on his lap.

After they playfully touched one another and the laughter died away, they kissed affectionately and his manhood was aroused by both her passion and the odour of her fragrance which he had not smelt for many months. He had missed her immensely and often wished that he could take her with him on his faraway duties.

Their lips eventually parted and she arose from his lap. She had missed what she had just experienced with her husband and she wished that he could stay in

Moscow more often. She looked at him affectionately and ran her fingers through his hair. She could not help but think how he appeared more like a German than a Russian. His blond hair was cut short to the scalp though it still reflected the waves in his mane and his attractive features were perfect for the Aryan race. His nose was disproportionate to the rest of his face, but this did not detract from his handsomeness. His shoulders, though wide, were rounded and dropped at forty five degrees from his neck making his appearance seem shorter than his actual height of just under two metres. Often Wandeczka had told him to lift his shoulders and to hold himself smartly.

'Bed?' Andrei suggested innocently completely forgetting the last question she had asked him.

She smiled at him, which only nurtured his faint erection.

'We cannot, not yet. I want you to meet Jan, my cousin who'll be visiting us.'

'Oh! Yes your cousin.' Andrei suddenly remembered where the conversation hadn't temporarily concluded.

'As soon as he goes, we'll retire.' she smiled and winked at him.

That pleased him and he grinned widely in satisfaction knowing what was on the menu next.

She leaned toward him as she sat down at her seat once again and pulled her chair up closely to him. Her low cut dress enhanced her cleavage and she took Andrei's hand and pressed it lightly to the bare part of her chest.

'Coming from Poland, he will need help Andrei and I hope you'll help him?' she pleaded seductively in a low sensuous intonation making sure the cadence of her voice was lower in sound for the early part of the sentence.

'If I can help, I will help.' he stated flatly. Although he had heard where her cousin was from he chose to ignore the fact. He was more interested at that moment in where his hand was and what was going to happen later between them than in helping her long lost cousin.

With that statement sounded she dropped the subject happy that she had extracted those words from him. Wandeczka knew that she was on the path to securing her cousin's safety. The first stage in the plan had succeeded. The next stage would be a formality she thought to herself as once again she arose from her chair and served her husband with his favoured dessert.

'The evening had been perfect, the remainder can only get better,' she told herself. Unhooking the clasp of her brassiere and ridding herself of the last piece of clothing, she eyed herself in the three quarter length mirror as she sat on the wicker chair in the bathroom pulling on her black knee length boots. She was pleased with what she saw as she flung her left leg out in front of her, pulling sharply, the upper leather of the boot which fitted snugly against the calf of her leg. She repeated the action for the right limb and stood upright in front of the mirror, again inspecting herself for any flaws. She hardened both nipples until the redness stood out from the pink surround like a coat peg sticking out from a wall, and selflessly thought to herself 'another treat for you Andrei.'

Completely naked, except for the boots, she opened the bathroom door and pressed herself up against the door support, purposely revealing her right breast for her husband to view plus a section of her body from the shoulder to the toes.

He called to her and she obeyed willingly, revealing herself completely, walking toward him alluringly. She sat by the side of him and as he fondled her she reached for his sexuality. He bent forward to caress her breasts with his lips and she held him there, an agreeable captive. Allowing him to suck into sheer pleasure, she too, felt herself losing out to love and lust and before she lost all control she made him promise that he would help her cousin.

'I'll help him, I'll help him,' he whispered breathlessly, 'I promise.'

She could have asked for anything at that moment and if it was in his power he would have supplied it. Touching her lower half with his lips, Wandeczka too was finally appeased and the night for her and Andrei held no boundaries in their fulfilment of one another.

Lying in bed awaiting his next and final surprise, Andrei could not contain his elation. He felt like an excited little boy and reminisced back to those tender years when he had always been eager to open presents which had been presented to him on his birthday. Although he felt sure he knew what was about to happen the final packaging and the exact identity of how it would appear and how it was dressed were still elusive to him. His mind summoned all possible fantasies, not all of which, he knew, would attain the reality, though any would be overwhelmingly rewarding.

The homecoming had been nothing short of perfect. It had always been worthwhile but on this occasion it was extra special. The meal she had prepared was succulent and tasty, bettered only, he thought, and only occasionally, by the chefs who displayed their culinary crafts at the very few selective Russian restaurants found in Moscow. The wine she had provided was his favourite French burgundy and had been retained by himself for special occasions and which, his connection had said, was purported to have come from the wine stocks of the last Czar. Andrei never knew whether the story was true and did not bother to find out. Tonight he had enjoyed the burgundy more than usual and the quantity overflowed which made him feel light-headed though happy and contented.

The visit of both Wandeczka's long lost cousin, Jan, and her friend, with whom Jan was spending the night, and which he had not been looking forward to, had been a measured success especially as they had not stayed too long. As a result of the fleeting visit he now found himself under Wandeczka's guidance, in bed, looking forward immensely to the next event.

Eventually the bathroom door opened and part of her appeared. His excitement became intense and he focused fully on the one large breast he could visibly see, paying particular attention to her red nipple. He scanned the rest of the right side of her body quickly and was pleased with what she wore on her leg. One of the earlier fantasies he visioned of her was complete. He beckoned her to him and she came willingly. Approaching him seductively, he sighed quietly and satisfyingly to himself pleased with the image that he now cast his eyes on. The awareness of his organ was overpowering and as they fondled he thought about how long he would last that night. It had been a long time and he did not want to spoil it. She searched for his erection and as she grasped it he felt sure that it had grown larger than ever before. Leaning toward her to feed on her plentiful breasts she accepted him eagerly and when he had caressed them long enough she made him promise to look after her cousin. Like a spider playing with its prey, Wandeczka had her husband where she wanted him; he sighed with satisfaction and answered in agreement to what she wanted. His promise was the last words either heard as his mouth left her breasts and she guided him down to her upper thighs to bury and smother his face in wild and lustful odours which she produced eagerly for both him and herself.

The Russian system of punishment adopted several contrasting institutions to penalise the criminal to varying degrees. The first institution being that of jail, of which there are an abundance of many differing types throughout Russia. The conditions in the jails are nearly always filthy and the inmates, prior to and after sentence is passed on them, can expect to spend an unlimited amount of time in a room very often filled to exhaustion with other criminals. Before his trial and whilst the questioning is underway by the authorities the convict spends the periods between interrogations alone in a cell with a single piercing light which burns continuously day and night.

The second institution for punishment is hard labour, better known to the Russians and their next door neighbours as 'lagier'. They are camps set up and controlled by the Russian NKVD to administrate groups of prisoners who are very often worked until they virtually die whilst working. This hard labour can take the form of mining and digging for metals or minerals, or clearing forests to use the wood for building material. Each lagier is self contained and the inmates are allowed certain powers of self government which is decided by the captives themselves. The prisoners are very often divided into brigades and certain decisions plus the overseeing of the work is in the hands of supervisors called 'brigade leaders', or 'pridurki' as named by their fellow inmates. These 'pridurki' are themselves inmates and elected by their fellow convicts.

The third form of punishment adopts the form of deportation, very often called 'free exile'. This form of punishment is applied to whole groups of people such as families, villages and other societies but can also be applied to individuals. These groups are taken without warning, frequently in the middle of the night, and transported to distant places and settled in isolated outposts called 'posiolki' in the remotest depths within the Russian countryside. The people are then dispersed individually or collectively, on collective or state farms known as 'kolkhozy' or 'sovkhozy.' Once again as in previous institutions the overall responsibility is that of the NKVD Officer, who in free exile is usually no higher in rank than a non-commissioned officer.

The majority of people in free exile were tried and convicted without being present at their own trial. The magnitude in numbers of the people who had been deported into free exile prevented this happening and sentences were passed on whole families and villages at the same time. Needless to say correspondence of the sentences was never related back to the victims, therefore they never knew how long their term of punishment was to last for or when they were going to be released.

Work which was completed whilst a person was in 'lagier' or in 'free exile' was supposed to be rewarded with some form of payment. This payment usually took the form of food. In certain circumstances in free exile money could have been paid but very rarely was. All three of the different institutions were controlled or influenced in some way by the Narody Komissariat Vnutrennikh. People's Commissariat of Internal Affairs, better known as the NKVD.

The judicial system in Russia, depending on where in the country the trial took place, and on what judge was sitting in judgement, resulted in very bizarre decisions for both serious crimes and those that were considered not as serious. One would assume that the nature of the crime should have fitted the punishment, that the hardcore criminal who had committed murder would serve his or her sentence in the institution of jail. This was not always the case. Many ordinary Polish people who were deported into free exile, simply because they were the husband or mother or some form of relative of a person who had spoken out against the Russian regime, found themselves sharing tasks and responsibilities and even accommodation with those who had committed the more serious crime of murder.

It was to the institution of free exile that Sophie and her family with her new found companion had arrived several months prior. The four of them together were housed with a Kazak woman and her son who were extremely hostile to them at first. Inside the dwelling, of which the walls were coated with mud, a meagre existence welcomed them to their new home. The house consisted of two rooms. The first, which was the largest, comprised of the living area and the sleeping area in one. The room was supplemented by one or two pieces of wood which was the only furniture found in the house. The second room, the cooking area, was much smaller and the majority of space was occupied by the stove which the inhabitants of the house slept on during the cold and bitter winter months. No room was set aside for bathing and washing oneself or for answering the call of nature. Many of the locals washed by spitting on their hands and then proceeded to wash their faces with it. Defecation was performed in the open outside at the rear of the house. The locals who were used to people passing by as they performed this action could not understand the reluctance of the Polish people who could not, at first, bring themselves to do such a thing. However, as the weeks moved on, the Poles too, soon accepted the daily routine in the same manner in which the locals did so. No germs or diseases emanated from the human waste material which was either dried up quickly during the summer months by the hot sun or covered and disintegrated by the cold snows in winter.

Inside the houses very little or no air permeated through the abode and the smell which first hit those newcomers on entering the premises was overpowering. The mixture of perspiration from the owners, who infrequently washed or changed their clothes, together with the warmth of the summer and the lack of ventilation, fused to make a potent stench in the dwelling. Very often during the summer months the occupants slept with the doors wide open due to the warm conditions.

None of the walls were ever completely free of lice and bugs. To endeavour to overcome the problem of these vermin whilst sleeping, the beds were made up above the ground to try and contain the movement of the nuisance. No amount of checking and re-checking could render the beds or the individual's clothing completely free of the parasites.

Outside, at the rear of the houses, could be found small gardens where a variety of vegetables were grown. Cooking by the Sagajlo family was undertaken by digging a small hole in the earth at the rear of the garden where a cooking pot was then placed over the hole and supported by bricks. Within the village and out over the steppes the cattle were allowed to roam free dropping their dung which was collected by the villagers at a later date and used as a source of fuel.

In the short time that Sophie and her family had been at the village the barriers between the Kazak people and the group of Polish deportees were slowly being broken down. Many of the villagers had become friendly and helpful although several still begrudged the attendance of the newcomers. The friendliness was more noticeable when the Polish visitors produced from their luggage the various trinkets and little luxuries they had managed to bring with them from their homeland. Out of all these the most popular items were tobacco and tea. The Kazak men were especially partial to the Polish tobacco. Many useful exchanges were bartered, not only with these two ingredients, but also with other provisions which they had brought with them. Helena Sagajlo was ever grateful for the package which Eva Bryevski had given her at the clearing station. The contents were useful to her now having arrived in this distant world. Even the shabbiest and smallest piece of lace which nobody would consider using was of great value in the village and its bartering powers were surprisingly valuable. The Kazak people had never seen articles of such luxury before and to them it was something new, a commodity which they desired and wanted.

The morning was warm and the sky was blue and free from cloud which interpreted the beauty of the surrounding scenery that lay around her. The small brook that dazzled from the rays of the sun which shone and glittered off the surface of the water enhanced the colour, strengthening the effect of the warm morning. She squatted on her knees in front of the cool running stream and leaned toward the clear free flowing water, cupping her hands as she pressed forward to drink her fill. Taking the handful of water, guiding it toward her mouth and swallowing refreshed her enormously. This simple pleasure in a cruel world where she now found herself reminded her of memories long ago. She drank in the same manner until her thirst was quenched.

Completely alone she bathed the top half of her body without discarding her clothes, pulling the light coloured blouse which Eva Bryevski had given, amongst other things, to her mother at the clearing station in Sverdlovsk, and which she now wore, away from her body to make her task easier. She repeated the duty to the bottom half of her body walking into and standing in the brook, but only after she had scrutinised the surrounding area in case any onlookers were watching. Satisfied that she was alone she lifted the short cotton skirt up above her lower body revealing the contrast in colours on her bare skin which the heat of the summer sun had bestowed on her without any warning.

After she had finished her duty she returned to the riverbank, sat and lay back supported by her elbows, to perceive the landscape around her. 'It too, is refreshingly beautiful in the heat and colour which radiates through and over the land this morning' she thought to herself. Across the stream and to the right side of her, the land undulated away. The grasses which had turned yellow, occasionally interrupted by the steppe thistles with their red heads, likened the earth to a large coconut matting covered as it is by dried up stalks of feather grasses which would serve as fertiliser for next year's growth.

Again memories returned to her as she now lay back on the ground. Sunshine days and picnics in the land where she truly belonged and the fun and gaiety she had enjoyed with her true love dazzled her mind. Questions pressed her as she looked up at the diamond blue empty sky. 'Would she see him again? If so how long would she have to wait? Would his feelings have changed?' The questions flowed, no answers accompanied them. Not for the last time her thoughts turned to the final day that she had spent with Jacob. The reassurances he had given to her and the plans they had made for the future. 'What now had become of them?'

Vladimir Stoich was finishing his usual morning stroll around the village and making his way back to his own house when he noticed the creature of extreme beauty disappearing out of view over the brow of the small incline which led out of the village no more than two hundred yards ahead. Immediately he decided to follow and make contact with her if the opportunity arose. Since her arrival approximately eight weeks earlier he had watched her and thought about her on many occasions. Changing his original thoughts, he decided conclusively that it was time to make contact.

Reaching the top of the incline he noticed her disappear once more from his view. Turning right at the bottom of the bank which he now stood on, she walked along the side of the brook behind some bushes. He descended in pursuit of his goal and followed her footsteps until they guided him to an area which opened into a clearing free from bushes and vegetation. In the nine months that he had resided at this village he had never before walked along the path which he now followed. He was surprised how pleasing the scenery appeared and the serenity around him relaxed his manner. To his surprise he found himself enjoying the walk as he pursued his target. He walked for almost fifteen minutes and by the time he spotted her again he had worked up a sizeable perspiration. 'I must take more exercise,' he thought to himself as he wiped his brow clear of the beads of salty sweat that now rippled down his face.

The brook he followed fell away down to his left and he walked out into the opening only after watching her again disappear over the bank no more than ten metres ahead of him. Creeping slowly toward the edge of the opening ever careful that she was not looking back on her tracks he peered over the incline and was grateful to find her kneeling forward over the brook drinking the refreshing liquid. Watching her drink, and the thought of the path he had moments earlier walked, his thirst became ever stronger. Momentarily he cogitated following her down the bank and joining her company. Deciding against this he turned and looked around to seek a suitable hiding place to watch this creature of beauty. To the right on the bank were some bushes, as he made his way toward them he was careful not to raise any alarm that someone had followed her.

'Perhaps now I should make my move instead of hiding here,' he thought to himself. Suddenly, crouching behind his camouflage, and as he considered the advantages and disadvantages of doing so, it was all decided for him.

Still kneeling over the water she was now pulling her blouse away from her body. Immediately Vladimir became even more interested. Without taking the garment off she wet her right hand and proceeded to wash the upper part of her body returning at intervals to soak her hand in the brook and repeat the process. The onlooker wished that she would take the clothing off and was disappointed his wish had not been carried out, but still the effect on him of what she was doing was satisfying. Finishing the first part of her cleaning process she stood and turned toward the bank behind her and looked up to ensure nobody was around. She now faced directly in front of Vladimir and though he was looking down on her he was protected by the bushes which afforded him ample camouflage. The view he gazed upon made him think he was in the land of pleasant dreams.

Her skin appeared soft and fresh like that of a new born baby. Her hair which her mother had cropped short to be rid of the bugs and lice, and which had grown back into a scraggy yet attractive collection of tresses, shone in the morning sun like the mane of a black thoroughbred stallion. Moving down her body, the water she had used to bathe herself acted like glue to the blouse, enhancing the shape of her upper frame and protruding the mammilla of her breast through the garment. Vladimir was entranced and he felt his emotion stir in his lower depths and harden quickly.

Turning back to the brook, happy that she could not see anyone in the vicinity, she raised the tattered skirt she was wearing which had been made out of the cotton blanket taken out of the boot of her father's vehicle the night they had been rounded up. Walking into the stream she completely revealed the lower rear part of her body and prepared to wash once more. The two-tone colour of her lower and upper thighs enhanced her femininity to the viewer.

Vladimir, who already had a perfectly good position to perceive this distant goddess, in greed, lunged head forward to seek a better view. In the process he overbalanced and nearly toppled over and down the bank. Regaining his composure he looked quickly in the direction to where she was standing hoping he had not caused any noise. She had heard none. He decided against moving any further forward satisfying himself on viewing from his present position. Settling himself down quickly, afraid that he may miss any of her actions, he watched as she angled forward revealing the expanse of her rear, though still petite in size. She bent forward to scoop and hold water in her hand raising it to her underneath before going through the process again. Repeating the action several times Vladimir was bewitched with her movements and his manhood ached with each rotation she performed. Finishing her second task she lowered her skirts and returned to the edge of the brook and sat down on the ground. He watched as she first briefly rested on her elbows and then lay back facing the wide open expanse of clear blue sky.

The pursuer decided to make his move. He retraced his steps out of the bushes and across the top of the bank, re-entering again from the access he had earlier approached from, pretending that that had been the first occasion he had appeared there that morning, if indeed she would see him approaching and may ask. Swiftly he decided his overtures to her should be subdued and to refute his authority on her in any way. He knew without having been introduced to her that she was a woman of the highest quality and he decided to treat her like one of the many genteel ladies he had experienced in Moscow.

Following the same path the second time above the bank, he sat down on the brow and picked up a small stone and launched it toward the stream. It hit the water breaking the surface with a gentle ripple. At once Sophie sat up and looked about her. The memories she had mustered became instantly forgotten as she viewed him no more than ten feet above her, sitting on the bank. Immediately she asked herself how long he had been there.

'I did not mean to disturb you.' He spoke to her calmly in his semi deep Russian voice. 'Please forgive me,' he continued apologetically. 'Do you come here often?'

There was still silence from her. Sophie had begun to learn Russian since arriving and she had grasped the language quickly. She could understand what he was saying though she was unsure what to do, whether to say anything or remain silent. Her decisiveness was blocked by apprehension and nervousness which now attacked her.

He arose and descended to where she was now standing. Again he spoke.

'I come here when I like to think of home,' he lied. 'I've never seen anyone here before. How often do you come here?'

Finally, and still nervous, she decided to answer.

'Not as often as I would like to.'

'It is a peaceful place? Yes?' he questioned, and then answered detecting some alarm in her manner.

She nodded her head. 'Yes, very peaceful.' And then, getting the better of her anxiety, she decided to ask, 'How long were you sitting there?' She pointed to the top of the bank where she had first seen him.

'Not long, perhaps two or three minutes,' again he lied with a straight face. He had mastered the expression over many years.

'Where are you from?' he enquired.

She was relieved that he had recently arrived and answered his question. Vladimir paid little attention. He was remembering how he had seen her minutes earlier with the blouse tight to her body revealing her shape. He dared not look down toward her chest as she faced him and he was careful to control his eye movement, determined not to let them stray. His law was never to let a lady know how she was lusted after.

'How long have you been here?' he asked knowing the answer before he had asked the question.

'Over two months,' she replied.

Again he repeated his earlier statement. 'This peacefulness makes me think of home.' He motioned to the other side of the brook to glimpse a better view of the picturesque scenery in front of them. 'It brings back good memories. Does it do the same for you?'

She turned and looked in the direction he was pointing, pausing before answering. 'Y…Yes it does,' she stammered due to her returning misgivings of suddenly realising that she was alone with this man.

When she turned to look, Vladimir cunningly glanced toward her blouse and was disgruntled to see the material had dried hiding the outline of her body.

Turning back to face and look at him once more she uttered an excuse that she should be returning.

He stepped aside and as he watched her climb the bank scrutinising her movements he called after her, 'Perhaps we will meet here again?'

She turned as she reached the top of the bank and nodded in the affirmative, and then hurried on her way.

Returning hastily to the village and the security of her family she could not help but question why she was hurrying and that her first thoughts on seeing him when she had entered the village two months ago could be wrong.

CHAPTER 18

From the moment of entering through the prison gates Jacob knew that the time had arrived when he would soon face the infamous interrogations which Russians had been famous for throughout their history. Interrogations not only been perpetrated against their own countrymen but on those people whose frontiers bordered Russia and beyond. Jacob himself knew the time was imminent and he prayed with each breath within him that his father would somehow be absolved from the proceedings though he feared that this was not possible.

The days came and went and the time they had spent in the hovel of a cell was slow and monotonous. Conditions inside were abhorrent. Inmates when sitting or lying on the floor were packed tightly together and resembled dead bodies compacted in a mass grave. At night it was not possible to move once everyone had agreed on a sleeping position. If one prisoner wished to move and change his position he would disturb others in contact with him which caused a lot of aggravation. To avoid this they first had to negotiate until all agreed to move and then do so en bloc.

If one person wanted to visit the pail closet or 'parasha' to urinate during the night, he would lose his sleeping place and before resuming a sleeping position again for the night would have to wait until another inmate visited the 'parasha.'

Some inmates, especially those who were close to death and whose abilities were failing day by day, never bothered to make their way to the 'parasha' and urinated where they lay. Others, who were too ill to move by themselves, both young and old, but who still had their faculties intact and where decency still marginally existed, were aided in their short journey if they requested help.

Food was provided for at least once daily and this could occur at anytime during the period. Herrings were the favoured menu and if these were not available then only bread was given. Occasionally soup, the contents of which were unknown, was provided. The portions supplied were small and never met the adequacies of a normal diet for a man. No exercise was allowed except for the cleaning of the toilets and the men devised rote so that each and everyone would have some respite from the hovel they were kept in day and night. Those that cleaned the latrines also had to empty the 'parasha' or pail bucket which was always full of urine.

To amuse themselves the guards would very often lock the doors to the toilets when the inmates who were designated to clean the area were inside. The chlorine compound supplied to the prisoners to disinfect the urinals was of a concentrated nature. To use it the cleaners needed the availability of fresh air to circulate through the latrines. Not only did this weaken the strong, overpowering smell of the chemical but it also allowed the inmates to breathe more easily. When the doors to the latrines were finally unlocked after the prisoners had completed their duty, they were very often blinded, temporarily, by the fumes from the chlorine and could barely see to find their way out of the toilet area. Through the constant massaging of their eyes, endeavouring to keep their eyesight uncontaminated and free from the effect of the chlorine, the skin around their eyes became reddened as did the eyeballs themselves.

After two weeks of the normal daily routine of sitting or lying and sleeping virtually whenever one chose, Jacob and his father were separated. Whilst Jacob's turn had come to undergo whatever plans the Russians had laid out for him, his father along with Anatoly was taken at the same time to another part of the prison.

Their parting was brief. With very little warning their messages were simple but their promise to one another to meet again held all the intention and fervour to do so above anything else. This small yet enormous assurance was enough to heighten their resolve.

With a guard either side Jacob was ushered along the corridor directly outside the cells. The floor was uneven, similar to the cell he had left behind but much cleaner, and made up of slabs of stone which had lost their grey colour being replaced by an off white tone as a result of decades of human traffic, the numbers of which had been lost over the years of time. The walls were a repeat of the cells, dark in colour but appearing free from vermin. The air he breathed was fresher and tasted less foul in the back of his throat. At the end of the corridor he was taken through an iron barred gate. Once through the darkness did not change significantly though he could see immediately ahead of him a flight of steps which led upward to a higher level. He had no time to take in the full view before he was redirected into another corridor which stood perpendicular to the first. As he passed through the metal entrance to this passage the light emanated from the lamps burning above increased threefold causing him initially to shy away from the brightness. He heard the metal door close quietly behind him.

His eyes slowly adjusted to the light and his senses became aware of the noises that were coming from the newly discovered cells that he now passed. His bowels tightened and relaxed spasmodically and his stomach turned against the rhythm of his innards as it raged inside his body. He could not control himself and as the cries echoed out from behind the closed cell doors he had passed and was still passing, he found that he was at war for the command of his form. More by intuition with his guards than commands from them, he came to a standstill in front of an opened door to a cell which housed two chairs situated opposite one another divided by a wooden table. That was all Jacob could see as he was pushed forward into his latest shelter. His private interrogation cell and therefore his personal hell, worse than that which he had experienced so far, would commence from this platform.

The door was slammed shut behind him. The actual noise seemed louder than all occasions before. 'How many times have I heard that?' he asked himself. 'First the trains, then the prison commune shared with another fifty inmates, and now this private room. My private room. For how long I wonder?'

A man walked from the dark shadows of the room, stood at the table and without waiting for Jacob to sit, sat down himself. Jacob was then beckoned to sit on the second chair which stood opposite the first across the table. Jacob's back was to the door. The room was dark except for the one bright light which hung from the ceiling and from which emerged brightness, the strength of which Jacob thought he had never seen before. He looked toward the corners and could not see anything. He sensed however, correctly, that some person or persons lurked there.

The man who sat opposite him spoke Russian in a squeaky mouse like voice which alienated his large fat appearance. Taking great pleasure in his manner, he extinguished the last remains of his cigarette on the small metal container used as an ashtray before commencing to speak in an eloquent and positive demeanour.

'You have been accused of raising arms against the people of the Soviet Union. In addition to this charge you have also been accused of working against the Communist party, spreading malicious information about that party in order to turn ordinary people against the party which has arrived to serve and assist them.'

He moved forward looking for any signs of guilt in Jacob's eyes. There were none. To Jacob these charges were completely false and he had nothing to hide. Although he hated the Communist party and their members he had said nothing to anyone, except his family, regarding his concerns. Now at this moment, in the prematurity of this investigation, he was grateful to his father who had warned him and the family that under no circumstances were they to utter one word to anyone outside the immediate family regarding the corruption, the rape, and the demise of their country since the Russians had arrived.

The Fatman sat back in his chair pausing before continuing. He slowly arose out of his seat picking up the documents which he had initially laid in front of himself on the table and came around to stand by Jacob. Placing the documents down in front of the victim he continued.

'You realise that all these are serious offences and carry heavy punishment if proven. We have witnesses who claim that you are guilty. Therefore we can do this the easy way or the hard way. Sign the documents in front of you now and you will merely carry out your sentence. Refuse to sign and you will be persuaded sooner or later to do so. I suggest you adopt the first method.' He patted Jacob on the shoulder and returned to his seat.

Jacob coughed, more through nervousness than the wish to clear his throat. The war in his stomach which had subsided rumbled with discontent once more.

'I have done nothing of which you have accused me and I will sign nothing that contains anything but the truth.'

'I hope that we are not going to need persuading Comrade Bryevski. If that is called for you will experience nothing like what is awaiting you.' He grinned toward Jacob seeming to take pleasure in his last words and the prospect of some form of cruelty about to begin.

'You may read the contents of the documents we have prepared for you.'

Jacob picked up the forms and slowly read through the words. He deliberately took his time keeping the inevitable commencement of torture at bay. At the same time he considered whether it was worth the delay for he knew that it would descend on him sooner or later.

After a considerable amount of time the interrogator interrupted.

'We know that you can speak and read Russian. Do not waste our time Comrade Bryevski. We are not stupid; you are not the first to adopt these tactics.' His squeaky tone deepened marginally indicating his growing anger. The victim was unaware of this.

Jacob was disillusioned and wondered how many had tried the same ploy only to suffer what he was about to suffer. The words in the documents were all lies, a complete fabrication and he wished that for what was certain to happen, he had actually performed those acts which were stated in the documents as his brother had done so since the Russians occupied their homeland.

'You will never get me to sign that document. Everything it contains is untrue.' He knew the words that he spoke were true. So long as his mind remained lucid Jacob would never sign the document. He continued. 'Fetch your witnesses, I have never heard of their names and no doubt they have been imagined. I will prove them wrong.' He was confident now and speaking bravely surprised that as yet, no physical contact had been aimed at him, either by the Fatman who interrogated him, or the two, perhaps three henchmen who he could now clearly hear breathing in the dark corners of the room.

What happened next was a complete shock to Jacob and he reeled heavily in the chair which rocked on two legs before returning to its rightful resting position on four legs. The blow to the left side of his head did not feel as though it had been performed by a human hand, it felt more like a heavier implement. He immediately felt immense pain which he had not encountered ever before and which continued longer than he had ever experienced previously. Visions of bright lights and stars affecting the mind quickly followed the pain. Jacob grabbed hold of the arms of the chair as the blow shuddered through his body, almost barrier free, carrying itself through the seat in a rocking movement before eventually dissipating.

He sat there slumped in the supporting vessel, still conscious but only just. He tried to focus on the Fatman and could see three and then four of him until he filled the room. Controlling his unawareness he somehow brought himself around, slowly regaining his composure. He sat up and immediately thought his over confidence had bestowed this on himself and decided to proceed with caution from now on with any answers and statements he made.

The interrogator was surprised how quickly this prisoner had adjusted himself after such a blow. Koronin, the giant like ape man who had stealthily moved from the shadows and now stood by the side of Jacob had never failed on his first punch to render the innocent party unconscious. The Fatman hoped that Jacob, and first conclusions were favourable, would put up a better fight than most of the others he had interviewed and interrogated and now looked forward to the contest intensely.

Taking full charge of his faculties and sitting himself composedly in the chair, Jacob focused on the Fatman ensuring there was only one of him and then sensed a second party standing by himself. He turned to his left and was not disappointed to see a monster of bone and human flesh standing like a sentinel no more than a foot alongside himself. He viewed the man next to him and continued his gaze until he reached his face and then lost the top of his head in the darkness of the room. Focussing on his face, the ugliness and abnormality of it shocked Jacob. Small lumps of skin protruded at various stages over his upper head and he resembled something man had made hideously wrong in its construction. He was unnatural and grotesque. Jacob returned his gaze back down the body of the man and stopped at the hands. They were enormously shovel like in appearance and were in direct proportion to the body that carried them. He noticed the spatter of blood on the monster's right hand. Jacob raised his own hand to his head to verify if the blood was his. It was. He also noticed at the same time that his skin had been broken, though not severely. He wondered, 'If this was the first weapon they were to throw at him, what were the others like?' He could still hear breathing coming from the shadows. 'Were they worse? Were they larger and bigger in creation than this beast they had set loose?' he asked himself. He was stirred out of his thoughts by the Fatman speaking once again.

'Well you are more arrogant than the rest Comrade Bryevski. Perhaps Koronin's actions will bring you back into line, even change your mind.' He squealed in a high pitch at Jacob grinning facinorously at the same time. His excitement was escalating.

Mustering himself once again Jacob simply ignored his interrogator's words.

His ignorance was to his detriment and the second punch that fell on him knocked him and the chair to the ground. It was worse, both in force and effect than the first, and there was nothing that Jacob could do to keep his mind blanking into oblivion. He felt himself slipping into unconsciousness as the chair started to topple over. Before he hit the floor he was in another world.

Koronin pulled his arm back and inspected the blood on his hand. Along with another accomplice who had walked out of the shadows of the room, and under the instructions of the Fatman, they picked both Jacob and the chair up of the floor and sat the occupier back on the seat ready to proceed when the victim would regain consciousness.

When Jacob came around the Fatman and his three henchmen, who included the barbarian who had commenced the beating, were talking across the table behind the Fatman's chair. When they noticed his attention, they too assumed their original positions. The interrogator sat down and the first of the three henchmen, Koronin, stood next to Jacob with the other two blending back into the shadows.

Again the Fatman grinned at Jacob and announced, 'A quick recovery Comrade Bryevski. You caught us unawares. Have you changed your mind?'

Jacob once again refused and the procedure was re-enacted. This time the victim took longer to regain consciousness and when he did the fat interrogator had gone from the cell.

Jacob's head throbbed from the pain which had been cruelly and mercilessly inflicted on him and he fought to keep his focus on objects within the room which he could now see due to the single, powerful light having been turned off to be replaced by three individual subdued lights in the cell being switched on. Without warning a vessel full of cold water was thrown into his face. He was both relieved and dreading this action. Relieved because the cold freshness of the water had restored his vision correctly, dread because they had done so only to revitalise him for the next round of pain.

No sooner had the thoughts elapsed from his mind when the torturers again resumed their work. It was as if they were reading Jacob's mind. On this occasion Koronin and a second henchman who was similar in size to his counterpart, though not as ugly, pulled Jacob out of the chair and spread eagled him across the table from the waist up. Whilst Jacob had been unconscious his persecutors had tied rope around his wrists. It was with the residue of this rope that the two largest henchmen were pulling his arms almost out of their sockets. He groaned painfully and fought with little force to restrain their wrenching. However that pain was quickly forgotten as the first of several scores of blows were inflicted on the back of his body, up and down his spine, by the third member of the torture party wielding a thick wooden stick. The action had started with very little build up and it took Jacob by surprise.

The Fatman returned. His facial expression changed to one of dejection as he witnessed what was happening on entering the cell. He noticed the shirt on his victim's back was partly torn and shredded resulting from the blows inflicted on him with the wooden baton. It revealed wields in the skin resembling scaled down tyre markings that a vehicle would make in the dirt. He looked with interest at the blood which ran freely down and over the sides of the captive's body like rivers of red wine when a glass had accidentally been knocked over, and he enthused at those lesions which had already commenced its healing action as the transparent liquid juices of the repairing process could clearly be seen, like some diaphanous substance eating away at the broken and bruised bodily fabric. His attention was drawn to the stick which had changed colour from off white, before the beating, to dark red during the flogging. In some areas it had collected small strips of skin which had fused with the blood resulting in congealed globules of dead matter. Shouting to the three men he screamed his disillusionment at what he had already missed.

'You had instructions to fetch me when he had regained consciousness. I wanted to see all the show not part of it.' This outburst gave some respite to Jacob as the beating momentarily halted.

When the Fatman could see that he had stopped his own pleasure he bellowed to his subordinates, 'Continue! Continue! ProdolzhAhytyie! ProdolzhAhytyie!'

Several minutes later Jacob was unconscious again.

His eyes opened to shining bright light which stood like a beacon in the cell and beat down on his countenance. Although his face took vision toward the floor he could see out of the corner of his eye the obstacle that gave rise to this pharos from the ceiling. He raised himself slowly from the support of the rickety old bed and the pain from the wounds inflicted on his back shot their messages to the brain recalling promptly what had happened before. With unbearable discomfort he returned almost immediately to the original position on his stomach. Laying there mustering sufficient mettle to cross his painful barrier he recollected most of the tortuous moments which he had been through. The complete anthology belonged to his subconscious. Again he tried to get up and again he submitted to the pain. On the third attempt he overcame his personal battle and sat unsteadily on the bunk which held a thin, well worn dirty coloured mattress.

With his hands he tried to reach behind to his back to certify the damage but could get nowhere near his goal and he surmised as to how serious an injury they had inflicted upon him. He leaned forward, the pain reared once more, the slightest movement caused immense agony, and strips of his shirt fell into view around the front of his waist. In his left hand he held one of the pieces as he assumed his upright position and, with the right hand, touched the material which had originally been white in colour but had now become dark red, almost brown. The cloth was, in parts, much thicker in texture and he could see as well as feel slivers of dried skin interwoven with the fabric of his garment. He pondered as to how long he could continue his abstention of signing the pack of lies they had written about him. Despite his pain he still felt strong and his will to fight their fabrications would continue to endure. He lay back on the bed on his stomach and tried to sleep.

Jacob had no idea of the length of time he had been sleeping and the fresh cold water soaked him and awoke him with startling alacrity. He leapt up sitting rigid on the bed only to see the culprit disappearing through the cell door, locking it firmly behind him. The pain from the wounds to his back, which he had temporarily forgot due to his slumber, again returned. This time he felt worse and could feel the spine itself throbbing as a result of the beating. He looked up toward the unrelenting single bulb powering away at its energy source and wondered, not for the first or last occasion, how long he had been sleeping. His tiredness had worn off. He was unsure whether it was because he had been allowed a lengthy rest or whether it was due to the effects of the cold water and decided on the latter. With great pain to his rear torso he turned the mattress onto the side which was dry and laid down to rest.

Again he was awakened by cold fresh water hurled at him from the guard vanishing through the door and throughout the night the same event was to happen whenever Jacob fell asleep. It was useless turning the mattress anymore as it was wet through. He made an effort to stay awake but eventually the calling of slumber, which his senses were desperate for, conquered him, and he fell, inevitably, into that which was unattainable for long periods.

They came for him again, the next morning Jacob thought; in fact it was the late afternoon, the same three monsters that had been in his company on the previous visit. They pulled him up onto his feet without awakening him and he came around as he was being escorted through the door of his cell. The pain in his back gripped him immediately like a vice tightening its jaws on his spine.

Returning him to the same interrogation chamber that he had occupied the day before, the process was repeated again with the Fatman smiling and intermittently asking, 'Are you ready to sign Comrade Bryevski? Tyepyery lee gotov podpisatch Tovarishch?'

The answer was the same from Jacob. 'No! Nyet!'

The punch came first which rendered him unconscious on the first attack and then, after regaining his senses, the beating.

A clean wooden baton was produced from the trouser pocket of the second henchman whose name was never announced. He smiled as he handed the appliance over to the third assistant who had carried out the beating on Jacob previously. Jacob had seen this man before though not as clearly as he viewed him now. His appearance resembled that of an inmate of the prison itself, very thin and gaunt looking. Unlike the prisoners he was fully clothed. His face had the manner of a mean person with two large ball bearing shaped eyes, infected by a hint of crimson colouring, which darted back and forth in the sockets rendering him completely alert and totally sinister at the same time. The cheeks were long drawn out flashes of flesh which together with the tightness of his skin over the rest of his cranium gave him a hungry expression. Hungry for torture Jacob rightly assumed.

He was not as tall in height or as broad shouldered as his two accomplices and for this Jacob was grateful. He considered the possibility of this henchman being of similar size to the first two, and shuddered at the thought. Jacob could not help thinking about the results which could be achieved if the authorities had let someone the size of Koronin loose on the prisoners. As he pondered on those thoughts he was aroused from them by the two largest men heaving him with ease, as if he were a lightweight, out of the chair and over the freshly cleaned table. The pain which he already felt exploded into an excruciatingly agonizing sensation as his healing skin was stretched out of proportion and the bones around his spine, including his ribs, were startlingly severed from their repairing process.

On this occasion he was spread eagled lengthways across the table. His legs were bound together at the ankles and the rope tied to one of the four legs of the table. Koronin and his associate gripped the ropes around the wrists as before and pulled his arms out wide. He was then manoeuvred and pulled diagonally across the table and his shape appeared like that of a human crucifix.

The first blow fell unsuspectingly on the back of his calves. More force was felt on the right leg and as the blows continued to be rained down on his defenceless lower half Jacob endeavoured to raise his left limb above the level of his right, trying to divide equally, the pain and certain, though hopefully reversible, damage to his walking apparatus.

Unlike the previous beating where Jacob had controlled his verbal outlays, when the time had arrived for the assailant to commence his assault on the top half of his legs the utterances which immediately came forth were foul and abusive against the regime and more specifically toward his current torturers. For a very short period this seemed to lessen the pain that he suffered but as the verbal abuses became worse, the persecutor increased his persecution quickly and easily winning the battle over the persecuted. Jacob's shouting quelled, his hope extinguished, his battle for this day lost.

The pain was intense. His lower calf muscles still throbbed from the remorseless beating. Above that pain Jacob could feel the muscles of the rear of his upper thighs at first being bruised, then cut and eventually lacerated. With each single blow the condition of his legs deteriorated, and in apposition the searing, concentrated suffering increased. Ultimately it rendered him unconscious and again he was eventually returned still comatose to his cell.

So the pattern continued over several days. In between sleep he was taken out to be questioned, beaten, and tortured. The questioning became shorter and the beatings and torture seemed to last longer. The reality was the reverse.

In the precious and increasingly shorter saner moments, whilst alone in his cell, he coaxed his mind to accept some degree of normality only to eventually succumb to the power of sleep. Along with the lucid moments came the bleaker stages which increased as the interrogation progressed. Whenever he awoke of his own accord it was always with a fear of the unknown hanging over him. Since the interrogation had begun this fear had steadily multiplied revealing itself suddenly, after one particular bad session, in all its powerful yet vacant force. He cried like a baby, frightening and scaring him like a child afraid of the emptiness which the darkness brings. For Jacob there was no solace from another human. He was alone with his fear and the terror had to be fought by him. Coupled with the phenomenon of the unknown, the deprivation of time gripped him. It was a void to him. All sense of it had been lost and he could vaguely remember being beaten on the first day. The seconds, minutes and hours were important and he had no way of measuring them. He had no idea how long he had been under interrogation. He wanted to know. He wanted to survive this ordeal to be able to tell others. In the absence of time he measured his existence by the amount of sleep he received. Despite his battered body, when he was allowed to rest for any length of time, usually due to an oversight by his guard, it strengthened him and he knew the more he received the better would be his chances. Though even here he knew he was to be cheated by them. Ultimately without the sleep which he was systematically denied, Jacob was slowly but surely losing the battle for control of his faculties. His mind began to play little tricks.

On the seventh day he was awoken and taken to a different part of the prison. In the middle of his new cell, which was colder in temperature, stood a small square chamber with pipes connected to it from the ceiling above? The entrance to this chamber was gained through the side of the cubicle. Made of metal on all sides except the front which was of glass, Jacob was locked in the compartment no more than a metre square in area. For further security the access was also bolted on the outside. From a small hole in the top of the compartment at one end, which one of the pipes was connected to, water was run through until the chamber was partly full. Worse was to come. When the cubicle was half filled, part liquefied and part solidified human excrement was passed through the two other holes from the two remaining pipes above, down on top of the victim. The level of the mixture inside the tank rose until almost full and only then did the waterfall of faeces cease to flow. The stench was overpowering and Jacob vomited violently inside the chamber. At intervals, to keep the mixture cold, the liquid inside was drained off at the bottom of the cell and replaced by fresh cold water and more excrement processed from the top.

Due to the dimensions of the chamber, efficiently calculated by the inventor, Jacob could neither sit nor stand and the only suitable position to adopt, and even this was uncomfortable, was one of kneeling. The kneeling position he selected forced him to use the muscles in his legs which had been severely beaten on previous days. The injuries were far from healed and as he crouched in this awkward position the existing pain to his upper and lower legs intensified. Also, whilst in this position, he had to turn his head over forty five degrees to enable himself to breathe as the water was filled to a level of three inches from the top of the chamber. Several air holes had been punched in the upper section to ensure the prisoner did not die from suffocation.

Jacob was kept in the tank for two hours. The combination of the cold water numbing the body, the pain in his legs becoming increasingly unbearable, the stench from the faeces and the fatigue which finally overcame him as he tried unsuccessfully to keep his circulation going through continually moving, eventually caused him to faint. He sank in a crumpled forlorn mess to the bottom of the tank completely immersed in the produce from the bowels of human life.

The process was repeated the next day. Jacob lasted thirty minutes. Each time he became unconscious he found himself back in his private cell with the lighted beacon for unwanted companionship. The excreta had not been washed from him and the faeces had dried in patches clinging to him like barnacles to a rock face. When he was awakened by the customary water bucket he spat and heaved the taste of defecation from his mouth and throat. The smell, still unbearable, caused him to faint.

His body ached like never before and he felt he was close to death. He prayed for the sleep he wanted and needed so badly and at the last moment when he was about to succumb and call to the guard and his interrogators that he would sign and admit defeat his mind strengthened in resolve and his original thoughts subsided. Somewhere in the hidden depths of his subconscious his whole nature would resurrect itself. He would remember his Polish nationality and what each and every one of the faithful had suffered and would continue to suffer in some form simply not to submit to the lies and misrepresentations of the Russian regime.

The inevitable was finally pronounced on Jacob in the middle of the second week. He remembered his wrists being secured with clean pieces of rope when they had finally cleaned the faeces off him. He had never been completely free of the ropes since almost the beginning of the interrogation and they were now used for his bondage to the chair once again. His trousers were ripped open around the groin area and the electrodes were connected to his testicles. He cried outwardly and unashamedly long before he felt any new pain.

He had been oblivious to his surroundings for the last several days and events which had occurred to him during that time were obscure to him now. He only felt the pain and the agony at the end of each exercise. It was different when the cold pieces of metal were being taped to his genitals. With renewed vigour he came back to life. He knew what this experiment was. He had been told of its effects on many occasions previously and the thought that after this he would be dead filled him with horror. There was no hesitation in his mind. Without question he knew he was going to die. To him there was no other outcome. He did not want to die. If he had to die why could he not spend his last moments with his loved ones? To Jacob the thought of spending the last seconds of his living life with the Russians filled him with revulsion and he continued to cry, not now because of death, but because his desire was to see his family for one last final moment. Whilst he cried the Fatman smiled, and Jacob, amongst his own tears, thought inhumane conceptions for this alleged person who grinned opposite him now.

He gazed upon the Fatman waiting for him to speak or nod or communicate some sign to the henchman behind who was controlling the power unit. If he did signal to throw the switch, Jacob never saw it, and the crackling and buzzing of the power surge coursed through his body. The sudden burst of pain, the like of which he had never experienced before, remained with him until the Fatman ordered its cessation only to utter the familiar words. 'Are you ready to sign Comrade Bryevski? Tyepyery lee gotov podpisatch Tovarishch?'

Smelling the odour of his own burnt skin and looking down to his groin region to verify the black scorch marks on the connected area of his body; no reply came forth from Jacob's mouth. He had long since given up answering the same question which was put to him over and over and both parties knew this lack of communication by him constituted a negative reply for his interrogators.

'Again! Higher! Yeshchaw Raz! Vishye!' squealed the Fatman an octave lower toward one of his henchmen who controlled the power unit, laughing in anticipated expectation at the undoubted pain his victim would suffer as he completed his order.

The pain was excruciating and incomparable with the first surge of power through his testicles and into his body. No human could have survived consciously the eddy of electric capacity which Jacob had experienced on the second circuit. Within moments Jacob had resumed the position which he had entered into more than a dozen times within the last nine days. Unconsciousness came to his rescue.

The Fatman sprang into action. The wide grin automatically wiped from his face. Peering with hate at the assistant who turned the power and back toward the victim, he surmised sternly to himself, 'this should not have happened.' After all they had been through he did not want this man killed. Since the first week of interrogation had been completed the Fatman had viewed this unknown with strange regard. On their first meeting he had assumed that this Pole, an ordinary Pole to him, would last no longer than the normal duration. He was wrong. Since the close of business on the first day and on subsequent days he had slowly come to respect his adversary with increasing admiration. He did not deny his sadistic delights in seeing this stranger slowly perishing under the beatings bestowed upon him by his own command. He would admit to the pleasantries he witnessed on seeing the skin being tarnished and severely broken allowing the inner tissue to flower then wither in exposition. The ecstasy of visualising the blood flowing in abundance and the bones being hammered and crushed with hideous relentlessness were difficult to put into words, but he would admit to enjoying every minute of it. That is what they had trained him for, to enjoy his work. What they had not prepared him for was the one victim in a hundred or more interrogations who stood out from the rest. Those singular men out of a thousand men who would not flinch from their beliefs, from their loves, from their complete resilience of whatever it was they abided by and protected so strongly that they would rather give their lives away rather than submit their cause. Here was one such man. The first he had encountered in his duty. Had they killed him prematurely whilst he as Interrogator had wanted him to survive? He himself was prepared to forge the signature required on the documents in order that he could survive under his charge. What the courts decided elsewhere was not his responsibility.

The Fatman walked slowly toward the henchman who had provided the upturn in power which buzzed through Jacob's body and suddenly lunged at the perpetrator.

'You dogshit.' He spat at him, foaming at the mouth. 'If you have killed him it will be your turn next.' He was pointing violently at the lean henchman and then, to emphasise first his anger then his intent, swivelled on his heels to point at the body in the chair where Jacob was now slumped in.

'Sir, it was you who ordered the power higher,' the torturer protested.

The Fatman turned and aimed a punch up toward the subordinate hitting him fully on the mouth. The action relieved part of his aggression. Blood was spilled immediately as the man's lip crushed against his teeth. The red liquid spouted like a fountain at first, quelling itself before finally running smoothly and controllably from the mouth.

'Do not answer me back. Dogshit!' And to make his position clear, and to vent his remaining anger, he slapped the man several times around the head.

Turning to the other two henchmen, he barked, 'Check him. Make sure he is alive.'

With haste Koronin and his aide bent over Jacob. Neither knew what to do, this part of the interrogation was new to them. Moving his head backward to see if he were still alive and with intentions of reviving him, both men breathed the stronger stench of burnt skin around the body into their lungs and immediately coughed it back. After several long seconds of inspection by the two, Jacob moaned in his oblivion and both men sighed with deep relief.

Disdainfully the Fatman turned back to the bloodied third assistant. 'You're a lucky bastard. Go, get out of my sight.'

The man disappeared from the interrogation room and the two remaining assistants, under the orders of their leader, carried Jacob back to his cell.

Having been returned to his private domain one more time, Jacob, again under the orders of the Fatman, was allowed to sleep longer than usual. Eight hours later and still in a deep sleep he began to dream of past memories. Good times and sad times came to him. Visions of when he was young and the different stages of his youth resurrected themselves. One dream formed more strongly than any other. It was stranger and appeared more vivid than those previous. The last occasion he had been with his mother formed in his mind but he conversed with her under different circumstances. Seeing her again soothed and calmed him.

'I shall return to see you Mama,' he told her.

'Yes, I know Jacob, though you should sign if you want to see me again.'

'Sign, I do not think I should sign Mama.' There was a pause before he spoke again. 'Yes I'll sign if that is what it means.'

Jacob's words which he spoke in his dream were clearly audible.

Each of the guards who kept watch on individual prisoners who were being interrogated was instructed that when victims start to dream and talk aloud in their delusions the main interrogator should be summoned immediately. The guard had followed his orders and sent for the Fatman to come at once.

The persecutor walked along to the cell where Jacob was held. Following in his wake were the three henchmen, the torturer who had increased the voltage, seemingly forgiven. His lip was swollen and he walked sheepishly in his leader's gait.

The Fatman himself bore a sullen expression on his face. Despite the fact that he knew the time was near when his victim was about to finally capitulate, he could not help wonder whether the overloaded charge of electricity had caused this turn of events and prematurely forwarded the submission of his treasured victim.

Bounding along he remarked to his associates, 'Our prized inmate has finally succumbed comrades and our sport for the moment is over. Let us hope that our next victim is as game as this one.'

He reached the cell door and looked in through the opened hatch.

Jacob continued his dream and his own words continued to be broadcast aloud.

The face of his mother had gone to be replaced by that of his old Great Aunt who now spoke to him in his dream.

'Yes Jacob if you want to see the family again you should sign.'

'Yes Aunt, you are correct, I will sign and then I can be with them.'

Totally oblivious to Jacob the cell door was opened and the documents were produced. The Fatman spoke to Jacob for the last time. On this occasion his voice, although still shrill like in tone, was much softer and he spoke in a perfect Polish accent.

'Jacob, Jacob,' he cajoled his victim, enticing him to momentarily give up his slumber. As he spoke he nudged him gently.

'Jacob. Come, wake up. Your family have sent me to you.'

It was several minutes before the Fatman was able to break through the huge barrier of deprived sleep and rest that Jacob's body had been denied for so long. Patiently he kept up his beguiling patter, repeating the important words of family, Aunt and mother. Eventually the final collapse of the victim was underway.

The words, once heard, acted like a trigger and Jacob came around slowly, breaking his slumber only slightly.

'Who is that?' he asked aloud.

'I'm from the family Jacob. They have sent me to help you.' The Fatman continued with his gentle tone. 'Come Jacob then you can return to them.'

His eyes opened marginally. He thought that he recognised the being that sat opposite him, though he could not remember from where or when. His eyes closed and the Fatman who was as patient now as he had been when he first ordered pain on the same human, again spoke.

'Jacob, is your Aunt there?' There was a pause and then Jacob broke the silence.

'Yes, she is with me.' Between the sacred hallowed-ness of sleep and the reality of awaking, Jacob still glimpsed the images of his Aunt in his mind and he smiled outwardly and sporadically as he perceived her floating in and out of his dream, the strength of which depended on whether Jacob was deeper in dormancy or slowly waking from his slumber. She was mouthing something which Jacob could not understand.

'Come Jacob, sign and you will be free.'

The voice did not come from his Aunt. She was still mouthing words but he could not understand her.

Finally after further inveigling by the temporarily reformed interrogator the victim spoke once more.

'Yes, I will sign.' With that statement and thinking he was obeying his Aunt's wishes, he opened his eyes, still not fully conscious, to find a pen being placed in his hand and the documents thrust under his nose.

'Good Jacob. Good.' The persecutor continued to coax and encourage his deceived victim until all the documents had been signed. 'You will be with your family very soon,' he purred smoothly.

With the signature on the forms Jacob fell back on the mattress and resumed his deep slumber from which he had unknowingly been awoken.

'Welcome to the end of your life swine. Dobro pozhalovatch eto konets tvoyay zheezny sveena.' The Fatman's parting words, spoken in his native tongue fell on deaf ears as Jacob curled up on the rickety bed for his long overdue repose, contented to resume his emollient dream.

Jacob finally awoke several days later stiff and very sore as a result of his suffering. The immense pain in his back and ribs continued though it had eased somewhat. His legs which had originally swollen to twice their size, enhancing the passageways of the veins and arteries, had now begun to diminish. The different shades of purples and blues colouring his skin verified the extent of his bruising which caused him severe discomfort. The suffering around his testicles had subsided unlike the dark patch around the area which testified to what had happened. He took solace in the knowledge that his inner body was already beginning to rebuild itself and the all over throbbing pain, although great, was slowly beginning to abate. He noticed, although he could not remember the timing or the actual incident, that he had been returned to his original cell with its fifty other occupants. The filth and stench had not changed and he imagined that it had become worse. 'Probably because he had been in a smell free environment' he explained to himself, 'and no doubt I will adjust to the frowzy odour very soon.'

Looking around he detected that there were new additions amongst the inmates and concluded they were replacements for those prisoners who had either disappeared during his recess from the dungeon, and like himself would return soon, or that as a result of being tortured they, unlike himself, had either died whilst being questioned, been moved to another penal institution or been executed.

One thing troubled Jacob as he found himself returned to his primary cell. In the normal course of events he should only have been returned if he had confessed. He could not remember confessing. He could remember his dreams and talking first with his mother, then his Aunt and a man who he did not recognise, about signing some documents, though that was in his dream. He could remember signing forms but that also was in his dream. As he pondered at length he became unsure as to whether it was a dream or reality. Continuing his thought process and sifting through the last moments he had endured the torture and its aftermath he realised that they had finally reached him whilst he was sleeping. The face he did not recognise and what he thought was part of his dream became clear to him and he knew it was the Fatman. Whilst he was confused and bewildered he had signed what they had wanted him to sign. Jacob cried quietly to himself realising that he had definitely endorsed the deceitful lies they had written. Crestfallen and broken, he cried himself into slumber.

The echoing sound of the key being inserted into the bulky lock and the grating noise of metal on metal as the key is turned, which he had heard on numerous occasions before, signalled to him that the door of the cell was opening. He mustered himself from the drowsy state bordering between sleep and consciousness and his mind became alert to the threat of all possible evils. Were they coming for him because he had concluded incorrectly that he had not confessed after all? His thoughts and emotions suddenly became confused again. If they had returned for him he did not want to go through the pain and suffering only for them to deceive him during his moment of weakness. At the same time he did not want to sign the documents which contained lies about him. Fighting over his torment of whether to submit without having to experience any further torture, his anguish was dispelled for him.

Glancing quickly in their path, two strangers whom he had not seen before had entered the cell. One dressed in civilian clothes approached in his direction. The second, a slightly taller man in uniform walked in the opposite course then retraced his steps and followed the first.

Jacob lowered his head to continue his slumber. He knew instantly by the way the two men walked that they were merely onlookers and it was extremely unlikely that any of the inhabitants of the cell would come to any harm whilst they were present.

No sooner had he looked away when he thought that one of the strangers who had entered the chamber resembled someone he knew. Jacob raised his head again peering at the person in civilian apparel. It was too late the stranger had turned away. Jacob contemplated whether it was who he originally thought and then questioned the accuracy of his eyesight especially after what he had recently been through. With hope of gazing on the visitor's face disappearing fast the individual turned and looked toward him once more. There was no recognition that the person had seen him. Jacob swallowed hard. His eyes watered and tears trickled down over his face. Despite his pain he was placated inwardly and he concentrated on whether and how he should gain the attention of the caller.

Before he could think or do anything the person moved further away to Jacob's left. Jacob's optimism ebbed, rapidly, the further the being moved aside. Then, again, similar to moments before, his expectations were lifted as the person turned and retraced his steps toward him. 'If only he knew what he was doing with my hope,' Jacob thought to himself at the same instance praying that on this occasion he had been seen.

He watched the person walking nearer and lowered his head to visualise his foot movements. Eventually, ever so slowly, they stopped directly in front of him. The visitor in civilian clothes shuffled his feet and then stood perfectly still inches from where Jacob's legs were outstretched. Lying there, totally oppressed, he glanced up at the man and glimpsed his features. The eyes of the two men fixed on each other and never moved.

The uniformed stranger who had originally taken his own route into the cell only to backtrack and follow the civilian now dismissed himself from the midden leaving the first man alone in the chamber.

Looking up at him through glazed chestnut coloured eyes, a second lump of emotion came to Jacob's throat, choking him. His face appeared as fresh as the night they had been taken and Jacob concluded, correctly, that he had found his goal who, in turn, had responded favourably to him. Jacob swallowed his emotion with difficulty as the stranger began to whisper. The whole time they conversed Jacob could not help but wonder how they had found each other amongst all the suffering and madness.

When their conversation ended both men bade a sad farewell. Meeting him had boosted Jacob's resolve at a time when it was at its very lowest. Although he did not look strong inside Jacob felt strong and he knew that the strength of the eagle deep down would rise once again.

CHAPTER 19

The vehicle slowed as it approached the opening gates and then proceeded to pass through the first bastions of defence. There was no need to stop the automobile for clearance; the guards were familiar with the high ranking officer behind the steering wheel. The driver, returning their complement, saluted the soldiers on duty.

Junior Major Andrei Valenti Tscharakova of the NKVD enjoyed the recognition he was automatically advanced from his former guards. Even though more than twelve months had passed since he had left his post in charge of the prison and taken up his new promotion he had frequently visited his previous subordinates when he had returned from his distant duties.

His career had started quietly and violently back in 1920 fighting for the Red Army against the Polish people who wanted to retain their independence and democracy from the reins of budding Leninist ideals. It was as a result of his experiences fighting against the brave, defiant and successful Poles that Andrei's hate for them had been derived.

Deciding quickly that physical combat, armed or unarmed was not for him, two years later, in 1922, he leapt at an opportunity to move into the administration section of the newly formed United Government Political Administration or OGPU, reorganised from the All Russian Extraordinary Commission for Repression of Counter Revolution and Sabotage, the infamous CHEKA.

There he stagnated over the next ten years in low key posts but out of harms way. When Stalin took control after Lenin's death and after grasping and manipulating the power to his own means, in 1934 he further reformed the OGPU into the Peoples Commissariat for Internal Affairs, better known as the NKVD. With this tool at his disposal, Stalin was to wield with unrelenting power its formidable force against both the exceptional, the ordinary and the lower class citizens, in civilian life and at all ranks within the military, who dared, either openly or clandestinely, to act or speak out against him. During the purges of the late thirties Stalin was to imprison millions of fellow Soviets many of whom were eventually executed or to die in abominable conditions in the labour camps.

Andrei Valenti Tscharakova kept a low profile throughout the years of the purges. After a half dozen tiers of officialdom had been liquidated systematically, one after the other with the minimum amount of time, Andrei Valenti, somehow avoiding any accusations of being a saboteur or suchlike, started to move up the ladder of success within the NKVD organisation. With so many levels of authority disposed of, a lower level of talent and supervision was being pushed through to fill the vacant places. A new horizon opened up for him and he quickly made his move for promotion applying for the empty positions of those who had been severely dealt with. Gaining adequate experience, using what limited yet reasonable intelligence he possessed, showing potential whilst introducing new ideas as and when required, hardly any of his own, performing no more than capably in all the positions he held, and progressing well in relation to the other mediocre candidates in similar posts at times showing a ruthlessness beyond his years, he climbed the ladder to promotional success rapidly. At all times he was careful never to befriend a higher official for fear that during further purges any suspicion would fall on him. In this way he avoided the fatality that so many others underwent. After completing a successful spell as head of the prison he was visiting today he was again promoted to his current position of Junior Major, one of the youngest to hold such a rank in the NKVD and which included the deportation of Poles into exile. This gave him powers to travel far and wide.

He had earlier phoned from his apartment to announce that he would be arriving in approximately thirty minutes with a visitor to show around the penal institution. The guards on duty therefore expected his arrival. Although he was still officially off duty until the following Monday, he preferred to wear his on duty uniform to exert his authority should the need arise which was highly unlikely. Sitting next to him was his wife's cousin, Jan Pilochka. This visit, which Jan knew nothing about until twenty minutes before leaving the apartment, was for his benefit. Though Jan had no idea of where they were going.

Accelerating slightly into the courtyard he finally brought the vehicle to a halt in the middle of the enclosure where another soldier was awaiting his arrival. The subordinate opened the driver's door of the vehicle and Andrei alighted. The two men exchanged conversational pleasantries and the senior of the men dismissed the underling giving instructions that he would first take his companion around the premises himself after which he would join the officer in charge of the complex, though not before he had returned his guest to the apartment.

'Come Jan and stay close to me.' Andrei opened the passenger door of the vehicle and beckoned him out.

Jan did as he was told and followed Andrei's instructions. He had not bothered to ask where they were going and wondered about the purpose of the building that his host had now brought him to. In the short time he had known him Jan could not help but question whether or not Andrei was a good Russian. He was obviously of high authority and previously Jan had automatically assumed that most Russians in high authority could be brutal and callous especially to the Poles. This had not been the case so far regarding Andrei. He knew that Jan was a Pole, an alien to his country. Despite that he had helped Jan enormously. The information on the documents he now possessed was genuine except for the origin, stamped and signed with the full authority of the relevant NKVD departments. A new set of clothes had been made available to him and he had been allowed to pick and choose as he wished. The accommodation which Wandeczka had said was available to certain members of the NKVD would be made available to him in less than two weeks. All this had been provided by Andrei. In addition to these favours he had formed a friendship, or so he thought, with the Russian Junior Major, 'completely against what I have heard from my countrymen,' Jan told himself. 'The only other alternative for performing these favours was that Wandeczka had a strong hold on him.' Jan knew it was early days and he wondered whether the hospitality from Andrei would continue and if so, for how long. He knew that he need fear no misconceptions from Wandeczka.

The large oak door they entered through into the building stood at the northern end of the premises. It led onto a large concrete platform to the left of which could be found a flight of concrete steps which led down below ground level. Andrei, followed closely by Jan, descended the stairs and the clattering of his boots on the stony concrete announced his visitation to anyone below.

When they reached the lower level the distinct smell which was recognisable on entering the building intensified. It had no effect on Andrei as he had long become accustomed to the odour. At first Jan held his breath for longer periods then reluctantly gave in to the stench, breathing without trying to smell at the same time.

The guards again acknowledged the officer and with a flick of the senior man's hand and without uttering one word, the guard dutifully opened the rolled iron barred gate. The two visitors stepped inside. The gate clanged shut behind them and they commenced their walk into the catacombs of the Lefortovo prison.

Both men walked on the uneven ashen coloured surface for several yards before Jan's eyes became adjusted to the dim light. The smell again seemed to increase in strength the further they progressed and his lungs already ached for the fresh air which they had abandoned outside. He said nothing but he now knew the purpose of the building and searched himself for the reason why Andrei had brought him to such a place.

Continuing to breathe the contaminated air which nurtured inside the complex, Jan suddenly realised where he had experienced the fetid odours before though not in such abundance and strength as they now emerged. The past memories of the people who produced the sweat, the urine, the death and the animalistic smells of the carriages together with the concentrated stronger stench within the building made him heave inwardly. He kept his suffering from Andrei and fought the swell inside of him.

Still with the odours threatening to overpower him he followed the path that Andrei walked. Looking at the man, ahead of him, who had brought him to this degradation, still he could not fathom out why he had done so. 'Perhaps he truly does hate me along with all the Polish people' he told himself, attempting to rationale the reason for them being here. Whilst Jan began to seriously question his earlier thoughts about his host Andrei stopped and crossed to the left hand side of the corridor. He pulled back the shutter on the closed door he now stood in front of and looked in. He turned to Jan and stated firmly almost ordering his companion. 'Look!'

Jan walked forward trembling at what he might see; hoping it was not what he envisaged it would be. He concealed his emotions from Andrei, concluding unequivocally that the person his cousin was married to was definitely a bastard and belonged to the devil himself.

Reaching the shutter, Andrei stepped aside as Jan peered through. Jan's thoughts were piteous and his facial movements were one of disgust. The internal disturbance he had moments earlier controlled welled inside him again. He almost vomited through the opening in the door. Fortunately, and using all his willpower, he again stemmed the tide.

Andrei watched his guest intently and enjoyed witnessing the heaving performance his cousin in law had just been through.

The mass of bodies which at first appeared intertwined, some half naked, lay stretched and crouched, languid and limp on the floor. Sores and lesions were detectable on those bodies he could see near to his view. They were crammed into a cell which should have occupied no more than perhaps twenty prisoners. There were at least fifty in the cell that Jan now perceived. In one corner he noticed a bucket had been placed for urinating. It was full and overflowed onto the floor into and up against the bodies which lay in close proximity to it. No windows were detectable and no fresh air flowed through the cesspit. The walls were partly covered in what appeared to be black wallpaper which seemed to move, before Jan realised that the areas were alive with bugs and lice. The heat which emanated from within the hovel was generated from the bodies themselves and was similar to that of a warm fire.

He turned away only to face Andrei. Jan still fought with all his willpower the feelings which continued to curdle inside him and which yearned to be free from his body. He wanted to shout his protests at the indecency and disgrace of it all, though he did not want to show his weakness to the Russian who now faced him. To do so, unknowingly to Jan, would have succumbed to Andrei's deepest wishes.

'Would you like to go in and take a closer look?' Andrei asked.

Without waiting for the answer the officer looked back down the corridor and called the guard. The subordinate marched quickly along the passage to where the two men stood, obeying the instructions and opening the locked door. It swung open freely and Andrei walked inside beckoning Jan after him.

Jan was not looking forward to this experience.

Inside, the cell and its contents looked even worse and the intensifying strength of the many different foul odours together with the heat, almost overpowered Jan. Faintness attacked him but he conquered the assault. There was no quick relief available to him. He would have to battle it out.

Andrei motioned to the right of the cell and Jan took the opposite direction. Quickly Andrei backtracked. Above everything he wanted to see more physical evidence of the revulsion Jan felt at what he now looked upon and which he had already verified outside moments earlier. With his warped sense of satisfaction it provided Andrei with a warm feeling of power, of victory over a lesser mortal. Viewing Jan now, only the look of amazement could be seen on his visage, no physical revulsion was apparent. Andrei's satisfaction was not fulfilled.

What Andrei had thought was the look of amazement on Jan's face was true, though it was not amazement as a result of the wretchedness in the midden, that had disappeared when he had cast his eyes, several moments earlier, on the person whom he now looked down upon and who he had first espied, despite his horrific condition, seconds after entering the cell. Jan was speechless and he did not know what to do. He wanted Andrei out of the way and as if someone had heard his thoughts and answered them, Andrei having been discontented with the appearance on Jan's face, turned to exit from the chamber.

'I shall wait outside for you Jan.'

Jan, still shocked, immediately bent over the body of his friend who had looked up and recognised him. His friend's face was stained as the tears which flowed partly cleansed the dirt from his skin.

'Jacob what have they done to you? How did you get here?' he whispered, automatically communicating in his native tongue. Then he started to whimper to the friend he loved but could not help.

Jacob put a swollen finger to his bruised and cracked lips beckoning Jan to remain silent. Waving his swollen hand, Jacob gestured to his friend to lower himself to his level. After wiping his tears he returned his paw to its original comfortable resting position. Jan did as summoned.

Kneeling close to his friend Jan gathered himself and checked his whimpering. 'Now is not the time to be weak,' he reaffirmed. Concernedly, he whispered, 'What can I do to help?'

Waiting for Jacob to speak he could not help but notice the bruising around his forehead and on the lower and upper cheeks of his face. He continued the inspection of his friend and became even more saddened at what he witnessed. His arms like his face were also bruised and on his wrists deep red imprints of where a rope had obviously been tied too tightly around the skin were prominent. All the fingers on both his hands were black with bruising as well as dirt. His shirt was ripped and torn and had changed to a brown colour. His trousers were open at his genitals to reveal, underneath, what looked like a separate black patch covering the area. At first Jan thought it was Jacob's underpants, though quickly realised it was bare skin. Without thinking he asked what had caused the discolouration knowing before the reply came that it would be something horrific. He wished that he hadn't asked the question.

'Electrocution,' Jacob answered simply and another tear came to his eyes.

Jan bit his tongue and swallowed hard pretending not to hear the reply but the image which had instantly formed in his mind of a body in contortion was difficult to erase. To rid himself of the picture he continued his observation of the wrecked human in front of him and now noted he legs which were inflamed to an abnormal size and the visible bruising resembled colours of the rainbow. Wherever Jan looked on Jacob's bare body there was injury of some sort. He motioned to help him sit up though his friend refuted his succour.

'I have found this position to be the most comfortable and would prefer to remain like so. Any movement increases the pain.'

Again Jan asked, 'What have they done to you?' and again he regretted asking.

'They have finished with me now Jan. Do not worry anymore, they have what they want. Now hopefully I can heal myself.' Jacob coughed weakly to clear his throat. His tears had stopped and he continued. 'There is too much to explain and not enough time.' Jacob spoke in a soft whisper which cracked and broke like that of a radio operator fighting with interference. 'Have you any money? With that I can buy time and a little hope.'

Wandeczka had given Jan money several weeks ago. He rifled his pockets unable to find it at first. Searching energetically he kept looking toward the door. Eventually on the second inspection he found what he was searching for and handed the notes to Jacob.

'This is all I have.'

'Insert it in the gap between the stones in the wall behind me. Make sure no one is looking.' Jacob pointed to the spot without moving from his position. 'Thank you my friend.'

Jan, ensuring nobody was peering, nestled the notes in a nook in the wall, only after he had cleared the bugs and lice out of their home to make way for the money.

'Jan what are you doing, do you want to join them?' Andrei suddenly asked bellowing back into the cell at the same time laughing with the soldier who had opened the door and whom he was now conversing with outside.

'Coming.' Jan replied, trying to answer calmly, hiding his alarm and surprise at being called by Andrei.

'Go! Go!' Jacob pleaded still whispering, 'or they'll suspect something.'

'I will try to return again.'

'No, no, never do that Jan, promise you will not return, promise.'

Jan promised.

'Now go.'

He kissed his friend on the forehead and he immediately tasted that which he had only been able to smell until now. As a sign of their friendship, and in great pain, Jacob clenched his hand to Jan's arm before finally parting. The small gesture was enough for both men to recognise the bond between one another.

Fighting the tears, Jan arose and walked out of the cell without glancing back.

Once outside in the corridor Jan looked toward his escort. Detecting a sneering smile on his face he felt the emotion of sadness held for Jacob being replaced by hate for the Russian soldiers and especially for this man who had helped him, but who, like other Russian officials, enjoyed the immense suffering created by them to be inflicted on the Polish people. He vowed, as he stared toward what had now become his enemy, that one day he would avenge his countrymen.

'Let us move on Jan, there is more to see.' Andrei announced calmly and satisfactorily and then dismissed the guard as he locked the door.

The deeper they progressed into the pithole of death the more intensified became the stench. Again Andrei turned to one of the doors that hid an incredible heap of desecration of human life and pulling back the shutter beckoned Jan to take another look.

Jan turned away at first then retraced his movements. 'Yes Andrei you bastard,' he thought to himself, 'I will look on anything you wish and from now on you will see no emotion from me.' It was as if the meeting with Jacob had some positive reaction on him. Jan felt stronger and more certain about what had to be done if the opportunity arose. He stared Andrei fully in the face as he passed his escort to look once more inside the chamber.

Peering through, he was confronted by the same situation as he had seen in the previous cell. On this occasion the chamber had fewer inmates. None of whom appeared to be moving. Jan surmised they were already dead. He scrutinised one body for a longer period to ensure his thoughts were not correct. Eventually the body moved by raising its right arm as if acknowledging Jan's concern. Satisfied, though hopelessly inadequate to help him, Jan closed the shutter and turned to continue his visitation.

Both men came to the end of the long corridor before stepping through the locked gates at the opposite end to where they had entered. The guard saluted both and closed the barred gate behind them. Turning to ascend the steps in the corner of the small area they now found themselves in, Jan was suddenly startled by a horrendous violent scream which echoed down the corridor that stood adjacent to the flight of stairs. He looked at Andrei who was unaffected by the sound and who had stopped because his guest had done so. Andrei looked down the corridor then turned to Jan and stated in a prosaic, unsympathetic voice, 'Oh yes, I had forgotten about them.'

There was a pause while Andrei pondered on his next move, toying with the idea of wanting to show Jan more suffering but remembering that he also wanted to visit his colleague who had replaced him as warder of the prison. Moving away from Jan and quickly ascending the steps he retorted, 'Come, you have seen enough.'

Jan swallowed and sighed deeply with relief, ensuring first that Andrei did not see. He surmised, judging by the sounds, that what he had already seen was nothing compared to the horrific cries emanating from the second corridor and gratefully acknowledged the fact that he would not be pursuing that route. An afterthought came to him that he had already seen the results of the screams on Jacob. Unhesitatingly he followed Andrei up the steps. As before, the boots echoed their sound on the concrete stairs, this time they notified his departure.

Out in the courtyard, while Andrei was his normal unemotional self, Jan breathed deeply the air which had been starved to the prisoners below. He remembered his days whilst travelling on the trains and thought of the sights he had seen underneath the very ground which he now stood on. Both were ghastly, both were incomprehensible, though the latter was abhorrent. He walked slowly toward the vehicle that Andrei had already reached and was climbing into. Whilst he walked he continued to breathe deeply, cleaning his lungs. 'Purging the mind of the stench and filth and degradation I've witnessed will be possible temporarily,' he told himself. He knew he could never forget permanently.

Jan sat in the front seat and looked toward Andrei who fired the ignition of the automobile bringing it to life. He appeared to be simpering as he stared out of the windscreen ready to pull off. Before doing so he turned to face Jan. The smile had subsided to be replaced by eyes which were liquefied and glowering like the deepest flames in the nucleus of a fire. To Jan he appeared demented. At first he spoke calmly, lucidly and without compassion.

'You could quite easily end up in one of those cells. Never step out of line whilst you are my guest in my country.' He stated quietly but firmly, emphasising the pronoun.

Jan noticed that his nostrils began to flare as he continued to speak and he was beginning to spit the words out of his mouth toward him. 'This is how the devil himself would speak' he thought.

'Stay away from Wandeczka as much as possible and never contaminate her with your filth. When you move to your own apartment I expect you to see less of her. Do you understand?'

Jan understood and nodded. Deep down, for the first time in his life, atavistic tendencies conjured inside him. He wanted to fight. He wanted to physically harm the man next to him even to kill him, anywhere and by any means, but he knew to do so under the present circumstances would be utterly futile. If he tried and failed, Andrei could quickly and easily have him disposed of without further worry. The only person who would be concerned and who would ask questions would be Wandeczka and Andrei would undoubtedly lie to her as to his whereabouts.

Andrei turned to look out through the windscreen and freeing the handbrake he guided the car out of the courtyard through the impending gates and into the main street.

Jan promised himself that he would get even with this man one day. He would wait patiently for that day to arrive.

For Jan the atmosphere was tense in the vehicle on the journey home. Neither of them spoke and Jan was certainly not in the mood to talk to his enemy anymore. He was grateful for this peace as his mind was racing with ideas.

'Come in, come in, Major,' Captain Sergei Sulin Shorkov who had taken command of the prison after Andrei's promotion welcomed his senior officer with enthusiasm as he had done so when he had worked directly for the man.

It was Andrei who had taken him under his wing and nurtured him over the last two years within the NKVD. 'Always sensible to make a few friends in the lower ranks when on the way up the promotional ladder, in the event that one may need them on the way down,' Andrei had decided when he semi adopted Comrade Shorkov from his first day of service in the Regime. Andrei adopted this attitude with those lower in rank even though he was against his superiors becoming too friendly with himself.

The relationship had flowered from day one. Not so much with trust, at least not in the early stages due to the continuance of the purges, but more with a quiet respect on both sides. When the time had arrived for Andrei to move on to his next promotion it was the name of Sergei Sulin Shorkov he had mentioned to his superiors who should be the one to take up the office from him.

Explaining to his principals that since his virtual forced arrival in the NKVD a little over two years ago, due to his cold blooded killing of a soldier who would not carry out an order to execute one of the peasants at a dispute in Georgia where he was posted at that time, Sergei had continued to work hard and conscientiously for both the NKVD and the ideals of Communism. Under Andrei's guidance he had proved a useful addition to the department. Several days later when the announcement was made, Andrei's satisfaction was complete. His superior officers had duly obliged and promoted Comrade Shorkov.

Due to the purges there were very few men available with suitable capabilities for the position anyway, and the Superiors, to their pleasure had found no cause for regrets so far. The continuity of the changeover was maintained with very little disruption experienced while the new man settled into the job, again proving Andrei to be correct, earning himself as well as Sergei further approval from their Commanding Officers.

'Sit down Andrei. Drink?' The formalities of rank between the two officers had been dispensed with now that the door of Sergei's office had been closed making it a safe haven from both prying ears and eyes. The two men conversed using their Christian names. 'What an unexpected pleasure.' Sergei continued and meant what he said.

Without waiting for both the reply or enquiring as to his preference, Sergei motioned toward the second of his filing cabinets which stood behind his desk in the far corner. The third and bottom drawer of the cabinet doubled as a drinks closet. He poured the Russian vodka from a Polish lead crystal decanter he had extracted and which had been given to him by a fellow colleague of his acquaintance who had visited the country. He knew Andrei was now in charge of Polish deportations and told him the origin of the vessel.

'What do you think? All the way from Poland. Taken from one of the elite houses in that country.'

Andrei arose from the leather backed chair in which he had been comfortably sitting and came around to the cabinet to inspect the receptacle from which Sergei poured the drinks. On his way he noticed the paperwork neatly placed on his protege's desk. Taking the decanter from Sergei he admired the exemplary workmanship and smiled at his colleague.

'They have many objects of beauty and somehow those objects end up with those who truly deserve them.' His smile turned to a laughter which was immediately reciprocated by Sergei. It was this type of humour which had fuelled their friendship, from one of purely respect, several weeks after their introduction. Neither liked the Polish people, or any foreigners for that matter, and both joked about the lack of well being against their foes whenever possible. The two men clasped each of their glasses, again lead crystal and part of the decanter set, and cheered one another and the Soviet Union.

'Interesting work?' Andrei enquired as he motioned to return to his commodious armchair nonchalantly perusing Sergei's documentation on the way and suddenly becoming interested in the particular heading of the page uppermost in the open folder which faced him.

'DEPORTATIONS FROM PINSK.' It read. Below the title was a list of names commencing with the surname, followed by the Christian names and any title that the person held. Usually a rank denoting that the individual was or had been in the military. What Andrei had first looked at tentatively quickly turned to a scrutiny before he realised that this information was not directly his concern anymore. Looking somewhat sheepishly toward Sergei he enquired whether the latter had any objections to his further perusal.

'Do you mind if I take a look?'

'Help yourself.' Sergei granted freely whilst he passed Andrei and sat in the second of two easy chairs.

Andrei need not have concerned himself and needed no more persuasion. He continued his examination of the list and noticed the pencilled marks against some of the men on the register.

'The pencil notations?' he queried. 'That denotes you have the men in the prison, yes?'

'Either in this prison or those that are scattered in and around Moscow,' Sergei replied.

'Those in the same prison, are they held together in the same cell?' Andrei was ignorant of the fact that this information was not of his delegation and was oblivious that his questioning began to increase rapidly like some teacher orally testing his pupil on a particular subject.

'No specific plan is used to keep them separate until they are interrogated.' Sergei arose and came around the desk to stand next to Andrei.

'Are these separated?'

Noticing Andrei's index finger pointing to that of the same surname he replied. 'Those men are father and son. They have been separated.'

Andrei gazed on the name Bryevski, followed by the Christian names, Pavel and Jacob.

'They have been tortured?' Andrei enquired running his finger up and down the list of names.

'Yes, if not all on the list, certainly the majority.'

'All these men have had military experience with the Polish Army at some stage in their lives?'

'Yes, that is correct.'

'What is next for them?'

'You know the usual. Some may go before the tribunal, others will not. Then, depending on the crime, either movement to another penal system or death. Some may even remain here. At the moment the prisons are filling too quickly and the interrogations and trials can't keep pace. Already many prisoners have remained here longer than is usual.'

'In a way, to increase their suffering, that is good news.' A wickedness appeared in Andrei's eyes. 'Keeping them here in suspense again adds to their suffering. It's a shame that they have to come before the troika. Then their destiny will be known to them.'

Andrei grinned, a wide facinorous smile, and then laughed aloud. Sergei immediately engaged his mind into the funny though warped side of the reasoning and joined in the strange merriment.

Amidst their mirth Andrei added, 'they will probably die in the cells eventually.' Both men continued their chortling.

Scrutinising the list further, Andrei then became serious as he noticed a name on the register which rang a bell deep in his mind though his powers of recall had eluded him.

'The name halfway down the list. There's nothing noted against him? Do you know why?' Andrei asked resuming his earlier determined approach.

'We heard that he had escaped from one of the trains that he was held on.'

Swallowing the remainder of his vodka and gesturing the empty glass in front of Sergei, the subordinate duly obliged, quickly finishing his own potion before crossing to the decanter and pouring a second measure into each of the glasses.

'I remember the incident,' Andrei stated, his memory had returned.

'You do?' asked Sergei somewhat surprised at first, then realising that Andrei was responsible for the names drafted for deportation from the region of Poland they were discussing and assumed that he would or should know about such matters.

'Yes. This man and another of his colleagues escaped. The dogs chased them, killed one of them and the soldiers who followed, also giving chase swore that they had killed the second man. When they returned a little later to clear the bodies only the body which had been torn by the dogs remained. There was no trace of the other supposed corpse. The two soldiers were reprimanded and transferred elsewhere.'

'There are several other Poles who have eluded us similar to this Sagajlo character.' Sergei raised his voice becoming concerned.

'Those few Poles,' Andrei reiterated Sergei's words deliberately contradicting his estimate. He did not see the problem as being as large as Sergei had voiced, 'are very fortunate people Sergei. No more than very fortunate.' He emphasised his point. 'I prefer to record this example,' indicating once again to the name on the list, 'as a blunder by one or two of our own less fortunate soldiers. We will catch up with them sooner or later, you will see.'

Sergei said nothing in reply, simply hoping that Andrei would be proved right. He handed one of the refilled glasses to his superior and both men drank a toast, on this occasion, to the NKVD and the sanity it held for the Soviet Union and its people.

After they had conversed further on both pleasure and business matters Andrei left the office of Captain Sergei Sulin Shorkov. Checking the outer room to confirm that his visitor had departed, the latter closed his office door and proceeded to open the third and bottom drawer of another cabinet. It contained special documents he had formulated himself on persons who had managed to repeatedly and successfully evade the clutches of the Russian NKVD even if they, at some stage, had been caught.

Reading the more detailed notes on a one Pieter Sagajlo and his escape from the Katyn, to be followed several months later by a second escape from the area around Pinsk, Sergei surmised to himself that a man of this calibre would indeed be a difficult target to pin down and once captured should immediately be executed. 'Let us hope Junior Major that you are correct.' He spoke aloud to himself closing the individual file, returning the folder to the bottom drawer and relocking the cabinet.

Descending the stairway to return to his vehicle in the courtyard, Andrei Valenti Tscharakova was both pleased and slightly disgruntled at what he had not perceived on the list. Pleased that all his devious and crooked work in drawing up and forging new lists without the one single name had worked perfectly, and not even Sergei Sulin Shorkov had detected anything. Andrei concerned himself as to whether, if in the same position, he would have noticed. Leaving the latter question unanswered and preferring to think that he would have spotted the missing name, he returned to his immediate mixed feelings and the drawback to the whole episode. The underlying fact that he had saved one Pole from what he truly deserved. 'Why did I have to marry a woman who is half Polish?' he asked himself. But he knew why. 'Fear not Jan Pilochka, Wandeczka keeps you alive. Should anything happen to her then your fate will surely be sealed, by myself personally.' The harbourer consoled his misgivings with that solemn promise to himself.

CHAPTER 20

Recovering slowly from his terrible wounds Jacob decided against approaching the guard immediately about providing additional food for himself and his inmates until he was both physically and mentally stronger. Whichever guard he contacted, Jacob knew, for whatever reason, that when money was involved, either of them would inflict his own brand of brutality on him by kicking or beating him. This was not a possibility but a certainty as far as Jacob was concerned. He knew it would happen and the results of such brutality could succeed in deterring his own recovery process beyond all boundaries of repair.

It had been well over a week after Jan had left the money before Jacob summoned the guard over to him. Waiting for him to walk within his confine and not wanting the other inmates to know what was being said through fear of being overheard and then denounced by a fellow inmate to the authorities; he called quietly to the soldier as he approached nearby. Speaking in Polish he called him the filthiest names he could muster, which gave him a bizarre though understandable sense of satisfaction.

'Scum. Scum. Szumowiny. Szumowiny.' He whispered, 'You who have no father,' he continued, and then a little louder, 'Bastard, Bekart.' The whispering of words in the cell which was usually so quiet, except for the groaning of those detainees who were savagely beaten, was sifted out by the soldier who looked toward Jacob's direction. Immediately he picked out with ease the one that spoke amongst the remainder of his whining companions.

Continuing to speak in Polish Jacob made eye to eye contact with the soldier as the latter kneeled to view the prisoner more closely. 'You have arrived quickly szumowiny. Would you like to earn money to buy things for the whore you married?'

The soldier looked at him with a blank expression ignorant of the insults being directed at him. Finally, laughing inwardly, Jacob spoke in the Russian language, the only dialect the soldier understood.

'I have money to exchange for food, money that you can spend on your wh…,' Jacob remembered at the last moment that now he was speaking in Russian and quickly repeated his sentence changing his last word from 'whore' to 'woman.' His mind had not fully recovered its quick perception and he reminded himself to be aware of this. Jacob held the rouble notes up to the soldier's face which immediately attained an expression of disbelief.

'Where did you get this?' he enquired, shocked that a prisoner had somehow managed to acquire the money and afraid that he would be blamed for firstly not finding the currency on the prisoner and secondly for not confiscating it.

'I will never relate the source of my good fortune.'

The soldier quickly became angry and grabbed Jacob around the back of the neck, pulling him forward. Pain was immediately felt, though nothing to what he had previously encountered.

'Where? Where did the money come from?' His whispering stopped and he started to shout at his prisoner. Suddenly afraid for himself that someone would overhear, he ceased his bellowing as quickly as it began. Then without warning, in anger and frustration at not being answered, with his free hand he punched Jacob in the face. Simultaneously the grip around his neck was sharply withdrawn and Jacob's head rocked backward, banging on the wall behind. The soldier laughed. Jacob laughed.

'You will never know my source.' He emphasised decisively. 'Take the money and say nothing.' He placed the notes in the top pocket of the sentry's uniform. The soldier looked at him undecidedly. If he were caught he would be brutally punished. He tried again to extract the information from the prisoner.

'Where did you get the money?' Again he grabbed Jacob, this time by the throat not giving him the chance to speak. Tightening his grip on the captive, Jacob did not fight back; he was not strong enough to do so. He looked the soldier fully in the eyes and nodded his head from side to side, mouthing the words, 'I will never tell.'

The soldier loosened his grip and Jacob whispered again, adamantly.

'You will never hear from me where the money has come from. Never. Bekart. Bastard.' The last word insulted at the soldier was uttered again in Polish.

'I have been tortured by those which make your efforts seem like that of a young boy. I will never tell. Do you want the money? Arsehole.' Jacob spoke in Russian and each time he finished a sentence, the last obscene word was uttered in Polish which the soldier did not understand.

'If you will not take the money I'm sure your colleague will. Shithouse.'

The soldier began to think about what the prisoner had said. Kurilov, the greedy swine, who guarded the cells with him, would surely take the money. He knew that for sure and without further hesitation he had made up his mind.

'Yes, I will do it. What do you want?'

'Food. Food for us all.'

'There are over fifty men in here.'

'I know. Either all of us receive something or nobody receives anything including you.' and he pointed to the notes still visible in the soldiers top pocket to enhance his point.

'It will cost.' The idea of suddenly receiving money excited him as he thought of what he could buy for his woman with it. 'Fifty roubles.' he whispered at Jacob, surmising that he could name his own price.

Jacob laughed. 'Never. Ten at the most and then you are robbing me.'

'I will get nothing for that outside.' The guard protested, the glint of greed in his eyes slowly dying as a result of the prisoner now bartering with him.

'Do not lie to me. You will take the rubbish from the streets before you pay for what we will receive from you. I have no doubt that the only service I will be paying for is that of the nuisance of getting the food into us. You low form of scum.' Again Jacob returned to the profanities which he had purposefully eluded and had now commenced once again, still careful to utter the obscenities at the end of the sentence only in Polish.

Jacob peered into his eyes awaiting the tell tale signs of guilt and confirmed his suspicions. The Russian soldier turned away pretending to look at the inmates who had mustered in the corner. Reverting back toward Jacob he fired one last price for the food.

'Twenty roubles and that is my final offer.'

'Agreed,' Jacob announced, 'but for twenty roubles you must find out where Pavel Bryevski is and whether he is alive and well?'

The soldier pondered. Before he could speak, Jacob continued.

'Without the information on Pavel Bryevski, the deal is off. No information, no food. Do you understand?'

The soldier understood. He could see the clothes he had visualised on his woman disappearing from his thoughts and without quibbling he agreed the extra condition. 'This Pole was a hard man to bargain with,' he concluded miserably.

'To prove that you have spoken with the correct person you must ask him the name of his eldest daughter. If that name is accurate, then you get the money. Is that clear?' Again the guard nodded his head.

'Good. Good,' Jacob announced, 'you have ten roubles,' he pointed to the money in the soldier's pocket, 'the balance will be given to you when you deliver the food with the information and your whore will be fully clothed unlike the guttersnipe that she surely is.'

The guard arose and turned to exit from the cell. As he locked the door on the inmates he could not understand why the Pole, at the end of his sentences, had lapsed into words of another language.

The guard kicked Jacob awake. A firm punt hard enough to disturb the prisoner on the first attempt. Jacob came alive to the pain and looked up to visualise the soldier who was carrying a dirty sack over his shoulder. The deliverer kneeled down and bent over his special prisoner at the same time opening the sack for him to look inside. The pain faded and taking a portion of the bread out of the sack Jacob was surprised to find that it was more edible than that which they usually received. He dug deep into the bag to confirm that the remainder was similar. It was and Jacob was pleased with the results. He leaned forward and before finishing his movement toward his shoe he relaxed to his original position.

'Pavel Bryevski. What is the name of his eldest daughter?' To Jacob this was the most important part of the bargain.

The guard replied and the smile on Jacob's face told him that he had completed the task successfully.

'And what of Pavel Bryevski?'

'He is well. Beaten but recovering.'

The words of his chronicler both strengthened and hurt Jacob. To think that an elderly man had been beaten into submission was despicable to him.

'Will he recover?' Jacob asked with desperation.

'He is in a better state than you. If you will recover, he certainly will,' replied the guard.

'How do I know you are not lying to me?'

'You do not know. But when he came to the door of the cell after I called him he told me the names of the whole of your family.' The soldier repeated the epithets and also mentioned that Pavel walked in a much better condition than Jacob did so.

Jacob was pleased. Although he had no idea how he could prove if the soldier were lying or telling the truth, he felt that what he had been told regarding his brothers and sisters names was good enough from a guard whose only interest was that of acquiring more money. Jacob also felt that a guard of his low intelligence would be clueless as to finding the sort of information that he had asked of him and also afraid that either his equals or his superiors would find out. Therefore his only source would be to actually seek out the person himself. He pulled his leg toward him and searched in the shoe under his foot for the remaining ten roubles. Extracting them he handed the money to the soldier who snatched the bounty from Jacob and counted it quickly, making sure nobody was looking.

'Perhaps I will need food again. Do I ask you or your colleague on the next occasion?' Jacob enquired knowing the answer before the reply.

The soldier stared at him, grabbed him by the throat and gestured, in words as well as deeds, that he was the only person to confront in future.

Jacob had angered him too much and now understood his limits. When the guard left, Jacob arose with difficulty and proceeded to distribute the food, occasionally making the comical excuse that the Russians had noticed the diet for the men was not as good as the hotels in Moscow and at long last they had decided to do something about the situation.

The hot summer was drawing to a close and the autumn conditions were beckoning their existence to come alive. Only once more that year would Vladimir spy on the woman who had taken such a high priority amongst the other duties he performed as a representative of the NKVD in the area. To enable him to experience, even though it was only by sight, once again the perfect femininity of this deity amongst women, Vladimir had positioned one of two old men he personally employed in the village at a crucial vantage point, discreetly out of sight, overlooking the incline of her path to her hideaway. He was there for one purpose only, to communicate to Vladimir her impending visitation to the area where she bathed.

He had waited patiently day in day out and the wait had been an extensive one raising serious doubts in his mind as to whether she would eventually revisit. 'What if she had found a new bathing area?' 'Perhaps I should take further steps to locate the new area?' he wondered.

Then one morning, just when he had given up all hope, one of the old men came scurrying to his shelter. Knocking faintly on the door, Vladimir, on answering the call did not wait for the scout to finish his news. He rewarded the carrier of good tidings, as both parties had earlier agreed, and immediately followed in pursuit.

He knew the direction well. Since that first encounter he had walked to the area on many occasions hoping that he would chance upon a meeting with her once more. He had seen her in the village several times and he knew that she had also seen him. Whilst she was around he acted with perfect manners, totally opposite to his normal character. When she was gone he would return to his normal ways. To her he was lenient, whilst with others he was hard, demanding and sometimes cruel. He had noticed how on the first day on arriving at the village she had looked at him with discomfort and apprehension eventually turning her gaze from him. Above everything he wanted to change her ideas toward him and to help the situation he instructed his subordinates to allow her to carry out the manageable tasks. In that way she would receive the full food quota, though still below normal adequacies for an adult.

With haste in his manner he hurried along the path to his long awaited second encounter with the vision he had looked upon once in reality, countless times in his slumber and even more in his imagination. Quickening his pace the nearer he approached, not wanting to miss anything which she performed, he perspired as never before and his heart beat with irregular rhythm. 'Slow down Vladimir,' he told himself, 'or you will never reach your goal.' His pace eased ephemerally only to ignore his original thoughts as he surmised what delights of the flesh may be lost to him.

Arriving at the opening with ungainly haste for a man of his size, he stumbled quietly across the divide. He tripped once and nearly fell headlong over the bank as a result of his still uncoordinated and rapid movement, before taking up his position in the bushes where he had last perused her.

To his immeasurable delight, and thanking the heavens, which, being an atheist was against his thoughts, she had scarcely started her performance. Pulling a red blouse away from her body she repeated the whole routine which she had undertaken before when Vladimir spied her including the survey in the middle of her act to see if anyone were looking.

The onlooker was ecstatic. Her actions had remained in his mind from the very first occasion she had performed them and he had seen her enact them in his brain over and over again. Now he was watching the performance live once more. Breathless, simply because he had witnessed what to him was a fulfilling and sensuous act, he gathered his senses and quickly decided how to make contact with her once more.

The approach was the same. On this occasion he waited until she climbed the bank and purposefully clashed with her as she came over the top of the slope. Apologising profusely he caught her before she tumbled back down the incline out of balance. Steadying herself as a result of his help and support, he immediately retracted his hands which had been holding and touching her body not wishing to convey his impure thoughts in some way. He had relished every moment that he had been in contact with her even though it appeared innocent enough. Although she felt a little thin and he did not usually find the type attractive, to him she was different. She was in the higher echelons of women. A class above all other classes. As well as possessing what to him was a good body, to most men an immensely divine body, it was his subconscious peculiar thoughts, deep in the darkness of his mind, that he could puncture the higher standards of morality of the true upper class ladies that gave him his greatest satisfaction. Contamination of the elite was his preference and his turn on.

'Sorry,' she also apologised, reciprocating his earlier gesture and hastily gathered her composure. Then as she heard him apologising again she thanked him.

'We meet again at the same spot.' Vladimir retorted hastily, wanting to keep the conversation alive and not for the first time pretending he had only recently arrived. He continued. 'I've been here often since our first encounter and I've never seen you here again?'

'No, I have not returned since that day.' She found herself more relaxed with him on this occasion and answered him with confidence.

'I must return to the village or my parents will be concerned.'

'Can you not stay awhile and converse?' he appealed to her. 'Do you have to rush back? I will not harm you.' he gesticulated with his arms spread wide in a pleading manner.

She wanted to change her mind, to give him a chance even though he was a Russian soldier, worse a member of the NKVD, and they were not to be trusted. But during her encounters with him and despite his reasonableness and certain respectability she was still unsure about him and his intentions. As she pondered on whether to change her decision he spoke again.

'If your parents will be concerned for your whereabouts then you must return. Perhaps we will talk again.'

Spontaneous relief overcame her. He had provided her with a way out. 'Yes we can talk another time.' She had replied without thinking and then, endeavouring to please him in some small way for the politeness he had shown her, she reiterated her last words a second time. Whilst she spoke she questioned herself as to whether she was taking the right course.

Vladimir watched as she went. After she had disappeared from his view he sat down at the top of the bank and reflected on the events of the last ten minutes. He grinned, wryly and confidently, believing that where his new ambition lay he was sowing the seeds for greener pastures.

It was several weeks later when Vladimir and Sophie came into contact with each other again, nature playing a major role in their encounter.

Sophie, on behalf of the family, before starting her work in the fields, elected to go to the village well for the water and was suddenly caught in one of the rapidly formed and powerful sandstorms 'burans' which developed with such speed that it would catch many of the local people unaware. The villagers, used to the effects of the 'burans', immediately dropped whatever they were carrying, unless it was of value, and hastily made their way back to their homes or took cover wherever possible out of its path.

Sophie who had filled her vessel with the water was now returning to her dwelling. Before she had completed half the distance she was engulfed by the storm.

Visibility in this weather was virtually zero and anybody who endeavoured to reach their intended destination could walk within feet of their goal and not see anything.

Vladimir, who had discreetly intensified the reconnaissance of the woman to cover all her movements outside the village especially in her spare time, was informed by the second of the two old men he employed. 'She is returning from the well Master and passing the house. The 'buran' has started to swallow her.'

'Make yourself scarce,' Vladimir demanded, and as the servant left, Vladimir, without waiting, rushed into the street, gladly put his hands around her waist and guided her toward his home.

Sophie did not struggle and was grateful that someone had seen her plight. She was a little frightened at the experience and although having been warned on many occasions about the 'burans,' she had neglected to react quickly enough in this particular instance.

Climbing the wooden steps to the entrance of his accommodation he closed the door hurriedly behind them, put up the wooden shutters and lit the lamp on the table in the room. She was grateful for the safety of the refuge even though it was with the Russian NKVD Officer.

'Thank you. I may have been lost if I had remained out there.'

Again Vladimir slipped into a totally different personality playing the part of the gentleman.

'It was my pleasure to help a lady in distress. If you would like to refresh yourself there is water already prepared in the next room.' He pointed to the area which stood at the rear of the house.

Sophie could see through the opened door that a bed lay in the corner. She refused the offer.

'Would you like some tea?' he asked. 'The sandstorm will continue for a while. You have time to keep me company and take a drink with me if you wish?'

The idea of drinking tea filled Sophie with delight. Although her mother had been given a little by Eva Bryevski at the clearing station, that had been used several weeks ago either through bartering or drinking the precious commodity themselves.

Sophie turned, walked toward and peered out of the window between the gaps in the wooden shutters which Vladimir had closed. She looked toward the area where her quarters were and could see nothing. Even the steps to the house where she now found herself had disappeared from view. Turning once more to face Vladimir she nodded her agreement to his suggestion.

He smiled at her and immediately walked toward then opened a cupboard in the corner of the room wide enough so that Sophie could see the contents inside.

Her expression was one of incredulity as she gazed on the stocks of food which filled the closet. Items which were common and accepted as ordinary goods in her household not so long ago were luxuries now. Those she could identify from where she was standing she began to savour in her mind. Her sensory organs became active and soon her mouth was awash with juices. She could not remember seeing such a cabinet full of provisions since leaving home. Utterly speechless and totally surprised at what she gazed upon, especially as where they now lived was virtually a deserted region, she thought of how many people could survive and for how long on what she observed. As Vladimir closed the door she was sure that the object he picked up of the floor as it fell from the top shelf was a bar of chocolate. He replaced the item in its original position and after taking the required contents from the cabinet to make the tea he locked the cupboard.

Whilst Vladimir brewed Sophie's interest turned to the interior of the dwelling. She was surprised to find it sparsely furnished with only the essentials available, a table and three chairs in the middle of the room with two cupboards and a stove standing in opposite corners. Above and to the left of the stove was a shelf on which a bowl sat, presumably to use for washing. Below the shelf stood a broom which had seen better days. There were two windows in the room both boarded due to the sandstorm and concealing the outside world. One of the windows had curtains hanging either side which were of surprisingly good quality. They looked out of place in the room. Below this window four pairs of well worn boots lay in an untidy heap on the floor. Amazingly to Sophie this was the only cluttered mess on show, even the wooden floor was swept clean and she was surprised that the neatness apparent inside the house was not extended to her host's personage. The dwelling was constructed of mud as were the majority of buildings in the village, and as she stood inside the house she confirmed her earlier theory that the abode was larger in size than any other in the village. She detected no vermin in the room but concluded that as the many houses she had visited in the village contained the menace this house must also have them somewhere.

Busying himself preparing the brew Vladimir looked across at his stunning guest dressed in rags. She appeared a poor second to Cinderella regarding clothing he thought, though a definite first in beauty. Vladimir made the first effort to converse.

'Please sit,' he beckoned walking toward her. Preparing a chair for her he chatted enthusiastically whilst he waited for the water to boil.

'It is not often that I have charming guests.' he smiled at her. 'The furniture is not fashionable but very functional.' She sat and continued to be surprised by his gentlemanly conduct. Again she thought to herself that she could be wrong about this man.

'I know we have met before but we have not introduced ourselves. My name is Vladimir Stoich.' He held out his hand awaiting her representation.

She looked at him and then hesitantly offered hers.

'Sophie Sagajlo,' she crooned.

'And where are you from Sophie Sagajlo?' he repeated her name deciding long ago that he liked it.

'Lyszcze (Wishche), a village outside Pinsk in eastern Poland,' she replied reflecting on how far away her family were from their true home.

'You miss your home very much I presume?'

'Yes. I do, very much.' she replied slowly and dejectedly. 'What makes this place more bearable is that I have my parents with me. Thankfully!' she stated as an important afterthought.

'Something which many of us do not have, including me,' he added after a brief pause as he returned to the stove.

She was surprised that he had made this statement and suddenly felt that perhaps he too was alone in a strange far off land and had been forced to come here against his wishes.

'The tea is ready,' he announced seconds later as he reapproached her carrying two tumblers and a lidded pot on a wooden tray. 'I hope it is to your liking.'

He placed the earthenware vessels on the black scorch marked table which was a consequence of placing boiling hot pots, pans and other receptacles on the surface without any protection.

She tasted the drink and announced with pleasure his success and her gratitude. Sophie returned to the part of their conversation which he had broken off, surprised at herself for having the temerity to ask such a question of a person whom she hardly knew and one in high authority.

'You mentioned that you were alone without your family out here?'

'Yes,' he replied also sitting on a chair which he pulled from under the table. Deliberately he forwarded no further information on the subject and at the same time tried to make her relax in his company by allowing her to progress the conversation.

'Were you also sent here without your consent?'

'I knew, although I did not want to come here.' He kept the reply purposefully short.

'You too, have been subjected in your own way to the punishment of the regime, a regime that you serve.'

'Yes.' Vladimir noticed the expression of her eyes change to one of sorrow. He knew the sorrow was for those victims of the regime though he also felt and wanted to feel that a small portion of the sadness he perceived in her luscious coloured eyes was for him too. He felt guilty that he did not say anymore to her about the consequences under which he had been sent to this part of the world and what the alternative would have been if he had refused. He knew that to offer such information would shatter his hopes forever.

'I will not be here forever and neither will you.' He roused her out of her unhappiness not wishing to see the melancholy look on her face.

She had been thinking of the thousands of Poles who were subjected to punishment by the regime. Now, for the first time, she had met one of its members who had also been punished and forced to come to such a place.

'If you were sent here as a form of punishment then you must have done something wrong?'

'Yes, that is true.'

Her confidence was growing and she felt more relaxed. 'What did you do to be sent here?'

'I misjudged someone. I was wrong about them.' Vladimir vaguely replied then continued quickly on another track of conversation. For some reason he did not want to lie to her. 'It's not such a bad place although it can be lonely and as I've said we will not be here forever.'

'Another?' he asked noticing her cup was empty, 'the storm is still strong'

She placed the beaker on the table and he happily poured a second measure into her receptacle.

As he poured she pondered on her original thoughts. 'Vladimir works for them and how many people are caught in its web? Thousands, millions,' she guessed, 'people who are looked on as criminals whether or not they have committed a crime. Even those who make a simple misjudgement whilst working for them are punished. Are they too not prisoners of the system? Isn't Vladimir a prisoner?' she questioned. 'But his circumstances are different. His sentence will be shorter than ours. He will return sooner. Her thoughts turned to those with the greatest need. Her family, herself, her people and especially Jacob.'

'Whilst we are a thousand miles from our homes we should try to get on as best we can.' Vladimir suggested.

He stirred her from her thoughts of Jacob and for the first time she smiled a lugubrious smile at him, though intended for a distant lover.

'If there is anything I can do for you Sophie, don't hesitate to ask me. Anything, do you understand?'

She nodded and again could not feel easy about what he had offered her.

CHAPTER 21

From the moment that Jan had crossed the threshold of her apartment and told her his story she knew that he was a genuine, kind and truthful person. His experiences had been alarming though he had survived them, a more competent individual, grateful for what he now received and what he would continue to receive in the future. He had told her himself that nothing would be taken for granted by him again and that he would cherish everyone and everything. His feelings however, would not and could not be extended to the Russian regime, together with its operators, who had and who would continue to perpetrate their havoc on the innocent.

This she had accepted and understood. She endeavoured however, to explain to Jan that not all Russians who held office in the regime were similar. Many of the members who held positions at all levels were not to be compared with those who committed these tortuous punishments on people. She had said this to Jan not only because she believed it but also because her husband was a member and she believed that he was of a kind nature. Whilst making the statement to Jan in defence of her spouse and those that she truly felt deserved defending, she realised that she did not know what Andrei's function was in the NKVD and questioned herself as to whether, in his work, he really was as gentle, kind and understanding as he could be at home with her. After her discussions with Jan on the subject the thought returned to her often and she could never truthfully answer herself.

Wandeczka too had changed. She had become more responsible in her attitude toward herself and Jan. Before he had arrived, selfishly she would not arise until midday, very often not until mid afternoon allowing herself to catch up on her sleep after performing at the club until the early hours of the morning. Now she had set a new task for herself, a new mission. Andrei had left specific instructions that she should teach Jan all there was to know about being Russian. 'The more he knows the better will be his chance of being accepted as a true Russian by all who he comes into contact with. He must be strong, especially if people comment scornfully on the Polish people and their country.'

Wandeczka knew this better than Andrei. Whenever her mother and father quarrelled, it was only over how one country treated another. She smiled as she thought of her parents all those years ago, and how, despite their infrequent arguments, they would always reconcile after their disagreements. It was a subject that she and Andrei never talked about, because like her mother, Wandeczka had warm feelings toward the Polish people. After all she was half Polish herself.

So she set about her task with gusto. Informing him of the Russian culinary skills including certain dishes such as 'pieroshki' which are common in both Poland and Russia but with subtle ingredient differences to each country. She made him aware of the important and not so important customs and traditions, the boundaries that the country engulfed stretching from Eastern Europe right across to China. She made clear to him what he could and could not speak about, both in his home and elsewhere whilst in conversation with other people. She instructed him in depth on the revolution and the Communist party and dwelled on its leader, Stalin. How he came to power and stayed in power which brought her to the purges of the thirties. At all times Jan listened intently. Every so often he would ask a question which in itself would encompass different facets of Russian life, and the talking point would move into a new area only to eventually return to the original topic at a later date. He was surprised at her knowledge and came to know that it was her father and Andrei who had told her so much about the politics of the country. The more touching human aspects of Russian life were divulged to her by her mother and it left Wandeczka with a much more balanced view of her people and country. The subject she left until last was that of religion. On this issue she told him no more than the authorities frowned on all denominations of faith, though she still believed in the Virgin Mary and Almighty God as did many of the older Russians, and she added, 'nobody would ever change my mind for me.' She was pleased that Jan felt the same way and both agreed to pray occasionally together.

Teaching and educating him in the varied topics brought her closer to him and his mannerisms at all times were of a perfect gentleman. The conversations between the two of them were varied and as she continued to educate Jan in the ways, the customs and the traditions of the Russian people they became close too in their relationship. She had always looked forward to the start of a new day, though now it was more fulfilling for her. Quickly, her affection for him grew and her own feelings for her husband began to be questioned by her.

Jan was very different to Andrei both physically and in character. Whilst Andrei was tall, broad and fair, Jan was also tall, though of slim build with layers of brown coloured hair. From Jan's large light brown eyes she could perceive a touch of wickedness in him, which periodically manifested in his conversation. His eyes continuously shined in their sockets lighting up the rest of his features which were good looking not handsome. Whilst Andrei always seemed aloof and she could not quite reach his inner depths even when he was completely relaxed, Jan had quickly trusted her and confided his worse fears to her. She admired Jan for still holding the substance of his roots together despite experiencing severe hostile circumstances and he still felt that the majority of the human population was good and not evil. He learned quickly, and rarely forgot a teaching once she had relayed it to him. On the odd occasion he ventured out alone he would buy a small gift for her, usually flowers. This touched her immensely. Nobody had given her presents in this way before. They laughed and joked in the middle of conversations and when the time came for her to prepare to depart for her nightly work; she begrudged the long intermission and the fact that it separated her from him. Occasionally, which was extraordinary for her, she would take the option of having her nights off, whereas before she nearly always worked.

When the time arrived, in less than a week, for Jan to leave her apartment for his place, her affection had changed considerably from one of simply a family connection.

She had waited long enough for him to make the advances she decided as she arose from her bed that morning. Sleep had been difficult to find and wherever she looked it was elusive to her for long periods during the previous night. She understood the reason and knew that her thoughts were for the man sleeping in the next bedroom. Looking at the clock she also knew that he would be awake, dressed, breakfasted and ready for what the day would bring, which was very little until she arose, usually several hours later. She decided immediately to visit him and somehow conjure the amorous side of the relationship which showed no signs, either verbally or physically, of existing between them.

Putting on her dressing gown she tied the belt of her garment tightly, concealing her nakedness, and ventured out of her bedroom and into the area where she thought Jan would be. He was not in the living area and she retraced her steps. Through the opened door of his bedroom she could see him sitting up on his bed fully clothed and reading.

She brushed in to his room and started conversing about how untidy he was, which wasn't true. Picking up the pillow lying on the bed she walked toward him and proceeded to fight him with the cushion. She yelped as he jumped up and grabbed her unsuspectingly, pulling her down as a result of his sudden burst of energy. She tumbled with ease onto his bed making sure she gripped him enough so that he was following her in her fall. 'I could not have planned it better myself,' she thought to herself as he landed across her. They jostled lightly and she yelped again as he bumped her chin accidentally and with little pain. He was concerned and after apologising the smiles became instantly more serious as they realised what either individual meant to each other.

She had seen it and witnessed it from the moment he had arrived and now she could see again the warmth and goodness of this young man percolating in his eyes as he lay on top gazing into hers. It was as if they were far away from any disturbance. Silence descended on the room. Nothing could be heard from the exterior. The traffic which passed outside the apartment seemed to have stood still. They heard nothing only the beat of each others hearts and she felt his lower body flicker to life. Seconds passed which seemed like minutes. The flicker became a flame. She wanted him to kiss her. She had wanted that, she realised, from the moment that Andrei had returned to his duties. In those few seconds she realised, that although she had enjoyed her husband's company and lovemaking, in the relatively short time she had known Jan she preferred his presence to that of her spouse. Wandeczka returned to the immediate situation knowing what should happen next and hoping that it would. He came to her slowly, very slowly. It agonised her. Then she realised that he was nervous and probably had few encounters with women. She had forgotten how young he was, though he talked and conversed with a wise head. 'I should have realised,' she told herself as his lips beckoned ever closer. She opened her mouth to invite him, and guided, with her hands, his head and mouth down toward her. His kiss was different. He had little experience with women, she now knew, but his caress conveyed the goodness and love which he felt for humanity and she felt fully contented and relaxed with his embrace like never before. Longing for it not to end, minutes later he was standing above her apologising.

'No. No apologies. I have wanted and waited for many days Jan.' She pressed her index finger against his lips and he became silent. Then she stretched up to gently kiss his lips, smiled at him as she left his room, and went to greet her colleague who was ringing the apartment doorbell, earlier than usual, for their alternative weekly visit to each other's home.

His atavistic tendencies had dulled in his mind but certainly not in his heart and he could easily resurrect those emotions whenever he dwelled for long periods on what he had witnessed. The promise to himself to seek revenge for his colleague in the prison would not be undone, no matter how long it would take.

He had changed enormously in stature since the journey by train had begun growing from strength to strength since his escape, and finding his own way to Moscow to locate his cousin had made him finally aware of his own capabilities. He had even overcome the unbearable mental torture, although nothing compared to what the actual inmates had undergone, of the visit to the prison where he observed hundreds of Poles becoming part of the living dead. 'I will come through,' he told himself and he had steeled himself for whatever lay ahead, 'though nothing can be worse than what I have experienced and seen already.'

Several weeks had elapsed since Andrei had reported back for duty. To where on this occasion, his wife never knew. By consequence, Jan did not know either. He did however, want to know. He wanted to know more about the function that Andrei carried out for the NKVD. 'It may be of use in the future,' he concluded to himself thinking ahead but unsure as to the precise relevance of his thoughts.

Wandeczka came into the room at that moment and stirred him from his deliberations. He looked toward her and could not help finding himself attracted to her. To him she was captivating, voluptuous and above all extremely kind and although he had testified to her brief bouts of spitefulness toward her friend he had never dreamt that this woman, his cousin, would have all these qualities. Perceiving her over the weeks he could not help but admire her precise figure and those long stunning legs. Her auburn glow of hair cascaded to her shoulders in curved waves like sand dunes meeting the shoreline. The dark greeny brown eyes glinted at him like the deepest shaded emeralds. At times he surmised the glint in her eyes enticing him to take advantage of her, but he was unsure. His uncertainty coupled with his innocence held him firm but how he wished otherwise. The dressing gown she now wore hugged her figure and he found it difficult to take his eyes from her. On many occasions he wanted to tell her how he felt. His naivety and shyness with women always prevented him from doing so.

He had grown close to her in the short time that he had arrived at her abode and they had conversed, joked and laughed with one another like two old school friends meeting after being apart for many years. 'Not what Andrei would have wanted,' he told himself without uttering a word to Wandeczka.

Perhaps it was his way of defying the man who had forced him to see what he did not want to see and now he was getting his own back on Andrei for punishing him. Though having been made to see the degradation of human life he was grateful, otherwise he would not have found Jacob. His stay would not last for much longer for Jan was leaving Wandeczka's apartment in two days for that of his own. At the same time he could not help feeling that he would miss his cousin and despite his protestations to the contrary they had agreed to visit one another at least once a week.

'Come on Jan, shake yourself,' she grumbled at him picking up his pillow that lay at the bottom end of the bed, marching toward him and hitting him over the head with it, continuing to verbally badger him at the same time. 'When you move into your new flat you will have to look after yourself.'

Again she thumped him over the head with the pillow only for him to suddenly jump up, grab her by the waist and twist her around and down on the bed. She giggled and laughed as did he, struggling with him and managing with her force to pull him over also. He laughed as he fell over her and managed not to land the whole weight of his body on her. Both laughed as he collapsed partly onto her, the top of his head bumped against her chin and she yelped, more through the sudden shock of the accident than the tingle of pain.

'Sorry,' he hurriedly apologised not wishing to harm her in anyway, and as he pulled his head up to inspect her chin to see if there were any damage she smiled at him and he realised that it was all a joke. In that moment their eyes met, the smile between them hung for a brief moment like a droplet from a tap, and then slowly disappeared to be replaced firstly by a more serious realisation followed by a deep long lasting stare into each others eyes.

Jan was unsure. He had been attracted to her from the moment he had gazed on her outside the club after they had collided into one another. That attraction had increased since their first encounter and never waned for him, but he felt that a woman of her substance and maturity would not have eyes in that manner for him. He had controlled his emotions without any problems, happy that he was near her. Now even that would not be for long. Lying there partly across her, the common mixture of ignorance due to innocence and the threat of what Andrei had said now confused his thoughts. He lingered on and on. To him the brief moment seemed like forever. The craving to simply touch those lips was irresistible. His loins began to react and the threat of Andrei vanished from his mind. He was left with only his innocence. Faltering as he wrestled with what his thoughts decided for him, he was aware that if she had not wanted to be kissed and caressed she would have arisen and made some lame excuse to get away by now. Finally, through the sheer want and need of touching her in a more than platonic form, he lowered his mouth closer to hers. She did not move, instead her lips parted wider and wider as he drew nearer to her. 'Does she too have a longing?' Jan fleetingly cogitated before committing himself. Then he had passed the point of no return and before he had time to ponder on any of his other mixed and desirable thoughts, they were replaced with willing actions. Their lips had met, touching each other with great emotion. For him it was indescribable and he knew that he wanted it to last forever. He had kissed other women, 'no girls' he corrected himself, but he had never been probed by another female in this manner. The enjoyment he experienced surprised him and he, in turn, reciprocated which added to his euphoria. Soon their tongues were fighting for the occupancy of each others mouths and their panting increased, the noise echoing all around them. On the point of exploring one another further, they were disturbed by the sound of the apartment doorbell.

The remainder of that day they spent in the company of Wandeczka's friend. She had arrived early because 'workmen were making repairs to the apartment block and causing a row.' With complete surprise to Wandeczka she decided to spend the whole of the day instead of the customary two to three hours with her and Jan. To confirm her intentions she had brought her outfit with her to take straight to the club when both women would leave in the late evening to perform their individual acts.

This was a surprise to Wandeczka and although she tried hinting to her friend that she wanted to be alone with Jan because they had much to talk about before he was to leave the apartment for good, no end of friendly persuasion would make her leave. Reluctantly Wandeczka realised that she would have to wait until another time to be alone with Jan.

That day had finally arrived and as promised Wandeczka had prepared a meal for them to eat in his new home. She supplied all the ingredients for the dinner including the wine and insisted before they sat down to commence the meal that Jan, like herself, make himself clean and presentable at the table.

The conversation over dinner returned to them as natural as it had done before their encounter on the bed in Wandeczka's apartment. For two days after the episode any dialogue amongst them had been reduced to two or three words with the occasional single sentence. Wandeczka was not perturbed by this hesitation in their relationship, concluding that it was as a result of Jan's inexperience of how to deal with the situation and a natural consequence of his naivety with women.

Jan, however, was concerned. He did not want to displease her in any way. She had been a tremendous support and of incalculable value. Above all that, he had grown to love her. He now knew that there was definitely some form of affection, not simply platonic, but something much stronger waiting for him, although he did not know how to conjure that special ingredient from her again. Besides that, after the passion between him and Wandeczka had subsided and when his thoughts were sensibly gathered, he was still concerned as to what Andrei had instructed outside the prison they had visited weeks ago. Yes, he had ignored the warning when he and Wandeczka were on the bed together. But with more time to dwell on what Andrei had said he was increasingly unsure as to whether he should pursue the relationship and decided to give up the pursuit himself and to let events take its course.

The nature of conversation which had resumed that evening over the dinner table was in the form of another lesson for Jan. Wandeczka had cleverly guided the dialogue along those lines, relaxing Jan into his old self prior to the encounter in her apartment. She knew that he was nervous as a result of what had happened, although if she had asked him outright he would have completely denied the allegation. Rather than do anything about the situation, no matter how much he cared for her, he would leave the issue, not knowing what to do, until she would decide to do something about it herself.

It had not taken her long and she had organised the dinner in his apartment on the day he would move in. At first he made some lame excuse about being busy with one or two tasks to perform in his new accommodation. She had waved down his feeble excuses and insisted that she would prepare dinner in his flat on the first evening. He had capitulated in his protestations and the evening had gone ahead as planned.

Wandeczka was pleased with herself and pleased with Jan that he did not withhold any of his natural exuberance for conversation from her. His attitude, at least on the surface, appeared normal and now she proceeded with the remainder of the evening happy and contented herself.

She was preparing coffee after the meal when Jan came out with the used crockery off the dinner table which he had cleared away. Placing the empty vessels on the worktop, he turned to take the coffee, which she had announced was ready, from her. As he turned, she also turned to give him the cup with its contents. Accidentally some of the hot drink spilled onto her dress and he immediately apologised.

'It's not your fault Jan,' she announced as she wiped the front of her garment with a clean cloth which Jan handed to her.

'I will have to change,' she continued.

'We're not in your apartment now Wandeczka. You don't have any clothes here.'

'No, but you do.' she smiled at him as she caught sight of his serious expression. 'I can borrow some of your clothes until this dries. Will you unzip me?' She asked him staring into his eyes. She was now teasing him and playing on his innocence. A gentle smirk dawned on her face.

Jan was perplexed. He didn't know what to say or do to her after her last request.

'Jan,' she whispered to him, 'don't worry I'm not going to eat you.' She turned her back on him and again instructed him pointing at the same time. 'Zip please.'

He did as requested, fumbling at first with the fastener. Then as the dress opened up in front of him he gazed on the back of her blue underwear which contrasted strikingly with her soft peach coloured skin. His movements immediately began to flow with ease.

She turned to him once more and noticed his facial colour slowly changing to a bright crimson red. She stared into his eyes. He stood motionless in front of her knowing he should turn away at the same time not wanting to be deprived of the aura he looked upon. More than anything he craved her attention to continue. Moving her hand up to his face she stroked his cheek and felt his soft skin, which as yet had not experienced the shaving blade. Then she stood on her toes to attain the height she needed to caress him, a long soothing, sensuous embrace which ignited the whole dormancy of manhood throughout his body. As she relaxed back onto the soles of her feet, he now leaned forward to her not wanting to let go of her lips. She tugged gently at her own dress with her free hand for she knew he would not dare to perform the act, and as it slipped from her shoulders down her waist and eventually to the floor he gasped as their embrace momentarily broke and he glimpsed much more of her peach textured skin amongst the light sky blue colouration of her matching French underwear. Her cleavage was deep, verifying his thoughts that her breasts were of ample size. His emotions were beginning to run away. He wanted to touch her and go on touching her but with pain he controlled himself.

With startling speed she had felt his erection forming and pressing against her. The time was ripe. With expertise and as they gazed with affection into one another's eyes, she unbuttoned his trousers, lowered them to the floor, at the same time giving room to his restricted hardness.

Walking him to the bedroom they continued to osculate and undress one another. She revealed her body to him slowly allowing him time to feast his eyes on her wonderment. She enticed his touch and he did so with delicate fingers and soft but firm hands. To him she was like a flower blossoming slowly with the first light of the day and he was the sun being allowed to gorge on the slow process of the revelation. He gasped at the first sight of her alluring symmetrical shaped breasts which stood out firm like his erection and again they stopped to touch one another. Before finally arriving in the bedroom completely naked she sat him down in the living room and beckoned him to take off her stockings and underwear. He exclaimed in awe as he looked on her sexuality. She pulled him gently to her burying his head, confirming that it was his for the taking.

She was careful what she did with him and although he was fully aroused she controlled him with precision. Even then, as she knew beforehand, when he entered her he did not last long. Though, with both the excitement that a child has over a new toy and the persistence of an animal in season, he continued often to confront her over and over during the night until finally, on the last encounter, with the shafts of the dawn light invading their private heaven, the passion and lovemaking was beautiful for both, though still not perfect for her. He collapsed by her side and the accumulated exhaustion allowed him to find slumber with speed.

Wandeczka realised that she had entered into the realms of a new teaching with her pupil and that she had already commenced those lessons in gently advising how to satisfy the teacher also. She would willingly continue to do so until the pupil would become a master. With wonderful visions of days and nights to come, Wandeczka also found a warm and easy slumber.

For the duration of the summer months and into the autumn Sophie and her family including Juliana worked on the collective farm 'kolkhoz.' The farm consisted of rows and rows of fields, some of which had already been tilled and sowed whilst others were left uncultivated. The unprepared pastures were the most difficult to work whilst the easiest task to perform was that of planting seeds. With the continuous kneeling and bending required to complete the planting, even this work was strenuous for those who were unused to the job.

After the planting the weeding then had to be performed and throughout the period irrigation of the fields had to be undertaken. The stream which ran by the pastures was diverted at various stages along its flow. The earth was dug out from the bank where the stream channelled itself and re-diverted into the numerous fields. A continuous process of digging and re-diverting the water through new channels was operated until all the fields were fully irrigated. When the operation had been completed the stream was allowed to resume its own course once more and the bank which had originally been gouged out was filled in. At the end of the summer the kholkozniks commenced the gathering of the produce which included vegetables, potatoes, cucumbers, onions and melons.

Meals were supplied by the workers themselves and consisted of whatever they were fortunate to acquire. The days commenced very early between four o clock and four thirty in the morning with a breakfast which usually comprised of warm milk and bread. To get to the 'kolkhoz' many labourers had to walk on foot for approximately one hour.

Work commenced at six in the morning and continued on many days until sunset. An hour was allowed for lunch when the people were given a portion of black bread. When the harvest was gathered the workers were also allowed to keep a small amount of the vegetables to eat with their lunch. In addition to this some usually brought other food with them which almost always consisted of milk. Soup was cooked occasionally, and comprised of a collection of whatever ingredients could be found. The worse feeding situation was hot water with bread. Again after completing the day's work the return journey of one hour awaited the farm workers before arriving home. The evening meal usually consisted of a few vegetables such as potatoes or cabbage as well as the customary bread. Seldom eggs were eaten as a main meal.

Sophie was often given the easier of the tasks as a result of direct instructions given by Vladimir who was the supreme authority above all in the area. The headman of the village also supervised the work performed in the fields but was under the jurisdiction of the NKVD Official. Helena worked alongside her daughter, and very often Sophie swapped duties with her especially when her mother was given the heavier tasks to perform. Her father, Yuri, the doctor, was allowed, infrequently, to perform his medical duties on those who needed it the most. With very few drugs and very little equipment there was a minimum amount of healing that he could do. Even then, for some unknown reason he was not always allowed to examine people who needed his attention the most. On many occasions he thought about complaining to the authority and then resisted at the last moment, knowing that if he did so his medical expertise may have been denied to the whole of the inhabitants of the village on a permanent basis.

His knowledge in medicine was wide and ranging, though unfortunately because of the lack of facilities and drugs in the village and even in the nearest town he found himself reverting back to the herbalist remedies, an avenue of medicine which he had studied long ago in medical school. Together with one of the Kazak villager's who represented his people on medical matters they built up a good relationship with many favoured results, some through trial and error rather than through certain knowledge.

The summer was a memory in the past as the autumn came and hurriedly pursued its path, seemingly to dwell only fleetingly on the steppes of Kazakstan. The coloured coat of the saiga, an odd looking antelope with a prominent moose like snout, changed from the yellow brown in summer to its grey shade in winter. The susliks or ground squirrels prepared for their hibernation by foraging, eating and storing their usual diet of seeds and produce from whatever the trees produced.

The winds which were continuously present over the steppes now became stronger and the first signs of winter, which dawned cruelly on the new inhabitants without any warning, took them by surprise. A great coat of white powder covered the ground outside their house and as far as the eye could see.

In preparation for winter and throughout the summer, whenever possible, Sophie and her family had been storing the essential commodities of fat, flour and fuel which were scarce during the winter months. These items were needed to sustain them through the hard and very cold season. The main source of fuel was provided by the cattle which wandered freely over the steppes. The only drawback for those that collected the dung 'buhary' was that very often they had to walk miles in search of the produce. When dry the 'buhary' burned quickly and lasted a very short amount of time. To allow it to burn for longer periods, 'buhary' firstly had to be mixed whilst wet with straw and earth and then left to dry, usually in the shape of bricks. This method also made it easier for transportation. These bricks of fuel were then stored ready for use in the winter to be used to feed the fire during the freezing months.

The first snowfalls had begun and the Sagajlo family were concerned. Despite their stock of food they were still worried that they would not have enough to sustain them during the winter months. They had written to relatives and friends in Poland to send whatever they could in the form of provisions. Only one friend had replied. His letter did not bring good news as it announced to them that many of their close circles of friends and relatives had either fled their own homes out of choice or had been forced by the Russians to move and had subsequently been deported.

The goods they did receive, and for which they were truly grateful, of tea, tobacco, matches and material as well as some other items, was almost all bartered or sold in the nearest main town of Sokolovka which Sophie and Juliana had visited. It was here also that Sophie sold, for a considerable amount of money, the tiara which she had worn on the night she had attended the ball. With great emotion she relinquished her heirloom. Knowing what comfort it would bring to herself and her family in the way of food and provisions softened the effect of its parting. With the money received, they then purchased the required food, commodities and clothing which they needed for the winter months.

The doctor estimated that they would have enough to last well into the winter, though perhaps not enough to see them through the whole period. In addition to their troubles there were other families in the village that they had travelled with who were also short of food for the oncoming period.

Sophie and her parents spent many hours discussing what they could do to alleviate the problem. After much deliberation their conclusion was unfounded. Sophie had ideas of her own which, for now, she did not want to divulge to others.

CHAPTER 22

Purveying the inside of the midden in which he had been incarcerated with the lazy, lacklustre eyes of someone who had become used to the dimness of such a place, his mind finally registered that nothing had changed. For the innumerable days that he had awoken from his slumber, his nightmare was a reality.

The first perception was always of the clutches of lice and bugs which moved in pockets of black hordes across the walls of the cell like dark unrecognisable shadows flickering in the moonlight. They did not occupy all areas of the walls at once, but had resided at some time, within their lifespan, over the majority of the area within the cell. Despite these unwelcoming visitors, in fact the prisoners quickly became used to the intruders; this was not the worse effect of the dungeon. The greatest annoyance was that of the inhumane conditions in which people had to occupy the cells. The simplest of amenities were not available. Due to these lower than lowlife circumstances the bodies of the men who dwelled in the chamber became tarnished and befouled. In certain individual cases the minds of the men had followed the same route as their bodies. Insanity had taken over. He spied on the figures of human degradation which resembled almost dead cadavers. Lifeless, listless, sapped of energy.

Sitting there, slowly awaking from his slumber, not wanting to visualise that which could not be ignored, the whole episode of recent months stealthily crept up on him and the realisation of his captivity in the jail had begun to take its toll. Not only physically, this had already been inflicted, but mentally also. He inspected himself with displeasure. His skin had changed colour. To him, at least, it appeared to have changed colour. The rancid, contaminated air and filthy conditions had finally camouflaged his original clean coloured body, overtaking, devouring, eventually, and finally, purging his pigmentation of all its cleanliness and liveliness, leaving him in a sorry putrefied mess. Even the hairs over his torso seemed to have changed colour from their normal dark shining glow to a lighter, yet contrasting duller effect.

The awareness of his state and condition became too large to be quelled inside of him. He cried without disgrace in front of his fellow inmates. Unafraid and carefree of whom might see, for they in their turn, if not already, would undergo what he was now experiencing himself. Extreme doubts as to whether he would or could survive this nightmare to defeat all other nightmares surmounted him. 'Cry!' he told himself. 'Cry and wash yourself of all that has happened to you so that you may allow yourself to survive and live to remember and relate what has been inflicted on you over these past months.'

And so he did. Weeping at length, he continued to remember the experiences that he had been through since arriving at his own personal hell. With each memory of the awesome past, a new stronger emotion of sadness developed freshly inside him. His sorrow was colossal yet bearable, silent yet public, a tumultuous relief yet not completely free. Those inmates who looked toward him detected his grief but said nothing. The majority of them understood what he was going through and they too, though not visibly, felt the affliction which engulfed him.

Then, when he thought there was no more to give and his distress started to abate, somewhere in the depths, his mind and body working in partnership would find more to dwell on and his misery would continue that much longer. Finally, when there was no more evil to recall and his mind had been cleansed of all the cruel and heartless remembrances, there was nothing. His mind became empty.

He sat there motionless, not even his eyelids blinked. His breathing appeared to have stopped. He was no more and yet he was still alive. Sitting there in a putrefied mess, the minutes passed by slowly, ever so slowly. Thirty minutes, then sixty. It was if his subconscious were taking over the control of his bodily functions to keep him alive, whilst the conscious element battled to decide whether he wanted to live or die, remain sane or become insane. The whole existence of his mind, his body and his life hung in the balance. Like those he had earlier recognised as being mad, he too, was on the brink of madness. Now, however, he recognised nothing. His whole existence was in the balance. His mind was in control yet he as a person was unaware of the perception. This state of undesired equilibrium remained with him for many hours.

Without warning, and as if the conscious and subconscious had fought their battle, though nobody would ever know who had won, not even the human within whom it was being fought, further movements deep in the mind began to grow. A series of thoughts, with lengthy intervals of nothing, mustered periodically. The nothingness was slowly being replaced and he was on his way back from the brink. His bodily functions gained their momentum. The recovery was quicker than the degeneration. The series of thoughts turned to a flow, more fulfilling and wholesome than those before, taking the place of the emptiness left behind. Rapidly with each second his memories came flooding back. Those memories of richness which made him happy. The gaiety and brightness, the laughter and merriment, the friendship and courtship which he had achieved during his lifespan and which to him had helped him to complete his life. All were from the past. Yet, as they came rushing forward in his mind he remembered them all as if it were yesterday. He dwelled long and hard on those good times and conjectured as to whether he would repeat any of those events again in his life.

Not wishing to retreat back into the antipathy of his earlier cogitations he dismissed his conjecture on the future and concentrated his thoughts on what had been. Strongest in his mind were those of the last twelve months. Uppermost in those thoughts was one main character. She was with him now as she was then. The feeling was strong. He could smell her and reach out and embrace her. He could feel his fingers running through her long black tresses. He lingered on the kiss from her soft lips and felt the touch and the warmth of his body against hers. The sensations and perceptions came to him with infinite strength, holding, comforting, and retaining him in the world of normality. Preserving and fighting the battle of him slipping into the possessiveness of the sphere of insanity.

With those wondrous thoughts, herculean in his mind, Jacob fell asleep, returning him briefly to a safe haven.

During the months that followed and whilst Andrei was away performing his duties for the NKVD, Jan, and Wandeczka continued to see one another as and when they wanted. They met almost every day and if they missed one day they made a point of seeing each other the next, even if it was for a brief moment.

During this time and to broaden his knowledge of the Russian capital and its people she took him into and around the streets of the city. She took him to visit the various sights which Moscow had to offer. He came to know and learn about much of the city and its buildings with its diverse streets and corners and its short cuts as if it were his own home town.

When they had nothing specific planned they simply walked and enjoyed each other's company talking about their memories, both happy and sad before progressing to the future and what it held for them. If they did not go out they remained indoors and conversed, quickly becoming embroiled in their dialogue. They always arranged to meet in Jan's apartment very rarely at Wandeczka's. Jan advocated this as occasionally, though more and more seldom, at the back of his mind the warning that Andrei had given to him outside the prison continued to rear itself. He felt more comfortable that he never went to their home to see her and that she always came to his flat to see him. If Andrei ever approached him about their continuing meetings he could justify and defend the point in that manner. In addition to their walks and conversations they made love frequently and very often she would be late for work as the passion between them eclipsed the time. She experienced pleasure with him like she had never known before and under her continued guidance he learned quickly to satisfy her. For him the initial novelty of sex was still strong though the mad dash had worn off to be replaced by a more calm, passionate and long lasting emotion. Still looking forward immensely to their lovemaking sessions, there were occasions, nonetheless, when he could not control himself long enough.

Her job, although she still enjoyed the work, had started to take second priority in her life. Now, unlike before, she regularly turned down the option to perform on her nights off. Her first concern had changed for the welfare and support of Jan and she felt her feelings growing stronger and stronger for him with the passing of each day. Feelings which she was unsure of and had no control over, but for which she was happy. Also, she could not remember developing similar emotions regarding her husband.

Andrei had been home one week of his two week leave. At the end of the first he had become annoyed with the relationship between his wife and her cousin. It was not how he wanted it to be and despite his warnings to Jan he had not stayed away from her. Although Wandeczka informed him that Jan had not visited their apartment, his wife had included him in many of her conversations about what she had been occupying herself with whilst he was away.

Wandeczka, for her part, had been sparse with the truth to her husband regarding her relationship with Jan and concentrated on the subjects of her teachings. She also mentioned that her job was still important to her which it was, although truthfully, not to the same degree as in the past.

Andrei decided to visit Jan himself and enquire as to what had been happening whilst he had been away. Purposely dressed in his uniform, as it always instilled some fear in both innocent and guilty people, even those that were members of the NKVD, plus the added delight in perceiving the nervous look of those he visited and questioned, he announced to Wandeczka that he was going out to attend to some business and that it would take some time to resolve.

Jan opened the door to his apartment in response to the rapping on the wooden entrance. He was concerned as to who the caller was. Usually Wandeczka visited him and she had insisted that she would not do so alone whilst

Andrei was home on leave unless her husband accompanied her. Opening the door slowly and gazing toward the floor he glimpsed the brilliant sheen on the shoes, the fine crease of the trouser uniform and immediately thought that he had been discovered by the authorities and they had come to seek him out. For a brief moment he felt sick. Seconds later he was somewhat relieved to look upon Andrei's face. Although more relaxed as a result of his original thoughts being unfounded he was not looking forward to discovering the reason for Andrei's visit. Jan knew that this man did not like him. The feeling was mutual. He knew that the purpose of Andrei's visit was probably to reprimand him for a reason which, as yet, was unknown.

'Andrei, c…come in.' Jan stuttered nervously signalling his unease to the visitor calling. The caller entered the apartment, instantly recognised the tone of the voice and was immediately pleased.

'Calm yourself Jan,' he urged himself. 'You have done nothing wrong,' and immediately he knew he had lied to himself. His mind was racing and he endeavoured to control it. 'You have been through enough already; do not let this one person agitate you anymore. Remember what Jacob told you, if there are any problems hit first ask questions later. There will be no need for actions of that sort,' Jan thought, and then questioningly continued to ask himself, 'will there?'

Andrei thankfully broke Jan's galloping conjecture.

'Nice apartment,' he sardonically announced to Jan as he looked directly toward him from a distance of several metres.

Jan ignored the comment and did not reply. Andrei continued.

'You want to remain here I presume?'

Jan looked at him now with a blank expression.

'Remain here in this apartment. In Moscow. In safety?' he emphasised every point.

His attitude and tone stirred Jan determinedly. 'Yes,' he stated with confidence.

'Why have you not heeded my words Jan. My advice? What was it I said to you before I left for my tour of duty? Do you remember?' Andrei's eyes, as on the previous occasion when they had talked in the vehicle outside in the courtyard of the prison, had begun to glitter like a madman once again.

Although the look disgusted him Jan was not disconcerted by the observation on this occasion, unlike the previous episode. He gathered and controlled the earlier nervousness in him, remained calm and replied simply.

'Yes, I remember, and I have noted what you have said and heeded your words.' Jan was more confident now than he had ever been before in Andrei's company and his answers were fluent and convincing.

'Then why are you still seeing Wandeczka. I thought I told you to stay away from her.' The deranged glint in his eyes continued, witnessed by Jan.

Both men remained standing. Jan walked toward Andrei before replying. Stopping no more than two feet from him he looked the interrogator straight in the eye. Andrei was taken aback although he did not relay his sudden surprise to the man who stood directly opposite him now.

'I have heeded your words,' he repeated with a certain amount of venom, 'and stayed away from Wandeczka. Whenever we have met it is because she has visited me here, in this apartment.' He lied, knowing he had met her outside on many occasions. This time he did not care. The man was certainly a liar and probably a murderer. Maybe he had never pulled a trigger or pushed a button himself to commit the murders but surely he had ordered those actions to be undertaken on his behalf. He was a man with very few morals who cared only about himself and the regime. Jan felt no guilt about lying to him and continued his reply.

'I have told nobody of your warning to me in the automobile outside the prison and I presume you have told nobody either, not even Wandeczka. I could have told her but decided against doing so. If she is unaware of what you have said to me then what can I do to stop her from visiting. At first I made excuses that I had tasks to do in the apartment, but I cannot continue to make the same excuse. I have no work to do here and no job outside to keep me occupied, therefore it is impossible for me not to see her especially if she visits me here. Her visits were fruitful though and thanks to her I have learned much about the Russian way of life.' With those last words Jan confirmed to Andrei what Wandeczka had already told him.

Andrei was quiet. The maniacal sparkle in his eyes had started to subside as Jan relayed the reasons for him and Wandeczka still meeting. By the end of Jan's reply the glinting had completely abated. 'The Pole has a sound argument and I did request that she teach him everything about the Russian life.' Andrei surmised to himself and instantly decided how he could now keep the man occupied.

After a brief pause in which Andrei sat in one of the unoccupied chairs without being invited to do so and still concerned over the Pole's direct approach and eye to eye contact which had temporarily unnerved him, he spoke.

'I can help with your unemployment situation.' He rubbed his chin with his hand as he spoke and was still thinking of all the details and piecing them together before he continued.

'Yes, I can help,' he finally and definitely announced. 'I will need a few days to coordinate and clear the matter but I do not see any problems which cannot be ironed out.'

'Good. Dobroyeh,' Jan immediately replied, pretending to be excited at the prospect of being able to do something though unsure whether he wanted work for fear that his true background would be found out and that it may hinder the amount of time he spent with Wandeczka. 'Good. Dobroyeh,' again he stated keeping up the pretence. 'Can you tell me what the job is to be?'

'No, not yet. Let me sort things out first. I will let you know in a day or two.'

Andrei arose and walked to the door. He said no more until he was outside the apartment. 'I will be in touch,' and ignorantly turned and walked off.

When he had disappeared down the stairs and Jan heard the door of the apartment block closing, signifying to him that Andrei had left the premises completely, he quickly closed his own door and motioned to open the bottle of vodka that Wandeczka had given to him on the day he had moved in. He poured himself a large glass from the contents, gulped a mouthful down and howled from him the warm effect of the drink as it slid down his throat. The bellowing noise was not only due to the drink but also as a result of the manner in which he handled the situation between himself and cousin in law. Although inwardly he was nervous at the beginning of his response, by the end of his answer he was calm and very confident. He felt that he could deal with the rhetoric which he had expected from Andrei but which never came. At that he was surprised. Jan also felt, but was not sure, that his close encounter standing near to Andrei as he gave his reply had produced a split second of nervous hesitation from his visitor. 'On a one to one situation he is probably a coward,' Jan cogitated to himself. He sat back; relaxing in the chair and smiled confidently to himself that perhaps he had the measure of the man now and contemplated on what job Andrei was perusing on his behalf.

The more he considered the prospect the more he looked forward to the task, whatever it was. He was definitely bored with the amount of time he had spent alone by himself in the apartment. Although Wandeczka had always told him to ask her for whatever he wanted, including money, he had refrained from doing so. Any money she had given him was usually spent on food with very little left over for other expenses. With little money to spend he never went out other than to shop for his necessities, unless of course it was with Wandeczka. Now he could be free of her succour although he was truly grateful for what she had done for him and he would never forget the enormity of her aid. With the job Andrei could fashion for him he could now purchase whatever he wanted from the money he was going to earn. Finishing the last drops of vodka in his glass he replenished with another large amount and decided that would be his last.

Andrei returned three days later. As before on the previous visit he arrived without any warning again dressed in complete Russian uniform. On this occasion Jan showed no nerves and was completely calm and confident as he opened the door for his unwanted visitor to gain access.

They did not exchange pleasantries with one another and on entering the apartment Andrei immediately sat down on the nearest chair in the living area.

'I have good news Jan.' He spoke laconically with an air of pomposity in his voice. 'You will take up a position in the NKVD directly under my supervision.'

Jan who had also sat down on a chair opposite Andrei and who had said nothing since Andrei's arrival, now fought to retain his initial calmness and control which had been disturbed as a result of Andrei's announcement. He was thankful that he was sitting down otherwise he would have fallen down. Clearing his throat, speaking slowly and clearly so that he understood what Andrei had said, he repeated his visitor's last words.

'A position in the NKVD.'

'Yes, that is correct.'

Jan swallowed heavily and Andrei noticed the action.

'Do not worry; you will have a position of no responsibility. You cannot,' he corrected himself; 'you will not do any harm in the task I have chosen for you.'

Recovering slowly from the initial shock of being told he was to work in the NKVD he ventured a question. 'What are my duties to be?'

'You will work for me as my driver as and when I require you. When you are not needed by me, you will carry out minor clerical duties.' He eyed Jan as he spoke looking for any further reaction. There was none. Jan had fully regained his composure and his control.

'Will I travel with you when you are away on duty?'

'Occasionally, yes. Though I do not see this happening too often.'

Jan was relieved at this. Whilst Andrei was away he would be able to see Wandeczka whenever he wanted. 'So long as it is outside my working hours,' he reminded himself.

'Are there any other questions?' Again Andrei returned to his earlier terse attitude realising he had mellowed in his manner of speech whilst he had been conversing with Jan.

'No. No more.' And then a final important question came back to him: 'When do I commence my duties?'

'I leave at the end of this week for a trip to Poland, I should now say the western Soviet Union,' he corrected himself, once more eyeing Jan crucially for any reaction but detecting none. 'I return in two weeks time. Then you will begin your duties.'

There was a pause. Jan had noted what Andrei had said and the comment certainly touched a nerve deep inside him. 'Bastard,' he thought. Outwardly he did not reveal his emotions and as Andrei continued, the feeling subsided but his memory held it firm in his mind.

'If there is nothing else I shall return home.' He arose and walked to the door in the same quick manner as he had entered.

He opened the door and Jan followed behind. Walking out over the threshold he turned back to Jan.

'There is one small problem Jan,' the listener became alert. 'From time to time you will see documents that will be confidential. If you ever relay any of this information to other sources, unless I have specifically given instructions to do so, then you will be shot. Do I make myself clear?'

'Yes,' Jan replied simply.

Andrei left without as much as a farewell.

Jan closed the apartment door, retraced his steps into his living area and dwelled on what Andrei had told him. He thought about the false background that Andrei had manufactured for him and what might happen now that he was going to work for the NKVD.

Andrei, Wandeczka and himself had been over his new background on many occasions. He was her long lost cousin from the south of Russia who had originally come to visit and then had decided to stay in Moscow and seek employment. The thought struck Jan at the same time that Andrei had never asked him about his true background. 'He knows everything' Jan concluded to himself and dwelled on it momentarily. Jan had other matters to think about. If Andrei was happy with the story, then why should he worry? Whilst he was apprehensive about the position he was taking up, somewhere deep inside of him an excitement began to muster at the thought, at some stage, of him being in the possession of first hand information. Of what he did not know, except that it could be very important and of use to someone or somebody outside of the Soviet Union.

At the end of the second week Andrei had left once more for his duties. Wandeczka waited until the next day to visit Jan and they spent the whole day together, most of it in bed, until Wandeczka had to finally and reluctantly leave in the evening for the club at which she performed.

Spending the day alone in their own company, they talked frankly about their relationship and their love for one another. They discussed in which direction their separate yet connected lives were leading to.

'There is nothing we can do at present,' Jan announced. 'Our country,' he corrected himself, 'sorry my country is occupied by two armies who only want to see its complete destruction. I cannot leave and go back until it is recognised and controlled by its own people once more.'

'Your country is my country Jan. Do not forget that I'm half Polish too. Does that mean you will remain here until our country needs you?'

'Yes. In the present circumstances, if I return there is nothing that I can do to help. Stalin has taken thousands probably millions of my people and either killed or transported them to far off places. If I go back and I'm caught, the same fate will await me. Poland is a shell of its former self with the cream of its inhabitants gone, perhaps forever. All I can do is wait until the moment arrives when I can return. One thing is for sure, I'm looking forward to the job even though it is as a member of the NKVD.'

'That was a complete shock to me. I never thought you would take up the position. It stands for everything you despise.'

'I know. But what else can I do? I'm indebted to you and Andrei for the help you have afforded me. I cannot refuse whatever he offers. He could dispose of me; throw me out in the street. It would be easy for him to do such a thing.'

Wandeczka sat up and leaned toward him. He glimpsed her bare breasts as the bed sheet fell to her waist and concentrated his vision on the left nipple he had been playing with whilst they conversed. She covered his mouth with her hand interrupting his chatter and reassured him. 'Firstly, Jan, you will never owe me anything for what I have done for you. There is no such thing as an obligation by you to me. You owe me nothing. You are free to go whenever you wish. If not now, then later when the time is right for you to move. Do you understand me? No debt. No obligation.'

He turned his attention from her body to her face as she spoke. She stared into his eyes and he could see the beauty suffusing with her kindness which emanated from her dark green brown sparkling optics. The look he gazed upon filled him with a warm comfortable and secure feeling that he had not known since before the Russians had invaded his homeland.

Again she asked with kindness. 'Do you understand?'

Jan simply nodded that he did.

Satisfied that he understood, she continued. 'Secondly, there is nothing Andrei would not do for me. He would never throw you out unless I wanted you out. Therefore you will be safe for as long as you wish, which I hope will be a long time.' There was a pause before she continued. Another thought had crossed her mind. 'If our love ends for whatever reason you need not fear. If you ever fall out of love with me Jan I need to know immediately. Do you understand? Even if that happened I would never turn Andrei or anyone against you.'

He clasped her hand tightly. She smiled at him and they caressed.

As they broke their embrace Jan could not help but remember the last words that Andrei stated before leaving. His mind dwelled on those thoughts now. 'From time to time you will see documents that will be confidential and that under no circumstances are you to reveal the contents to anybody except those that I specifically name.'

Jan's eyes lit up with the prospect of diverting that information to those who really wanted to know. The Polish people. He had thought about the idea many times since Andrei had mentioned the fact and Jan had dwelled on the cogitations of helping his country in this way. He said nothing more to Wandeczka about the idea, simply because if anyone ever found out she would be innocent and would therefore be unharmed.

'Where you go Jan, I too may choose to follow.' She whispered as if propositioning him and immediately she climbed onto his lower abdomen. With her hand she nurtured his half erection to its full complement. Then she put his slim, though powerful, rhythmic body through the motions of pleasure and ecstasy once again.

Fleetingly he dwelled on her last words, which didn't alarm him, and then became sidetracked as his attention was all hers for a more immediate pleasurable outlet.

Dressed in his new dun coloured uniform, with distinctive red collar patches on the shirt, afforded to lower ranks of the NKVD, Jan's feelings were twofold as he left his apartment and climbed into Andrei's automobile to commence his first day of duty with the Regime. His internal disgust at becoming a member of such an institution was only placated by his desire at some stage to be able to acquire information, any information, which maybe of use to outside sources especially that of his Polish government. Seating himself next to Andrei in the passenger area, he first reminded himself that he would have to be patient and allow sufficient time to elapse for people he was about to work with to be able to trust him, if they ever did trust anyone. With that understanding in himself he turned his attention to the immediate journey and the impending commencement of his first day duties.

Although he had travelled only once in that direction with Andrei, which was several months ago, as a result of his many walks with Wandeczka through the streets of Moscow during their long periods alone together, Jan recognised instantly the route the vehicle was taking. His stomach began to twitch eerily at the prospect of revisiting the prison once more. Despite his faintest feelings of disgust which had risen, Jan was prepared, and had been so since the first encounter, for any situation that his host might introduce him to in future.

He did not have long to wait to confirm whether or not it was their final destination. 'I'm prepared for any depraved and debauched exhibition which you may present for my pleasure Andrei Tscharakova,' Jan vehemently mouthed to himself as the automobile sped past the large wooden gates of the Lefortovo and on toward its final destination which they reached ten minutes later.

They drove through what appeared to be a similar set of gates which they had earlier passed by. On this occasion Andrei parked his automobile along with several other vehicles at the opposite end to the entrance which they had come through.

The Senior Officer alighted from the vehicle and took pleasure in welcoming Jan to the building as if it was his own domain. His pride and pleasure. 'The Lubyanka.' Andrei announced almost merrily. 'The headquarters of the NKVD which also serves as a prison similar to the Lefortovo we visited before. Do you remember Jan?' Andrei asked his expression changing quickly as he eyed him sardonically. He did not wait for a reply and continued. 'Certain people have been heard to remark that the cells here underground' he happily pointed downward, 'can be worse than the Lefortovo. One other thing, periodically you will be visiting the Lefortovo to carry messages.' His expression became serious again. 'Do not forget our talk several months ago and how you too could find yourself in those cells, or if you prefer in the cells below where we stand now.' The warning was given with venom and disdain echoing through his voice.

Although he knew the nefarious streak in the man, the declaration still stunned Jan and it showed on his face.

Andrei continued to laugh inwardly, sure of the fact that his inferior in-law had initially surmised he was being taken again to visit the filth and degradation he had visited in the Lefortovo months earlier. Andrei also could not help but think that the possibility of Jan arriving here, at the Lubyanka, everyday for work, and the fact that he now knew the conditions in the cells were similar to, if not worse than those at the Lefortovo, would not allow him to forget the obscene visions that he had witnessed on their earlier visit to the prison and that those visions would continue to conjure themselves in his mind. Andrei, above all, hoped that Jan would not be able to forget.

Jan listened to Andrei. His thoughts paralleled Andrei's hopes. Though Jan was pondering on the cesspits that lay hidden in the depths of the Lefortovo and, as he had been cheerfully informed, the Lubyanka, it was not as to how he could end up there, but of how to devise a plan so that he could visit his friend, whom, when he had last called, had lain so badly beaten in the hovel. 'Andrei has presented me with the perfect opportunity in an official capacity. Somehow I must find a way to get below,' he surmised to himself as his superior rank stirred him out of his busy mind.

'Come, Jan, we have work to do.' Andrei ordered as they climbed the few steps to the building which Jan would soon become accustomed to. Andrei continued his instructions. 'You will walk or find your own form of transport to this place of work from now on as do all my subordinates.' He emphasised the last word. 'We may be related as a result of my marriage to your cousin but that will not help you anymore. I do not want our family connection broadcast either. Understand?' He moved ahead hastily without waiting for the reply.

Walking through the corridors of the headquarters of the Secret Police, the first and immediate observation Jan noticed and was surprised at was the quietness of the interior of the building. Entering Andrei's department, the silence was partly broken as his superior introduced Jan to a man of large stoutness who stood several inches shorter than himself. His portly figure was too large for his clothing and the folds of skin bulged from under the dull brown material of his uniform. His hair was thin and combed in such a way to hide an almost bald scalp and his tiny pale blue eyes inspected Jan all over in seconds.

'Jan Pilochka, meet Philip Vaseli Vorolenko, my personal secretary.'

'Welcome Jan,' he hissed as he held out his hand to be introduced to the new subordinate. Shaking hands Jan felt the opposite number's warm sweaty palm almost sticking to his own before finally separating.

The newcomer reciprocated and his first hypothesis was that the man could not be trusted and was probably Andrei's personal spy as well as his personal secretary. 'One to watch,' Jan warned himself.

The day was relatively quiet for the new recruit. Philip showed him around the relevant offices and areas of the building which Jan was likely to frequent. Wishing to keep suspicions away from him Jan decided on his earlier agreed plan to settle into the job quietly before asking any questions which may be of use to him in the future.

CHAPTER 23

Winter arrived with a vengeance bringing with it the short days and the very long nights. The temperatures dropped to well below zero and the land all around was covered with a thick layer of snow. There was very little to do when the premature nights descended and entertainment reverberated around conversations of past memories of the Sagajlo family.

Juliana listened with enthusiasm to her new family as they conversed over many happy moments. A trace of animosity crept into her thoughts as she compared her own childhood and upbringing to that of Sophie. Although her childhood had also, in the main been happy, at the same time it was much harder. She felt guilty at her disloyal thoughts toward her new friend who had become like a sister to her. Inwardly she was disappointed with herself and made up for her slight by grasping Sophie's hand.

The conversations continued on most nights. Each night several new stories would surface as well as a repetition of those already recollected. If the conversation subsided early the family either read by whatever light was available usually candlelight, or fell into an early slumber.

Very few books were available to read and those that were present were read over and over many times. The days passed by without any warning of the months following. Christmas was upon them quickly, taking them by surprise. They were unprepared for the occasion in every aspect. There was little food to be had and a feast was out of the question. No money or spare provisions were accessible to purchase or barter for presents. Even if they had the necessary purchasing power the selection of goods on offer was very limited.

The Kazaks and Russians in the village never celebrated Christmas. This year they would be joined by the deported Polish people. On the evening before Christmas and during the next day the Sagajlo family remembered and talked continuously of the celebrations back home and the important part they played in their lives.

Along with most countries in the world it was primarily a family affair. On Christmas Eve the children searched for the first star in the sky signalling the end of the fasting and that supper would soon be served. The tree would be decorated by the parents and the door to the room was kept locked until the meal was ready to be served. Before commencing the meal the parents would give each of the children a piece of the blessed bread and wish them happiness in the coming year. Under the tablecloth hay was spread over in remembrance of Jesus in the manger. Preferably twelve dishes should be served in memory of the Apostles. If the number was unavailable then the settings should be even to avoid any misfortune in the future.

'Borsch' was usually served as the first course which was soup made of beetroot with dumplings and mushrooms. The second course was a selection of fish cooked in different ways, some fried, and some in gelatine. This was followed by a choice of 'pieroshki' ravioli. The last course being served was the sweet dishes such as pastries called 'mazurki.'

After supper the whole family would take any food that remained over to the barns and stables and give it to the animals and the birds so that all should have a share of the feast on the holy night and none should feel lonely. The country people had many charming superstitions one of them being that on Christmas night all animals can speak and that good people can understand them.

When feeding the animals was completed the family returned to the house to receive their presents. Carol singing followed and those carol singers who visited the houses were invited inside. This gathering continued until it was time to attend Midnight Mass.

Almost from the first day of their arrival, Yuri Sagajlo was looked upon as the leader of the small contingent of Polish people who had arrived in the village. Whether this was because he was a doctor who had endeavoured to provide succour during the journey to those who needed help, or whether it was down to the fact that he was always available to simply listen to their problems and concerns and if he could not help them in some small way, then at least they had been able to confide their troubles to someone, sharing the unseen burden that weighed heavy on their minds. For the relief it brought to them they were truly grateful and they looked to him frequently for guidance and assistance.

'You have enough problems of your own to worry about,' Helena, his wife, would tell him when he occasionally became very disillusioned because he knew he could not help someone to overcome their difficulties. It was useless for her to utter her disagreement, which she only voiced to him when he became dejected, mainly to prompt him out of his mood. She knew full well that he had always been this way and deep down she loved him for it. He was strong and resolute, and he thrived on dealing with other people's problems and she felt sure that this is what he lived for, even more now that he was in a distant land.

It was like this once more on a bitterly cold night at the beginning of January when Krysia Voseskaya arrived at the abode where Yuri Sagajlo was staying with his wife and daughter together with Juliana. The woman was crying hysterically the moment the door was opened and she cast her eyes upon the large appearance in front of her. His black coloured hair had started to grey many years before and since their short period in Siberia the process had accelerated. The large round nose appeared as though it had been stuck on his face like a bulbous lump of plasticine and together with his hazel coloured eyes much tenderness emanated from his oval friendly face. The red cheeks he appeared with on opening the door had quickly disappeared as the cold winter outside stole the warmth from his face replacing its own brand of severity over the man's features.

'Come in! Come in! Roscie prawo! Roscie prawo!' He beckoned Krysia hastily indoors, keeping her from catching her deathly cold and preserving the warmth in the house from escaping forever into the bitter cold night air. He spoke in his native tongue which was deep and reverberating but strangely comforting to those who knew him.

'What is the problem?' he asked soothingly as he placed his arm around her at the same time guiding her to their own private warmth in one of the two rooms within the house. Although they shared the abode with another local family the heating and cooking in the dwelling were separate concerns for the two different parties.

Entering the house and being assuaged by the Doctor immediately calmed her and the tears started to subside but her sobbing continued. 'M…my little boy, T…Tomus, h…he is h…hungry and I have no f…food for him. I'm sure I can see his belly swell as I w…watch him each day.' Her weeping strengthened as she finished her sentence and Yuri looked upward for help and guidance. He left the warm area around the stove and went to his store of food, took out some bread and on returning gave it to the woman.

'Give him this for tonight and tomorrow I will try to get more. Have you eaten?' he asked tenderly.

'Not since yesterday, but I will be all right. Some food has been promised to me tomorrow.' His benevolence stemmed her tears.

Yuri again crossed to his store and handing her a second portion of bread gestured her to take the food.

'I cannot,' she declined the offer.

'Take it,' he insisted.

'No, this will be enough for Tomus tonight. I can wait till tomorrow. You may receive other callers Doctor.' She turned and walked to the door without accepting the second offer of food, uttering her thanks as she disappeared into the night air closing the exit behind her.

After her visit there was silence in the house. Sophie broke the quiescence by asking a general question of everybody. 'What can we do? Three other people have died already. Tomus may follow.'

There was a long silence as the remainder dwelled on her words and the lengthy pause was broken by her father answering her enquiry. 'There is nothing we can really do without food.'

'Will the boy die Papa?' she ventured wanting confirmation of her earlier statement.

'I will examine him tomorrow. Perhaps there is still a chance.'

'A chance, what do you mean?'

'If we can acquire some food, then he may live.' A morbid silence fell over the conversation. Then Yuri continued, correcting himself. 'That is not true. I examined the boy last week and then he was well past the early stages of malnutrition. I think it is too late to save Tomus at this stage.'

'Why Papa? Why?' Sophie anxiously enquired raising her voice, almost pleading with him to do something, anything, and knowing full well that there was nothing he could do to save the child otherwise he would have done so already.

'With hunger and starvation there comes a stage when it is too late and the body rejects all that it is offered. No amount of food can save the person. In hygienic circumstances, with the proper care and nursing and with sufficient food, the boy may have stood a chance. In this lower world where we now find ourselves, there is no hope.' He nodded his head to reiterate his point. 'Only a miracle will save him now.'

'How can we prevent other children like Tomus from dying Papa?'

'As I have said food is the best medicine and it is the main ingredient that we lack.'

The conversation ended with that statement and not for the first occasion did the whole group sit and pray together. Uppermost in their prayers was the dying child, Tomus, and the strongest prayers were for the hope that there would be no more children who would suffer like him.

Tomus Voseskaya died four days later. The cause of death, as far as Yuri Sagajlo could diagnose with the inadequate equipment he possessed, was due to severe malnutrition in its later stages which had in turn broken down the defences of the body allowing pneumonia to invade, develop and proliferate.

The grave took several days to excavate due to the severe weather conditions and the hardness of the ground. The ablest of men and women from the Polish community were divided into separate groups which worked in one hour relays to prepare the sepulchre for the funeral. Whilst the people in the village awoke that morning a fresh fall of snow had descended during the night and more work had to be completed before the grave was finally prepared.

The entire Polish contingent, including the sick, attended the funeral. Sophie stood in her inadequate winter wear, as did the majority of mourners. The freezing cold belied the midday sun beating down on the body of the small boy as the shivering bier of human beings slowly delivered the small corpse to the graveside. The cadaver was wrapped in an old rag, his clothes already taken and dispersed to those families with children.

With the corpse of the dead boy lying in full view of her, the rictus set full in his jaws, his stretched stomach swelled to a hideous size resembling an abnormal growth as a result of the hunger he had battled through against insurmountable odds, Sophie vowed that something would have to be done to stop this nightmare from occurring again. She knew what she had to do and it should be done immediately rather than at some time in the future. 'Haste will save lives' she told herself. Deciding on her course of action, she knew that this was the acid test of her relationship with him.

The body was lowered into the ground with the mother of the dead child collapsing and almost following her son into the grave. Two friends rushed to her aid.

Wasting precious time, Sophie waited until all mourners had left the graveside and made their way back to their lodgings. She walked by herself and as she entered the village she made a detour around the back of the houses without anybody seeing her movements and approached Vladimir's residence from the side. Not wishing anyone to see or hear her, she knocked lightly on the door. Almost immediately the occupier replied and opened the door smiling delightedly at his unexpected but most welcome visitor.

'Come in, come in,' he welcomed her. 'Sit down,' he gestured motioning a chair in her direction.

She sat and smiled toward him. An insecure smile infringed with melancholy at the thought of where she had just come from. 'Should I be here?' she asked herself knowing the answer as she questioned further her confidence in him.

She had never visited him voluntarily before and instantly he speculated that she required something from him. Without prolonging the suspense, he asked pleasantly. 'I do not think this is a personal visit. I suspect you want something. What can I do for you?'

Sophie was taken aback by his directness. He had never been so forthright with her before. She was unsure what to say and decided to start at the beginning. Unfolding her story she explained how the Polish people in the village, virtually since the commencement of winter, had survived on meagre provisions. Now, for many, those provisions were desperately low. For others they had been completely consumed. 'Already we have four dead amongst us, one of those a child. We do not want anymore to die. I have come here....' and she hesitated before asking the question.

'Come Sophie we have known each other long enough,' he cajoled her into continuing with her conversation.

'I have come here to ask you for a favour. You will be repaid in full as soon as it is possible.'

'What is your favour Sophie?' Inwardly he was delighted she had asked.

'I need food. Enough to feed the people through to the end of the winter when we can start to work again and earn money to buy our own.'

He had finally heard her request. A request that he felt sure would have been forthcoming long before it actually did. He knew that the food which had been put aside by the Polish people for the winter would not be adequate and that sooner or later one of them, maybe more, would come to him and ask for aid. He was delighted that it was Sophie who had visited as he had hoped all along that she would. He had formulated the plan and put it into action. He had played the waiting game. He had stalked her without her knowledge over the months and with the help of his two Kazak watchmen, like a predator cat pursuing its prey. Now he would pounce gently on her, unlike the ravaging animal. He had been patient, very patient with her, and she had come to him. Now he would take what he wanted in return for what she wanted. Their exchange of goods would be completely opposite though exactly what each other wished for, in his case longingly. She would not however enjoy her part of the bargain to him. No woman of high morals would. Vladimir sighed deeply, and contemplated how he was going to communicate to her what he had desired so much almost since the day she had arrived.

Sitting down opposite her, he gazed on her exquisite beauty which had encapsulated him from the first moments on viewing her. There was no easy way to explain.

'Sophie you know that I can help you and I will help you.' She detected a wavering in his voice, and she smiled a sceptical smile still believing that he wanted to help though unsure as to whether her request would be as straightforward as she seemed. Vladimir continued.

'There is something that I want from you,' he pointed at her and then moved his eyes away under a whim of guilt.

'We will do whatever you want Vladimir.'

Sophie had misconstrued his words and he calmly reiterated them emphasising the pronoun. 'No, no, Sophie. You. From you alone.'

Her worse fears which she had originally sensed on first meeting him, and which he had successfully quelled in her mind over the preceding months that he had occasionally spent in her company, now reared their ugliness again as she realised what he had really wanted all this time. The thoughts that she had deduced so long ago about him, and which had been allayed, were finally coming to fruition and she did not want to ask him to confirm what it was that he wanted.

There was a pause, and then he spoke again. 'Do you understand?' He did not wait for a reply and continued without interruption. 'I have wanted you from almost the first moment. I have waited and waited. The price is you and I will pay you with enough food supplies for many weeks.'

Sophie was muted as she listened to him speak, verifying what she already knew. With speed she considered her fellow villagers and the many lives that were in jeopardy and she knew immediately that she must suffer herself to fulfil her part of the bargain in order that others may survive. 'If it is to save lives, the consequences, although unbearable, would have to be tolerated,' she told herself.

Whispering, almost whimpering, she arose from her seat and enquired simply, 'When?' and then realising that time was of the essence she answered for him, 'tonight will be appropriate.'

Vladimir arose also. Her demeanour touched him. A sudden blaze of moral concern raced through his mind and he almost wished that he had not asked of her what he desperately wanted and had simply complied with her wishes instead. Over the months that he had come to know her his infatuation had developed into something stronger. Not love, but a desire so deep that it had gnawed away at his inner depths for what seemed like an age. To simply touch and experience her body, that is all he longed for. Then as quickly as his ephemeral, honourable obligations developed, it withered, and with muted success in his voice he simply replied, 'I shall await your visit.'

The remainder of that day lingered unbearably. Vladimir watched as the hours moved on at a snail's pace. Each hour seemed like a day in itself. He prepared himself thoroughly washing once on the hour before her arrival and then, after pouring himself a large brandy and spilling part of the liquor down his shirt, he washed a second time, no more than minutes before her feeble knock was answered by him ordering her to enter. Exiting from his bedroom he welcomed her and finished the remains of the brandy as he approached her. Despite his confidence with women for some reason he was apprehensive with her visit. The liquor helped to hide his misgivings.

Talking to her she appeared oblivious to his words and assumed correctly that she was nervous and perhaps a little frightened. Not wishing to waste time, and afraid that she would change her mind, he helped her out of the coat she was wearing and placed the article over the back of one of the chairs. Whilst he did this Sophie removed the scarves from around her head and took off from her feet the heavy felt boots, 'valonki,' which she had managed to purchase on a visit to Sokolovka, the nearest town. Returning to stand and smile in front of her he moved her cardigan out of the way and pressed his hand to her blouse and against her breast, touching it gently. Feeling the firmness of her bosom underneath, his reaction was instant. The touch nurtured a movement in his lower body and he furthered his exploration by advancing onto her second breast. Touching her, also brought an instant opposite reaction from her, and as he felt and gazed on her pronounced breasts through the garment she wore, it resurrected memories of the summer and the first occasion when he had viewed her similar to that now. This vision only served to intensify his groping. Without warning she motioned past him and walked toward the room he had recently vacated.

This reaction immediately reminded him that she did not have any aspirations toward him and that she was only performing this act as a duty for the benefit of her fellow creatures. Despite this cognisance, he still desired her and wanted her as quickly as possible. He knew that the likelihood of her changing course and pulling out of their contract was still a possibility and he did not wish to resort to violence with her. Turning to follow her into the bedroom he clumsily unbuttoned his shirt, disrobed and let it drop to the floor. Entering the room he was silenced by the rapidity of Sophie undressing. Her cardigan and blouse were already hanging over the single chair which was the only piece of furniture in the room beside the bed and side cabinet.

Seeing her so closely in a state of undress was breathtaking. Although her breasts were not large they were well proportioned in shape and firm as he had always surmised them to be. Now he verified the fact. Whilst she lowered the zip on her skirt he noticed her ribs impressing their shape on her skin. He immediately winced with distaste for he preferred his women to be meatier around the midriff. His disfavour abated as he witnessed her winning her battle with the zip, which had momentarily become stuck, and successfully lowering the garment together with her underwear to the floor. It revealed a mass of black plumage which now motioned him into a frenzy of undress to keep up with her.

As Sophie awaited his arrival in bed, through his haste, he nearly fell on her after fighting to take the last leg of his trousers off. Gratefully he won his conflict and joined her. He knew before he mounted her that he would be too heavy and as they changed positions he could feel the swell deep in his loins begin to muster as she nestled herself on top of him gripping him and guiding him to her. His performance disappointed him. Time had been forgotten when he had last been so rapid. He reasoned to himself that it was his monumental desire for her which he had harboured over the months that had caused the quick, though for him, delirious effect.

She went to him early that night, the memory of the boy's funeral strong in her mind and the body fresh in the grave. It was those thoughts as well as the cause of his death which drove her on to the ultimate loathsome encounter.

Closing the door behind her and making an excuse that she needed fresh air; she headed for her rendezvous, continually peering behind to ensure nobody was following. The snow lay several feet deep around her. In some places the drifts were double the height. Only a few days earlier the younger and stronger inhabitants of the village had dug the remaining houses, including Sophie's, out of the huge drifts. The night sky was clear. The temperature very cold and the stars hung like fairy lights in the sky lighting up the individual paths which led from each house and which had been cut through the snow like a mass of causeways. She hurried along to her destination full of apprehension of what lay ahead, shivering not as a result of the cold night air, but at what type of fornication she had to endure to receive her much needed and desperate rewards. 'It is not possible that he will be pure and simple. He will probably be a beast,' she whispered to herself. Her thoughts began to run away with unknown expectations and with them her already despondent manner increased. She gathered herself and corrected her depression as best she could.

Darkness had not only fallen over the village it had also fallen over her soul. That which she was about to embark on was against her moral attitude and deepest wishes. 'However,' she told herself, 'the gains are enormous. Do not pour scorn on yourself, you are about to save lives.' She continued haranguing herself, fighting the guilt that lay, like a heavy weight, deep down inside her. Looking piously to the heavens she whispered to her Lord, 'what I'm about to do will be for the benefit of others. If it is wrong, then please forgive me.' Stopping briefly to perform the sign of the cross and to genuflect she continued on her path.

The nearer she approached her goal the more her thoughts returned to what was expected of her that night. The act was simple enough she had performed it with Jacob many times and in many ways. Almost every time it had been richly rewarding. Her mind carried her back once again to the last day they had spent together which seemed so long ago. She dwelled on the afternoon of that last occasion when Jacob had held her in his arms and lowered her playfully into the river soaking her lower body. How they helped one another out of the river and she had let him go. The final act of ecstasy as they made love while their clothes dried. Tears formed in her eyes as, not for the first time, she wondered what had become of her Jacob.

Wiping her sorrow away, she washed her face in the pure white snow to rid all trace of her lamentation. Approaching the house and climbing the three steps to the entrance, her anxiety increased causing her stomach to rumble like distant thunder.

She knocked at the wooden door and could hear a muffled voice beckoning her to enter. With her knees almost careering together, she entered with immense reluctance. Closing the door behind her she turned to view her oppressor coming out of the room where he slept. He grinned happily and uttered words toward her. She could see his lips moving, though the words floated to and through her and she heard nothing. She was petrified. 'Control yourself Sophie for all will be lost,' she reprimanded herself.

Approaching her in his ungainly walk which for his size was natural, he stopped to pick up the drink off the table and finished it in one gulp. Breathing out heavily, resulting from the effects of the drink in his throat, he continued toward her.

She gazed on him with increasing repulsion and her instincts immediately told her to flee and vacate the place. Fighting with her initial reaction she held her ground. Deep in her mind her subconscious reminded her that she had come for the benefit of others and to save lives. 'The end result would be successful,' she told herself.

She froze to the spot and Vladimir, without asking, helped her out of her coat. Immediately after discarding the other articles of clothing which she had dressed in to keep warm, he stood directly in front of her and wasted no time in gently placing his hand on her breast. As he moved his hand across to her second breast and pressed against it more firmly, the goose pimples that sprouted over her body immediately verified to her that his touch was cold and lecherous. Unfortunately, his touch also nurtured her nipples to stand hard and erect and the protrusion acted like a trigger to him as he caressed her bosom even more. She closed her eyes and tried to think of Jacob and how he had touched her, though the vision would not present itself. She felt sick and to stop the contact she walked past him toward the bedroom. At first, as he followed her into the room she thought about turning away whilst she undressed, then decided against doing so. She wanted the performance over with as quickly as possible and if he watched her undress, hopefully it would stimulate him even more keeping their actual intercourse short. She noticed him gazing on her as she struggled briefly with the zip on her skirt and she hoped that his perusal was having the required effect. Eventually the zip came free and after discarding the rest of her clothing she brushed past him onto the bed.

Sophie climbed under the bedclothes and awaited his massive presence. Desperately, she wanted this over quickly. He followed her seconds later and his size was so heavy that she changed positions. She guided his erection, nurturing it as she did so, inside, and the coldness she had experienced as he fondled her minutes earlier, multiplied out of all proportion. It was not the warmth that Jacob had shown to her she remembered and again she endeavoured to surmise an apparition of her loved one to see her through the ordeal, but again it eluded her. 'Please let it be over quickly,' she pleaded in her mind to someone, something, as she lay on top of him with his paws reaching for every part of her body.

Thankfully it was not long and she gave thanks to the heavens as she hurried back to her abode weeping with relief that on the first encounter he had not called upon her to perform some inhumane indecent act.

Half an hour later Vladimir kept his part of the bargain and the selection of food which was delivered to Sophie reminded her family of the choice which had always been available to them in Poland.

'Whatever made him share with us?' Sophie's father asked incredulously as he closed the door behind the old Kazak men who had delivered the goods. 'Thank the Lord for one so generous. We must divide this amongst the others immediately,' he concluded.

Sophie smiled. Outwardly a feeble smile, inwardly it was a sickening smile as she nodded in simple agreement with her father.

Looking toward her, he could not help considering that somehow, more than he knew; his daughter had been responsible for this gift. He chose at this stage not to question her further.

Sophie estimated that two more visits to Vladimir would provide sufficient provisions for the contingent of Polish people, including her family, to be able to survive the remainder of the winter. Then each individual could return to some form of labour where they could earn their pittance in order to purchase food and feed themselves.

The second visit was similar to the first. Sophie was terrified of the encounter but there was nothing else that could be done to save her people. She had to continue with her ordeal.

On this occasion Vladimir was robust and rougher, frequently ordering her to change position. It lasted only minutes longer than the first confrontation and Sophie was greatly relieved whilst Vladimir was despondent.

Although it was late in the evening, after the performance was over, Vladimir had to visit one of the Kazak men in the village to discuss another matter. Trusting Sophie implicitly, even though he had abused her, he left the keys to his cupboard and locker on the table for her to take what she had earned.

Sophie ran to fetch Juliana, mumbling some excuse that Vladimir owed her a favour. Completely under Sophie's trust, Juliana with her counterpart, worked vigorously, and between them the two women almost emptied the cupboard and half the locker of a large amount of food that the cabinets contained as well as other items which were of use. Over three trips, both women transported the goods to their dwelling, during which Sophie continually prayed that Vladimir would not return. She knew that she was taking more than she had bargained for and that which she knew she should not touch, which excluded a bottle of his beloved brandy. She also realised that the amount she was taking could also prevent her from visiting Vladimir ever again to prostitute for him. She knew she could be tempting fate and the wrath of Vladimir could result in dire consequences for her, but she was willing to take that chance.

Before they settled for the night, Sophie, in fear that Vladimir would return and demand the repossession of his goods over and above what they had agreed on, decided to distribute the provisions to the other Poles in the village. With the continued assistance of Juliana she completed the task with haste.

When Vladimir eventually returned he unlocked the first cupboard to see what she had taken and proceeded rapidly to open the locker. His fury turned to anger and he slept fitfully that night. The next morning he summoned her to his abode.

'You have abused my kindness and respect for you.' He shouted at her as he stomped back and forth in the room.

Whilst he spoke she faced toward him but she was watching the fresh fall of snow through the window, in front of which Vladimir paraded, and could not help but think that his temper now was as strong as the blizzard outside.

'You know that you have taken more than we agreed. You owe me! You owe me!' he exclaimed in an angry tirade halting in front of her, raising his fist in unison then lowering it the next moment as he remembered how, before, the consequences of the act toward a woman had concluded in his arrival at such a remote backdrop as where he now stood.

Sophie closed her eyes expecting the impact of his force to rain heavily down on her. It never came and she opened her eyes to visualise the blizzard subsiding and Vladimir's voice toned with a more placid lilt. The harmony between his moods and the weather at that instance alarmed her.

'What shall I do with you Sophie?' he asked himself aloud. His anger quelled, he continued. 'What do you have to say for yourself?' and before waiting for an answer to his question, ventured his own reply. 'There will be another time Sophie. I know. When that time comes, you will pay for what you have done.' He was unsure whether there ever would be another occasion but he longed for the possibility of the opportunity.

She wanted to speak, to say something in her defence though she knew her protests would be in vain. Taking so much from him was wrong. Perhaps she had taken too much of his supplies. Perhaps he was left with nothing, though she found this hard to believe. If it was so then she was wrong but Sophie took comfort in the knowledge that what he was doing to her was even worse. As the guilt for what she had done slowly grew on her conscience, and on the verge of apologising for what she had taken, in walked the two old Kazak men who had delivered the food to her house after the first part of the bargain had been completed with Vladimir. Astonishment raced across her countenance as the two men carried, in their arms, a replenishment of supplies. On witnessing them refilling the cupboard in full view of her, Sophie wondered where the replacement of food was coming from. Completely dumbfounded she asked the question, 'Where? How do you manage to replace the stock so quickly?'

The oppressor simply smiled and then laughed at her.

The two old men left and they were alone again.

He crossed to where she stood. The smile was replaced by a more vicious grin and he grabbed hold of her. 'I think I should get full payment for what you received from me last night,' he garbled at her with a lecherous grin.

He was hurting her though she did not show it. His sudden change of attitude took her by surprise and she was afraid that he would carry out any act to get his revenge. The beat of her heart began to increase in pace. Her mind considered the options of what she would do if he proceeded there and then against her wishes. 'Should I fight? Should I submit?' She kept herself reticent and her silence enhanced the respectability he had for her. The pause lingered long between them. Her eyes pierced his and she was determined not to look away.

Eventually his grip relaxed before finally freeing her. He turned and walked toward the still opened cupboard, locked it, and retrieved his key placing it in the rear pocket of his trousers. As he did so, Sophie rubbed her upper arms to help recirculate the flow of blood which, as a result of his strong grip, had momentarily been severed from supplying her lower arms. She stopped immediately he turned and looked her way.

'Forgive me. I did not mean to harm you. Go!' he said waving his arms as he dismissed her, allowing her to go freely. He wanted her again. The effect on him was drug like. Now that he had tasted her he wanted her even more. The more he wanted her the less he could do about his addiction. He was not a fool. He knew he could only have her without force for a minimum amount of time. That period was drawing ever closer. The spring would soon return followed by the summer and then there was no possibility ever of holding her for ransom over the lives she held dearly to her and which she wanted to see survive the bitter cold, and even more, the deep strong pangs of hunger echoing in their bellies which many of them had tasted and were still experiencing. He wanted to perform with her and go further than he had done with any other women, except for the sluts he had debauched and they meant nothing. 'Why was this so?' he kept asking himself. 'Do not worry Sophie; I will have what I want from you. You must surely come again, for although you have taken many provisions from me, even those will not be enough to sustain you all through the remainder of the winter.' Again, more with hope than certain knowledge, he wished his thoughts to come true.

She left, pretending not to hurry from his abode. Walking out of the door she nearly crashed into the two old men who were returning with more goods for his cupboards. Gazing at them carrying the provisions, any lingering guilty thoughts she might have had disappeared completely. She felt no sadness for Vladimir as she headed for her own house wrapping herself warm against the cold and bitter Siberian winds.

The winter which had been coming to a close was unexpectedly prolonged by another fall of snow which covered the village and the surrounding countryside in a further cold blanket of ebony white flakes. The foreboding landscape was broken only by the splendid deep blue colour of the sky, interlaced with cumulus, contradicting the severe coldness of the day. This unpredicted late burst of harsh weather meant only one thing for Sophie. The chance for the village to resume normal work would be delayed further. Postponing the querulous event by one day would be crucial to the amount of food which was left to sustain them all. A week would be catastrophic. 'How long would this spell last?' Sophie agonised over the problem. She knew the consequences of this act of nature which had treated a cruel blow. It would mean only one thing. She would have to pay a visit to her undesirable host once more.

It was almost six weeks earlier at the beginning of February that Sophie went to him for what she thought would be the last occasion. This call, the third of its kind, would surely be her last she thought and no doubt her toughest. Forced into her purgatory acts for a third occasion she considered the hard facts that she would never be able to forget the events which she had participated in. Ejecting the rotten, painful memories from her mind she decided to bargain for one final substantial amount of food which would subsidise her family, and the remaining Poles in the village, through what she hoped would be the last bitter spell of winter weather and beyond into the spring.

Approaching the house that Vladimir occupied, her anxiety was greater than on the first instance when she had appealed to him. On this occasion there were further complications. Both parties had not talked since their last meeting where he had rebuked her for almost clearing his food stores and manhandled her roughly. Yes he had apologised, though she was concerned that he no longer had any time for her. If that was the case, then many of the Poles in the village would not last the extended winter period even though it was slowly coming to an end. She needed Vladimir to accept her now otherwise the two previous visits would be virtually to no avail. In the back of her mind she even contemplated offering herself willingly to any sexual connotation, even to plead with him, as long as she could save some of her people.

Before she had time to think any further she found herself knocking his door. He replied sharply to her announcement. Perceiving her in front of him he smiled at her and invited her in. Entering his abode she was grateful that her original thoughts of him not wanting her were unfounded.

Their bargaining took longer than usual and Sophie knew that for some reason he wanted her more than ever. She could not understand why, for although she had not told him so, she felt sure he knew that he repulsed her and from the amount of food she had bartered herself for, he would surely know that this would be her last visit. Leaving the house she hoped and prayed that he would do nothing obscene to her, though this she felt was probably impossible.

'No Sophie,' he mumbled to himself as he closed the door behind her, 'it will not be easy for you on this occasion. If you want that much food you will have to pay for it, unlike the last occasion.' Vladimir had not forgotten. 'The amount of food you have asked for will carry you through into the spring and I will never have the opportunity again. This time you will surely pay.'

To pay she was. Stripping naked by the side of him in the bedroom he took her completely unawares, seizing her from behind and around the waist. She was lightweight and no match for his strength. She struggled violently but in vain as she felt his erection searching for her in the wrong area.

He pulled her backward and down onto his stand and she felt the monster tear into her passage. 'Don't scream or you'll receive nothing,' he barked at her.

Tunnelling further into her, she wailed in a lower, muffled tone, always remembering his words. The pain was agonising. She had never been entered that way before and the experience lasted longer than her two previous encounters with him. Then finally, before the satisfaction of his erection was completely vented, he withdrew with almost as much pain to her as when he had entered, and still from behind, he inserted correctly. His discharge thrust its way up toward her inner belly as he sighed with delirious satisfaction. With pain in her body and revulsion in her mind, she deliberated to herself as he spoilt her, 'you have made me pay tonight as you said you would.'

Later that night the two old Kazak men delivered Vladimir's part of the bargain.

CHAPTER 24

It was for no particular reason that he had gone there that afternoon but uncannily he had found himself near to where she lived. The snow had stopped falling. It was a Saturday afternoon and he had decided to go for a walk. Passing the time in this manner helped him to sort things out, especially when decisions which affected him weighed heavy on his mind. In this particular instance the direction that his life was taking had come to the forefront. He seriously considered looking for a way to return to his native land convinced that his function in the NKVD would be of no use to those he wanted to help. 'Perhaps you should give yourself more time' he told himself. 'You've only been in the regime several months and already your thinking of going home. How will you be able to make a contribution even if you do manage to get home safely?' His mind talked to and questioned itself continually. Arguing the advantages and disadvantages of whether to stay or leave.

The one reason not to return was that of his family. When he had left to attend the evening's celebrations all those months ago he had no idea that he would be leaving his home for a long period, perhaps now for good. There was only his mother remaining. His father had died several years earlier. Although he was concerned for her he knew that she was a strong person who had, and who would, continue to survive most events, whether good or bad, in her life. After he had settled in Moscow he pondered at length on the merits and demerits of contacting her. Firmly he decided against doing so, judging that it would be safer for both parties that way.

Whilst deliberating these matters he suddenly realised that he was feeling colder. The winter in Moscow was particularly harsh and the fresh fall of snow was already strong enough to cover the old footprints of pedestrians. The steady flow of the few vehicles that passed had ploughed trenches in the road allowing the ebb of traffic to continue. At the side of the road the vehicles which spat up the flakes from under their wheels had turned the whiteness to a grey black which, from a distance, appeared like channels of mud. On his left the trees that habited the park creaked and groaned, like old people, with the burden of the produce from its seasonal visitor resting on its branches. He looked to the sky for a remission from the weather; at least until he could get home, but knew without a second glance that the snow clouds were visiting for a long period. The light was disappearing fast, it seemed with each footstep he trod, and he looked around and about him and realised where he was.

He was quite a distance from his own apartment and although he wanted to get home, he was feeling tired as a result of walking for almost two hours and much of that had been through heavy snow. He considered the idea of calling on her, only for a brief respite, and finding his way home later. Although he knew Andrei was due to arrive that night, without arguing with himself as he had done all afternoon, Jan decided to take a chance and call on her anyway.

Turning into the street where she lived the memories of his arrival in the capital over six months earlier revived in his mind. He had come so far and survived so much. Was it worth throwing it all away to the probability of being recaptured and deported once again if he returned to Poland? Approaching Wandeczka's home his mind was made up. He would not return to his country. Not yet. He was looked upon as one of them, a Russian. Only Andrei knew his true background and he would keep quiet provided Jan didn't cause too much trouble. With his cover his task to succeed could be that much easier. Fighting for his country, if it was possible, from within Russia could be difficult but surely not as difficult as if he fought with his true background being known. Perhaps after all there is a way of succeeding here in the capital. 'Be patient, your time will come,' Jan cautioned himself.

Immediately on hearing his voice she opened the downstairs door to the apartment block. The very late start to her day had improved immeasurably.

Knowing that Andrei was returning from one of his distant visits whilst in service with the NKVD, both Wandeczka and Jan, sticking to their original and proved plan that they wouldn't visit or contact one another two days prior to Andrei's return, had reverted to their normal lives, empty of each other. Wandeczka had performed at the club the previous night and had not returned home until the late hours of the morning. That was the reason for her late awakening. When she greeted Jan at the door she was pleased to see him but also concerned that he had broken their code of practice.

'Is anything the matter?' she asked worriedly.

'No. No. Everything is all right.' He immediately put her mind at rest explaining his reasons for being there.

She kissed him affectionately with a tenderness which partly revived the warmth in his body and then, after taking his heavy woollen coat and boots from him, she went to make him a warm drink.

'When exactly is he due home?' Jan asked. Whenever they were together they very rarely talked about Andrei. If the subject reared itself they always referred to him in the pronoun.

'I had a phone call last night, at the club. He's been delayed due to the weather. He expects to arrive late tomorrow.'

'I took a chance coming here. Perhaps I should have gone home.'

'No you were correct to come here. Even if he was here your reasons for visiting are understandable even to Andrei. And I would have protected you if he had said anything.' She wanted him to know that she was still here for him whenever he needed despite his acquired independence.

Jan understood her message and was grateful for her concern. He watched her walking toward him, carrying the hot drink, from the small cooking area in the apartment. Most apartments in Moscow shared their cooking facilities with several other families living in the block. Andrei through his status had managed to acquire an apartment which was more private than most. In addition to the cooking area it also had a second smaller bedroom and a small bathroom where it was possible to have a hot bath.

Jan noticed for the first time since his entrance, as she approached, that she was still in her dressing gown which clung to her figure. The shape was enhanced by the tightness of the belt around her waist. As she walked her right leg thrust out in front, unknowingly kicking the bottom part of the gown away from her to reveal a measurable length of her inner limb. He watched her avidly as her deportment intensified his pleasure. Whilst following her he could not help but wonder what she was like on stage.

'Drink this while it's hot,' she ordered as she arrived in front of him. 'Deep in thought?' she enquired further.

He told her what had been in his mind and added. 'You have a tremendous effect on my mind. Whenever I'm around you my problems seem to disappear, at least temporarily.'

'I wonder why,' she grinned as she undid her waistband and opened her dressing gown to reveal her naked breasts and a red pair of French knickers. She took his hand and pressed it to her left breast. The nipple hardened quickly testifying the coldness outside which his hands still retained.

She shivered and laughed at her bodily response and he followed.

'What about y...' He didn't have time to finish voicing his question about her husband as she knelt, open legged, across him and pulled his mouth onto her nipple.

'Don't worry about him. We have another twenty four hours together.' she whispered confidently as she then fed him her right breast.

Five minutes later she arose and rid herself of her lower garment and at the same time removed Jan's clothing. As she undressed him they groped for one another like two naive lovers exploring as if it was their first occasion. Returning to the chair, she stood above him and lowered herself onto his mouth. He entered and probed her as no man had done before and as she felt her private inner body being wantonly and pleasurably violated she could feel herself running away with the freedom and immense desire that came hand in hand. Her lasting was not long. Her waiting was quick. Her climax was utopian and Jan realised that he had been part of a new realisation in finding new pleasures in which to satisfy her. In the process he had become a master in helping her achieve that expectation.

An hour later Wandeczka phoned her club making an excuse that she would not be in that evening. She returned to the bedroom eager for more of what she had achieved earlier. On this occasion the process was longer. Both were ecstatic and fell asleep almost immediately after satisfaction had been met.

Throughout the winter of 1940 and into the spring of 1941 Jan worked hard at his duties in the NKVD headquarters of the Lubyanka. Without raising suspicion or asking any questions which were not out of the ordinary he had come to understand quickly the methods of administration within the department where he worked. He soon learned that Philip Vorolenko was a confidential person in his private as well as his working life and talked little about what he did in his spare time. Jan also noticed that his immediate Superior was not a clever person whilst at work, preferring, out of intransigence, to continue his working practices as he had always done rather than adopt any new methods to improve efficiency within their particular network. In addition to this, when Jan would recommend, from time to time, implementing a new filing system or making a change to a particular procedure, Philip would dismiss the scheme out of hand without considering the merits of the new proposal. After several occasions when this occurred, Jan decided on a new approach. He would drop subtle hints to Andrei regarding his ideas on improving the administration processes, careful not to suggest the whole revision and purposefully leave out certain points. Andrei would take note and after reviewing the new procedure himself, that Jan had informed him of, would order Philip to adopt the new method with the additional changes which Jan had wanted but had left for Andrei to work out and finalise himself.

After six months in the NKVD, Andrei recognised that Jan had settled into the job and that it was he, and very often only he, who had done anything to change and improve the day to day working of the department over the period he had been instated, rendering the section more efficient. When the prospect of promotion reared itself in the area there was really only one candidate for that position. Although Andrei did not want to give it to Jan, he knew without any doubt, that Jan was the best and the only person for the job.

The junior major lingered at length on who he should award the promotion to. Although Jan had approached his duties with care and consideration and had worked hard and conscientiously Andrei was not one hundred percent certain that his cousin by marriage was performing the job for the right reasons even though he had no concrete proof of this. At the back of his mind the fact that he was a Pole continued to irritate him. Continuing his deliberations for over a week, Andrei concluded that if he gave the post to Jan there was nothing of significance in the job, over and above what he was already doing, that could allow him to use any useful information he would see for some other purpose. Also, he did not envisage a problem with Jan supervising two maybe three men occasionally. Satisfied that there was nothing to worry about and that he could still keep a close watch on him, Andrei announced in the office the next morning that Jan had been successful in gaining promotion. The latter was astonished at the announcement. At the same time he realised that nobody deserved it more than him. His efforts were beginning to bear fruit and he was pleased with his movement upward in the NKVD. The only person chagrined by the announcement was Philip Vorolenko. Jan could not understand why and promised himself to make the effort to somehow befriend him. 'He is the closest link to Andrei's work and I need him on my side,' he surmised to himself.

Only twice, since joining the regime, had Jan been away on visits with Andrei. On each occasion, at some stage of the journey, Jan chauffeured for the junior major. Andrei assured him that despite his promotion Jan would continue to accompany him on occasional trips in the future.

Jan still managed to see Wandeczka whenever possible and they continued to make love. Although Jan had accompanied Andrei on two trips, the junior major had taken an additional half dozen excursions on special duty for the regime without his accompaniment. On those occasions, whilst Andrei was away, Wandeczka would spend the majority of the days and nights at Jan's apartment. When the time had quickly come around for them to once more lead their own separate lives both would find it difficult at first to return to their normal routines.

Several months after commencing his duties with the NKVD, the first opportunity arose for Jan to re-visit the Lefortovo premises since Andrei had taken him on his depraved inauguration of the prison dungeons. Jan dreaded the return but knew he would have to go ahead. Each subsequent visit became easier to accept until eventually it became part of his job routine.

Despite his initial and understandable misgivings about returning to the Lefortovo his desire to visit the filth that lay below ground level to see if his colleague and friend were still alive was strong. Each time his mind warned him to be careful and also to heed Jacob's words, 'Promise me you will never return.' So far he had never done so.

It was now after his promotion and on further subsequent visits to the Lefortovo that his confidence grew and he felt sure that he would have no problem in gaining access to the cells below and visiting his missing, though not forgotten, colleague. Jan's rank was higher than that of the guards on duty patrolling the dungeons. The only concern he had was if any inspections by higher ranking personnel would occur at the same time as he would be visiting. That was a chance he was willing to take. Above all, his curiosity as well as his concern for his friend was getting the better of him.

Exiting from the administration block of the Lefortovo, where he had earlier delivered documents in exchange for those he was returning, Jan looked across the courtyard that he had passed on many occasions previous. Today his path differed as he turned right and walked along the paved area toward the oak door that he had entered through unofficially with Andrei almost nine months prior.

Descending the steps inside, the stench he had forgotten returned to him immediately, unchanged. The lower he descended the stronger it became triggering his subconscious and all his previous wretched encounters of bestiality since his journey had begun spiralled in his mind like a continuous kaleidoscope of horrific events. Unlike before he was now able to control his nightmares.

Showing his papers, he explained to the guard that he worked in the administration departments of the Lubyanka. Jan mentioned Andrei's full name and title and that he had been given permission by the Junior Major to view for himself, whenever he wished, the dungeons below the Lefortovo. Unsurprisingly the avenues opened with ease for him to inspect the area he was now entering. Once through the gate he was along the corridor perusing the chambers that he had once looked upon with Andrei. On this occasion the proceedings were more sedate and Jan was completely calm.

Nonchalantly making his way toward the cell where he remembered his friend to be, hoping at the same time that he had not been moved for any reason, he stopped at two other dungeons on the opposite side of the corridor not to arouse any suspicion to the guard that he knew where he was heading. Finally he crossed over, peered through the opened slot in the door of the cell he had intended to visit, breathed the strong stench of human filth inside and asked if the door could be opened for him to enter. The guard did so without any questions, slightly surprised that he had not been ordered to do so by the member of the NKVD. The stench heightened immediately the door swung open and the heat doubled its exposure. Again Jan passed and witnessed the path of human filth and degradation that he had experienced on the first visit. Nothing had changed except perhaps for the men themselves.

Walking in the opposite direction to where he remembered Jacob to be, he moved slowly between the disgusting bodies that individually smelled abhorrent and collectively was overwhelming. The breeze through the opened cell door, to those inhabitants inside, marginally relaxed the stench, though to Jan it was still unimaginably powerful. Moving in a complete circle he espied Jacob against the same wall in a different area to where he had last perceived him. Several minutes later, and after bending to inspect one of the other captives in the cell, he stood over his friend. Scrutinising the body of the man he now looked down upon, he was relieved that the evidence of his friend's beating that he had witnessed before had healed significantly although several scars and bruises were still apparent. Kneeling in front of him, Jan winced at one or two lesions that had not healed as quickly as the others. From one wound fluid still wept. 'Nine months and still he is not recovered,' he thought sickly to himself. From the moment that Jan had arrived in front of Jacob the latter had not made a single move.

Lifting Jacob's face to ensure he was alive, Jan gazed on terror in his friend's eyes and immediately knew not to utter a single word. He winked toward him and before arising, purposefully dropped his folder containing several documents over the prisoner's feet. The guard, who had accompanied Jan on his tour, motioned to help and halted as the latter announced firmly that everything was under control. During the process of retrieving the papers and replacing them in the folder, Jan placed a bundle of rouble notes in the opened sole of Jacob's left shoe, out of view of the attending guard.

Before finally making his exit from the cell Jan repeated the process of inspection with another of the inmates, on this occasion without the benevolent gesture of donations of money. He had given his last rouble notes to Jacob.

The bastard she was carrying was of Russian origin. The realisation of what had happened disgusted her and the fact that it was not conceived out of love increased her aversion.

The Official had corrupted her on several occasions. She knew the risks and was willing to take them. Now she could not complain although she felt that she would never conceive due to her erratic menstruation periods. Without seeing a cycle since before Christmas, and before that only sporadically from the time she had embarked on the original train journey over ten months earlier, she had assumed, incorrectly, that conception would be impossible.

She reminisced on the events that had resulted in her present condition. What else could she have done? Before Tomus had died, which was the turning point for her, three other people had tasted death due to hunger, not directly perhaps, but in the end it was the root evil. Parents, her friend and herself were feeling the pangs of starvation and were slowly wasting away through lack of food which had expired when there were several more months of the cold, freezing winter to endure. The other members of the party who had accompanied her family to the village had also experienced the same dilemma.

The doctor and Sophie alone, in more detail, had discussed the problems of surviving the winter months without any food the day after Tomus's mother had visited their house.

'Your mother will never last through the remaining winter period either Sophie.' Her father had now decided to speak after withholding the information regarding Helena from her. 'Her malnutrition is more advanced than ours. She will be in need of food sooner or she will never survive.'

The news was a shock to Sophie and she decided to wait several more days considering the options open to her. But when Tomus died the final decision was made for her. Sustenance from another source without any payment was extremely unlikely. She now had to pursue her own course to save her people including her mother whom she realised was ill, though not as seriously, until her father had warned otherwise.

Now, two months after the last episode with Vladimir, she was pregnant. That meant that she had conceived on the second meeting with the NKVD pig. Continuing her recall she asked herself whether the pain, the agony and the suffering that she experienced was worthy of her cause. Counting the number of people who were alive today as a result of her efforts, there was only one answer. It had been a success, even though she was carrying an unwanted child, the stigma of which preyed heavy on her mind. Now it was her turn to find solace for that is what she needed desperately. She had to tell her story to someone, to relieve herself of the burden of the whole saga and its dire consequences. It was her turn to seek help. The person who was more able to listen at first and then to aid her was her father.

Waiting until darkness had fallen and both her parents and Juliana were sound asleep, she awoke her father and urged the importance of conversing with him now whilst everyone was in slumber.

Arising and sitting on the bed with her, Sophie recalled how he had not only been a quiet dependable source throughout their stay in Kazakstan so far, but also throughout her young life. Not only did he listen to his family's concerns but also to the people who had arrived at the village with them.

'What is it my daughter,' he enquired as he put his arm around her immediately bringing comfort and warmth to her. She remembered instantly when, on many occasions as a little girl, he had performed the same act of protecting and consoling her with his massive arms, that she had felt immediately better.

Sophie began to weep quietly.

'Come Sophie, there is nothing that you cannot tell me that I have not heard before. I understand that it must be important otherwise you would not have woken me at this hour.' He continued to cajole her wanting her to speak to him. 'There is nothing I can be ashamed of Sophie.'

The words he spoke made her think twice of announcing her tale of woe for she was sure that what she was about to relate would even horrify her father. Biting her tongue for self-assurance and fighting back the tears eventually the floodgates opened and her words spilled from her mouth candidly, like a child finally relieved at unburdening itself with the guilt it has carried for far too long. She, too, was like a child now, babbling the words in implausible and incoherent utterances.

'I did not want to do it father. There was nothing else to do. The only way out, a chance for us all to live. He had what we wanted. I had what he wanted. Now it is over and I will pay for the consequences. Oh father, help me. I'm sorry for what I did and now I will pay. Pay for my shamefulness.' Repeatedly her confused utterances continued and as her father held her tight to him to control her and to bring her back to some form of normality; she turned to him and with a last sentence which was completely intelligible she spouted the words which had eluded her during her gibbering. 'I'm pregnant.'

After her understandable verbosity had subsided, amazingly there was still silence in the room. This signalled to father and daughter, huddled together in one corner, that Helena and Juliana were still asleep. The tears which had fleetingly subsided nurtured once more. They fell freely over the soured complexion of Sophie's skin and she bothered not to wipe them away.

With the final utterance of her words he had understood everything else that she had previously rambled at him. A lump came to his throat and he felt himself screaming inside. His emotions were always well controlled but now he fought the battle not to cry. To help him fight he thought about what had happened. No, he did not like the outcome of the proceedings. His daughter was pregnant. However, his feelings for her increased tenfold and he felt no shame for her only admiration. She had done more to help not only her family but also the other Polish people in the village. 'She is worthy of all their respect and admiration' he told himself, 'and they will never know the true story.'

After a silence which seemed like forever, though only minutes had passed, her father spoke. He cleared his throat quietly for only now had his emotions begun to abate after attacking him on realising the immense value of his daughter's quest.

'My poor daughter. That is how you were able to get the food for us to survive. Vladimir wanted you and you wanted the food.' He repeated what she had been trying to say, ensuring her that he understood everything. There was another smaller pause before he continued.

'Both my admiration and love is boundless for you Sophie. No father could reject a daughter who has sacrificed so much to help so many. Your decision was magnanimous and your gesture not worthy of this world or the people on it. I'm in awe of you; I do not think I could have pursued the same path.' He held her tightly to him wanting to supply her with all the comfort that he possibly could. Embracing her in his arms as she snuggled up against his body, it was his turn to remember, when as a small child, how she felt more secure when they were close to each other as now. Again he thought about her experiences and the enormity of her sacrifice overwhelmed him. He spoke with emotion in his voice, slowly and deliberately.

'If we had not discussed the problem of getting through the winter and if I had not told you about Tomus and your mother, then this would not have happened.' He went to continue with his conversation and, placing her hand over his mouth, she stopped him in mid sentence knowing where the conversation was going. She felt a tear touch her finger. His sadness touched her deeply and she began to whimper quietly as she spoke to him.

'Do not say anymore father. It was nothing to do with you. I thought long and hard about what I was doing. Every second of the day and most of the night I deliberated on what to do. Finally, at the graveside looking at Tomus' wracked body, I knew what had to be done. In the end the decision was mine and mine alone. You were never to blame. The problem was discussed by all. Only I had the solution.'

'My little girl has grown up into a mature woman. I love you,' he whispered to her.

Emotions under control, Yuri Sagajlo broke the temporary peace that had descended and suggested that he examine her to confirm her pregnancy. In the deep darkness of the night the doctor verified to his patient, on this occasion his daughter, her worse fears.

With the terror now definitely assured, for her the conversation had not finished. Sophie readied herself for the next decision which she had also made alone and for which she needed her father's assistance.

'Papa, I have come to another decision. One where I need your help.'

The instant she had told him of her predicament, and throughout their conversation, he had asked himself would she go through with the pregnancy to the end. What he thought she was about to ask of him was against his principals. Still, with gentleness in his tone he encouraged her conversation.

'What is it?'

'I cannot give birth to this child, Papa.' Sophie had returned to her normal relaxed manner with her father now that she had told him the worse, or what she thought was the worse. Whenever a serious discussion had occurred between them she had always addressed him as father. Now she had reverted to Papa.

'It is a bastard and was not conceived out of love. The means for its conception are evil and corrupt. I cannot and will not give birth to that which is inside me.' Again silence descended on the room before Sophie banished it with the sound of her voice. 'Will you help me Papa? I want it to go away for good.'

She had finally requested what he did not want to be asked. Even before she spoke he knew he could not deny her his help. What she had undertaken was of immense importance. As she relayed her reasons for not proceeding with the pregnancy it had only strengthened his resolve to help her.

'I will help you little one and I will be near you at all times. If ever you need me you have only to call.'

Her emotion stirred inside once more as she heard the words 'my little one' being directed at her. Her father had not spoken those words to her since her teenage years and it was she who had asked him to refrain from calling the name in front of her friends. She was fourteen and he had used the terminology from her earliest memories. It was his pet name for her, a private name which gave an added meaning of affection between father and daughter alone. It had strengthened the bond between them. As she heard the words now, an aching came to her. She had missed being called that epithet and how, despite her circumstances, now in the middle of the steppes of Kazakstan, on hearing the words again they filled her with satisfaction, a little hope and immense joy. She knew that her father was on her side and it would no longer be a lonesome battle.

'What will I have to do father.'

'Nothing, leave it to me. I do not know of an herbal concoction to help you, but the medical man of the Kazaks has a solution. I will see him tomorrow.' He was unsure whether to inform her of the effects after having taken the drug and immediately decided to disclose them to her now.

'There is one thing Sophie, you will feel pain when the foetus aborts.' He held her tightly to him as he explained to her the details and consequences of what would happen.

'I have already lived through enough pain Papa that will be a small price to bear when the moment arrives.

She huddled into the pit of his arm and chest and Sophie was contented and at ease with herself for the first time since before her physical experiences with Vladimir had commenced. She felt now that the immense burden was off her solitary conscience and that after her final battle inside her had been fought she could at last return to some form of normality. Eventually, father and daughter fell asleep together where they sat.

Two days later at the end of a long exhausting day, Yuri and Sophie, alone together, walked out of the village. As they strolled they conversed about the day's events and the commencement of preparing the fields for the annual planting. The winter had escaped several months earlier taking its white produce and the bitter wind with itself. Although cold days still occasionally cultivated themselves they were of a dwindling species and the duration for which they came grew further apart as the old season grappled with the onset of the impending summer to continue its periodic existence.

Sophie and her father walked, perceiving at the same time the splendid colour of the steppes around and about them which came to life during spring and early summer. The wild red and yellow tulips, yellow and blue tinted steppe irises, dark red peonies together with purple hyacinths and blue sage blossomed in the late spring. Mingled with the varied species of tufted grasses they highlighted the plains in vibrant colour. The herds of wild horses on the steppes had completed their copulation months earlier, and now the males had left their females to foal alone. The bustards were out foraging for food and transported themselves more by walking and running than by flying. Their smaller cousins, half their size, the little bustard also joined them in their exploration. Occasionally, a demoiselle crane with its black breast and white crest contrasting elegantly with its grey plumage, could also be glimpsed. The surrounding area had come to life in such a short space of time and the seasons were taking turns in nurturing themselves once more in the New Year.

'Thank you Papa,' Sophie responded as her father handed to her a small vessel with the herbal concoction which the Khazak's medical man had produced for him.

'How will I know when it works?' she continued to ask him, concerned at the unknown experience she was about to go through.

'You will know my little one. There will be no need for you to worry whether the foetus has aborted. You will know.' There was a pause as they continued to peruse the beauty of the landscape around before her father continued. 'There is one thing that I do not know Sophie.'

'What is that Papa?'

'I do not know how long the mixture will take to react. There are three doses in the bottle. You are to take three equal amounts on three consecutive mornings. He told me that within three perhaps four days of taking the first dosage it would be all over. Do you understand?'

'Yes,' was the simple reply though she was afraid, afraid that her God would not forgive her. Afraid as to whether she was making the correct decision and she was also afraid of the pain which she would undoubtedly experience. The latter though was the least of her worries. She turned to her father, stopped him, looked up and confided her concerns to him.

'Papa, I'm afraid of so many things.' Instantly, with the knowledge of knowing what each loved one wanted, they embraced.

'Don't be afraid, I will be with you now and always. Remember that,' he reassured her.

With great relief, knowing that he was one hundred percent behind her, she sighed deeply and kissed him on the cheek. Then she announced to him as she held the potion up to the sky, 'Tomorrow will be the first day and by the end of the week it will be over.'

Looking at her, Yuri was still concerned for her. He had noticed that her outward appearance had changed. The glossy shine of her hair had dulled over the last several weeks. The complexion which had always been smooth to look at and even softer to touch had roughened and hardened visibly. Her peach coloured skin had soured to a jaundice tone and dark grey bulges grew under her eyes. 'Perhaps it was as a result of the pregnancy' he thought to himself even though he knew most women blossomed in that condition. 'But most women do not live in such bad conditions,' he reminded himself. Deciding not to question her on the subject as she already had much to concern herself with, he turned with his daughter and they retraced their steps back to the village.

The reaction which followed on the morning of the second day that she had taken the herbal potion was almost instant. It was as if the foetus which was being denied the gift of life somehow had knowledge of what the destructor was inflicting on it. Nausea came over Sophie as she returned inside the house to prepare herself for the day's task. With each passing minute the nausea increased steadily. She knew that she would not be able to partake in any form of work that day. Warning her father what was happening, he in turn, made some excuse to his wife that today he would be attending to the one or two sick people in the village, including Sophie, who were remaining at home.

'Will you be all right Sophie by yourself?' her mother enquired of her daughter before she left.

'I will be fine Mama, you go ahead. Someone has to earn money to feed us,' she replied trying to keep the effects of her increasing pain from authenticating itself on her face as she made an effort to sound jocular at the same time.

Her mother made some funny remark in return before concluding her comments with a final affectionate utterance to her daughter. As she came out of the house with her husband she turned to him and counselled him, although there was no need, to watch over Sophie.

Placing his arm around his wife he confirmed that he would check on her periodically throughout the day. He could not remember ever lying to Helena before and tremendous guilt now descended in his mind. 'It is not too late, you still have time to tell her,' he cogitated to himself. His indecision whether to confide in his wife was finally resolved for him as the landlady of the house called to Helena to walk with her to the fields. The guilt he felt subsided ever so slowly.

'Do not forget Yuri, look after her,' Helena reminded again.

He waved her goodbye and waited until they were out of sight over the incline of the dirt track road before re-entering the house.

Yuri arrived to an earth shattering sound as he closed the door of the house behind him. Quickly he walked through the small home and out into the small courtyard in the rear. Entering the house once more, he piled several layers of loose hay on the floor of the room that his family occupied. He then helped Sophie to walk from the second room into the first where the golden matting of hay awaited her usage. She was beginning to perspire and the droplets of sweat ran in tiny globules down over her forehead.

'I feel sick Papa.'

Immediately her father grasped at the nearest container which he thought was suitable for her to vomit in. She heaved once. Nothing regurgitated.

Suddenly, and without any warning, another scream came forth from her. Although it was not as loud as the first, the suddenness of the outcry startled Yuri.

Sophie, in increasing pain, did not want anyone to witness what was happening. She wanted to be alone with her own pain and suffering.

'Fa...Father,' she gasped in between her heavy breathing, 'I must be al...alone.'

'Will you be able to manage?' he asked helplessly.

She spoke no more, conserving her energy and simply nodded her head.

'If you need me then call.' He left and as he closed the door he could hear her panting increasing before being broken by another cry. He wanted to return to help, something held him back. He was unsure whether it was because of his own cowardliness at the inhuman sounds he heard emanating from his daughter or simply out of respect to comply with Sophie's wishes. He would never know.

She was relieved. Yes, she loved her father and she was grateful that he was prepared to be with her and at her disposal. Her initial thoughts were that she would need someone with her. Someone to fight the battle with her. Within moments of her father preparing the straw matting which she now sat on and then stood on, depending on what made her feel more comfortable, she knew that she had to fight this battle alone. Despite the nausea making her feel weak she still felt strong. She was scared no longer and she was determined to carry this fight to the bitter end. She wiped the perspiration from her forehead and ran her fingers through her sweat ridden hair. Peering down between her legs she awaited the full onslaught of the battle.

The panting and screaming chased each other for their share of the performance. The cries she echoed, at first she felt, and then when they continued, she knew, were for the tiny life form developing inside her. She was denying its existence. Denying its chance of life to be part of a world where good and evil existed side by side. Deprived of the opportunity to be a success or a failure. Refuted the ability of perceiving all the beauty and an equal amount of ugliness throughout the globe. The foetus was beginning the end of its short life and twilight had descended on it with venom of tremendous vengeance. Before the poison would take its final hold and before it would relinquish the fight, a battle which it would assuredly lose, had to be fought.

The screams of the unborn child continued. She looked upon it as the cries from a foetus of the devil. After all, was that not what the father was? He who had reaped his desire on the victim several months earlier, not once but on several occasions, each occasion worse and viler than the previous. Pondering on those moments she was interrupted by another shriek which momentarily deafened her. After it subsided her thoughts returned. Thoughts of her conception and now the final solution. She rallied herself in her decision that it was not wrong to end the life which continued to struggle to remain inside her now. It had begun in such a horrid, debauched manner. A life not born out of love and affection but out of lust, lewdness and immoral tendencies. Yes, she had consented, and what a price to pay. She was not ashamed of why she had participated even though, to her, the actual act with him was obscene and grotesque. She felt no guilt, no remorse for the act in question. She had saved the lives of many people, including her own family. But she had been dealt a cruel blow as a result of her actions. Whilst mindfully reassured that she had made the right decision to be rid of the child, the pain heightened once more as if in retaliation. The surety of her judgement wavered slightly and the guilt persisted, slowly creeping into her mind, endeavouring to reverse her original decision to rid herself of the baby. The foetus, by the only means open to it, called to her that it wanted its chance to live. The scream sounded horrifying as the pain in her lower body shot into her womb and returned to reverberate back to her lower area once more. The thoughts which passed through her mind and the screams which vocally echoed into the room, eventually gave way to the heavy panting which had returned more frequently.

'It was over,' she thought to herself as the deep red blood spurted then dripped slowly from her underneath. The pain had elapsed and her contorted body, which expressed the discomfort on her face, straightened itself once more. She breathed more easily and as the minutes passed some form of normality resumed to her bodily functions. Her perspiration abated and she felt steadier on her feet. She looked down past her lifted skirt at the tiny mess below her that lay on the yellow nest of straw. There was silence in the room.

Without warning, and as if the foetus, unknown to her and still inside, had seen part of its life system laying on the golden coloured carpet, it raised its last final attack on the one person who could give it life. The first battle was lost, though the war was not over yet. Almost collapsing with the massive spasm of pain which lasted longer than any other she had experienced since the episode had started, she rocked and fell forward only saving herself with her outstretched hand which grasped the rear of the chair no more than a foot away from her. Steadying herself, she managed to stay on her feet and let out a cry of such terrific force that her father entered the house seconds later calling her name.

'L…leave me. L…leave m…meeee.' she cried at him with a devilish scream of huge proportion between her gasps for the air which she found hard to acquire and with the pain still rampant in her body.

Without questioning he disappeared back through the door worried and concerned for the daughter he loved so much and for which he could do nothing. He had never noticed, ever before, such an expression which she carried on her face. For once in her life she was alone fighting her own personal war.

Rebounding again from her lower body, through her uterus and into her womb only to backtrack along its own path to repeat itself over and over again, the pain surged to such power that Sophie felt as though she were being beaten and kicked by some assailant. Perspiration returned in torrents. Almost capitulating and fainting with the pain she vomited several times which kept her conscious. As she regurgitated, her initial horrendous wail was now replaced by quieter cries in tune to her retching. As suddenly as the massive pain started it abated, moderating itself to a slow rhythmical bearable throb. Finally, having fought its last battle and accepting defeat, the last remnants of the infant not to be, fell away from her in a small glob of thick dark red blood. There was no recognisable shape; nevertheless she knew she had killed someone. She cried uncontrollably as she looked upon the sanguine life form which she had denied. Her feelings were mixed. Some of regret, which soon abated. Mostly of relief, but no sadness. The realisation of her resolve for not feeling guilty confirmed to her how the last year had hardened her to life. She panted heavily as she regained her breath and wondered whether that was the end of the saga. She waited and waited. No more globules of matter came. Droplets of blood initially fell from her to be replaced by a slower yet constant flow. Five minutes passed then ten, 'surely there can be no more' she said to herself. There was no more except for the continued flow, like that of a period, accompanied by the throbbing though acceptable pain. The whole experience had been worse than her father had foretold.

CHAPTER 25

Nearly a month had elapsed since her terrifying self inflicted ordeal. Before that day her nights were restful. Since that day her nights had been sleepless and her dreams, which were always of the same theme though of different versions of her abortion, had always been grotesque. She lived the experience over and over again as the realism entered her dreams building into a climax to suddenly awaken its mentor only for her to realise that it had all been a vision in her slumber. She would lie awake too afraid to sleep for the remainder of the night. Once again her father had been correct and the nightmares had slowly subsided to eventually disappear as the weeks passed by. She had not dreamt about the episode for nearly a week. Her sleepless nights left her and she returned to some form of normality. Both her parents were of immense strength to her although her mother knew nothing of the reality that had befallen her.

Sophie had only seen Vladimir twice, and then at a distance. She was grateful for that as her hate and loathing of him was complete.

Often she would walk out of the village on her own making sure she was not followed by anyone especially Vladimir. Since the abortion she had enjoyed her own company more than ever. Whether this was because of the guilt which she still felt occasionally deep inside or whether it was the fact that she had kept the secret from everyone, especially her mother, and only her father knew, she was unsure. But for the present time she planned to continue to enjoy her own company and looked toward an inner peace within herself. It was whilst on one of her long walks that she discovered another secluded area of the river which was suitable for bathing. Sophie had never returned to that part of the stream which she had located on first arriving at the village. Whenever she thought about the place and its beauty, it still held horrifying thoughts of her encounters, although not then impure, with Vladimir. For that reason alone she could not return to the place and had never done so. Although the new ground she had discovered was some distance walk away from the village, she did not mind. It appeared completely cut off behind large tufts of grasses and was well away from the normal path that people travelled on. She bathed in this new area in similar fashion as she had done so in the old area before, occasionally choosing to bathe completely naked.

Almost three months after their last encounter had expired Vladimir continued to reflect on his moments of fornication with Sophie. During his dalliances with her he had kept himself away from the other women in the village. Since his last occasion with Sophie he had returned to his old ways and had slept with several of the sluts who offered their services for a small price. After sleeping with them his thoughts would always return to the lady that he had so badly abused. He knew now that there were no circumstances in which he could have her unless it was by brute force. He reminisced on his spying missions of the previous year, when he gazed on her as she bathed herself in the stream. Continuing to dwell on the same thought over and over in his mind he decided to once again call his two watchmen together to find out whether she ever returned to the area she visited that previous year. It was summer once more and he felt sure that she would continue with her old habits.

Over a week passed before news came to him that she did not visit the place anymore. His disappointed expression immediately changed when the first of the two old Kazak men told him of their new findings, quite by accident, though this piece of information they kept from him, that she had found another place to visit approximately one kilometre to the north outside the village.

Vladimir clapped his hands together and smiled with glee. 'Come,' he beckoned to his assistants, 'show me where.' Walking in the direction toward the area, Vladimir surmised to himself, 'perhaps I cannot have you Sophie but I can still spy on you.' He smiled as his path took him north of the village and he knew that remembrances of yester-year could soon be exhibiting themselves once more.

Another week elapsed before Vladimir was given the good news that she was on her way to visit her secluded place. Hurriedly dismissing the whore he was about to exploit, he threw a few roubles at her to quickly rid her from the house. She went without arguing. It was not often that the NKVD pig had given willingly for nothing in return. She disappeared out of sight before Vladimir had pulled his trousers on. Hastily he made his way to the area where to him his new dreams and apparitions would come true.

Sophie had gone there after a particularly hard day's work in the field. She did not mind the walk as it helped her to unwind and relax from the strenuous tasks of the day. All along the path to her hidden bathing area she repeatedly peered behind to ensure nobody was following. Before she arrived at the spot, and after she was well away from the main area of the road, she began to undress. The sun was particularly warm that day and even now in the evening it continued to generate much heat. Arriving at the new domain she had completely undressed except for her undergarments. Leaving her fresh clean clothes at the side of the stream and taking those that she had worked in during the day into the water with her, she sat and then lay down, immersing herself fully in the cool but soothing waters. She disrobed completely and washed the working clothes and herself before finally continuing her relaxation in the stream.

An occasional light breeze disturbed the warmth of the evening, negligibly, and the sparkling blue water rushed around her freshly cleaned body, cleansing her skin even further. The coolness of the stream nourished a tingling sensation over the whole of her form and she felt surprisingly refreshing after a short period. Lying back once more, she watched her body playing games with the flow of water. Her feet rose to the surface and she floated herself momentarily. Then, submerging herself completely, her breasts defied her wishes and they rose to the surface, her nipples standing toward the evening sun like flower buds seeking the warmth before opening. She felt good about herself despite all that had happened to her. Finally coming to terms with her horrid encounters over the previous few days, her confidence had been restored and she was quietly proud of herself as she realised, at that moment, how many lives she had saved. Dismissing a thought on whether to return to the village, she continued to enjoy the solitude of the surrounding area and her pleasing thoughts. As ever her reminiscences returned to happier events of her past life with the parents and brother she adored before finally resting with the man she loved. Whilst she dwelled on the past she automatically sat up and washed herself and her working clothes a second time.

His perspiration ran in torrents down his forehead and fell onto his shirt, heavily soaking and staining the cotton material. He had broken new ground in his haste to reach the area and not to miss anything that she may have performed and that which he had steadfastly embellished in his mind. On arriving he blundered into the area without keeping his arrival a secret or surveying the area to see where she actually was. He glimpsed her in the water. She had her back to him and therefore was not aware of his intrusion. Rapidly searching for somewhere to hide, Vladimir could locate nothing substantial in the immediate vicinity to take cover behind. It was not like the old spot where he could view her from the bushes above the incline. He noticed the small clump of trees on the bank on the opposite side of the stream but to get there would surely announce his arrival beforehand. As she sat up, in the water, naked, bathing her clothes, he became entranced by her motions and completely forgot that he was out in the open.

It was a number of minutes before she sensed that she was not alone, as if some mystic phenomenon had warned her. The wondrous thoughts she reminisced, vanished immediately and before she turned to look behind she was terrified of what she would find. Swivelling around, she gasped in astonishment and trembled in the water. Her body stiffened and the response in Vladimir's loins was similar as she rose out of the water like some nymph. Although he had seen her before as she appeared now, her nudity was still stunning for him to perceive. He wanted to say something, to put her at ease, though the words would not formulate.

'Stay away!' she shouted at him. 'Stay away!'

He held out his hand limply hoping it would stop her from shouting, and to stem her obvious concern, he walked toward her clumsily. She immediately thought the worse as he approached. Forgetting the clothes which she had taken into the stream to wash, she grabbed the clean garments from the water's edge, turned and ran up the opposite bank to late to notice that he had pressed his fingers to his lips beseeching her not to shout or to be alarmed. He started after her in a quick trot, not quite running. The shape of her body from behind captivating him with each stride she took. He too was now through the stream and she had taken a run up the facing bank. Nearing the top she lost her balance and screamed as she fell back down, the clothes she gripped falling from her hands. She tumbled, her legs and arms spread-eagled and her nakedness clear and precise for Vladimir to enthuse on. He watched her falling and she landed at the bottom of the slope in front of where he now stood. Her heart was beating faster and faster and thumping against the diaphragm of her body as she recovered her balance and sat up on her haunches. A little composure was regained though she was clueless as to her next move. She covered herself and her nudity as best she could with her arms and hands. It was not enough. He continued to view parts of her, the parts which he had dreamed of repeatedly. He was transfixed by her nudity and his manly instincts turned atavistically. Somewhere in the depths of his mind a message came forth to treat her respectfully but his craving blotted out any sense of responsibility. Subconsciously he convinced himself that she was now beyond rapprochement of any kind. He leaned forward pulling her head toward him hitting her full on the side of the face with the rear of his hand. She reeled back against the sloping ground and her senses lapsed into semi-consciousness. Her hands fell away to the side of her body as she lost control and her knees parted. He looked at her salaciously and automatically unhitched his leather holster with its pistol in the scabbard, throwing it out of the way. It landed no further than five yards from where he stood. After unhooking the belt of his trousers, the breeches dropped instantly, revealing his throbbing erection. His instincts were mechanical. He had done it so many times before. She was still concussed as he lowered himself onto his stunned victim.

Juliana sat up immediately she heard the words being shouted. She looked around her and could find nobody. Instantly the words came again and she felt sure the voice was that of her friend. She arose from out of the water and dressed as she walked in a northerly direction to where the sounds came which was further up the stream from where she had bathed. Following the flow of water for several hundred yards and about to turn and make her way back to the village thinking that she had imagined the cries, she heard a second scream, nothing coherent, coming from the direction in front of where she now stood. She advanced further, careful to keep her presence secret from whoever was in the area. Creeping stealthily through a clump of mature grasses, Juliana came out onto an open area of land alongside the stream. Approximately fifty yards in front of her she perceived Sophie sitting in a crouched position, completely naked, at the bottom of the slope on the other side of the stream. Nervously, Juliana watched as the NKVD official leaned forward and hit Sophie with considerable force. With trepidation she watched the large, obese man throw his weapon to the floor and proceed to unbuckle his trousers. Thoughts instantaneously returned to her of events over twelve months earlier and the three soldiers who had raped her then. She began to tremble and tears of anger formed inside her. She walked forward, stealthily. Something outside of her had started to take control over her normal senses and she viewed, in her subconscious, the whole depraved act that she had once been through herself. Quickening her step as she viewed Vladimir's trousers falling to the ground, she whispered to herself, 'I cannot let this happen to Sophie. She cannot go through with this debased act.' She spied the holster on the floor several yards away from the two people in front of her and ran to gain access before her presence was known. When she was no more than twenty yards away she saw the Official lower himself closer to the helpless victim and noticed that Sophie had hardly moved and surmised correctly that she was still stunned. The next moment Juliana was by the holster, grasping the object. She fought to unbuckle the flap and free the weapon inside. Struggling in her haste with the leather case, she continually looked across at Vladimir to ensure he had not noticed her. Flashbacks of her own ordeal continued in her mind as she was visualising the present experience with Sophie and the past experience of her own suffering. Her own mind was re-echoing her own rape all those months ago. By the time she freed the leather flap and pulled the pistol from the holster she was seething with rage and looking for revenge, unsure whether it was for Sophie or for herself.

Entering the concussed victim, Sophie came around, and as he raised his hand to stun her once more he felt the cold touch of steel against the back of his neck. He stopped and slowly turned his head to find Juliana, in a bath of perspiration, holding the pistol in front of him. Her facial features, void of all colour, enhanced the shock and terror that she felt both for her friend and for herself as her knowledge of her own forced ordeal had returned to her so vividly. Sophie moved from under her attacker, to the side and out of the way. Vladimir turned over and sat on his bare buttocks. Fear was in his eyes also even more so now that he had a better view of Juliana's terrified features. Before he was able to speak, to reason or to plead with the holder of the weapon, Juliana, at close range, lowered the pistol, pulled the trigger and fired the first bullet into his groin. His penis severed from the rest of the genitals. The blood spurted forward from the wound splashing Juliana on the lower part of her legs. He was not dead and as he clasped his hand over his disjointed loins she pulled the trigger once more and shot him through the eye, leaving him alive long enough to feel the horrendous pain and to hear his shattering screams. She fired the third bullet into his heart before allowing the gun to drop freely to the floor. Sophie walked toward Juliana. They cried as they gripped one another tightly, comforting each other from their different though terrifying ordeals.

In the early part of June 1941, it was with total surprise that Andrei came out of his office and announced to Jan that they would both be leaving at first light the next morning on an important and necessary journey. Before Jan had the time to enquire where they would be going and unsure whether Andrei would have replied in any event, the junior major left the office immediately he had made the announcement. Presumably, Jan thought, to prepare for the journey the next day.

Jan realised that the trip must be of great importance as rumours abounded throughout the military establishments within the capital that the Germans had amassed troops near to the new German-Soviet border. Intelligence reports had secretly announced that some eventuality was about to break due to the movement. As a result of this action, senior officers, both military and civilian, were requested to remain at their posts unless unusual consequences prevailed to do otherwise. 'It must be extremely urgent if he is leaving his position,' Jan cogitated to himself as he too left the department early that evening also to prepare for the next day's journey.

At four thirty the next morning with the dawn breaking and the sun promising another warm day, Jan rendezvoused, as instructed, with Andrei at the relevant terminus to board the train. Not until they had travelled for most of the morning did Jan realise that they were heading south east. He had learnt long ago that once the journey had commenced, obtaining any further information out of Andrei was not easy. Any information would have to be volunteered by the officer of his own accord.

The journey by train lasted ten days. Jan had never travelled this far before with Andrei, the previous longest duration being of one week. The differing views and sceneries he passed made him think that he had ventured into and through several separate countries. Enquiring of Andrei as to their whereabouts along the journey, all the latter would reply was, 'we are still in Russia,' and he would simply return to his work and bury his head in his papers, occasionally ordering Jan to perform some simple task. As members of the NKVD, they were afforded the best accommodation and facilities on the train. Lower ranking members usually travelled in the lower class carriages but on this journey they had all been taken. So Jan travelled in comfort with Andrei. The whole saga provided new experiences for Jan.

Disembarking from the train early in the morning at the end of their journey, the local NKVD attachment had obviously been forewarned of their arrival. Six men were especially placed at the disposal of Andrei, one of whom was a sergeant. The necessary transport, a truck and automobile, were made available and Jan chauffeured Andrei on their final part of the journey. After the pomp of the welcoming party was over, which thankfully to Andrei did not last too long, he ordered, without further delay, that the party continue immediately to their required destination without any further stoppages.

The official party travelled by road passing scenery that was both beautiful and plain. The terrain was as contrasting as the scenery. The roads, usually passable with much discomfort, occasionally disappeared completely only to be rediscovered several kilometres further on. Having stopped for only two half hour rest periods, they arrived in the early evening at the small village which was to be their final destination. To Jan the houses were extremely small and he had never viewed anything of the like before.

Several days earlier other Officers of the NKVD, of lower rank, had visited the village and so the head Kazak man had been expecting the further arrival of members of the regime, although not so soon. Again after the introductions had taken place which on this occasion lasted no more than several minutes, Andrei gave instructions for the headman to line up the whole of the village, male and female, including his own people. Whilst this was being performed, the Junior Major further requested to view that which he had travelled the long distance to see. After issuing orders to his own subordinates, who together with the six NKVD men, proceeded to assemble all occupants of the village in an orderly manner, the headman turned and accompanied Andrei, with Jan close on his heels, in the direction of the local hall.

Entering the building, which appeared twice as large as the local houses, though still small in size, the two visitors viewed one large room. Both men were disgusted by the amount of vermin that crawled on the walls. The whitewash paint resembled darkened damp spots where the bugs and lice clustered in large groups. At the end of the room against the furthest wall was a makeshift table supported by wooden trestles. On top of the table, a blanket covered that which adopted the shape of a human body. The three men, led by the headman, walked toward the corpse. The odour they had smelled on entering the building, intensified the nearer they approached the body. The heat of the summer had hindered its preservation and as they now stood over the covered torso the stench was unbearable. Without being asked the Kazak headman leaned forward, pulled back the makeshift blanket, and glimpsed the body which by now, under normal circumstances, would have been buried. Andrei unflinchingly scrutinised the corpse. The first noticeable difference he recognised was the size of the trunk. It had shrunk since the last occasion he had perceived it and was unsure whether this was because the cadaver had been dead for so long or whether it was due to the limited choice of food in Siberia. Knowing the person as he knew him, he decided that it was due to the former reason. The cicatrice down the right cheek of the corpse's face immediately brought back memories to Andrei of the reasons why the man had arrived in this wilderness.

Having read the detailed report on the death of this Official, which had been given to him after disembarking from the train, Andrei continued his inspection of the cadaver looking for the three bullet holes. He could only find the two and turning to the headman he apathetically enquired, 'The third bullet, where did it enter?'

The headman gripped either side of the dishevelled trousers around the corpse's waist and pulled the garment down with little difficulty. Andrei was somewhat reviled as he lastly fixed his gaze on the damage that the bullet had caused, shattering the man's groin region. He realised immediately that probably he had been caught once again carrying out that which he was not supposed to do. The thought crossed his mind that the killer was a woman. About to command the Kazak to cover the body once more he noticed something crawl from the area of the groin and was ephemerally disturbed to see one of the bugs scurrying away.

Jan looked on the corpse with surprising calmness. He noticed from the trousers of the uniform, the only part of clothing left on the body, which was clearly unkempt, that it was the dress of the NKVD. He could not help surmising why they had travelled all this way simply because the death of a member of the NKVD had occurred. He ventured a question toward Andrei. 'Who did this to him?'

'One of the people outside.'

'What for?'

'Who knows? They are scum and will kill for no reason.'

Jan was standing behind the junior major and the Kazak headman who stood slightly to the left side of Andrei but also out of his view. Whilst the Officer uttered his last words, Jan detected a faint grimace on the face of the headman. The onlooker said nothing.

Jan's final thought was not of sadness but of acceptance, even relief, that there was one less member of the establishment to execute its severity on those still alive.

The three men reappeared outside in the cooler sunshine. The whole village had been ready assembled in some order outside the building for their purpose. Without further delay Andrei walked away from the building toward the gathering of, what appeared to him, grossly dishevelled and deviant looking human beings. Halting no more than ten feet away from the first row of people, he announced his intentions.

'Inside this hall,' he pointed behind himself to the building where he had moments earlier emerged from, 'a Russian who is a member of the Police force has been brutally murdered.'

Andrei talked and Jan's eyes gazed on the members of the village who had been assembled for their benefit. Despite the warmth of the early evening, the atmosphere in the village was tenebrous and as he looked at the different faces, all appeared worn and tired and miserable. He recognised the differences between the Kazak people and those with features like himself and immediately thought whether he too would have ended up like these wretched souls in the middle of nowhere. Struggling day in day out to survive and earn, in whatever way possible, enough money or goods to purchase or barter for an adequate supply of food to be able to live and breath and then, perhaps, eventually, to find a better life when their sentences were finally completed. They will probably be dead long before then he concluded. Staring on the misery of the scores who stood before him and who were being addressed by Andrei, Jan was immediately stirred out of his melancholy thoughts to words fraught with evil deeds as he heard the final summation in Andrei's speech which echoed above everything else he had said and was the conclusion of his rhetoric.

'In one minute, if the murderer does not come forward, I will execute five people at random. When they have been executed I will choose another five. This will be repeated until the whole village is exterminated. I know there are Poles amongst you here. Those of you who speak Russian should communicate the message to those of you who do not understand.'

As Andrei uttered his words, Jan's gaze, which still purveyed the sullied masses, fell on one face which stood out above the other members of the village. He recognised the features immediately and he looked to see if he could identify others. They were there also. His daughter and his wife. All three had aged beyond their years, and the emotion that Jan felt for them temporarily drowned out his fear of the threat that Andrei had seconds earlier communicated to the whole village. Despite his persistent stare in their direction, his counterparts did not notice him.

Within the space of ten metres, between the area where the military stood and that of where the village people waited, atmospheres of completely differing genres were experienced. On the military side it was one of soldier like business as opposed to that of the people which was tense and extremely frightening. It was as if a curtain had been pulled across the void to intensify the separate climates.

Andrei stepped forward after the one minute had elapsed and proceeded to walk along the lines of people who stood in abeyance. He tapped the shoulder of every twentieth person he walked past. On his instructions they in turn stepped forward. When the vigesimation was complete the five people he had chosen, who were all Poles of both sexes, were manhandled by himself out into the open beyond the rest of the villagers. He then ordered them to line up at the northerly end of the village still in full view of the congregation. Further orders were bellowed, on this occasion to his sergeant, who in turn commanded his men to prepare to execute the five innocent people that had been selected. The five soldiers burst into life and took up their positions almost instinctively due to the format always being similar and changing only slightly if at all with previous executions. The silence over the village was unparalleled, broken only by the sound of the guns being prepared for action and the occasional bleating of several women in the audience who anticipated the imminent massacre. The command was given to take aim. The precision timing and action of the soldiers was exercised for all to see. A loud shrieking sound was uttered from somewhere amongst the standing villagers. At first it shattered, then intensified the depressing atmosphere out of all proportion. 'No! No! No! Nyet! Nyet! Nyet!'

The soldiers, without lowering their weapons, together with the inhabitants of the village looked in the direction from where the sound had emanated. A woman, aged beyond her years, stepped forward and thrust herself through the folds of lined people appearing before the assembled audience and in front of the guns which still kept their sights on the targets. The soldiers who were ready to fire only retrieved their rifles to the normal position when ordered to do so by the sergeant.

In perfect silence the superior officer stepped forward to the woman. The deadly silence had returned as before. He looked at her scornfully, walked around her and talked to her from behind.

'It was you who killed the official?' he enquired and emphasised at the same time.

Jan witnessed all before. Although he knew what was about to happen he wanted to turn away, to avoid the inevitable outcome. As much as he wished to avoid what was happening it also held him engrossed.

Juliana remained silent and exceptionally calm. She did not understand Russian. The only Russian words she had ever learnt were no and yes. Again Andrei repeated the question. This time she replied in Polish, 'I cannot speak Russian.'

Andrei turned to the villagers and addressed them once more enquiring in his native tongue for any Poles who could translate. Yuri stepped forward. Although he was scared, his altruistic, spirited attitude continued to override his initial thoughts. In addition to this, Juliana had been like a second daughter to him since their odyssey had begun. Andrei repeated to Yuri his question for the third time, and he in turn translated for his adopted daughter.

'Yes.' Juliana simply replied in answer to the officer's question.

If she wanted to say anything else she had no time. The Junior Major had understood her one word reply. Indeed he had known all along whom the murderer was. At once he pulled his pistol out of its holder, pressed the barrel to the side of her head and calmly and leisurely pulled the trigger. The bullet flew out the other side taking part of her brain with it. As the missile continued on its path, the bulbous globules of brain matter fell to the ground landing in front of Yuri. Whilst the body of Juliana dropped instantly dead, Yuri instinctively and pathetically fought to catch hold of it as if he were somehow able to ease its descent. There were shrieks from several of the remaining members of the assembly. Seconds later, Yuri, realising a fatality had occurred, with tears in his eyes, fell to his knees and held the partly shattered head in his arms. Helena and Sophie who had looked on in bewilderment soon joined him in his grief.

'If it should ever happen again, five of you will be executed in addition to the murderer.' The officer calmly turned and announced to the remainder of the village. He replaced his revolver, walked to the Kazak headman and ordered him to clean up the house where the official lived as he would be staying the night and returning first thing in the morning.

Jan who was sickened by the whole episode gathered himself and followed Andrei, as ordered, back into the building which housed the corpse. He promised himself once more that this evil man must die at the earliest opportunity. He also warned that cunning and guile must be uppermost in any plan.

The lengthy silence was broken by Jan venturing a question toward Andrei. 'What I don't understand is why you have come all this way for this dead NKVD man?' He pointed at the corpse still lying covered on the table at the opposite wall.

Andrei turned to Jan and simply stated. 'Vladimir Stoich was my half brother. I had to come to ensure it was him.'

Totally stunned, the subordinate continued the questioning. 'S…So that is why you killed the woman, because he was your brother?' he asked, having great difficulty in hiding his incredulity of the whole sordid event.

'No, no Jan. There was no affection for him on my part and he probably felt the same for me. I killed her because he was a member of the NKVD. People should respect the uniform.' Andrei smiled disrespectfully as he spoke the last words.

Jan was more sickened and he now knew that Andrei, if not yet mad must surely be close to madness. Either that or there was an unexplainable reason for the man's complete disregard for human life. The promise he had made moments earlier returned to him. 'One day I will see you die for what you have wreaked on innocent people,' he reminded himself. Jan's precious attitude to life had changed completely under the influence of this man.

CHAPTER 26

Junior Major Andrei Valenti Tscharakova had been left to adjust himself to his forthcoming night's accommodation in the house which his half brother, until his death, had occupied. The dwelling was not much cleaner than a hovel, verifying that Vladimir Stoich had slipped into old habits after Sophie had stopped visiting. In the short time allowed the place had been cleaned, but ridding the whole house of all vermin for any length of time was difficult, especially with no cleaning agents available on the steppes of Kazakstan. The whole ambience both inside the house and outside disgusted Andrei. It was worse knowing that his brother had, until recently, occupied the place.

The fact that Andrei had to sleep there filled Jan with a certain delight. 'Now you have seen and will experience what the majority of ordinary people have to constantly live with,' Jan whispered to nobody as he excused himself for the evening announcing that he was going for a walk. The real purpose of his parting was to make contact with Sophie and her family. Satisfied too, that the rest of the Russian party in addition to Andrei had settled for the night in the village hall, the former, with several bottles of liquor left over from Vladimir's stocks, Jan went in search of his target with interest and a little trepidation.

He had observed where the family lived, realised they had not detected who he was, and decided the best approach was the direct route and headed straight for the house to make contact. His stay on the steppes was short and he had much to talk about with the Sagajlos before he returned early the next morning. Knocking on the door of Sophie's abode, Jan hoped that Andrei would not require his presence for any minor task that needed doing. If such an event occurred he could quite easily volunteer the excuse that he had temporarily lost his bearings whilst out walking. That excuse would undoubtedly amuse Andrei and temper any wrath he would feel if Jan wasn't there to do his bidding. As Jan waited for the reply, above all else, he hoped that Sophie and her family would welcome him.

The door was opened by an elderly woman whose expression on viewing him immediately appeared frightened and concerned. Jan had no doubts that it was the uniform which caused the effect. Immediately he assured her that she had nothing to be afraid of. Happy that she was somewhat relieved, at least on the surface, he then requested to see the Sagajlo family. The woman proceeded to invite the NKVD stranger indoors and then dismissed herself.

On entering the dwelling Jan was shaken to view the size and the state of the house. Again he was astonished by the amount of lice and bugs which crawled over the walls, although he needn't have been because he had earlier witnessed a similar sight in Vladimir's house before that was cleaned. The three people he had come to visit recognised him immediately and were stunned by his presence in such a remote outpost as where they found themselves. Though all three were concerned by the uniform he wore, Sophie ignored this aspect, deciding that she knew him well enough to know he could not have changed for the worse. She went to him almost instantly, throwing her arms around him. He reciprocated, picking her up and swinging her around. They both laughed which in turn broke the doubts that Yuri and Helena had momentarily held.

Putting Sophie down he kissed her on each cheek and then viewed her critically. Although he did not know what hardships she had been through, he knew, nevertheless, by the evidence on her face that her period in Siberia had been a difficult one. Her beautiful features which he had remembered so well were still present, only now they were broken by thin lines appearing across her forehead. The complexion of her skin had paled from the creamy soft coloured texture he had witnessed to a harder whiter shade and her eyes protruded from their sockets as a result of her ghostlike appearance. He noticed also that her once smooth and rounded lips were now partially contaminated by ulcers. Instantly he felt sorrow for what she had obviously been through, though, as yet he had no idea of what she had encountered. After purveying Sophie he motioned toward her parents who he also wanted to embrace.

Approaching them, Helena instantly spoke out and stated with venom in her cadence. 'You were the Onlooker in uniform who witnessed the shooting earlier today.'

Jan was surprised by the tone and insinuation in her voice but he understood perfectly why she had arrived at her conclusion.

'Yes,' he replied, 'but please do not be afraid. Although I wear the uniform I do not hold their views or support their beliefs. I can and will explain everything in time.'

His explanation had mellowed her opinion and she held out one hand allowing him to shake it. Yuri followed, more enthusiastically, and he was grateful and totally surprised that they had met someone from their home town. After their salutations were over Jan looked upon her parents and was surprised to notice that they did not appear, at least outwardly, to have suffered as severely as Sophie. Finally he announced that he had much to relate and again assured them over his position in the NKVD.

'Please do not disturb yourselves over the uniform. It is a long story as to how I became a member, one which you will understand when I have told you of the consequences leading up to my enrolment.'

'Let's go outside,' Sophie suggested, 'the evening is warm and out there we will not be bothered as much by the vermin.' All four moved into the back courtyard.

After making themselves comfortable in the open air, Jan began his story.

'First Sophie I must tell you about Jacob?' he addressed her directly, smiling as he did so, choosing his words carefully. 'You must understand that what I'm about to say will sadden you, but there is hope.'

Her eagerness was ahead of her. As soon as Jan mentioned his name her tears started flowing numbing her vocal chords. Expecting the worse she waited patiently for any news he had to relate of Jacob.

'At first when I saw him he had been tortured by the NKVD and physically was in a deplorable state. He has recovered though he is still not himself. When he gets out, whenever that may be, it will take a period of time for him to return to normality.'

Sophie cried without hindrance while her mother grasped her hand in comfort. At length Sophie enquired. 'What happened to him?'

'I cannot describe what happened during his interrogation. I do not know.' Jan partly lied to her for although he did not know much he knew that Jacob had definitely been electrocuted. He continued quickly, hoping she would not question him further on the matter. 'I spoke to him briefly, very briefly for there was little time to discuss anything on the first occasion. He did assure me that he was all right.' Again Jan did not relate Jacob's exact words hoping to build Sophie's confidence that her man would survive. 'Before I left him he made me promise not to visit again.' Sophie looked at him hanging on his every word. 'Eventually I had to go. The second visit was worse. We did not speak at all. He was probably afraid that if someone saw us talking that person would denounce him. It can be dangerous for the inmates to talk to supposed strangers. The Poles usually remain loyal to one another, but those inmates who are of different nationality often inform the authorities on anything the others might say or do, so long as it would ease their own burden. All I can say is that, thankfully, Jacob looked better physically.

Sophie continued to weep. Jan leaned forward gently taking hold of her hands.

'I'm sorry Sophie perhaps I shouldn't have told you everything.'

'You were correct to tell me all Jan.' She fought to speak amongst her sorrow. 'What about his mental state? Will he survive?

'I don't know anything about his mental state. From the few words we spoke on the first occasion I would say that mentally he was strong and he will survive.' There was a pause before he continued reassuringly for her benefit. 'Knowing Jacob as I do, I would say that both mentally and physically he will recover. But he will need time,' he warned.

Sophie was comforted by his words. Freeing her hands she wiped her tears away. 'I want to know everything you can tell me about him and his family,' she added. 'Spare no details.'

Jan continued his stories commencing at the very beginning from the night of the ball when the disturbance had occurred a little over twelve months previous. Although the three attendees already knew of certain events as a result of meeting Eva Bryevski at one of the clearing stations, they did not interrupt Jan from repeating the story once more, except for two occasions. The first was to confirm that it was her brother and his colleague who had been shot at the terminus by the guards. A silence fell over the group of four and after a short prayer had automatically been recited by Helena for her son and his friend, the conversation continued once more. The second time was to tell Jan that Jacob, along with his father and friends had been taken from the train.

'I didn't see Kazik in the prison. Was he taken there?' It was Jan's turn to ask eagerly.

'No Kazik remained on the train.'

'Thank goodness. He is too young and probably wouldn't have survived any interrogation,' Jan surmised aloud. 'But you say Jacob's father is there?'

Sophie nodded. 'Along with Stefan and Anatoly.'

'They are not with Jacob any longer, at least not in his cell. Probably they are elsewhere.' Jan decided that on his return to Moscow he would try to locate where the other three men were being held.

Continuing, Jan related the events in the order in which they had occurred to him. All three of the listeners were surprised that the Jan they had known had the temerity to escape from one of the trains. They also had the greatest admiration for him.

Completing his explanation of how he met Wandeczka, he then described his relationship with her husband Andrei. How he had been taken by him to the Lefortovo, and, without the latter's knowledge, how he had made contact with Jacob.

'Can you see him anytime?' Sophie eagerly asked.

'No, not anytime Sophie that would be too dangerous and Jacob's made me promise never to visit him. As I have said I have already broken that promise once and will never do so again.'

'You must break it one more time Jan.' Sophie arose and went into the house. Returning seconds later with something clasped tightly in her hand she stood by Jan and went to place the object in his hand.

'You must take this to him for me when you get back. Promise me you will do this Jan?' she pleaded with him.

He hesitated taking the article from her. Then before she pressed the object into his hand she proceeded to open the ornament and show him the individual photographs of her and Jacob inside. He looked down toward the item. Taking it from her he admired the articulate detail of the locket and the obvious love and affection the two portraits that faced one another, portrayed for each other.

'You must give this to him Jan,' she ordered and then she requested his agreement. 'Promise me you will do this,' she continued to plead.

Jan continued to show reluctance at carrying out the suggestion. He looked at Sophie. Her love and pain for Jacob was obvious to see. Her imploring eyes bored across at him. It did not take long for him to relent and he promised that when the opportunity arose he would re-visit Jacob. Then she continued.

'It was given to me by my parents on my eighteenth birthday.' She looked toward them both and returned her gaze with adoration. 'He knows this is precious to me and it will verify to him that my love is strong and shall never wane. Hopefully it will help him to fight and overcome his current hardship. If he knows I will be waiting for him he will succeed and come through his own personal battle.'

There was a momentary pause as the whole party allowed the conversation and the conjured memories to linger in their minds. Eventually, Helena arose to leave the trio announcing that she was going to prepare a little food for their guest.

Jan stopped her immediately. 'No, you must not do that. I can see how you have suffered and you probably have very little food yourselves. Don't make anything for me. I've already eaten well today.' With that Jan stood and took his wallet out of his pocket and opened the leather case. He grasped all the rouble notes and handed them to Helena. 'Please.' It was his turn to plead. 'You must take this money and use it to your benefit. Before I go I will leave my address. If you need more money, or if you need anything else, write to me there and I will see what I can do. Do you understand?'

There was silence between the groups. It was against Helena's principles to accept money in this manner. She did not want to, but Helena half accepted, still with reluctance. Never before had she done such a thing. Never before had she been in such circumstances as which she now found herself. 'Besides,' she thought to herself, 'it is for others too.' She realised that her husband and daughter had said nothing. Jan had said it all for them.

Jan continued with his persuasion still noticing her hesitancy. 'I know what character of people you are and I know under normal circumstances you would refuse what I have offered you. Under normal conditions I wouldn't have been as tactless to offer as abruptly as I have, for I know you wouldn't have accepted. But now, time is of the essence. These situations that we find ourselves in are not normal and I know desperately that your need is much greater than mine.' There was a pause as Jan placed the money firmly in Helena's palm and clenched it tightly shut for her. He then sat and returned to where their original conversation interrupted.

The acceptance of money was soon forgotten as Jan, Sophie, Helena, and Yuri became entrenched in the story that Jan related of how he had set up home in Moscow and had become a member of the NKVD. Whenever possible he heaped praise on the female cousin who had aided him so much.

'My heart is still with Poland and her people and I'm simply waiting and searching for the moment when I can serve my country in the best way possible.' Jan, for the purpose of his long lost friends, had brought his life of the past twelve months right up to date and had condensed his story into several hours. By the time he had finished darkness had fallen.

'I've been talking for most of the evening and haven't given you decent people a chance to tell me what has happened to yourselves. I know it's not good, though I have no idea how distressing it has been for you all.'

There was a long pause and Jan in the moonlit night could see the faces of those friends he had spent many hours with. Hours which were painful to relive and yet strangely enjoyable as it dawned on him that he had successfully survived a difficult period. He knew that it was not as difficult as that of the Sagajlo family. For Jan it proved that the Polish people were survivors and could live through extremes of hardship unimaginable anywhere else in the world. Hardship which he felt was equivalent to dwelling in hell, if there were such a place. He said nothing to break the silence amongst them. Eventually as Yuri prepared to speak, his wife, Helena, left the group, bid Jan farewell and uttered some excuse as she entered the house.

Before continuing Yuri cleared his throat. The simple trigger of Jan innocently enquiring of their existence in Siberia had such a rapid recovery of thought for

Yuri that his emotions instantly trembled internally. He spoke with a low melancholy tone. His features took on a lugubrious expression accompanying his speech, both portent signs of what he was about to disclose.

'To remember alone, by oneself, as to what has happened in the twelve months that we have been here is painful, extremely painful.' He paused deliberately before continuing. 'To talk about what has happened in the last twelve months would be to relive the whole nightmare again, and for that our minds and our bodies are not prepared. Perhaps they will never be prepared. We have all been through so much. Once through the horrors and nightmares, the mind absorbs them and wants to forget what it has encountered. The individual wants to forget what he or she has been through.' Yuri spoke with deliberation, slowly encapsulating in words the whole horrific scene which was nurturing in his mind without detailing any individual happening. He pondered fleetingly between his phrases, waiting to portray the worst possible outline for Jan of what had occurred to him, his family and the rest of their party over the previous year. It had been full of destitution and depravity. No words could depict their picture of meaningless existence. Relaying any story, any event, would come nowhere near the horrific reality. Yuri, however, endeavoured to continue to explain.

'We could not and cannot relate the whole twelve month episode in one single period. We would be left empty of emotion of love and compassion, for that is what the experiences here, in this hell, would have left for us if it were not for each other.' Whilst speaking, he looked toward his daughter and their eyes met. There were tears in both sets of eyes. Jan too, was filled with emotion. There was perfect silence once more between all three, occasionally broken by the now gentle Siberian wind which whistled at different tones from high to low pitch and very rarely left the company of those who had ever lived their lives, wholly or partly, on the steppes of Kazakstan.

'You must tell him what has happened to me Papa. If it's possible he can then relate the story to Jacob when he sees him next.' Sophie finally broke the long sad silence between the three, urging her father to narrate the events of the previous weeks, knowing that she could not have done so herself. Living through the experience once was adequate enough. With her wishes announced she too arose and went indoors.

Yuri Sagajlo waited until his daughter had disappeared inside before revealing the incidents which she requested should be made known to their visitor. 'The execution in the square today of the young woman was perpetrated as an act of revenge and not as punishment for any murderous deed. The woman who was killed saved Sophie from a prolonged rape ordeal, perhaps even from her murder.'

The announcement stunned Jan and in astonishment he partly repeated what Yuri had already told him.

The doctor continued: 'The two women, unknown to one another, were bathing in the stream further north from this village no more than two hundred yards from each other. A quiet secluded spot where each of them went to bathe privately out of view of prying eyes. Only they were not alone. At least Sophie was not alone. The NKVD Officer, whose body you have seen, had ordered two old Kazak men to keep watch on Sophie whenever she was not working. The men followed her in turn and when she visited the area they discovered her hideaway. On the last occasion Sophie was disturbed during her bathing. After grasping her clothes she tried to escape up the opposite bank only to stumble and fall backward down the slope to where the NKVD Official was waiting for her. Hitting her once, rendering her momentarily unconscious, he then proceeded to rape her.' Yuri breathed heavily and fought the tears cultivating inside him. Calming himself, he continued. 'Several hundred yards away, Juliana, that is the young woman's name, heard Sophie's cries and went to investigate what was happening. Glimpsing from a distance, the NKVD Official and Sophie, she knew immediately that her friend was in trouble.' There was another pause before he continued. 'Juliana had been raped by three Russian soldiers over twelve months ago in her own home back in Poland. She had been through what Sophie was about to go through. As the Official lowered himself she ran and picked up his pistol from the holster which he had discarded and shot the man dead.'

If Jan had not been able to see his host's face in the moonlight he would never have known. Yuri now had tears streaming from his eyes. The tone of his voice gave nothing away and he conversed in his normal manner.

Jan was shocked and did not know what to say. Finally he asked, 'how did the authorities find out?'

'The two old Kazak men had also followed keeping well out of sight. They had seen everything.'

'So Andrei knew who had shot the NKVD official beforehand.' Jan spoke aloud, realising that his cousin by marriage already had the answers.

Yuri looked at him puzzled and the visitor expanded his statement. 'He would have killed those five people he had selected beforehand if she had not come forward, even though he already knew who had committed the deed.'

'It does not surprise me, and another five would have followed, and so on, probably until the whole village would be exterminated.'

The horror of the possible massacre was difficult to comprehend for Jan as he reflected on what might have been. 'What kind of human being would allow that?' he asked aloud.

'The worse kind,' Yuri replied simply. 'But no amount of wickedness surprises me anymore.'

There was a long pause. Again the Doctor spoke first, returning to the episode regarding the dead official. Though what he was about to say was shattering news and on this occasion his speech was markedly disturbed by his grief.

'The man is dead but he has left his mark.' A silence once again descended as Yuri chewed on his next words before continuing. 'Sophie has syphilis. The symptoms are already evident. Chancres around her mouth have started to develop.' Another pause lapsed as he gathered himself to resume his narration. 'Apparently he had been with most of the whores in the village.' Yuri held his head in his hands and let the tears flow through his fingers to fall like salted raindrops to the ground. After several minutes he gathered his composure and looked at Jan.

'There are no drugs here Jan to help her ailment. If I can acquire the penicillin and the needles I can cure her.'

Jan who was speechless at the latter disclosure was eager to help and reassured the doctor. 'When I return I will acquire what you need and send them onto you immediately.'

'There is more Jan which Jacob should also know about.' Clearing his throat again, he related the events of how Sophie and the Russian Official had come to know one another. Commencing with the circumstances around Tomus Voseskaya dying which prompted Sophie to offer herself to Vladimir. How she was left with no option but to progress on her own path and the number of occasions she had been with him. He repeated at intervals how she had saved the lives of the Polish contingent in the village and how many people owed their lives to her, although they would never really know the truth. His final comment was on the aborted foetus which again Sophie had decided to proceed with. Yuri tried to explain to Jan as conclusively and positively as Sophie had explained to him, why she had decided on such an option. There was no need for him to be concerned. Jan understood why she had been so positive on her solution to the problem. Using Sophie's own words, unknown to him Jan stated, 'it was not a child born of love.' With that statement he had settled Yuri's expectations of most people not approving of any form of abortion.

Jan was overwhelmed with admiration for this woman. His sense of achievement for himself was suddenly eclipsed to him by the massive responsibility Sophie had encountered, willingly, by herself, to save so many during her sojourn in Siberia.

Late that night, Jan left the trio of friends he had found briefly and unexpectedly in the middle of a vast land governed by fear and tyranny. He turned to Yuri and openly promised him 'that he would belligerently seek revenge for what Andrei and his like had been responsible for, today, and on numerous other occasions.' Embracing one another as they bade farewell, Yuri did not raise any objections to Jan's promise and instantly felt guilty that he too would condemn the life of this man who had inflicted so much pain and suffering in a short space of time on the innocent. A life of a human being which until this day had always been so precious to him.

The goal for Jan now was to devise a plan to enable him to reach the higher positions of the NKVD and to use whatever information came into his hands against the people who were repressing his country. 'To do that Andrei would surely have to be removed,' Jan told himself, and then questioned whether, if a scheme could be conceived of, he was ready to carry out such a plan.

CHAPTER 27

The summer of 1941 was to prove a major turning point in the war. Early on the morning of 22nd June, without any warning, operation Barbarossa was launched by the German Wermacht from its positions inside Poland. Changing the Germans direction and attacking its former allies, the Russians, the action ultimately ended the Nazi-Soviet Pact in one single blow. Three million men in Wehrmacht grey, Panzer black and Luftwaffe blue surged forward, side by side with men from Finland and Rumania.

The Red Army, its command structure paralysed by the terrible purges of the 1930s, its men half trained and its weapons outclassed, were routed. Within two weeks the Germans had swept the Soviets from eastern Poland and spread its grip on Europe as the advance continued unrelentlessly into Russian territory.

Pieter Sagajlo, since his relationship with Irena had commenced and stabilised, had made contact once again with the Polish underground in his country. Using false papers, very often he had run dangerous errands for the movement passing information to different areas within Poland occupied by both the Germans and the Russians. With the advancement of the German army he now sensed that the moment would soon arrive when he could commence what he considered to be his duty. To seek out the perpetrators and exact his vengeance firstly for those hundreds of men who had been executed by the Russians in the spring of 1940, some of whom were his close colleagues, and secondly for the millions of Poles who had been forcibly deported into exile, innocent of the fabricated crimes they were supposed to have committed and amongst whom numbered his family. He had no preference as to which retribution he was to carry out first. He did know that as long as he could breath he would continue, relentlessly, to pursue those who gave the orders and those who carried out the actions, until they were slain.

Working in the fields, toiling the rich earth, he pondered on whether to fight with the Germans as they advanced further eastward or to bide his time a little longer and await an opportunity to strike at the Russians on another occasion. Deciding to discuss the matter with the woman he had grown to love and respect, he left his place of work and made his way across the fields toward the direction of the house. Approximately half a kilometre from the dwelling stood a small hillock which overlooked the whole area of land that Irena and he had continued to cultivate. Gazing on the crops that had ripened from the seeds they had sown together months earlier, he also viewed two soldiers in Russian uniform entering the abode he was now heading for.

Over the last forty eight hours, an abundance of Russian personnel movement had crossed through their land pulling back as a result of the German advancement. Taken by surprise, many Russian soldiers had been left behind in the retreat of the main armies to find their own way back to their ever changing and diminishing territory. It was of minor concern to Pieter to see these soldiers entering the house. He assumed that they were looking for food to help them on their way. Descending the hillock, and approaching within two hundred yards of the building, he heard screams from inside which immediately foretold that Irena was in trouble.

His reaction was instinctive and his athletic body allowed him to cover the remaining distance to the house in a matter of seconds without breaking sweat. A further scream reminded him that he must find a weapon of sorts before bursting into the house. Running silently to the barn he picked up the old Lee Enfield rifle which Irena had originally pointed at him all those months ago, and which they both had decided to hide in a safe place in the event that the Russians came looking for such weapons to confiscate. Flinging the bales of straw, underneath which the rifle was hidden, to one side, he yanked open the wooden box and pulled the weapon from its hideaway. Running toward the house he checked the performance of the firearm to ensure it still functioned correctly. Knowing there were only two soldiers who had entered the premises and chancing that there were no more, without reconnoitring the situation further, which he would have done previously before commencing combat, he lifted the latch off the hinge and burst in through the door. His rage intensified as he gazed on the bare anus of one of the soldiers bending over the table. Below him were the spread-eagled legs of a woman. The second soldier was at the other end of the table holding down the top half of the female against the support she lay on.

Pieter's actions were automatic, like that of a soldier in armed or unarmed combat. Instantly, before his thoughts had become engaged, as if he knew before entering the house what he had to do, he flung himself into action. His surprise was more incredulous as he viewed the crop of coloured hair of the furthest invader who faced him. Then, gazing on the face of the first soldier who now turned to do battle with him, both soldiers became instantly recognisable. As the rapist lunged forward to hammer his flying fist into Pieter's jaw, the latter swung his right foot forward connecting fully with the unprotected scrotum of the assailant. The man let out an indescribable wail and dropped his hands to cradle his lower area. Pieter reacted further by hammering the butt of the rifle down on the attacker's head. The man dropped like a stone to the floor, unconscious and for the moment oblivious to pain.

Seeing the first aggressor dropping to the floor, Pieter looked for the second. He had freed Irena from his hold only for her to further distract him whilst Pieter had tackled his colleague. Freeing himself from Irena a second time, the second Russian reached for his Tula Tokarev pistol to fire a single shot at Pieter. A fraction of a second before pulling the trigger Irena once again knocked him off balance and the bullet veered into the ceiling.

'Drop down,' Pieter ordered Irena, who was now in his line of fire.

The soldier stared disbelievingly at the rifle pointed toward him as he fought to regain his balance to fire a second shot. Catching sight of the man's strabismus, Pieter confirmed to himself that the two murderers were still together and in partnership.

Falling to the floor the boom of the rifle seemed to accompany Irena's descent and she watched the second soldier fall backward with the force of the bullet. Pieter moved forward, rifle prepared, and gazed on the second man who now lay on the floor, like his companion, unconscious. The bullet had hit him in the left shoulder rendering the arm useless until it would heal completely. For confirmation he peered at the face and remembered easily when and where he had last viewed it. Retrieving the Tokarev pistol, Pieter immediately directed his attentions to the woman he had saved.

Dropping the guns on the table, he grasped her and held her tightly to him not daring to ask whether the worst had been done. She cried and whimpered in his arms and her relief was boundless, as was his, when she finally spoke and ensured him that she had been untouched. He continued to hold her firmly to him as if protecting some precious jewel. To him she was priceless and he told her so. She became limp in his arms and her crying eventually subsided. Finally their embrace was interrupted by the first half naked assailant moaning with the pain which had returned to him the moment he regained consciousness.

'What shall we do with them?' Pieter enquired, knowing all along what he wanted to do.

'I don't know. If we let them go, what do you think will happen?'

'One of two things.' Pieter replied and Irena awaited his conclusions.

'They may return here and seek revenge or they'll probably pick on other innocent women and continue with this routine until they eventually find their army units.'

Irena looked disgusted and was horrified by what Pieter had related to her. She knew he was correct and nothing would stop these men, these animals, from inflicting themselves on other unsuspecting females.

'There is something else about these two soldiers.' Irena turned to pay attention to what he was about to tell her. As she did so the soldier who had started groaning sat up and endeavoured to cover his naked parts.

'Move one more inch of any part of your body and I'll blow your prick into your arse.' Pieter informed the soldier quietly and firmly, in Russian, with no compassion in his voice and without looking directly at the man. He emphasised what he meant by reaching for the pistol and cocked it ready for use. The soldier froze. The icy calm tone of the young man coupled with the readiness of the gun, frightened him into immobility. 'Put your hands on your head.'

'What did you say to him?' she asked.

Pieter repeated what he had said to the soldier for Irena's benefit, excluding the profanities.

'You were about to mention something before he attracted your attention,' she picked up where the original conversation had tailed off.

'Yes, when I first arrived here I told you about my friend and colleague being shot cold bloodedly?' Irena nodded as she recalled his words all those months ago. 'Well these are the two soldiers who performed that atrocity.'

'Are you sure?' Irena asked in total surprise.

'I have never forgotten their faces,' he positively replied. 'The colour of the hair and the squint are unmistakable.'

Irena interrupted him. 'You want revenge Pieter, I know.'

Pieter nodded in agreement. 'I swore that day, to avenge him. That I must do.' There was silence between them and then Pieter spoke once more.

'It's ironic, though I want revenge that is not the reason why these two must die.'

'No. I know.' Irena understood what he was saying.

'They will strike again without mercy, without compassion if we set them free.' All the time he spoke he kept an eye on the Russian who sat quietly and perfectly still.

'Yes, you're right. Take them and do what you have to do. I'm concerned now that he,' pointing at the culprit, who was alert, 'may be planning something while he sits there.'

'It's unlikely he or his partner will do anything. They are cowards. Their only concern now is whether they will be able to get away without suffering any pain or retribution.'

'I'll leave you now to deal with the matter.' She smiled poignantly at him. Although she had nearly been raped by the men she still felt some compassion for them. Climbing the stairs to visit her baby son, who thankfully had been sleeping through the commotion, she heard Pieter bark pitilessly in a language which she knew to be Russian though she could understand very little of what was being said.

The first soldier arose, pulling and fastening his trousers. He motioned to the other end of the table where his compatriot still lay unconscious on the floor. The blood which had first gushed from the wound now seeped gently from it.

'Wake him,' Pieter ordered.

After quietly shaking his colleague, the latter stood up with great pain.

'Outside,' Pieter ordered both men gesturing with the rifle also.

Once outside Pieter commanded the uninjured first soldier to pick up the shovel which was leaning against the wall of the house. Again, without hesitation, the man complied. Pieter walked the men in the direction from which he had approached the house back toward the hillock. Passing the mound they walked for another thirty minutes, longer than normal due to the injured soldier, along the edge of the fields. The wounded soldier was now being supported by his colleague.

At the far end of the farm holding, a small clump of trees stood, in the middle of which could be found a clearing. The trees sheltered the open area from all sides of the farm and out of sight of anybody who may have strayed onto the surrounding land.

Pieter brought the small party to a halt in the middle of the clearing and commanded the first soldier to commence digging. The perspiration from the man poured over his face, partly due to exertion and partly due to anxiety. Anxiety for a punishment which had to come but of which he knew not what form it would take. Occasionally he would look up to Pieter and beg forgiveness. The young, confident and inexorable captor ignored his protests and simply directed him to continue with his task. The second soldier sat, still in pain, in front of where Pieter stood. Almost one hour later the hole was large enough and Pieter ordered the man to stop.

'Get out,' he bellowed, 'and sit down by your comrade.' Similar to previous instructions, the man climbed out and simply obeyed.

Pieter continued. 'I want you to think back to nearly one year ago to this very month, a summer's morning in Pinsk at the railway terminus in the town.'

Both soldiers looked at one another surprised and utterly clueless as to what he was talking about. Then without warning, and bellowing at both men, he thrust the barrel of the Russian Tokarev pistol into the mouth of the soldier who had completed the excavation. 'Think or I will blow your head off, now.' Seconds later he retrieved the pistol from the open mouth and repeated the action to the second injured soldier. In sequence, as if they had undergone precision training, they whimpered individually. Their eyes lit up with fright, seeming to duel with the shafts of light that were piercing through the thick wooded area into the clearing. Retrieving the weapon from the mouth of the wounded second assailant, under orders the whimpering stopped and Pieter continued his tale.

'Wagons loaded with people, innocent people whose only guilt was to be born of Polish origin.' He deliberately paused before continuing, letting his words sink into the minds of his captives.

'Suddenly from the wagons two men escape and flee toward the buildings which stand at the edge of the terminus compound. Halfway across the open ground the men are spotted. Two soldiers with two dogs give chase. While one man runs to the buildings for shelter, the second man stumbles and falls. The dogs arrive first. The fallen man is mauled and mangled almost to death by the animals.' He was reliving his experience from twelve months previous and the terrifying ordeal came flooding back in his mind with vivid clarity. The turmoil in his mind ventured nothing on his face. He looked toward the soldiers and realised that they too had remembered the occasion. Their worried pale expressions hurriedly gathered pace and spread across their faces like white clouds blotting out a coloured sky. Then their appearances changed further as they caught sight of each others visages. A deeper realisation crept across their faces as they remembered that only one corpse had been recovered that day.

The pause from Pieter lasted an eternity for the men. They had no idea what was about to happen next and only expected the worse. The agonising wait caused the abler of the two men to urinate with fright and anticipation. The flow of urine down his leg fell onto his boot and the resultant dripping noise seemed to resound heavily within the glade enhancing the solitary surroundings they found themselves within.

Pieter continued. The sound of his voice deliberately low, like that of a whisper, magnifying the solitude of the three men and the possible deathly conclusion for the two captives. 'The two soldiers call the remaining dog off. One soldier prepares his gun and fires into the mutilated body ensuring death.' A further silence ensues as Pieter visually remembers the butchered body of the colleague that fell. The silence between the three deepens.

Finally Pieter breaks the stillness again. Pulling the cross and chain from within his shirt and showing the flattened part of the metal, he confirms what they already know. Announcing to them with a deep satisfaction, belying his calm outwardly expression. 'Yes, it is I, the second escapee who emerged from the buildings to be shot down cold bloodedly.' He stared at the red haired man, for it was he who had pulled the trigger on him. 'I did not die and I never ever thought that I would meet my murderers again so quickly. Do you remember the face?' Pieter leaned toward them in turn, allowing them a closer look. 'I have never forgotten yours,' he whispered to them.

The carroty coloured man began to whimper and Pieter slapped him around the head with the palm of his hand. 'Shut up. Are you a man or a baby?' Through sheer fright the blubbering instantly stopped. Without waiting for confirmation he continued.

'I don't know why I should do this.' He paused before commencing. The two men sat up immediately sensing from Pieter's voice that there could be a way out for them. The Interrogator immediately knew his tone had produced the required results. 'There are two pieces of information which I need. Two names that I must know. If you supply me with those names I will spare your lives.' He peered at the men making sure they understood. 'The first name I want is the man who orders the deportations of my countrymen.' Again there was a pause, only a brief pause. The wounded man whimpering between his words spoke first.

'The m...man or m....men whose idea it was will be unknown to us. D...different areas in P....Poland had d...different officer's ass...signed to carry out the deportations. The man in charge of the area in and around Pinsk was...' Before the soldier could finish, his counterpart joined in, blurting the name out, hoping that as he did so it would save his skin before that of his colleague.

'Tscharakova.'

'Junior Major Andrei Valenti Tscharakova.'

Pieter looked at the soldier who had interrupted and then back toward the soldier who had firstly spoken.

'Is that correct?' he asked.

'Y...Yes. Yes. Junior Major Andrei Valenti Tscharakova is the officer in charge.' The injured soldier confirmed.

'How can you be so sure this is the man?'

'It was he who personally p...punished us for not ch...checking that you had been killed.' The man started to stammer again, conscious that he was admitting his part in the act and afraid of the consequences.

'Where would I find him?' Pieter now wanted to know more about the man and his whereabouts. 'Take your time.'

'He would reside in Moscow at the headquarters of the NKVD.' The soldier had composed himself and now spoke without stammering. 'He also travels a great deal, or would have done until recently. With the Germans advancing he will probably travel only within the Soviet Union now.'

'Good. Good.' Pieter encouragingly stated, giving the soldier confidence to talk further.

The Interrogator asked his next question. 'In the spring of 1940 hundreds of Polish soldiers were marched to a forest outside Smolensk. There the men were executed, again in cold blood. Who would have been responsible for that slaughter?'

The two soldiers looked at one another astonished at what they had heard from this man. Pieter once more witnessed their expressions which answered the question for him.

The soldier with the carrot coloured hair replied, only too willing to do so. His colleague seemed to have gained the confidence of their interrogator and having already answered his questions, appeared to be winning him over.

'What you have told us is unknown amongst the ordinary soldiers of the Russian Army, probably unknown amongst the lower members of the NKVD. If what you say is true then the order would have come from very high up in the regime.'

'How high up?'

'The highest level.'

'Is that true?' Pieter asked turning to the wounded man once again for confirmation.

'It is true.' the man replied simply. 'And we wouldn't know how high up that would be. We have been told that all orders are sanctioned from the highest ranks.'

The first crack of the pistol splattered the brains of the wounded man over his colleague. The body slumped, almost in slow motion, into the already made grave enhancing the final consequence of what was to happen to his comrade. The second soldier howled as he turned to see his colleague slide forward with the top part of his head blown away. His howling intensified as he gazed on the brains that fell on his lap. The second crack of the pistol, which had the same effect as the first, immediately drowned the crazed screaming of the second soldier echoing loudly before all noise slowly dissipated itself amongst the protecting trees.

Pieter kicked the second dead soldier into the grave to accompany his comrade. He then filled in the burying place and returned with the weapons and identity papers to the house. His first step to avenge those who had poured humiliation, degradation, cruelty and above all depravation on all things that he had loved and known, had been taken. He had a name and his next goal, no matter what he had to endure, was the extermination of the person who carried that name.

Junior Major Andrei Valenti Tscharakova was now on the wanted list of two men.

The small but effective contingent of military personnel left early the next morning, a little over twelve hours since their arrival. They brought with them the intent of vengeance, so final, and which until their visit the villagers had mainly experienced through natural causes, that it took the inhabitants completely unaware.

Having reaped their revenge on a victim who had simply defended an innocent party from the brutality and destruction it was helplessly about to receive, they now departed, having resolved what they thought was the problem with the swiftest sentence possible, death. They now took with them their brief encounter of carnage. The sinister aura which had descended on the village whilst they were present also disappeared.

Returning to the NKVD building within Petropavlosk where the additional six military personnel had been seconded to Junior Major Andrei Valenti Tscharakova, he and Jan were informed that the train scheduled to leave for Moscow would be delayed by up to one hour. Due to the hold up the NKVD Officer in charge of the district then offered to take the two men on a tour of the official premises.

The second department they visited was a small medical centre situated on the upper floor of the two storey building. Discovering this fact, what then became uppermost in Jan's mind were the supplies which Yuri Sagajlo urgently required for his daughter. Instinctively he struck up a conversation with the medical officer in charge, who was equivalent to a senior nurse, whilst Andrei and his counterpart continued with their obviously compatible dialogue. As the small entourage left to proceed to the next department, Andrei turned and looked for Jan. He could see that he was in deep conference with the medical leader, thought nothing of their intense communication, and simply ordered Jan to meet him in approximately forty five minutes in the downstairs reception area.

Conversing about something which he knew very little of, Jan concocted a story that he too had worked in the medical section within the NKVD headquarters in Moscow. At the same time he slipped into the conversation that one of the reasons for this journey was that it was part of a larger tour by himself and his superior, and if time allowed, he was to take an inventory of medical supplies for their possible future transfer to other parts of the Union in the event that Russia was attacked by her neighbouring countries. Jan then went on to describe in complete confidence the military reports that were circulating in Moscow headquarters about the imminent invasion of Soviet territory by the Germans. Stressing the confidentiality of the information he made the medical officer swear his silence until any news regarding the event was made official. Jan then proceeded to name three drugs, two of which he was especially searching for, to use on severe burns. These first two names he fabricated, along with their remedies. The third drug he named as penicillin, a relatively new drug which had been distributed in the Soviet Union. Jan did not exaggerate the medical effect of this drug having been told by Yuri that it was both a new and powerful medicine.

Throughout Jan's conversation the medical officer was very attentive. Now, Jan thought, is the crucial moment. 'Do you happen to have any of the drugs I've mentioned?' he enquired innocently, stating that firstly the drugs only needed to be inventoried.

Wishing only to help the NKVD official who worked in the supreme headquarters, and thinking of what future prospects might open up for him if he assisted this person, the M.O. immediately volunteered what he knew. 'I've never heard of the first two drugs,' he happily announced whilst opening the medical supply cupboard, 'but we do have a small supply of penicillin here,' he declared. Instantly he showed Jan the store of penicillin that the department held.

'Excellent,' Jan commended the man, 'and what is the total amount of this drug that you have available if headquarters should need anymore?'

The medical officer reeled off the quantity of the medication that the sector currently retained together with further information on expected deliveries. Jan, pretending to be officious, made a few points on a small notebook he carried around with him. After annotating the amount he motioned to pick up a sample and accidentally knocked several other specimens of a different drug off the shelf.

Jan was apologetic. Whilst the M.O. kneeled to clear the mess on the floor, at the same time assuring him that no harm was done, Jan pocketed a bottle of the drug he required plus several syringes. The medical officer replaced the disturbed supplies and noticed nothing missing as he locked the cupboard.

Before he left the room Jan once again stressed the importance of keeping the whole affair confidential, asked the Official for his name, and purposefully made a note of it in the same notepad. Thanking him profusely, he clasped hold of the man passionately, as a top ranking General would do when bidding farewell to an equivalent rank prior to departing. Rendezvousing with Andrei as earlier planned, both men left the NKVD building and were driven back to the station where they boarded the train to return to Moscow.

The journey was uneventful. Foremost in Jan's mind was how he could post the medical supplies of penicillin and syringes he had acquired to Yuri sooner rather than later when they arrived in the capital. He was unsure of when the train was scheduled to stop and decided against enquiring of Andrei for the necessary information. Five days later they arose and after breakfasting they disembarked from their original carriage. By mid morning they were awaiting a connecting train which would take them on to Moscow. Whilst awaiting the connection, which would take approximately one hour to arrive, Andrei informed Jan that he would telephone Wandeczka to announce that they were homeward bound and advise her of their estimated time of arrival in approximately three to four days. This was the perfect opportunity for Jan who acted quickly by visiting the postal area in the town and forwarded his acquisitions to the village they had left behind.

They travelled a further two more days when the train made another routine stop at one of its terminals. As usual, Andrei disembarked and purchased the latest edition of the Pravda newspaper. Within seconds of picking up the chronicle he was transfixed to the spot. Taking root he read with amazement and disbelief the headlines emblazoned across the front page:

'Germany attacks Russia'

The report went on to state that the German-Soviet pact of Non-Aggression between the two countries had been treacherously broken by the German attack on Russian territory. Andrei's fixation to the newspaper continued as he studied the report and the shattering words he read reverberated in the astounding expressions on his face. Jan perceived this from where he stood, inside the carriage, and immediately knew that the news was anything but welcoming.

Finally, the Officer boarded the train silently. It was as if he were carrying the burden of the invasion on himself. His features had paled significantly and at that moment, having witnessed the corpse of Andrei's half brother Vladimir, the likeness between the two men startled Jan.

Andrei dropped the newspaper to the floor by the side of Jan who had sat again seconds before. The subordinate picked up the daily publication and confirmed the news to himself, which Andrei already knew. Whilst Jan read the report, he could not understand Andrei's mind. Having gazed on his brother's corpse several days earlier and shown no sign of shock, grief or sadness, after reading this newspaper report, his expression became instantly melancholic and deepened to one of extreme unhappiness. Mystified, Jan thought to himself, 'the invasion is catastrophic news on a larger scale, but your brother's death is also painful, and yet you showed no remorse.' His thought process was interrupted.

Breaking the silence and feeling guilty that he had been away from his post, although the journey was necessary to satisfy his own weird mind that his half brother was dead, Andrei informed Jan. 'We must return as quickly as possible to the capital. Our country needs us now.'

The words were futile to Jan as they already were taking the quickest route and proceeding on the fastest transport available.

'It is not my country,' Jan muttered to himself and concluded that Andrei had probably meant himself alone and the statement had been said whilst in a state of shock.

The remainder of the journey was completed in virtual silence. After a further five days of travelling, one day had been added to their journey by troop movements from the south to the west of the country, they reached Moscow where Andrei ordered his underling to accompany him immediately to headquarters.

Rumours were abundant in the Lubyanka, the NKVD headquarters, and in other military establishments within Moscow, that Stalin was about to declare some form of allegiance with Poland. Despite the overwhelming silence within the offices and corridors of the Lubyanka where the daily control of the functions of the secret police is performed, these rumours managed to filter their way down to the lowest level of members.

Finally on 30 July 1941 the rumours became reality and it was announced that Russia would establish diplomatic relations with Poland. Two weeks later on 12 August 1941 a military convention was signed where Russia allowed the formation of a Polish Army on Soviet territory. An amnesty was granted to all Polish internees, even though, in the majority of cases, they had never committed any crimes.

The news astonished Jan, but excited him also. After the initial euphoria the sadness crept in and his excitement turned sour. The realisation of what had happened to his people overwhelmed him. 'How many people will be freed?'

he asked himself. 'How many people will actually be informed of the amnesty? The process of communication in a land so vast causes many problems. Will they learn of it before Stalin changes his mind?' These questions rifled his mind. The announcement held no comfort for him. Continuing to ponder on the dilemma his countrymen would face, within minutes he was crying like a baby, muttering to himself, 'What a waste! What a waste!' as now the torment and devastation of the last two years which had been inflicted on his people came to the fore. 'All is not lost,' he told himself. 'Many will be freed. It is better that some are saved rather than none whatsoever. Then, as suddenly as the sadness manifested itself, it left him to be replaced by the original though now temperate excitement, for with those that were freed he visioned new ideas, new futures, which could, if directed in the proper channels, bring forth a new Poland.

The irony of the whole situation between the two countries, Poland and Russia, was hard for him to believe. But it was happening. 'So finally the Red terror has returned for assistance from its much devoured neighbour,' Jan murmured to himself. 'Devoured by those who now seek its help. Devoured by a system that has already consumed a portion of itself over the years, probably the best part.' He paused for reflection on which way the government in exile would turn and then continued to himself. 'There is nothing that Poland can do except to fight with you and alongside you. There will however, be those who will watch you and deceive you whenever possible especially those who have already suffered and lost a great deal. Many will forgive and forget and when it is over will return, hopefully to normal lives, as it once was provided you, the Soviet Union will forgive and forget and allow them to return? And even if you do, with all your terror and might, there will still be those whom you have damaged beyond repair. Those who will not and cannot forgive. It is they who will seek revenge. Beware, for now you will have enemies from within your borders. Those enemies within will be your undoing. It will take years, even decades, perhaps generations, but we will survive and in the end we will conquer. Not necessarily your land but certainly your repression and it will be achieved through our own determination to survive and eventually to be free.

In the quiet and peaceful calm of his apartment Jan sat and drank a toast to his beloved and beleaguered Poland and its subjects. 'To those who have suffered under terror. To those who have become part of the holocaust. To those who will become part of the forgotten journeys. Let your countrymen fight for your freedom by whatever means possible. Poland!' Deliberately with passion and commitment, he whispered the words. His surrogate home was in the middle of an NKVD apartment block.